William Landay is the author of the highly acclaimed *Mission Flats*, which was awarded the John Creasey Memorial Dagger for best début crime novel of 2003. A graduate of Yale University and Boston College Law School, he was an assistant district attorney before turning to writing. He lives in Boston, where he is at work on his next novel.

Acclaim for *Mission Flats*

'A most assured début, cleverly plotted with unguessable ending' *Sunday Telegraph*

'Compelling ... Marks the blooding of a major new talent with shades of Scott Turow' *Guardian*

An impressive and constantly surprising début ... The main plot-twist knocks you sideways and there's more to come. A marvellous, unexpected novel' *Time Out*

'A mixture of poignant, literary Americana and dialogue driven suspense, this impressive début novel delivers a well-judged final shock' *Morning Star*

'A gripping and thrilling read which has you completely hooked from its violent and shocking opening' *What's On*

'A first-time novelist has to bring something new to the table – something like the trumps that Landay throws down in his high stakes police procedural' *New York Times*

Also by William Landay

MISSION FLATS

and published by Corgi Books

THE STRANGLER

William Landay

CORGI BOOKS

TRANSWORLD PUBLISHERS
61-63 Uxbridge Road, London W5 5SA
A Random House Group Company
www.rbooks.co.uk

THE STRANGLER
A CORGI BOOK: 9780552149457

First published in Great Britain
in 2007 by Bantam Press
a division of Transworld Publishers
Corgi edition published 2008

Addresses for Random House Group Ltd companies outside the
UK can be found at: www.randomhouse.co.uk
The Random House Group Ltd Reg. No. 954009

The Random House Group Limited supports The Forest
Stewardship Council (FSC), the leading international forest
certification organisation. All our titles that are printed on
Greenpeace approved FSC certified paper carry the FSC logo.
Our paper procurement policy can be found at
www.rbooks.co.uk/environment

Typeset in 10.5/12.5pt Palatino by
Falcon Oast Graphic Art Ltd.

Printed in the UK by CPI Cox & Wyman, Reading, RG1 8EX.

2 4 6 8 10 9 7 5 3 1

Mixed Sources
Product group from well-managed
forests and other controlled sources
www.fsc.org Cert no. TT-COC-2139
© 1996 Forest Stewardship Council
FSC

For Henry and Ted, brothers

THE STRANGLER

The Hub of Business and Pleasure . . .

BOSTON

If you haven't seen the *New Boston* lately, you're in for a surprise—America's city of history is now a city of tomorrow.

Fostered by the unmatched universities here, hundreds of research-based industries have sprung up on all sides, probing the mysteries of the space age—atomics, nucleonics, electronics, automation in all its forms.

Here the executive and the R&D man alike feel at home. They live in new apartment towers right in town, minutes from work. Their children attend top-flight schools. Their wives shop at bright modern shopping centers. The whole family enjoys the unique cultural advantages for which Boston is world famous. And best of all, they are surrounded by the friendly faces of Bostonians. Year-round, there's fun afoot!

For a week, a while, a lifetime...you'll love Boston. Come see for yourself!

—MAGAZINE AD, 1962

Part One

1

Ricky Daley

In the subway: twenty swaying grief-stunned faces.
A man insensible of his own leg pistoning up and
down, tapping *tat-tat-tat-tat-tat* on the floor. At
Boylston Street the track curved, the steel wheels
shrieked against the rails, and the lights flickered
off. Passengers let their eyes close, like a congre-
gation beginning a silent prayer. When the lights
came on again and their eyes opened, Ricky Daley
was watching them.

At Park Street station, Ricky jogged up the stairs
to the street, into a stagnant crowd. Offices had
closed early, creating an early rush hour, but there
was nowhere to go. The news was everywhere, still
sensational though everyone had already heard it.
Newsboys squawked "Extra!" and "Read it *hee-
yuh!*" and "Exclusive!" They lingered on the
hissing alien word "Ass-*sass*-inated!" Over on
Tremont Street, crowds clumped against parked
cars to listen to the news on WBZ; they bowed their
heads toward the car radios. But there was no real

news, no one knew anything, so eventually they turned away, they loitered on the sidewalk, and shambled in and out of the Common. It was mid-afternoon, three hours or so after—*after* President Kennedy first slapped at his neck as if he'd been stung by a bee—three hours after but the concussed mood was not dissipating. It was deepening, and more and more the stupor was infused with anxiety: What was next? From what direction would the attack come? How in the hell would they all get through this?

Ricky strolled right through them, working his way west. It was quieter in the Common, away from the street. No one seemed to be speaking. No one knew what to say. In the quiet he could make out the murmur of the city, distant engines and car horns and cops' whistles. He wore a gray overcoat and an itchy hundred-and-twenty-five-dollar suit. His shoes, new black brogans, made squinching sounds when he walked. He had tried to soften them by wearing them around his apartment, but they still pinched across the top of his feet. He had succeeded, at least, in dulling the gloss of the leather by rubbing it with saliva. The shoes should look polished but not new. New shoes might draw attention.

By the Frog Pond, a woman on a slatted park bench held a handkerchief to her mouth, balled up in her fist. Her eyes were watery. Ricky stopped to offer her the stiff new handkerchief tri-folded in his jacket pocket.

"Here," he said.

"I'm alright."

"Go on, I don't use them. It's just for show."

Ricky gazed up, granting her the privacy to mop her nose.

"Who would do such a thing?" The woman sniffled.

Ricky looked down again, and he detected a shy grin at the corners of her mouth. Smile, he thought. Go on.

"Who would do this?"

Go ahead and smile. Because who could deny there was a little secret pleasure in it? Kennedy was dead, but they had never felt quite so alive. All these nine-to-five suckers, all the secretaries and waitresses and Edison men—it was as if they had all been drowsing for years only to snap awake, here, together, inside this Great Day. Ricky thought that, if he wanted to, he could explore this girl for information (where did she work? did she have a key? was there an opportunity there?). She was available. Probably she felt a little intoxicated by this feeling of nowness. Until today, she had never felt so thrillingly present in each moment. It was a limitation of human consciousness: We live only in the future and past, we cannot perceive now. Now occupies no space, a hypothetical gap between future and past. Only an exceptional few could feel *now*, athletes and jazzmen and, yes, thieves like Ricky Daley, and even for them the sensation was fleeting, limited to the instant of creative action. Cousy knew the feeling; Miles Davis, too. The boundless improvisational moment. Today this girl was experiencing it, and she wanted to share the experience even with a stranger. Well, Ricky figured, it made sense—Kennedy's murder was exciting. It was a good day to work.

"Castro," she decided. "That's all I can think, is Castro."

"Maybe."

"I messed up your handkerchief. I'm sorry. Must be expensive."

"It's okay. I stole it."

"You . . . ? Oh." She smiled, appraising him. "You're very nice. What's your name?"

"It's a long story."

He left her there. He walked on through the Public Garden. His breath made little clouds in the cold.

At Arlington Street, the doors to the church were propped open. The interior was warm and eggshell white. Through the open doors, Ricky could see an organist, a young man with flushed cheeks and a lick of blond hair that flopped in his eyes until he flipped it back with a toss of his head like a horse. The young man played in a sort of rapture. His eyes were shut, his torso swayed expressively.

Ricky walked on, west through the Back Bay, in a series of zigs and zags. On the residential side streets, he turned each corner, stopped, and looked back for a good long while. He hadn't noticed any tails, but you never knew. Even on a day like this, with everyone smashed by the news, cops included, it was important to maintain your technique.

At the Copley Plaza Hotel, a doorman in a long overcoat with gold braiding and epaulettes held the door. "Good afternoon, sir."

"Afternoon." Ricky took care to glance at the man only for an instant.

He moved quickly through the lobby, but not too quickly. Purposeful, proprietary, calibrating his movements to the room. He had a fingerman at the front desk, who gave Ricky a nod.

On the house phone he dialed room 404. No answer.

He sauntered into the Oak Room to wait at the bar for fifteen minutes, to be sure. A guest might go back up to his room for a forgotten item in the first few minutes after walking out, but he almost never returned once he'd been out for a quarter hour or more. Ricky made a point of checking his coat and tipping the girl a quarter. At the bar he ordered a highball and settled in. Rather than gawk at the luxurious room with its carved plaster ceiling and heavy furniture, he watched the door. He folded his arms across his chest, straining his suit jacket, because he'd noticed that rich people were comfortable in their expensive clothes. They wore a good suit as if it were an old sweater. They didn't care.

After a half hour of this business, pleased with the way he'd blended into the herd (no one, not even the bartender, would remember him later), he called room 404 again on the house phone and again got no answer. He drained his highball and in a tipsy voice he told the bartender an old joke— about the giraffe who walks into a bar and announces, "The highballs are on me"—before leaving. The bartender's face puckered: Didn't this jackass know Kennedy was dead?

Elevator to the fourth floor.

At room 404 he gave a brushy knock, then took a key from his pocket and let himself in.

He checked the room. Empty.

Back to the door. Gloves on. A glance up and down the hallway. He took a paper clip from his pocket, broke an inch of wire from it, slid the wire into the keyhole to plug it, then closed the door.

Checked the dresser. Checked the closets. He worked quickly but without noise and without leaving a mess. Found what he was looking for duct-taped to the inside of the toilet tank (clever prick): a yellow silk jewelry bag.

Ricky emptied the bag onto the bed. Loose diamonds. Some small jewelry pieces. Packets of hundred-dollar bills, banded. He separated out some of the jewelry, the gold plate, the pieces too bulky to conceal. That left a glassy heap. There might have been a half million dollars mounded up there. A cool little cone of diamonds.

The corners of Ricky's mouth tried to curl up into the tiniest unprofessional smirk, which he smothered.

2

Michael Daley

A bulge rippled across his view. It was, he thought, like looking at the bottom of a stream as a little wave passes over: a transparent swell traveled from right to left across his field of vision. It bloated the damask curtains, the walls, the men's faces, the bald head of a man at a lectern—and at that point Michael closed his eyes.

He knew what the hallucination signaled. The pain was coming. Soon. Ten, maybe fifteen minutes.

His right hand tingled, and a drink slipped out of his fingers and dropped away. The glass remained upright as it fell, as if it were falling straight down a tube. He gazed down into the top of the glass, at the undisturbed ice cubes and soda water and lime wedge, until the floor punched the bottom of the glass and the drink erupted onto the carpet and splattered his shoes.

The spill made no noise, but a little gasp went up from the crowd around Michael. From the lectern, the speaker quipped, "Yes, it's shocking, I know," and everyone laughed. Someone chucked Michael on the shoulder, and he mustered a smile for them, though he was not the sort who liked to be looked at, much less laughed at. He picked up the empty glass and made a feeble gesture with it, like a toast, to ward them off, to direct all those eyes back to Farley Sonnenshein and his speech.

Sonnenshein resumed, the usual developer-speak, although he made his pitch with unusual flair. "Gentlemen, let's not forget where this city was only a few short years ago. Decaying, rotting, shrinking—dying. Young people leaving in droves. Businesses closing. Blight was spreading like cancer in an old man. And the only hope for this man—this ravaged, dying old man—was surgery. Radical surgery."

Another wave rolled through Sonnenshein. The developer seemed to ripple like a flag in a light breeze. Michael looked down, pretending to concentrate on the speech. He thought he could hold this pose for a moment before the hallucinations got worse and he would have to leave the room.

This was the aura that preceded a migraine. The word aura was a clinical term, but it captured the experience perfectly. The migraine aura swept in like fog; by the time you'd detected it, you were already enveloped, isolated. This particular hallucination—those rolling undulations in his visual field—was new to Michael. He had some-times seen shivery radiations around the edges of things, like heat rising off hot asphalt, before a migraine set in. But this was new. He wanted to remember it clearly so he could describe it to his doctor.

And he wanted to get out.

Sonnenshein's voice: "The West End—a crowded ghetto, all fifty-some-odd acres of it—gone! Swept away! Soon it will be replaced with a streamlined complex of shops and apartments. We've broken ground on our new Central Artery, an elevated high-speed expressway that will whisk cars right through downtown, relieve our crowded streets, and speed local commerce. Even Scollay Square—"

A mock plea went up, in thick Bostonese, "*Nöt Skully Squay-uh!*"

"Yes, gentlemen, even Scollay Square! Goodbye, burlesque houses! Goodbye, tattoo parlors! *Arrivederci*, Scollay Square, you will not be missed. Not when this city has a new, modern Government Center in your place."

"You call that progress?" someone shouted, and there was a gust of laughter.

Sonnenshein waited for the room to fall quiet. "I call it the New Boston," he answered, as if this new city were a gift he was granting them. "That's the Boston your children will know. And the old Boston, my friends, *our* Boston, will seem as vanished and quaint to them as Pompeii."

Michael looked up. A test. For a moment he saw the scene clearly: Sonnenshein with his hand still poised on the white cloth; the roomful of men watching him, eager, excited at the nearness of Sonnenshein, the Man to See. The picture held for a moment, then it billowed once, and again, and again. Michael closed his eyes only to be dazzled by phosphenes, flashbursts of light that he sensed rather than saw, as if he'd been staring into the sun. He began to make his way toward the door, through the crowd, his eyes open only a crack.

Somewhere behind Michael was Sonnenshein's voice: "President Kennedy told that wonderful story about the great French marshal, Lyautey. One day Marshal Lyautey asked his gardener to plant a tree. The gardener objected that the tree was slow-growing and would not bloom for a hundred years. The marshal replied,'In that case,there is no time to lose. Plant it this afternoon.' Gentlemen, we too have trees to plant. Let's plant them this afternoon. That is how we will honor Jack Kennedy's memory. With a living memorial in his old hometown. I give you the next piece of the New Boston: JFK Park."

Michael dared to look back as Sonnenshein slipped the cloth off an architect's model, a Corbusian apartment complex, four soaring towers set in a swell of green. The model was white, immaculate, futuristic, fantastic. There was an audible contented *mmm*. Applause. Mayor Collins, in his wheelchair, peered between the little clay buildings at eye level, beaming. The Cardinal craned his neck.

"To the future!" someone toasted.

"The future!" came the answer, and a cheer went up.

A blind spot, a white hole, now occupied the center of Michael's field of vision. He tried to blink it away. The hole faded, scintillated at the edges, and through it he saw Sonnenshein scanning the room, gauging the reaction to his model.

Michael's boss, an assistant A.G. named Wamsley, materialized at Michael's side. Jug-eared, grinning his familiar toothy grin. "What's wrong, Daley, you don't like the future?"

"Not the immediate future, no." Michael struggled to hold himself still, to present himself as a healthy man.

"You alright, Michael?"

"No. I have a headache."

He stumbled out onto School Street. A doorman in his smart Parker House uniform offered a cab, and somehow Michael fell into the back seat. He was holding his head now, pressing two fingers at each temple. Still no pain, but it was coming.

"Beacon and Clarendon," he told the cabbie.

"You want to take a cab six blocks?"

"Yes."

"You could walk it quicka."

"Just do it."

"Oh, for Christ's sake. These people."

Michael lay down on the back seat. It smelled of vinyl and sweat and gasoline and cold. The aura would end, all the kaleidoscopic visions and the exalted, privileged intoxication that accompanied them—all the phenomena that so fascinated the doctors, the *scotomata* and *spectra* of a *classical migraine aura*—they would fade, soon, and in their place would be the first little swell of pain, a bony hump inside the forehead, pressing, always on the right side. You passed through the aura like a dream, and then the dream receded and you were only your body, you were bone and meat, a wounded mortal animal. Your brain, impossibly delicate, would be squeezed. That was what the aura signaled: Pain was coming.

The taxi bounced down Beacon Street. Michael lay with his eyes open. No pain yet. Soon. Soon.

3

Joe Daley

Joe Daley filled the door of the Chantilly Lounge.
He paused to let his eyes adjust to the gloom inside.
Joe had an enormous block of a head, like a slightly
oversized statue, and all that squinting and blinking caused his mouth to turn up in a bullyboy
smirk, which he did not intend but did not mind,
either.

The bar was nearly empty. It was three o'clock on
a Wednesday afternoon. In a booth a dingy man sat
with a few newspapers in front of him. Joe greeted
this man as he passed the booth, "Hey, Fish."

Fish ignored him.

The bartender ignored Joe, too. He busied himself with stocking a beer cooler from a case of
Narragansett.

"Hey, I'll have one of those," Joe said.

The bartender opened a bottle from the case, not
the cooler, and put it in front of Joe. He slid an
envelope onto the bar beside it.

The envelope disappeared into Joe's black

leather jacket. "Thanks, neighbor," he said with a tip of his bottle, echoing a line from the Narragansett ads.

The bartender did not acknowledge the little joke, but went right back to filling the beer cooler.

Joe gave up on him. He tossed a dime on the bar as a tip, then moved over to the booth. "What's going on, Fish?"

No one knew why this man was called Fish. His real name was not Fish or anything like it, nor had he ever been involved with fishes or fishing, at least not that anyone knew of. But Fish he was, a small-time bookie who, after paying out the rent he owed to the North End mobsters and to the Chantilly and to the cops, barely had anything to show for his bookmaking efforts. It had been easier before Capobianco took over, before the dagos decided to consolidate all the bookmaking in the city. Then, you paid the cops and that was that. Now you paid everybody. You couldn't live off the crumbs they left you. Not like the old days.

Joe slid onto the bench opposite Fish. "Let me see the Army," he said. This was *Armstrong's*, a daily racing form that covered the East Coast tracks. "What looks good today, Fish, anything?"

"I don't get involved, Officer."

"Hey, what's with the 'officer'? I ain't working, not till five."

"Before five, after five, I don't get involved. Just make your own picks. I don't give a shit."

Joe opened the paper and studied the handicapping information closely. He muttered as he read, "Feeling good today, Fish, fee-lin' good."

Fish shared a glance with the bartender.

"How about this one," Joe said. "Sixth race at Suffolk, Lord Jim. I like that name. Can I get one down for three oh five? Time is it?"

Fish took the Army with a little frown and found the listing. "Lord Jim," he mumbled, "ten to one. Ten to one."

"No guts, no glory."

"What do you know about him?"

"I know I like him. What, you gonna talk me out of it now?"

"How much?"

"A fin. Make it interesting."

"To win, you mean?"

"Yeah, to win. Of course to win. What do I look like?"

"Let me see the cash."

Joe dug in his pocket but came up with just two crumpled singles. He felt the envelope, hesitated. The bartender was watching. Ah, what the fuck, right? It was Joe's money, some of it anyway. He peeked inside the envelope. Nothing smaller than a ten.

"That ain't all for you," the bartender said.

"I'll put it back."

"It's not yours in the first place."

"I said I'll put it back."

Fish shook his head. He produced a battered black notebook from his coat and he noted the bet, encoding Joe's name in a cipher of his own invention. He folded the *Armstrong's* and put it aside, went back to reading the *Observer*.

The bartender returned to his work, avoiding Joe's eyes. His movements were sulky, miffed.

"I told you, I'm good for it."

"Yeah, alright, Joe, you're good for it. Whatever you say."

"Good."

"I just don't want to hear the envelope was light. Some sergeant comes down here—"

"I'm good for it, I said." In the sixth race at Suffolk Downs, Lord Jim finished sixth in a field of six.

4

Joanne Feeney's apartment on Grove Street had a kitchen window overlooking the West End, or what was left of it. The old neighborhood had been leveled. Rubble, acres and acres of nothing. Only a few buildings had been spared, a couple of churches, Mass. General Hospital. Outside the window now, in the distance, a crane idly swung a wrecking ball into the remains of a tenement. With each tap of the ball, the building shed a few crumbs.

Mrs. Feeney hadn't had much to do—she was sixty-three—so she had formed a habit of watching the demolition day by day. From her window she studied the wasteland, overlaying it with her memories of the West End, the narrow streets where she'd grown up. When she was a girl, there had been a bicycle shop on Chambers Street where you could rent a bike for a nickel an hour, and Mrs. Feeney had ridden around and around those vanished streets: Chambers Street, Allen, Blossom.

Now the window was open. Cold air blew in.

Classical music played on the hifi set. Her son had bought the hifi for her; she could barely work

29

the thing. But now it was playing Sibelius, the Fifth Symphony. The record ticked and crackled, but oh, the music! It swayed in a three-note theme, over and over, over and over—the long, gathering crescendo.

A long smear of blood.

A red handprint.

Mrs. Feeney lay on the floor. Her robe ripped open, legs wrenched apart, ankles pinned in the slats of two diningroom chairs to hold them spread, a pillow tucked under her rear end to prop it so that her pudendum was aimed at the front door. A pillowcase and stockings were wrapped around her neck, tied off with a big bow. Bluish bruises and the pink lividity of pooling blood mottled her skin around the garrote. Her mouth was still moist. In her eyes were tiny red spiders, capillaries that had burst.

The Sibelius symphony reached its climax. Five identical chords—irregularly spaced, like a dying heartbeat—each chord separated by a long, breathless pause. In an unstable B flat, the music pulsed twice—three—four—five times—then fell, exhausted, into its natural key of E flat—and it was over. The needle caught in the gutter and scratched there.

A fly, a lethargic November fly, flicked onto the dead woman's cheek. It tasted the corner of her mouth and scrubbed its forelegs together.

5

Michael, on the front porch. He paced. He hunched inside his winter coat, dragged on a cigarette, picked at the spongy floorboards with his toe. The planks were rotting, flaking apart. What a fucking dump. Whole place was falling apart. It was amazing how quickly a house began to disintegrate, how opportunistic the rot and damp were. One good stomp and he could crack any of these boards.

The screen door creaked and Ricky's head extended horizontally out of the door frame. "Supper."

"Be in in a minute."

Ricky's head retracted into the house, the screen door slammed, then the door snicked shut behind it.

But a few seconds later Ricky's head was out again. "She says now."

"Tell her in a minute."

"I told her. She says 'in a minute' isn't 'now.'"

"I know 'in a minute' isn't 'now.' That's why I said 'in a minute,' because that's when I'm coming in: in a minute. Jesus."

31

Ricky came out onto the porch, shut the door behind him. "The fuck are you doing out here? It's freezing."

Michael held up the cigarette.

"So come inside and smoke it. It's freezing."

"You seen this?" Michael nudged a long splinter in one of the floorboards with the toe of his penny loafer. He worked it back and forth until it flaked off. "Look at this."

"I know. It's a fuckin' mess. We'll fix it in the spring maybe. Come on, let's go. It's cold, I'm hungry."

Michael scowled.

"What's a matter, Mikey? You got a headache?"

"No, I'm fine."

"Then what's the problem?"

"I don't have a problem."

"You've got a puss on."

"No, I don't."

"You do. I'm looking right at it. Puss."

"I don't have a puss."

"You do. *I'll be in in a minute.*"

"Fuck you, Rick."

"*Fuck you, Rick.*"

Ricky smirked. The same charmed, blithe, princely grin he'd been deploying since the day he was born, four years after Michael. Ricky had smirked before he even had teeth, as if he knew, even as an infant, that he was no ordinary child.

The gloom Michael was feeling lifted a little, enough that he could shake his head and say "fuck you" again, warmer this time, *fuck you* meaning *stick around*.

"Let me bum one of those, Mikey."

Michael dug the pack of Larks from his pocket, and Ricky lit up using the end of Michael's cigarette.

"Jesus, would you look at this," Michael said.

The brothers peered through the window into the dining room, where an enormous redfaced man was taking his place at the head of the table. Brendan Conroy settled back in his chair, made various adjustments to his fork and knife, then shared an inaudible uproarious laugh with Joe Daley, who sat at his left hand.

"Honestly," Michael said, "I think I'm going to hang myself."

"Don't like your new daddy?"

"What ever happened to waiting a decent interval?"

"Dad's dead a year. How long do you want him to wait?"

"Longer." Michael considered. "A lot longer."

Ricky turned away. He took a deep, contented pull on his cigarette and gazed out at the street, at the unbroken line of little houses, all looking drab in the winter twilight. December in Savin Hill. Cars were parked nose-to-tail up and down the street. Soon there would be fights over who owned those spots; around here, shoveling a parking spot was tantamount to buying it for the season. Christmas lights were beginning to appear. Across the street the Daughertys had already put up their five ludicrous plastic reindeer, which were lit from the inside. There had used to be six. Joe had broken one in high school when he came home drunk one night and tried to ride it. The next day Joe Senior had made Joe march across the street and apologize for riding Mr. Daugherty's reindeer. What he ought to have apologized for was riding Mr. Daugherty's daughters, which Joe did with the same gleeful *droit du seigneur* he exercised over all the neighborhood girls. Even Eileen Daugherty, the youngest of the three, took her turn—in Joe's car, if Ricky was remembering right. That last coupling precipitated a brawl between Joe and Michael, because Michael had loved Eileen ever since kindergarten. He'd imagined that Eileen had somehow defied her genes and was not like that, until Joe set Michael straight, explaining that his conquest of the Daugherty sisters was really a sort of territorial obligation, like Manifest Destiny, and he'd needed Eileen to complete the hat trick, and anyway she had been a screamer. All of which had led Michael to throw himself at Joe, despite Joe's size, because he couldn't stop loving Eileen Daugherty even after she had offered herself up to Joe for the ritual goring. Maybe Michael loved her even now, deep down, the memory of her at least. He was that kind of kid. What ever happened to Eileen? Ricky turned back to his brother, "Hey, whatever happened to—?"

But Michael was still engrossed in what was behind the window, a fresher outrage. "Would you look at this? Look at Joe! What the hell does he think he's doing?"

34

Inside, Joe Daley and Brendan Conroy were holding up their glasses of pale beer, laughing.

"Look at him, with his head up Conroy's ass. He's like a tapeworm."

"Conroy could use a tapeworm."

"Really, Rick, the whole thing, it's just— Doesn't this bother you?"

"Not really. Hey, whatever happened to Eileen from across the street? You ever hear about her?"

"No." Michael did not glance away from the window.

Joe's wife, Kat, came out onto the porch. "Are you guys coming in or you want your supper out here?"

"Michael's mad."

"I'm not mad—"

"He thinks Mum's going to lose her virginity—"

"I didn't say—"

"—to Brendan."

Kat thought it over. "Well," she concluded, "she'll probably wait till after dinner anyways."

"There, see?" Ricky smiled. "Nothing to worry about."

"Come on. In." Kat herded them inside with a dish towel, and in they went. There was something about Kat—Kathleen—that suggested she wasn't taking any shit. She was just Joe's type, big and hippy and goodlooking and stolid, and the Daley boys as a rule did not fuck with her.

Michael went in first, wearing a sour-mouthed pucker. Ricky gave him a playful biff on the back of

35

the head, and Kat rubbed his shoulder, both gestures intended to cheer him up.

The house smelled of garlic, and the girls were bustling from the kitchen to the table with a few last things.

Amy sped past: "Hey, Michael. Thought we'd lost you."

Little Joe passed without a word. Joe's son, Little Joe, was thirteen and had taken over the title "Little Joe" from his father, who had been Little Joe to his own father's Big Joe. The Daleys did not believe in Juniors and III's and IV's; too Yankee. So each succeeding Joe got a new middle name. The current Little Joe was Joseph Patrick. At the moment he was sulking, Michael had no idea about what.

Margaret Daley, the materfamilias, tweaked Michael about a "disappearing act," which tipped his mood downward again. Over the years Michael had evolved an exquisite sensitivity to his mother's voice, so that he could detect the slightest reprimand or disapproval. Margaret was well aware of this sensitivity—Michael was her most finely calibrated son, the quickest to take offense and the slowest to forgive—but Margaret simply did not know how to speak without setting him off, without triggering one of those little sensors, and so she could not help but resent him for being thin-skinned and fragile, though in this respect he reminded her of Joe Senior, another man she'd never quite known, even after sleeping in the same bed with him for thirty-some-odd years. She saw

Michael's face fall when she mentioned his disappearing act. She regretted the comment for a moment, then decided not to regret it. Let *him* regret it. He was the one who should regret it. Margaret would regret only that Michael might spoil their Sunday dinner with his sulking.

Michael stood behind a seat in the middle of the table, feeling awkward, a guest in the house where he had grown up.

"Sit down." Conroy grinned. "You're making me nervous."

"Yeah, sit down, Michael. What *is* this?"

Michael looked at Joe, who continued to regard him with a quizzical, supercilious expression that said *What is this?* Joe was imitating Conroy; that was the insufferable part. Well, Michael sighed, dinner would only last an hour or two. The sooner it started, the sooner it would end. He could already see himself at home looking back on it.

Michael took his place and the others filled in around him. Margaret at the head, opposite Conroy, in the same chair she'd occupied forever. Ricky at the corner opposite Joe, as far from Joe as he could get, to minimize the fighting. Kat positioned herself next to Joe, where she could keep a stern eye on him. Michael liked Kat and liked Joe for liking her. God bless her, Kat would take a bullet for Joe or put one in him, as the occasion required.

But opposite Michael was his favorite, Amy Ryan, whose cool redheaded presence was the best part of these Sunday dinners. Amy was Ricky's girlfriend, and Michael harbored an illicit, quasi-romantic affection for her. Amy was wry, Amy was brave, Amy was funny, Amy was lovely, Amy was hip, Amy was profane, Amy was smart— her merits jostled for attention and it would have been impossible for Michael to name the one or two he liked best. Tonight she was wearing a white oxford shirt that may or may not have been Ricky's, which struck Michael as a poignant gesture. She wore Ricky's shirt as other girls had worn his varsity jacket once. There was a little of the bachelor's yearning in Michael's feelings for Amy. She made him question his instinct for solitude.

The group was still unfolding their napkins when Amy mentioned, "So, Brendan, I hear Alvan Byron is going to take over the Strangler case." She spent a few seconds surveying the dishes on the table in a nonchalant way—noodles and gravy and garlic bread—as if the answer would not make a bit of difference to her.

But Amy Ryan was a reporter, one of only two women on the staff of the *Observer*, and Brendan Conroy wasn't falling for any of her career-girl tricks."Are we on the record or off?"

"Oh, Brendan, come on. Listen to you. We're just talking. Alright, you tell me, on or off?"

"Off."

"Okay, off. Remember that, Margaret," Amy said, "we're off the record."

"Who could forget it?" the older woman drawled.

Conroy folded his arms. "Alright, then, here it is. Alvan Byron will not take over the Strangler case

38

for the simple reason that he could not solve the Strangler case. He hasn't got the people or the resources or the know-how."

"He's got Michael," Ricky said.

"And we've got Joe."

"Exactly."

"Ricky-y-y," his mother growled.

Michael forked a tangle of spaghetti onto his plate and, head down, he mixed red sauce into it with extraordinary care.

Conroy turned back to Amy. "Let me tell you something, girly-girl, before you go dancing off and write some story about the great Alvan Byron. Your Mr. Byron is not a cop, has never been, will never be a cop. What Alvan Byron knows about police work would fit on the head of a pin, with room for a few dancing angels."

Ricky: "The great Conroy has spoken."

Amy: "He *is* the Attorney General, Brendan. Doesn't that count for something?"

"No. See, you don't understand. Byron's the Attorney General— that's just the problem. You don't go to a dentist for a broken leg, and you don't send a lawyer to do a cop's work. I look at the Attorney General's office and do you know what I see? A law firm. Yankees and goo-goos and Hebrews, and the one lonely Irishman named Daley, and the whole place run by a colored fellow." He smiled at his witticism. "Whole outfit is upside down."

"And you," Michael said, "have got thirteen dead women."

Ricky: "Plus Joe, don't forget. Thirteen dead women—and Joe."

Conroy held Michael's gaze. "We'll find him."

Kat said, "Better find him fast. I don't sleep at night, with Joe off working and this lunatic running around. I feel like he's hiding in the closet somewhere, and if I fall asleep . . ."

"We'll catch him. Don't you worry. It'll all be over soon."

"Brendan," Ricky said, "no offense, but Mike'd catch your strangler before Joe gets through his first dozen doughnuts."

Joe waved his knife.

"Well." Amy sighed. "I'm just telling you what I hear, Brendan. Byron is going to take the Strangler case. Bet on it."

"I'll take that bet, girly. It's Boston PD's case. I can't imagine why on earth we would ever give it up."

"If Byron says you're out," Michael said, "you're out."

"That's what you think."

"That's the way it is. He's the A.G., he's got statewide jurisdiction. If he wants the Strangler case, he can just take it."

"See, now that just shows how little you know, smart guy. I'm sure you're right about the legalities. But there's what's legal and there's what's practical, and Byron can't solve that case without BPD's support. Doesn't matter what's in your law books. This is the real world. And in the real world you can't solve a homicide without homicide detectives. Byron doesn't have them; we do."

"Yeah, Mikey," Ricky said, "you've been spending too much time with your Hebrews and goo-goos."

"And your coloreds," Joe added.

"And Yankees," said Amy.

Michael: "Well, maybe you're right, Brendan. You don't need any help. It's, what, a year and a half? And what have you got? Thirteen dead girls and not one arrest. City's scared half to death. Hell of a job."

"Michael," Margaret cautioned, "that's enough."

Michael shook his head. He was not sure how he'd got into this position. He did not care much about the Strangler or Alvan Byron. He simply felt an irresistible urge to contradict Brendan Conroy. Something about Conroy's voice, that sententious tone of his, brought out the worst in Michael.

Conroy seemed willing to let the whole thing pass. He would not grant Michael the satisfaction of goading him into a reaction. "We'll catch him," he repeated without any real conviction. "You wait and see."

"So," Amy cut in, "you still want that bet, Brendan?"

"That Byron won't butt in? Sure. I just hate to take your money, girly-girl. How's two bits, can you afford that? They pay you enough at that fish wrapper?"

"Doesn't matter. I won't be paying it."

Conroy grinned and raised his glass to Amy. "I like your style."

Michael rolled his eyes.

Joe saw Michael's eyerolling and misinterpreted it. "It's easy to make fun from the cheap seats, Mikey."

"I didn't say anything to you, Joe."

"I'm a cop, too."

"I wasn't talking about you, Joe. Just let it alone."

"Yeah, you were. You were talking about cops. I'm a cop."

"Your dad was a cop, too," Conroy threw in.

"Let's leave him out of it," Michael said.

"I was just saying—"

"Leave him out."

"Sorry, Michael. I didn't mean anything."

"He didn't mean anything," Joe seconded.

From the police reports, Michael had formed an image of his father's death: In an alley in East Boston, his heart pierced by a bullet, Joe Senior had shimmered down to the ground, hands pinned to his sides. That was the image Michael saw now, and it made him venomous.

"Brendan, you might have let that chair cool off before you sat down in it."

"Michael!" Margaret's tone was more astonished than angry.

Conroy was unruffled."I see."He simply had not understood and now everything was clear. "Maybe I should go."

"So go," Michael said.

Joe pounded the table with the butt of his fist.

Conroy dabbed the corners of his mouth with his napkin. "I'm sorry, I shouldn't have come.

Margaret, ladies, thank you for all this. Excuse me."

"Brendan,"Margaret instructed, "you sit down. This is my house, you're my guest. It's enough of this." Mother Daley could be magnificently huffy. Her late husband had called her Princess Margaret. The three boys, more accurately, called her Queen Margaret.

"No, Margaret. Maybe Michael's right, it's too soon."

"Michael is *not* right."

"Some other time. I don't want to spoil this beautiful meal."

"Brendan! You sit down. Michael is going to apologize."

Ricky said, "What's he got to apologize? He didn't do anything."

"Mind your own business, you."

Brendan Conroy smiled gallantly. All the arguing was pointless. There was no swaying him from a grand gesture. "Some other time," he repeated. He excused himself, got his coat, and left.

The seven Daleys listened as Conroy started his car and drove off.

A moment of silence.

"Michael," Ricky said, "let me have those noodles."

For as long as the Daley boys could remember, there had been a basket attached to the phone pole in front of the house. They had gone through a few of them. Winters killed the steel hoops and especially the flimsy backboards from Lechmere's,

43

and every few years Joe Senior would swap in a new set, adjusting it slightly up or down the pole to avoid the holes left by the big lag screws he used. The current model, which had lasted the longest, had a faded, undersized fan-shaped aluminum backboard. It was hung a few inches too high and seemed to rise even higher as you got closer to the curb, where the pavement dipped. The boys thought of this hoop and the pavement in front of it as their private court. Even now, with the Daley boys all long gone from the house, there were neighbors who did not park in front of the basket, out of old habit, as if it were a fire hydrant. Occasionally a new neighbor or visitor or other interloper, ignorant of the local etiquette, would leave his car under the hoop, and the boys took it as a sign of the decline of their city. Back in the day, no one would dream of parking there because, as a general rule, you did not fuck with the Daleys, particularly Joe, and in any case there was always a game going on there.

These games were a deadly serious business. A *Code Napoléon* of unspoken rules governed play. One must never take the feet out from under a player near the basket lest he land on his back on the curbstone, as Jimmy Reilly once did. The Daleys' ball was never to be used in a game at which no Daley was present, even if the ball was sitting right there in the yard. All parked cars were inbounds. But the sidewalk was out-of-bounds, to discourage smaller players from running behind the basket and using the pole to rub off a defender, a strategy deemed so chickenshit that Joe forbid it outright. These were technicalities, though. The real secret knowledge of these games—their whole purpose—was the hierarchy of the boys involved. There were a dozen local boys who regularly played, mostly Irish, all linked through school or St. Margaret's parish, and every one of them knew precisely where he ranked from number one to number twelve. There was no allowance for age or size. Nor did it matter who you were. Michael Daley never rose above the middle of the pack, even on his home court; Leo Madden, though his father was in and out of Deer Island and his mother weighed three bills, was a rebounding machine and therefore he was completely respected here. Prestige to the winners, shame to the losers. All of it real and perfectly quantifiable and precious as money in the lives of boys, and men.

So, when the three brothers drifted out to play after dinner under the streetlight, the women gathered at the windows to watch. They arranged themselves at the livingroom windows, which looked across the porch and over a shallow yard to the street. Margaret and Kat stood together at one window, Amy at the other. The younger women wore similar expressions, sharp, bemused, scornful. Queen Margaret had the same sharp smirk, but there was bleary concern in her eyes. She could not completely share in the womanly skepticism of boys' games, knowing that, however it turned out, one of her boys would lose. She felt Kat's arm curled around her lower back; that helped a little.

"Margaret," Kat said, "you should have had one more. Two against one, it's not fair."

"Fair to who?"

"True." Kat considered the problem. "You know, Ricky should let them win, just once."

Margaret emitted a skeptical sniff. Cigarette smoke piped out of her nostrils.

"Amy, why don't you talk to him? Ricky's got to let Joe win sometime." Kat gave Amy a sidelong look. "Come on, Aim, you could find a way to convince him, couldn't you?"

Amy raised two fingers, scissored her cigarette between them, and removed the cigarette with a flourish. "Ladies, let me assure you, I could lie down in my altogether on a bed of roses and it wouldn't make one bit of difference. Ricky'd cut off his right arm before he'd let Joe win."

"Well," Kat sighed, "if Joe beats him then, it'll be fair and square."

"He's got to win sometime, right? I mean, if they play enough times?"

Amy: "I just hope Joe doesn't kill him, after that fiasco."

Margaret: "If he's going to kill anyone, it'll be poor Michael. I don't know what's got into him. Michael's crazy lately."

"Don't worry, Mum, Joe won't kill him. Maybe just, you know, shake him around a little."

"Well, that's a comfort, dear."

Outside, Michael was hopping up and down to stay warm.

"I don't know what Michael's got against poor Brendan, I really don't."

Amy: "I do."

Kat: "Margaret, maybe you should enter a convent."

"I'm not entering any convents."

"Still got some wild oats to sow?"

Margaret turned to face the two younger women. "Now why should that be so funny?"

Kat made a face at Amy: eyebrows raised, impressed smile, Wow!

Amy: "Nothing's funny. So, Mum, is Brendan . . . ?"

Kat covered her ears. "Oh, stop! Ick."

"Brendan is—"

"Stop, stop, stop!"

"I didn't know you girls were so squeamish."

Amy said, "I'm not squeamish."

Kat watched Joe as he stood waiting for a rebound, arms up. "Amy, you want to make this interesting?"

"Sure."

"Six points okay?"

"Sure, whatever."

"Margaret, how about you? Michael's feeling feisty tonight. Care to put a little cash down on the middle son?"

"You want me to bet against my own sons?"

"Only one of them."

Margaret shook her head.

"Go on, Mum," Amy urged, "it's just for fun."

"We'll never tell," Kat added. "Promise."

47

"No, thanks, dear."

"Take Joe," Kat pleaded. "The poor thing."

Margaret considered it. "I'll put a nickel on Ricky."

"Oh!" Kat yelped. "You're a horrible mother."

Through the window they could hear the brothers ragging each other as the game got going. Joe and Michael were a team, as usual, and at the start they exploited their two-to-one advantage by spreading out, forcing Ricky to cover one or the other, then passing to the free man for easy shots. Michael was a careful player, a lurker. He liked to slide into open spaces for unmolested set shots. At times he moved out of the lighted area altogether, and the women had to squint to find him in the darkness. Joe's game was all muscle. He moved like a bear chasing a butterfly, but his size ensured he would always have the best position under the basket. Together they made a decent inside-outside combination. As their lead climbed, 2–0, 3–0, 4–0, Joe's taunting got louder and louder. Amy was right: Joe was pissed about the way Brendan Conroy had been treated, and, though Michael had been Conroy's main tormenter, Joe directed his anger at Ricky. There was a tacit understanding that Michael was somehow disengaged from the grander struggle between Joe and Ricky. So if Joe was angry, it seemed perfectly natural for him to target Ricky, not Michael. The insults from Joe were all variations on a theme: "Come on, Mary . . . Does your husband play? . . . What, are you afraid of a little contact? . . . Pussy . . ."

And then, in an instant, the game changed. Michael put up one of his little jumpers, the kind he knocked down over and over, but this time the shot was flat. It caught the back rim and rebounded high, out into the street, away from the hoop where Joe was hanging. Ricky snagged it in the air.

"Shit!" Kat hissed.

A little smiled wriggled across Amy's lips.

What happened next happened very quickly. Ricky bounced the ball once with his left hand, once with his right. Michael swiped at it, and Ricky avoided him by threading the ball between his own legs, from back to front, which left Michael behind him and out of the play. Joe took a step toward him, like a palace guard blocking a gate. Ricky paused for an instant to eye him up. He slow-dribbled the ball low and to his right, extending it a few inches toward Joe, who finally took the bait, leaning then stepping toward the ball, a reluctant irresistible stuttery step. But it was enough. Ricky crossed the ball over to his left hand, and he was behind Joe. He laid the ball in: 6–1.

Kat groaned, "*Mmm*. It's not fair. The way Ricky shows off!"

"He's not showing off."

"Oh, Amy!"

"Alright," Amy allowed, "maybe a little."

But Amy could not take her eyes off him. Because he was showing off *for her*. And because he was beautiful. His game was jazzy and gliding and fast, she thought, but more than anything it was beautiful. The way he moved. The way the ball moved

49

with him, the way it yoyoed back to his hand. The way he spun, his body in flight. Amy had not known Ricky when he was a high-school hero—when he was Tricky Ricky Daley, point guard and captain at Boston English, All-Scholastic, All-Everything; when he'd been offered a scholarship to Holy Cross, alma mater of the great Cousy himself—and she was glad for that. She did not want to think of Ricky as one of those arrested men who were such stars in high school or college that everything after was tinged with anticlimax and nostalgia. She did not want to define him by what he *had been*. And she particularly did not want to define him as a jock because he wasn't, not anymore. Anyway, Ricky never talked about it. For a long time after they'd met, Amy had had no idea the man she was dating had a glorious past, until she'd finally met his family and Margaret had shown her a book of clippings. In fact, for Amy the defining moment of Ricky's basketball career was the way it had ended, the way he'd thrown it all away in a romantic, stupid gesture. He'd got himself pinched with a cartrunkful of Mighty Mac parkas that had "fallen off a truck," as the saying went. That was the end of Holy Cross and basketball and Tricky Ricky Daley, and good riddance. It was all so clumsy—so un-Rickylike—it seemed like a setup. Amy saw something heroic in the whole episode. Ricky had been true to some obscure, prickly, self-destructive impulse that no one, not Amy, probably not Ricky himself, could quite understand. He just had not felt like being Tricky

Ricky anymore, so he had stopped. And yet Amy could not deny that she loved him more—at least she loved him differently, saw him differently—when she watched him play. She thought she understood in some intuitive, inarticulable way what made Ricky do the things he did. It was something about doing the opposite of what everyone else wanted him to do. My Lord, how could she not love such a beautiful, wasteful man?

Ricky spun and tricky-dribbled and flew by his brothers. His hair flopped over his forehead, grew damp and drippy. He did not say much; his virtuosity was not news to anyone.

But Joe grew more incensed with each basket. His feet got sluggish and he was reduced to pawing Ricky as he rushed past, or elbowing him, or hip-checking him.

None of it mattered. Ricky scored with leaners and fades and baby hooks, and at 19–6 Joe finally exploded. He pushed Ricky hard into the chainlink fence behind the hoop.

"Nineteen," Ricky said as he lay on the sidewalk. "Hey, Mike, wanna switch teams?"

"Hey, Ricky," Joe said, "blow me."

"Oh, that's good, Joe. 'Blow me.' That's clever."

Joe gave Ricky the finger and held it there.

"Some brother you turn out to be, Joe." Ricky got to his feet. "First you take Conroy's side against Michael, now this. Tsk, tsk, tsk."

Joe took a step toward him. "You want to say that again?"

"Oh, come on, Joe, be a good loser. You've had

plenty of practice." Ricky jogged out to the street and tossed the ball to Michael for the customary check.

"You ready, Joe?" Michael asked.

Joe growled that he was, and Michael lobbed Ricky the ball.

Ricky eyed Joe again. He could end it by shooting from out here, over Michael, but he wanted Joe to know he was going to victimize *him*. Joe would not have the excuse that his teammate had let him down. Ricky jab-stepped left and with one of his whirling-dervish spins he put Michael behind him. He pulled up to shoot a little bunny directly in Joe's face. Joe waved at the shot then gave Ricky a hard shove on the left side of his chest, which sent him sprawling once more on the street.

"Jesus, Joe!" Michael shouted.

"Just play defense, Michael. It's like I'm the only one working out here. You play like a fuckin' homo."

Michael offered Ricky a hand and pulled him up.

"Twenty," Ricky said.

"I'm out,"Michael said. "This is bullshit."He stalked back toward the house.

"Go ahead, leave," Joe called after him. "I'll fuckin' do it myself. Fuckin' homo."

Ricky tossed the ball to Joe. "Check."

"The fuck are you laughing at?"

"I just thought you'd want to know what I'm gonna do."

"What are you talking about?"

"How I'm going to win. It's gonna be a jump shot, right from here, right over you. Just so you know."

Joe's brow crumpled.Was it a trick? Or just more showing off? It would be just like Ricky to promise a jump shot then race by Joe, just to make him look foolish. Then again . . .

Joe flipped the ball back. "Check."

Ricky stab-stepped to his right, a long, convincing lunge with the ball whipping far ahead of him, almost behind Joe, and despite what Ricky had said, Joe reacted, couldn't help himself—he stepped back. Just one fatal fucking step. Ricky pulled back and shot over him. Joe's chin dropped even before the shot hit.

"Game," Ricky said.

Joe glared.

Ricky might have left it there. But the sight of Joe with that seething expression, that muscle twitching in his cheek—Joe looked like he might actually burst—seemed funny to him. Ricky watched Joe watching him, and because it was the only thing he could think of

at the moment, Ricky finally blurted, "*Boo!*"

Joe took off after him.

"Oh, good gracious," Margaret moaned, from the window. An image flashed in her mind: the two boys rolling on the sidewalk, punching, arms flailing, hugging each other close so neither could extend his arm and land a solid shot. They had been, what, eleven and sixteen? And determined to kill each other if she hadn't rushed out and pulled them apart. And why? Over a basketball game. Good gracious!

Ricky was sprinting back toward the house now. He leaped up onto the ten-foot chainlink fence that separated the Daleys' driveway from the neighbor's. Joe jumped too, but too late. Ricky scrambled up and over the fence and dropped down on the other side. Behind the diamondmesh he grinned and panted, looking straight at Joe. "Where's a cop when you need one?" he said.

Amy covered her smile with her hand, as if it was impolite to laugh at the whole thing.

"Oh, Joe." Kat sighed. "Well, girls, we couldn't all bet on Ricky now, could we?"

6

Walter Cronkite, in voiceover: "The focus of our report is a key store in Boston, Massachusetts. Address: three-six-four Massachusetts Avenue. Until recently this was the busiest store in the neighborhood, perhaps one of the busiest key stores in the world, open for business six days a week, nine hours a day in the winter, twelve hours a day in the summer. During business hours cars double-parked in front, and on some days more than one thousand customers entered this door. Many proceeded to a room in the rear of the store. We followed with a concealed microphone and camera."

A wide shot of a storefront. The picture was in black and white, though the TV set was a new four-hundred-dollar color console model, one of Ricky's mysterious lavish gifts. In front of the store hung a sign in the shape of a key, its teeth facing up. The sign read,

SWARTZ'S
KEYS MADE WHILE U WAIT

Cut to a tighter shot of the storefront: People sauntered in and out of the front door, men and women, white and colored, in suits and T-shirts. Then an interior shot, blurry, the frame jerking around, the perspective a low angle, elbow height, as if the camera was being held under the cameraman's arm. Cigar-chewing men behind a counter. Amid the ambient chatter, a voice was overheard: "Gimme number six in the fifth, for one."

Cronkite's voice again, grave and rhythmic: "The men behind the counter are called bookies. They are taking offtrack bets on horses and dog races and selling chances on the numbers game, a form of lottery. What they are doing is illegal in every state of the union except Nevada. They are among thousands of bookies engaged in a nationwide multi-billion-dollar-a-year business, a business that has been called 'the treasure chest of the underworld.' "

Onscreen a cop in uniform—police cap, white shirt, dark necktie, jacket, and slacks—strolled out of the key shop. He got into the passenger seat of a marked BPD cruiser which was parked directly in front of the shop.

"Shit," Ricky said. His hair was still damp and tendriled from the basketball game.

Cronkite, still in voice-over: "How does organized gambling operate? How does this business continue despite laws against it? And when the laws are not enforced by police officers, how does this affect the community and the nation?"

The police cruiser pulled away from the shop.

Music swelled, Copland's *Appalachian Spring*. The cruiser froze onscreen, and a title was superimposed over it: BIOGRAPHY OF A BOOKIE JOINT.

"*CBS Reports: Biography of a Bookie Joint* is brought to you by pink-lotion Lux Liquid, the liquid for Lux-lovely hands and sparkling dishes . . ."

"Hey, Joe," Michael called from the couch, "you better get in here and see this."

"Mikey, we're in the middle of something here." Joe and Kat had been arguing in the kitchen, in shouting whispers. No doubt she was reaming him out for losing it with Ricky during the basketball game.

"No, you better come watch this."

Joe came out with a scowl. What now? He saw the slackjawed gawp on his brothers' faces. He glanced at the screen, which still displayed an ad for dish-washing liquid. "What? You guys look like someone just farted in church."

"They're doing a show on The Monkey," Ricky explained, "that key place on Mass. Ave." The Monkey was the locals' name for Abe Swartz, the old man who ran the bookie shop as part of Doc Sagansky's operation.

"Get the fuck out," Joe said skeptically.

"Just sit down, Joe," Michael said.

Joe shooed Little Joe off the couch and sat down. The house, which had never seemed small to the boys growing up, now felt comically miniature. Joe and Michael contorted themselves on the couch so as not to touch each other. Little Joe arranged himself on the floor in front of the TV.

The show resumed with Cronkite in a wood-paneled studio, sitting on an unseen stool, his shoulders at an angle to the camera. He wore a gray suit, white shirt, dark tie, handkerchief folded in his coat pocket. Hair Brylcreemed straight back, bushy eyebrows, a thin mustache. He was not handsome—his chin was weak, his nose drooped—but maybe that was his secret. That sonorous, earnest, authoritative voice, the voice of Truth Revealed, issued forth from a guy who looked like your barber. Over Cronkite's shoulder, in the upper left corner of the screen, was a still shot of the exterior of the key shop.

"This is Walter Cronkite. Experts agree that organized gambling is the most lucrative, most corrupting, and most widely tolerated form of crime in the nation. This huge business pits the government of the underworld against the government of the people. The corner bookie, to be found in most American cities, is at the base of the problem. He is the so-called Little Man, but he is the funnel through which billions of dollars a year flow into the underworld. It is our purpose tonight to examine the consequences of the nickels, the dimes, and the dollars wagered with the corner bookie. He and his associates might operate out of a hotel room in New York or a tavern in San Francisco or, as in the case of this report, a key store on Massachusetts Avenue."

The brothers stared.

On screen, a blank map of the United States. A line sprouted from Boston and stretched to a point that might have been Chicago. Then another, to Vegas. Another to L.A. To Miami. Montreal. New York. Soon the map looked like an airline route map, with every line originating in Boston. ". . . In August 1961, testimony at McClellan Committee hearings on illegal gambling alleged that Boston itself is one of the major layoff centers in the nation . . ."

Amy wandered in from the dining room. "What's this?"

"Shhhh!"

On screen, smoke rose from a trash can on the sidewalk in front of the key shop. A bettor came out of the shop and casually dropped a piece of paper into the smoldering can. ". . . It is a violation of a city ordinance to burn trash on the sidewalk, but here the smoke of burning betting slips remained a common sight, a beacon for bettors."

Kat and Amy and finally Margaret joined the group. From the men's faces, they knew this program was not leading anywhere good.

A narrator's voice, over grainy footage of people placing bets in the back room of the key shop: "The bettors at this bookie shop are not breaking the law; the bookies are. Most of the bookies' business in the afternoon is in bets on horse races. The minimum you can bet on a horse race at a racetrack is two dollars. Here the minimum is one dollar and fifty cents. We watched some of the customers bet as much as fifty dollars; we're told that a one-hundred-dollar bet is not unusual. The bookies claim that they pay the same betting odds as the racetracks; it's generally reported that most bookies pay lower odds than the track. According to some of the customers, bookies at the key shop have never been known to welsh on a bet. As one customer put it, 'This is a first-class bookie joint.' "

The program cut from the bookie shop to a montage of horseracing scenes: a bugler calling the horses to the post, crowds milling, money thrown down at the betting window, horses racing.

Cronkite again: "Here the bettor who has the time and inclination can bet his entire bankroll legally. Pari-mutuel horse tracks are licensed in twenty-five states. Total attendance at these tracks last year: fortyeight and a half million persons. The handle, or total amount of money bet: three and a half billion dollars—one billion dollars more than the nation spent last year on new schools, class-rooms, and textbooks. From the three and a half billions in bets on horses, the states received two hundred and fifty-eight million dollars in tax revenue. For every bet made here legally, it is estimated that at least three bets are made off-track, illegally, at places like the key store."

Another montage: an establishing shot of the entrance gate to the Wonderland dog track, more crowds and betting windows, dogs racing.

Cronkite, in voice-over: "By seven-thirty P.M., Boston's Wonderland, the world's largest dog track, is open for business. Here gambling on dog races is legal. Attendance at this track during the racing season averages twelve thousand persons a night. Total yearly attendance: over one million, two hundred thousand. Pari-mutuel wagering on dogs is legal at thirty-five tracks in eight states. At Wonderland, more than six hundred and eighty-three thousand dollars was wagered in one night. The total amount wagered at dog tracks throughout the nation exceeds two billion dollars a year. Two hundred million dollars of this went to the states in tax revenue. It has been estimated that for each bet made at a pari-mutuel dog track, at least one other bet is made off-track. The states receive no tax revenue from off-track bets made with bookies at places like the key store."

Cronkite again appeared on screen, unruffled by all this troubling news: "Evidence to be detailed later in the program indicates that the gross income of the key store in Boston may have exceeded twenty-five thousand dollars a week. That's a million and a half dollars a year, and that's no penny-ante operation by any means. But there are larger bookie operations. Experts generally agree that illegal off-track bookmaking is a multi-billion-dollar-a-year business. And the experts also agree on another thing: illegal gambling cannot flourish for long unless it is protected."

A montage of police officers ambling in and out of the key shop, all in full uniform, including motorcycle officers in jackboots and jodhpurs, and traffic cops in white hats.

A narrator's voice: "Some government estimates put the cost of police protection at fifty percent of the net profits of the gaming operation. Several bookies told us the costs were getting so high that it was becoming more a police business than a bookie business."

More cops were shown coming and going. One was temporarily impeded by the trash can full of smoldering betting slips, which a bookie kindly moved out of his way. The cop tipped his cap to the bookie.

Cronkite, voice-over: "From June the first to June third, 1963, we filmed ten members of the Boston police force entering or leaving the key store. We don't know why they came to the key store or what they did inside. We only know that they were there."

A man in plain clothes came out of the key shop. Big guy with a barrel torso. He wore a dark coat, open collar, and flat-brim fedora.

"Oh my God—" Kat muttered.

But Cronkite cut her off. "The man coming out of the door now is a detective. We found that he comes from Station Sixteen, Boston Police Department, just a few blocks away."

The camera lingered on Joe as he loitered on the sidewalk outside the shop. He looked, even to the Daleys, like the very face of police corruption.

"Oh my God," Kat repeated. She had covered her mouth with both hands, as if to catch any words that might slip out.

Cronkite: "Other Boston police officers were seen entering the key store during the course of our investigation. We must emphasize again that we do not know the nature of their business in the key store."

A white-haired gent appeared onscreen to opine on the matter of cops and bookies: "I think most of the policemen on the Boston Police Department are honest and want to do their sworn duty. However, some of them have been in touch with me, by calls and letters, and have written on police department letterhead, although unsigned, about suspected illegal gambling operations which they hope we will do something about."

And Cronkite again, now in close-up. "It has been said that police corruption can be found in every city where illegal gambling flourishes. The story has been told in headlines from cities across the nation time and time again. It is in part an answer to the question 'What harm can there be in a little two-dollar bet at the corner bookie?' "

"Fuckin' Walter Cronkite."

"Shush, Joe!"

"What, Mum? He can't just— I mean, for Christ's sake, I went in there for a key!"

Ricky snorted.

"Yeah?" Michael asked. "A key to what?"

"What is this, cross-examination? I needed a key. So what?"

Margaret turned to Amy as a representative of the news media.

"Amy, can they do this? Just, just put up someone's pitcher like that and say whatever they want?"

Amy made a fatalistic shrug and turned her palms up. *What can you do?*

Now the program displayed a banner headline

from the Boston *Traveler*, "Commr. Sullivan May Be on Probation," with the subhead "Volpe Has His Eye on Him." Cronkite in voiceover: ". . . At a press conference Governor John A. Volpe said he expects the Boston police commissioner to fulfill his responsibilities in full compliance with the law."

Cronkite appeared onscreen again, in the wood-paneled studio. "We extended an invitation to Boston Police Commissioner Leo J. Sullivan to appear on this program to comment on the difficulties facing local police departments in coping with illegal gambling as reflected by the history of the key shop operation. Commissioner Sullivan has replied to our invitation with a letter outlining problems confronting local police. He points out that legalized on-track betting stimulates illegal off-track betting; that placing a bet off-track is not an offense; and that bookmaking is only a minor misdemeanor."

"Yeah, okay, Commissioner, I'm sure that's gonna be good enough."

"Shush, Ricky."

Cronkite: "He went on to say that the local police administrator has limited manpower and funds, and that the combined efforts of all law enforcement agencies have failed to dent the framework of illegal gambling. 'It would therefore be a grave injustice,' said the police commissioner, 'to denigrate an entire police department and to destroy the public image created by the fine accomplishments of many dedicated police officers on the basis of one such gambling establishment. In the final analysis, the people of this and every other community must come to the realization that it is their small individual bet that finances the illegal gambling empire and complete enforcement is not possible without the active assistance of all good citizens.' Those were the words of Boston Police Commissioner Leo Sullivan."

"What a fuckin' rat," Joe said.

The camera moved in on Cronkite. "At this point you may be inclined to say, 'Well, those people in Boston certainly have their problems.' Don't deceive yourself. The chances are very great you have the same problem in your community. This is Walter Cronkite. Goodnight."

The Daleys were silent.

The TV prattled awhile—"A word about the next *CBS Reports* in a moment . . ."—until Amy shut it off.

"Fuckin' Walter Cronkite," Joe muttered.

"Stop that."

"Fuck Walter Cronkite."

"Stop it. It's not Walter Cronkite's fault."

"Well, it's not true." Joe seemed to believe in the transformative power of his own confidence. A thing was not true because Joe Daley said it was not true. "They're not gonna get away with this."

Amy said, "If you know any good lawyers, Joe . . ."

"Why do I need a lawyer? I didn't do anything. I just got done telling you."

"Joe," Michael advised softly, "call Brendan."

7

The hearing looked like a trial but it wasn't. It was a bag job. The "judge" was a deputy appointed by the Commissioner, serving at the pleasure of the Commissioner, there to do the Commissioner's bidding. The prosecutor was an I.A. lieutenant whose evidence consisted of a transcript of the CBS documentary and not much else. Joe had been forced to hire a lawyer, a shifty shyster he knew from the BMC, who made a few desultory objections. But everyone knew the verdict. Walter Cronkite had announced it on TV: Joe Daley was a bag man for the crooked cops in Station Sixteen. The inconvenient fact that the charge was true did not make the whole thing any easier for Joe to take.

After he testified, Joe paced the hallway on the sixth floor of BPD headquarters, where the hearing took place. There were no reporters, no crowds. It was a family matter, for now.

Brendan Conroy was still inside, shilling for Joe. His muffled voice carried through the door: Joe was a good kid, a good soldier. Third-generation Boston police. Son of a fallen cop. No one was defending what the kid did, of course. Of course. But then, there was honor in the way Joe'd come in there and kept his mouth shut and refused to roll over on anyone. Now, there was a time when cops were brothers, let's remember. Did they mean to throw out the baby with the bath water? Did they really want to lose a kid like Joe Daley? Let's not be more Catholic than the Pope here, fellas—if they were going to start canning every cop who ever took a few bucks, or who ate dinner at the kitchen door of a restaurant, well, let's face it, before long there wouldn't be a police department left. Anyway, the last Brendan Conroy had heard, Walter Cronkite had not been appointed commissioner of the Boston police.

Joe tried not to listen. He trusted that Conroy would pull it off. Conroy knew which strings to pull. He'd take care of the whole thing. No big deal. In time everyone would come to realize that this whole bookie thing was no big deal.

So why did Joe feel so aggrieved? It could have been worse, after all. The Monkey's was not the only place Joe had ever picked up an envelope or put down a few bucks on a puppy or on his badge number. For Christ's sake, if they had followed Joe around with a camera, Walter Cronkite would have shat in his CBS trousers. As it was, no one was going to throw Joe under the train for stopping by The Monkey's once or twice. So it wasn't the accusation that was so troubling to Joe. It was the sense of unseen forces, the infuriating aware-ness that he would never quite understand what had gone on here. He wasn't fucking smart enough to figure it all out, to see the connections, the complexities. Why on earth had Walter fucking Cronkite come to Boston? Why the key shop? Why him? Joe thought he had it sometimes, that the truth was about to come shivering through, but it never quite did. So the answers hovered out there in the air somewhere, just out of sight. He was like a kid. He could hear it in the way they spoke to him, that pizzicato pickpickpick tone the deputy had lectured him with—*Detective Daley, you've embarrassed this en-tire department in front of the en-tire country*. It was precisely the pissy tone Joe used with his own kid when he did bad. Now the adults were meeting behind closed doors to pass sentence on *him*. Well, so what could he do about it? He was not Michael or Ricky or Conroy. Guys like Joe had to just hold on to what they knew, cling to the catechism that had worked for cops for a hundred years. Rule one: Keep your mouth shut when you're supposed to keep your mouth shut. He leaned his forehead against the wall, mashed it against the dusty ancient plaster. What he wouldn't give to have Mikey's brain just for an hour or two, just to see things clear, to figure out what he should do, then he could happily go back to just bulling his way ahead without all this worry and frustration. The decision, the right decision, would already be made. But he would never have that kind of peace. Joe was forty-two; he was what he was.

Conroy came out of the room and marched up to

Joe with his arms extended in a conciliatory way. A reassuring smile. Everything was taken care of.

"How bad?"

"Not so bad, boyo, not so bad. You'll keep your job—"

"My job! Jesus, Bren! For Christ's sake, I'm just the fucking errand boy."

"Keep your voice down—"

"Half the department's on the sleeve, *you* know that!"

"This is the New Boston. Maybe you haven't heard."

"What fucking new Boston?"

"Just keep your voice down, Joe. You'll keep your job and your lieutenant's rank. But you're off the detective bureau."

Joe shook his head and sniffed at the injustice of it.

"Joe, what did you expect? You're lucky you're still in Station Sixteen. You know where they wanted to send you? Roxbury. How would you like that, chasing spooks all day?"

"Jesus, Brendan. What the fuck am I supposed to do?"

"Show up in uniform for last half tomorrow."

"You gotta be shitting me."

"Be smart, son. Report in uniform for last half tomorrow."

"And do what? Walk a beat?"

"Yes."

"For how long? What, am I gonna walk a fucking beat the rest of my life?"

"No. You're going to be patient and do what I tell you. You're going to take the deal and lie low, play the game. This is just politics. It'll blow over. Remember, boyo"—Brendan hoisted a thumb over his shoulder toward the hearing room—"they come and go; we stay. You think your old man and I didn't look out for each other?"

Joe shook his head. Whatever.

"Answer me."

"Yes."

"Alright, then. What are you going to do tomorrow?"

"Show up in uniform for last half."

"Attsaboy."

"Brendan. When am I gonna be a detective again?"

Conroy patted Joe's meaty cheek. "When the time comes."

8

A little before eleven, the cold deepened. A frigid current streamed past. Long strings of Christmas lights stirred on snow-shagged trees.

The baby Jesus trembled in his wheelbarrow. Long way from Bethlehem.

Joe stomped his feet, paced in circles. His shoes were the only thing that fit him. His pants and shirt collar were unbuttoned. The whole damn uniform had shrunk. He'd have to ask Kat to let the pants out a little. The wool overcoat was good, at least. But the exposed parts, his nose and ears and eyes, were singed. He kept an eye on the Union Club across Park Street. They'd got to know him there the past few nights, and they were pretty good about letting him come in out of the cold. The bartender even stood him a nip before he closed up every night. In a few minutes he'd go across and warm up a little. He could keep an eye on the crèche from there for a while.

This was Joe's penance, standing guard over the Nativity scene on Boston Common overnight. The same punishment befell a lot of cops in Station

71

Sixteen at Christmastime, but in the case of Joe Daley, with his televised humiliation and his demotion and his obdurate swagger, the assignment struck his brother cops as particularly laughable. Not that Joe meant to stand there all night. After midnight, he would relocate to the lobby of the nearest hotel, the Parker House, leaving his Lord and Savior to fend for Himself. He would circle past the manger scene a few times during the night and check in from the call box on Tremont Street, but he did not mean to freeze to death out here guarding a fucking doll collection.

At 10:55—Joe knew the time precisely because he was counting down to eleven o'clock when he would walk across to the Union Club to warm up—there was a loud smash from the bottom of the hill, somewhere on Tremont. It was glass shattering, but in the cold the noise was a dull crack, like the snap of a heavy branch. A smash-and-grab, probably, or drunks down on Washington Street. Joe took off running as fast as he dared on the icy downhill. He had to admit, as much as he wanted to call himself a detective, this was the sort of police work he was meant for. This was Joe at his most natural. He was a good reactor, he could impose himself on a situation, he could make things right, or at least make things better. Detective work was infuriatingly slow and irresolute. It was Miss Marple stuff, not police work. This—running like hell after a bad guy—was police work.

Meanwhile, in the manger all was peaceful. The wind shivered the statuettes and the tufts of grimy hay. The Virgin Mary listed fifteen degrees to starboard.

From the top of Park Street, the direction opposite the smashing glass, came Ricky. He was slightly out of breath. He wore a wool cap and leather jacket and Jack Purcells. His hands were plunged deep in his pockets, his shoulders hunched. In the Common he took a few mincing slidesteps over the ice to the Nativity scene and stood before it. *Bless me, Father, for I am about to sin*. He glanced around, then one by one he turned the statues around so they would see nothing, Mary, Joseph, the Magi, a donkey, two sheep, a family of very pious and awestruck Bakelite bunnies. He would leave no witnesses. When he'd rearranged the others, he lifted the baby Jesus out of His straw bed. "Now who left you out here in just a diaper?" he asked the child, who stared back with a conspiratorial beatific smile. He tucked the statue under his arm like a football and strolled off, his sneakers crunching in the snow.

There was a soft knock and Amy, still in her work dress, went to the door. "Who is it?"

"The Strangler."

"Very funny. What do you want?"

"Um, to strangle you? That's, you know, what I do."

"Sorry, not interested."

"Come on, just a little?"

"I said no. Go strangle yourself."

"That's how I got through high school. Come on, help me out."

She opened the door a crack to see Ricky posing cheek to cheek with the statue of the Christ child. "Oh, Jesus," she said.

"Precisely."

"Does this mean I'm dying?"

"No, no. He just came to visit."

"Oh, thank God. I mean, thank You." Amy stood back to let him pass. "I suppose you have an explanation."

"Yes. I found Jesus."

"Ha, ha. Let me guess. That's the one Joe is supposed to be watching."

"*Exactamente.*"

"And what do you intend to do with . . . Him?"

"I'm not exactly sure. I thought maybe you could hold on to Him for a while."

"Like a hostage."

"No, like a goodluck charm. That's His job, you know."

"You'll rot in hell for this."

"Anything for a scoop, Aim. You want the story? I'll give you an exclusive: 'Jesus Statue Stolen; Brazen Theft Right Under Dumb-Ass Cop's Nose.' Now, if that doesn't move paper, then I give up."

"You know, you Daleys aren't nearly as fascinating to anyone else as you are to yourselves. Why don't you leave poor Joe alone? He's got enough trouble."

"Come on, this is news. The public has a right to know."

"Sorry. We're a family newspaper. We don't blaspheme."

Ricky wandered over to the dining room table, which was covered with papers, manila folders, handwritten notes, photos of women bloody and contorted. "What's all this?"

"It's work. Try it sometime."

"Hey, I work."

Amy sniffed.

"Since when are you covering the Strangler thing?"

"They assigned the story today. We're reviewing it, me and Claire." Claire Downey was the other girl reporter at the *Observer*. The paper liked to team them up. They were good, and the two-girl byline was a novelty, especially on crime cases.

"Hasn't that story been written to death? What's the new angle?"

"Between us?"

"Between us."

"The angle is that BPD screwed up the investigation."

"Did they?"

"All I know is I'm looking through these reports and even I can see the mistakes. The crime scenes, the interviews, the leads they've missed—it's a disaster, Ricky. Well, you can read it in the paper, same as everyone else."

He picked up one of the photos and examined it idly. It showed a room, a stained carpet, various marks and arrows drawn on it. "Maybe you'd better keep this little guy. You might need Him." He propped the statue on a counter.

"Just take it with you. I'm not stashing your stolen property."

"Now that's blasphemy."

"No, that's your . . . work. I wish you wouldn't bring it here."

Ricky frowned. But he was feeling buoyant at the thought of Joe and the empty manger, and he did not want to argue. Ricky was determined not to acknowledge her sour mood, not to become snarled in it. He shuffled to the refrigerator. A few eggs, a block of American cheese, a loaf of Wonder bread. "You know what you need, Miss Ryan? A wife."

"The job's yours if you want it. You know that."

"Maybe just for tonight." He came to her and put his arms around her waist. "I'll be the wife. You can be the Fuller brush salesman."

She forced a smile but it faded.

"What?"

"You know what."

He groaned.

"Don't worry, Ricky, we won't talk about it. It's late."

"It's not that late. Come on, let's go somewhere. Down to Wally's. We'll have a drink, hear some music, take your mind off things."

"Ricky, some people have to get up for work."

"Oh, that."

"Yeah, that."

"Maybe I should go."

"No." She laid her head on his chest. "You can stick around if you want."

Ricky blinked uncertainly. He was not used to

seeing Amy unnerved. He was not used to—and had no interest in—comforting her. "What is it?"

"I don't know."

"The Strangler stuff? Those pictures?"

She shrugged.

"Come on. Did you read the paper today? The police commissioner says the odds of getting attacked by the Strangler are two million to one. Two million to one! The whole city's in a panic—for what? You're more likely to get run over by a car."

"I know, I know."

She felt his collarbone against her forehead. Under her hands, Ricky's lower back was hard as a shell. He had a little boy's wiry body. It felt unbreakable.

"Ricky, maybe we could just stay in tonight."

"Nah, I need to get out. Come on. One beer. You can sleep when you get old."

Amy felt with the tips of her fingers for the furrow at the center of Ricky's back. She traced the backbone as it rose to the flat of the coccyx, and her anxiety receded.

"I never thought you were a worrier, Aim."

"I'm not a worrier. I don't care about the Strangler."

She felt Ricky tap her shoulder blades in mock comfort. The gesture conveyed *there, there* and at the same time *stop hugging me, let me go*. A little chill went through her. Ricky was a consummate faker, but tonight he could not even be bothered to fake for her. He just wanted a playmate. Maybe that was all there was to Ricky, at least that was as much of him as Amy would ever have. Was it enough? A sentence repeated in her mind: *I don't know if I can do this anymore*. But she did not say it. Probably she never would say it. She would never possess him, she knew that. Ricky was nimble and sheathed in an athlete's confidence, and of course he was a man; he was not available to be possessed. She wanted him anyway. And if he never married her? Was it worth spinsterhood, did she want him even at that price? Yes, she thought. Yes yes yes yes yes.

"Ricky, I love you, you know."

"Okay."

"No, the correct response is 'I love you too, Amy.' "

"I love you too, Amy."

She squeezed him. Yes yes yes. Maybe a few months earlier, she might have felt differently. But now she and Ricky were entangled. And in the year of the Strangler, well, even if all Ricky had to offer was his charm and his good strong back, Amy thought it might be enough. She had a sense that the city's mood—the Strangler hysteria, all that mean, selfish, instinctive fear which everyone seemed to feel—carried with it an insight. What was happening in Boston was a passing revelation: The Strangler had taught them there was no safety inside the herd. Everyone was vulnerable. Death could strike out of a clear blue sky, like Oswald's bullet. If that was true . . . then yes yes yes, she did want him, at any price.

"Come on, let's go. We'll hear some music, you'll feel better."

"Okay," she said.

He bustled around, gathering up her coat and purse before she changed her mind. He held up the statue. "Bring Him?"

She shook her head.

"Right, there might be a cover." Ricky turned to place the statue back on the counter carefully. "You know, for a second there I thought you were going soft on me."

"Never," she said to his back.

9

Suffolk Superior Court, Thursday afternoon.

There was a sense in the courtroom at times like
these that they were not adversaries. They were a
team, fielding their different positions—judge,
lawyer, clerk—working together toward a common
goal. The outcome of the case was certain. All that
remained was the tying up of loose ends, reading
the correct words into the record. It was an unspoken awareness. You tended to feel it when
weekends or holidays loomed, in summer
especially, on Friday afternoons when everyone
was anxious to bug out. A certain contented lassi-
tude crept into the lawyers' voices. They referred to
one another with amiable, anachronistic formality
as "my brother." The familiar formulas spilled out
of their mouths quickly and with evident pleasure.
They were insiders, technicians, and they were
wrapping up.

Michael—who relished these moments of team-
work, these truces—spoke without notes, one hand
resting in the pocket of his suit coat, JFK style. "It is
a hard case, obviously, and the Commonwealth

is not unsympathetic to the situation Mr. and Mrs. Cavalcante find themselves in. But then, they are all hard cases and this is all settled law. Like most of these old tenements in the West End, the Cavalcantes' building was taken by the government in a proper exercise of its power of eminent domain. As tenants in the building, the Cavalcantes' lease was immediately terminated by operation of law and they became tenants by sufferance, with no standing to raise these sorts of Fifth Amendment or Article Ten objections." Michael heard the facile, bloodless tone in his own voice, but hadn't they been through the drill before with these old West Enders? It occurred to him there might be time for a haircut that afternoon, and his pace quickened again. "However, to touch on the merits of the plaintiffs' claims: First, there is no merit to the argument that the government's use of its eminent domain power is improper merely because it benefits a private developer. If Farley Sonnenshein can make a buck rebuilding the West End, then so be it. The project still serves a valid public interest by converting a blighted area, a slum really, into a new neighborhood of obvious benefit to the city. As for the claim that the Cavalcantes have been inadequately compensated for the costs of moving, that's really something they can take up with the Redevelopment Authority. As the court is well aware, the Authority has gone to great lengths to assist West Enders in relocating to new homes. The bottom line is that, without a valid legal claim, we can sympathize with the Cavalcantes but we can't do anything to help them. They simply have to move. The whole point of eminent domain is that sometimes a few will be called upon to make sacrifices for the common good. 'Ask not' and all that."

Michael lobbed an apologetic smile toward the older couple seated in the gallery. They blinked back at him as if he were speaking a foreign language—which he was, that is, he was not speaking Italian. And with that Michael nodded smartly to the judge, throwing the ball to him just as a second baseman turning a double play will pivot and whip the ball on to first base.

"Well." The judge sighed. "I find for the Commonwealth essentially on the grounds that counsel just stated."

Afterward, as Michael stuffed his files back into his trial bag, a court officer and the Cavalcantes approached him from different directions.

Mr. Cavalcante hesitated behind the bar railing. He was a small man, turned out in an old three-piece suit made from a rough, nappy wool. He held his hat over his heart. "Why did you say nothing about the, the"—he turned to his wife—"*delinquenti*."

"*Mafiosi*, eh, gangsters, bad guys."

"Gengsters. Why did you say nothing about the gengsters?"

The court officer handed Michael a slip of paper: *Call Wamsley ASAP.*

"You can talk to the Redevelopment Authority," Michael answered absently.

"The Redevelopment don't do nothing. They sent the gengsters. Now you send me back to the Redevelopment?"

Michael tried to focus on the old man, but his mind was on the message from his boss. It was rare that Wamsley or anyone from the office would bother him in court. That was the best thing about being on trial: You could not be disturbed. The joke in every lawyer's office was that there were only two places where you could not be called to the telephone, the bathroom and the courtroom.

"The Redevelopment says, 'Go to Medford, there is an apartment for you.' That's all they know, over and over, 'there is an apartment for you, there is an apartment for you.' Nothing about the gengsters."

"Look, just call the police. If you want to report a crime, call the police. I'm sorry, Mr. Cavalcante, Mrs. Cavalcante, I've got to go, I'm sorry."

The old couple stood staring. The man turned his head slightly, as if he had not heard the answer or was expecting to hear more.

George Wamsley bore a faint resemblance to Mr. Wizard. His ears protruded like a butterfly's wings. His hair was forever mussed though he was forever combing it. His teeth were big and horsey. He was rumored to be a genius, and inside the Eminent Domain Division of the A.G.'s office, which Wamsley headed, he was revered. He would sweep through the office with loping strides and a whooping laugh, lavishing extravagant praise on the young lawyers who worked for him, complimenting them on this motion or that brief, engaging in earnest discussions of mundane cases, and in his wake would be a sort of turbulence, a high. You felt ravished and energized by him. Somehow some of his wet and goofy enthusiasm got into you, and you in turn churned up his enthusiasm with your work. Your work! No longer were you a bureaucrat or some mustache-twirling villain out of Dickens, preying on the poor in the name of progress (a turnpike, a parking garage). You were part of a grand, historic effort to build a great city out of a decrepit one. Never had eminent domain seemed so damn interesting.

No doubt at any other time a man like George Wamsley would never have accepted the job of running the Eminent Domain Division. He had had choices. He was a Lowell cousin, a friend of the poet. A gentleman dilettante before the war—the sort of cultivated Yankee crank who dabbled in Negro music and sailboat racing and Oriental mysticism—Wamsley first found his stride after the fighting stopped, as an adjutant in the American sector of Berlin. In the straitened chaos of 1945 and '46 Berlin, an energetic polymath like George Wamsley could get things done. He spoke three of the four languages that were about. He enjoyed the dives on the Ku'damm and the improvised bar in the ruins of the Hotel Adlon. He collected antiques in exchange for Army beef and Lucky Strikes. War, at least the ruins of it, turned out to be a great adventure. When he returned to the States, Wamsley had drifted back to Mother Harvard, the law school this time, with the vague idea that a law practice might be a nice roost from which to pursue other interests. And then he had ingested the New Boston bug, another city in need of rebuilding, another project of a scale commensurate with his bounding energy. By now he'd even taken up an interest in modernist architecture; he thought he might try architecture school at some point.

Michael never knew what to make of Wamsley. He considered his boss a curiosity, a strange exotic bird from a faraway WASP country of which he'd heard rumors. Wamsley considered Michael a sort of exotic, too, a policeman's son and an inveterate laconic, maybe a little dull but a Harvard man, a good sober presence to have at one's right hand. Wamsley had recruited Michael to be *his* adjutant, and Michael felt a suitable gratitude, even affection, for his loony and possibly brilliant boss.

That afternoon when Michael entered the corner office of the Attorney General, it was Wamsley he noticed first. Wamsley was seated in a wing chair facing the A.G.'s desk, and from behind Michael saw only his skinny legs double-crossed. Wamsley unwound his legs and twisted around to peer at Michael over the back of the chair, as a child might. "Ah, Michael. The indispensable man."

The Attorney General, Alvan Byron, emerged from a bathroom off the office, wiping his hands with a paper towel. "Graveyards are filled with indispensable men. That's what de Gaulle said."

"Cheerful thought," Michael responded.

Alvan Byron was a big man, his torso one

enormous barrel. The A.G. favored big collars, French cuffs, and peaked lapels despite the prevailing fashion. His anachronistic suits seemed to place him in an earlier, more glamorous era. Though he was onequarter Scot, Byron was at the moment considered the highestranking Negro elected politician in the country, and his career already seemed to have acquired an irresistible velocity. Alvan Byron was bigger than Boston.

"Big news, Mr. Daley." Byron settled himself at the desk. "We're taking over the Strangler case."

Michael let slip an undecorous guffaw.

"Something funny?"

"No. Just, I know someone who'll be happy to hear it."

"A lot of people will be happy to hear it. It's time for a fresh pair of eyes."

"Boston PD isn't going to be happy to hear it."

"No." Byron gave Wamsley a glance. "We have some ideas about that, too."

Michael sat there nodding, with a dumb, bemused grin. He thought, *You two have absolutely no idea. You could put Sherlock fucking Holmes on the Strangler case and nothing—nothing—you could do would satisfy Boston Homicide.* What he said was: "Well, Criminal Division has a lot of good guys. I'm sure they'll do a good job."

"That wasn't exactly what we had in mind—"

"Criminal Division isn't getting it," Wamsley interjected.

"No? Who then?"

"A special bureau we're creating," Wamsley enthused."Kind of an allstar team. With all the men and resources they'll need, regardless of jurisdiction or expense." "Did you see this?" Byron tossed a copy of the morning's *Observer* across the desk. A splashy three-column headline:

STRANGLER INVESTIGATION RIDDLED WITH ERRORS

The byline read, Amy Ryan and Claire Downey.

"Yes, I saw it."

"That's your sister-in-law, isn't it, this Amy Ryan?" Byron bored in.

"Something like that."

"Well,"Wamsley continued,"we think she's hit the nail square on the head. BPD had its chance. They tried the old-fashioned way. Now it's our turn."

"Meaning what, exactly?"

"Meaning the case is just too big for one department, even Boston's. You have thirteen women dead, a serial-murder investigation that spans four cities and three counties. These local departments aren't used to working together. They don't know how to communicate. The left hand doesn't know what the right hand is doing. What's needed is a coordinated approach. It's just the sort of case we should be intervening on. Even more important, what you have in this case is a killer who is canny enough or unpredictable enough or just crazy enough that traditional methods have failed utterly. What's needed is new thinking."

"New thinking?"

"Yes, yes." Wamsley was giddy and sincere, and what he was saying made a superficial sort of sense. You could almost believe it. "An inter-disciplinary, unconventional, scientific approach. Detectives unblinkered by experience, by what they know, or think they know, is the right way to investigate a homicide. If experience shows anything, it's that people tend to see only what they're looking for. They will overlook the most obvious evidence because it does not fit their preconceived notion of what clues *ought* to look like or where they *should* be found. We think this case could benefit from a fresh approach. We think the answer—the critical clue, the correct suspect— is probably already there in the data, somewhere in that haystack. The trick is to find it, to isolate it from all the background noise, and to do that before the strangler strikes again. If we could just aggregate all the evidence we have, synthesize it, and subject it to rigorous scientific methodology, we could really crack this thing. We could subject all that data to computer analysis—"

"Alright, George," Byron said. "I think he's got it."

"Well," Michael ventured, "it all sounds very interesting. You mind if I ask why you pulled me out of court to tell me all this?"

"The new bureau is going to be headed up by Mr. Wamsley."

"It is?"

Wamsley grinned. "It is."

"George, you don't have any experience investigating homicides. Do you?"

"Absolutely none."

Michael thought at this point that he knew why he was here. Nutty as it was, they meant to put Wamsley in charge of the new Strangler bureau, and Michael would be asked to take over Eminent Domain. Michael thought he was up to it despite his relative lack of experience, he thought the others would accept him. And in the New Boston era, who knew where it might lead?

"Michael, George has asked that you be detailed to the new bureau as well."

"What! I've never investigated a homicide in my life."

"Precisely!" Wamsley boomed.

"Precisely? Look, all I know is eminent domain. What am I gonna do—take away the Strangler's parking space? This is crazy."

"It's not all that crazy, Michael," Byron insisted. "You're a bright guy. Your dad was in Boston Homicide, which will give you a little credibility with these guys. And you probably absorbed more from him than you realize. Anyway, your primary responsibility will be administrative. The bureau will be staffed up with detectives and experts and whatnot. Your job, with George here, will just be to synthesize it all, to keep everybody pulling in the same direction. We're not asking you to do anything you're unqualified for. We're not stupid. You underestimate yourself, Michael."

"No, no, I estimate myself just right. I'm not a detective. I can't even figure out the cases on *Perry Mason*."

Byron chortled."No one's asking you to be a detective.We're asking you—no, we're telling you—to be part of a team, a team that needs your particular skills."

"What skills? I don't have skills. Ask anyone."

"Michael, do you know what I see when I look at you?" Byron fixed his eyes on Michael."I see a bright young lawyer who is satisfied doing work that is beneath him. He comes from a family of cops, he has a good mind, yet he wants no part of the biggest murder case that ever happened in this city. It makes me wonder, what is he so afraid of? What does he want?"

"Maybe I just don't want to touch murder cases. Cuts a little close to home, you know?"

"I see. Your father." The city rustled outside. Byron considered it a moment. "Well, I'll tell you what, Michael. You help me here, catch me a strangler, and I promise you, you can try eminent domain cases to your heart's content."

10

It had begun in the summer of 1962. On June 14, a rainy Thursday evening, a fifty-six-year-old woman named Helena Jalakian was raped and murdered in her apartment near Symphony Hall. The case drew little attention. The newspapers reported that she had been strangled but no details were given. Boston averaged about a murder a week; there did not appear to be anything exceptional about this one. But the stranglings continued. Four more in the next four weeks. And by July, in the humid heat of summer, the panic was on. There was a lull from mid-July to mid-August— no murders. Then two in two days, August 19 and 21. There could be no doubt that the seven stranglings were all the work of one man. At first the newspapers did not know what to call him. They tried out Phantom and Fiend, even The Silk Stocking Murderer, before they finally settled on The Strangler. But they believed in him, they believed he had murdered all those women, and so did everyone else.

And why not? The cases were similar. The

victims were all older white women. The youngest, Jalakian, was fifty-six; the oldest was seventy-five. All lived alone, quietly, in smaller apartment buildings, three to six stories high, mostly nineteenth-century structures of stone or brick with thick walls which, it was noted, were highly soundproof. The victims dressed neatly. They looked younger than their true ages. To some, they even resembled one another. With one exception, they had been killed midweek, Monday through Thursday; perhaps the Strangler prowled on his way to or from work. The killer left a signature, too: the garrotes, which were braided together from the victims' own stockings and cords from their housecoats, were tied off in a big theatrical bow around their necks. The murder scenes were all bloody; the victims had been beaten and raped. Some of the corpses were mutilated. Some were arranged in obscene poses.

The police had no witnesses, no physical evidence of any real value, no sign of forced entry. The police commissioner, a former college football player and by-the-book FBI man named Edmund McNamara, could not do much more than order more and more overtime for detectives. Over and over, he admonished women to keep their doors locked and not open them to strangers, to buy a watchdog, and to call a special emergency phone number if they had any information—DE 81212. It became known as the "Strangler Number." But no arrests.

It was the summer of the Strangler, the summer no one slept.

Then the Strangler went quiet. September passed without a murder, and October and November.

On December 5, he struck. The victim was a twenty-year-old colored girl, very pretty, a student, killed in the apartment she shared with two roommates. On New Year's Eve, he killed another young girl, this one white, twenty-three, a lovely blonde secretary. These two cases did not fit the Strangler pattern. The victims were young, one was a Negro. Both had been strangled, but neither had any external injuries, nor had they been raped. The secretary was found lying in bed, neatly tucked in. She looked like she was sleeping peacefully. To the city Homicide cops, it seemed unlikely that the Strangler had killed these girls. But the press and public instantly credited them to the Strangler. A lone villain in the classical mode made a neater story—easier for the newspapermen to write, easier for readers to grasp.

In 1963 the stranglings were erratic and widely spaced: in March, a sixty-eight-year-old woman in the city of Lawrence, a half-hour's drive from Boston; in May, a young girl in Cambridge; nothing all summer, then another young girl in September, again outside the city. Through it all, the police and public retained their different views of the cases. The cops saw a dozen murder cases, perhaps related, perhaps not. The public saw only the Boston Strangler.

On November 22, hours after President Kennedy died, the Strangler struck one last time, killing Joanne Feeney in the West End. Another old woman, another obscenely posed corpse. It was a return to the form of those first killings in the summer of '62, as if the Strangler was announcing, *I'm still here.*

11

The murder books. In each there was a photo of the victim as she had looked around the time of her murder. There was more, of course. A murder book was the repository of every scrap of paper the police had compiled about a homicide, and Michael dutifully slogged through all thirteen of the Strangler books—detectives' reports, witness statements, field interrogation reports, autopsy and crime-lab reports, mug shots. But it was the snapshots of the victims' faces that gave him a frisson of mortality. They were such ordinary women, stern-looking older ladies with outdated names, Eva, Helena, Lillian, Margaret, and smiling pretty young girls named Beverly and Judy and Patty.

In the murder-scene photos Michael searched for those same faces, as if the reality in the earlier photograph would continue until canceled; only a photograph could disprove another photograph. But he could not recognize the women's faces on their dead bodies. In the wide shots, of bodies outstretched, or trussed, or tossed like rag dolls, the victims seemed to have no faces at all. A smudge, a stain, that was all he could make out. Even in the remorseless granular closeups of the victims' heads, he could not find the living women's faces.

Soon, too soon, he decided he could not stare at the pictures anymore. Enough. It was morbid. The cycle of emotions stirred by violent images was similar to that stirred by pornographic ones: shock, fascination, monotony, finally revulsion. Worse, mortal questions— what did it mean, exactly, to die?—were yawning before him. He slipped the pictures back into their manila envelopes. Decided he would maintain from the outset a greater emotional distance from the whole business. He would reduce these thirteen murders to data. He would organize the essential facts of each case, chart it all in columns labeled *Date, Location, V's Age, Details of Attack, Other Evidence, Witnesses, Suspects.* Patterns would naturally emerge.

"6/14/62 . . . Back Bay . . . 56 . . . no semen . . . blood in vagina indicates rape with object . . . blood in right ear . . . laceration at rear scalp . . . neck scratched and bruised . . . contusion on chin . . . strangled with cord of light blue housecoat; cord found still tied around neck, in bow . . . no sign of struggle . . . Arthur Nast . . ."

"6/20/62 . . . Brighton . . . 68 . . . external genitalia lacerated . . . blood and mucus in vagina . . . blood in both ears . . . open wine bottle on kitchen counter . . ."

An image lit up in Michael's mind, briefly, a strobe flash: a woman thrashing, arms flailing—shrieking, *NO!*—her face, grimaced, teeth clenched—darkhair—a scream—furniture clattering.

And then it was gone. He blinked away the memory of it. He had only the papers on his desk. And the clock ticking.

"8/19/62 ... Lawrence ... 53 y.o. .... supine on bed, R leg dangling, naked except for open blouse ... 3 ligatures on neck (2 stockings, 1 leg of brown leotard) ... external vagina bruised, bloody ... 2 halfmoon contusions below R nipple, 2 abrasions above and L of it ... R thigh contused ... raped ... V a devout churchgoer ..."

"8/21/62 .. .Columbia Rd., Dorchester ... 67 ... no forced entry to apt ... blood on floors in kitchen, hall ... bra on bathroom floor ... V found in bathtub, on her knees, face down in 6 inches water, feet over back of tub, butt up in air ... underpants tugged down but no trauma to vagina or anus ... blood on R of scalp ... two stockings around neck ... R hyoid bone fractured ... pocketbook open ..."

The investigators had only Before and After. The living woman and the broken body. Not the moment of horror. Not the dying. The reality of murder had been excised, like an obscenity. But Michael's imagination insistently re-created it.

A woman thrashed before him. Her hands shoving—he felt it on his skin. Her scream vibrated his ear.

"12/5/62 . . . Huntington Ave . . . 20, college student, Negro, engaged...wearing housecoat, menstrual harness, sanitary napkin . . . mouth gagged . . . no external injury to genitalia . . . no head trauma . . . no blood or menstrual discharge in vagina or rectum . . . strangulation by ligature . . . Salem cigarette in toilet . . . semen stain on rug near body . . . itinerant seen in stairwell . . ."

"3/9/63 . . . Lawrence . . . 68, white . . . beaten, stabbed, strangled . . . cause of death: blunt force trauma . . . sperm in vagina: raped . . . body naked on floor, girdle pulled down to left foot . . . clothes still on, pulled over head . . . throat badly contused . . . head and surrounding floor covered with blood . . . knife or fork stuck in left breast to handle . . ."

"5/7/63 . . .Cambridge . . . 26, nurse at Boston State Hospital, a mental facility . . . stabbed 17 times around left breast... 2 parallel horizontal incisions on each side of throat . . . nude but no evid of rape or sex assault . . . no injuries to genitalia, no sperm in vagina, rectum or mouth . . . body supine on bed, hands tied behind her back with scarf . . . stockings and blouse around neck but no ligature marks . . ."

"9/8/63 . . . Salem . . . 23 . . . found on bed,

lying on back, right arm under body, left leg dangling, torso covered with bedspread . . . bloodstain on bed under head . . . 2 stockings tied around neck . . . panties on floor with lipstick stain above crotch (used as gag?) . . . sperm in V's mouth . . . crumpled tissues on floor smeared with semen, lipstick . . ."

"11/22/63 . . . Grove St.,West End . . . 63 . . . blood . . . blood covers entire head, face and ears . . . slight injuries to external genitalia . . . no sperm in vagina...manual and ligature strangulation . . . classical LP (Sibelius) still turning . . . tied spreadeagle to chair . . . posed, facing door . . ."

Already Michael knew he did not have the stomach for this sort of work. He could not live with months of that shrieking woman in his mind's eye. It had been a mistake to let Byron and Wamsley talk him into this.

He slipped the photos of the last victim out of their envelope. The old woman in the West End, the Sibelius fan. *My God, what did you go through?*

Somewhere there was a murder book for Michael's father, too. Buried in a file at BPD Homicide. No doubt it contained the same sort of photographs, of Joe Daley, Sr., lying dead. It was a scene Michael had imagined a thousand times. He had created for himself a still life, a formal composition of a few elements arranged in a painterly way: body, scally cap, pavement. But had he got it right? The body—had the old man sprawled, or curled, or crumpled? Michael pictured him lying stiff as a fallen tree, a carryover of the distinctive toy-soldier posture Joe Senior had had in life. There would be a tight shot of the face, too, to document the victim's identity. What had his expression been? Grimaced or peaceful? One cheek on the pavement, or looking straight up to the sky?

In his fingers, Michael adjusted the photo of the murdered old woman in the West End. *My God, what did you go through?*

He wanted out. He'd tell Wamsley, maybe tomorrow, but soon. He just wasn't cut out for this work. He'd had enough of murder books.

12

The night lieutenant in Station Sixteen was a white-haired, florid man. He had a long nose but his every other feature was weak, a combination that gave his face the snouted look of certain rodents or streamlined locomotives. This lieutenant—his name does not matter here—was among the last of the generation of cops that joined the force during the Boston police strike of 1919, when standards were not so much lowered as thrown out entirely. These men were always at a disadvantage in their relationships with other cops, who regarded them as second-rate and incorrigibly lazy, if not scabs. There was something fraudulent about them. They were not quite cops. The wave of young men that poured into the BPD after World War II was particularly disdainful. The young guys were in a hurry. They had a lot of time to make up for. They had fought in the war, then come home and got married and set up house and passed the police exam—only to find their path blocked by these indolent potbellied old men who, if they could be counted on for anything, dependably sought out the least taxing duty in the least busy precincts. Of course there were lazy and second-rate cops among the younger generation, too, and decent cops among the 1919 strikebreakers, but the perception was settled. So, to deflect it, the 1919 men often adopted a showy scrupulousness about the military formalities of BPD life, the saluting and yes-sirring. That sort of punctilio drove the young guys up the fucking wall. They had done their share of saluting, and done it when it counted. But the night lieutenant was positively Prussian in this regard, and it showed in the way he relished the roll call before each shift.

He read out a few advisories. There had been several purse snatches on Boylston Street, and homosexuals loitering in the Public Garden. The men were to remember that the "Strangler corps"—properly called the Tactical Patrol Force, a police unit formed to calm the mounting public hysteria—would be appearing at certain calls. Finally, he called the men to attention and strolled among them as they held up their notebooks and callbox keys for inspection. He marched back to the podium and returned the cops' lethargic salute with a smarter one of his own. And the whole thing was about to break up, the men about to head out to their beats, when the lieutenant seemed to recall one last thing. "Wait, wait! Sit! I nearly forgot the most important case we have!" He reached into his coat and produced, grandly, an envelope. Inside was a note composed of letters cut from magazines and pasted to the page, a prototypical ransom note.

"We have a missing person case, a missing child. Let me see now." He put on his reading glasses. "'i HaVE TAKEn yOuR LoRd aNd mEssiaH hosTAGe.'"

The room broke up.

"'hIs blOOd bE upON JOsePh DaLEy.'"

In the back of the room, Joe groaned. He had been suffering already. Bone-tired from working last-halfs. Fish was dogging him to pay off his bookie tab. There was a woman in Brookline who kept calling and wouldn't get lost, and now she was threatening to call Joe's wife and spill the whole story. Worse, he was squashed into his uniform pants, which Kat had let out as much as the remaining material would allow. And he was choking on the stiff white collar that he'd crafted years before from a cheap plastic belt, an old cops' trick to spare their wives from scrubbing the collars of their uniform shirts every night—but he'd made this one when he still wore a seventeen-inch collar. And now this.

The lieutenant basked in the laughter. He was more often the butt of the joke. "The missing child is described as follows. Height: twenty inches. Hair: none. Age: approximately two thousand years, give or take. Last seen wearing a diaper and blanket and emitting a strange heavenly glow."

The lieutenant had to pause until the laughing subsided.

"The boy's father—hold on, fellas, hold on now—the boy's father is a very powerful man. I can vouch for that: I used to be an altar boy—I worked for the guy."

Joe slouched, tugged the brim of his hat down over his eyes. He smiled defensively.

"Officer Daley," the lieutenant called. Of course Joe had not lost his rank, but it was no time to quibble. "Shall I send this case up to the detectives?"

"No, sir."

"You have a suspect then, I trust?"

"Oh yes I do."

"And who might the . . . malefactor be?"

"I'd rather not say."

"Alright then, Daley. Just get this poor child back. His birthday's coming up."

Standing guard on the Common that night, the baby Jesus's vacant straw bed inspired in Joe a single thought: *Kill Ricky. Kill that fuckin' little prick.* He paced. *Skinny little shit. Kill him, wake him up, then kill him again.* The weather had warmed up the last few days and most of the snow had melted, but Joe wouldn't have felt the cold anyway. He wouldn't need a shot to warm himself up and he wouldn't be hiding out in no hotel lobby because his anger at his dickhead little brother could have melted the North fucking Pole. His hands hung bucket-heavy at the ends of his arms. There was twitchy energy loose in his shoulders, his triceps. Ricky just loved making Joe look like a fool and a fuckup, he always fucking had. But it was okay because this time—this time—Joe was going to kick Ricky's ass but good—

A woman screamed. Somewhere.

The trees rustled.

Joe rucked up his sleeve to check his watch: 11:50.

The scream was choked off. Distant.

Joe listened—

there it was again—

and he was already running.

A third scream, a panicky shriek: "No! Get away! Get—!"

And already Joe's legs were driving him, arms pumping, mouth chuffing, down the Hill, down Tremont toward Scollay Square, the Square already beginning to vanish building by building, street by street, the whole city dematerializing like a dream, different every time you saw it, disorienting—

Another yelp, short, softer, a chirrup.

He was running so fast now it felt like one long fall, felt like he had to keep throwing his legs forward just to keep from spilling face-first on the street.

There was a couple on the street, the man pointing, "That way!"

Down Bromfield. A clatter, from an alley.

And there it was, this sudden tableau: A guy, no, a giant, gaunt and gawky but towering. He had a girl pinned against the wall, one hand fisted around her neck, the other exploring under her coat, between her legs. The girl's feet wavered a few inches off the ground. One shoe had fallen off.

"Hey!"

The giant turned and glared, confused then angry, offended at the cop for intruding.

His face was cadaverous—starved and

105

narrow-skulled, pale skin taut over the cheekbones, bulgy dark eyes, a distinctly ridged brow— and in the alley's gloom, deeply shadowed, that mask was grotesque enough to freeze Joe for a second. Joe blinked and turned his head slightly, as if refocusing would bring the man's features back into proportion, convert the monster back into something familiar, a derelict or punk or some other nightwalker.

The man, apparently misapprehending some tolerant impulse in the cop's hesitation—sympathy, brotherhood, fear, who knew what?— clamped his hand hard between the girl's legs and agitated her hips against the wall. He gave the cop a little wrinkle-nosed smirk. *Yeah! See that?*

Joe decided then and there to fuck this guy up but good. He charged forward.

The giant released his grip on the girl. She landed unevenly on one shoe but righted herself, and stood long enough to watch the cop fly right past her without so much as a glance to see if she was okay— he passed very close, so close that she felt a little draft on her cheek, heard metal equipment clinking under his coat—and she decided just to lower herself to the ground and sit there.

Joe knew after a few steps that this guy wasn't going to get far. The guy ran like a fuckin' retard, all high-stepping Lincoln-long crazy-legs, and Joe had time to ruminate over how best to take him down with maximum injury. As they neared the opposite end of the alley, which opened out onto Winter Street, Joe launched himself—enjoyed a horizontal ecstatic moment—and fell on the guy's back, engulfed him like some enormous flapping bird. He hugged the giant's arms to his sides and allowed his own stout legs to become entangled with the giant's. His intention was to prevent the guy from breaking his own fall, ideally to bounce his face off the pavement.

But immediately it felt wrong.

There was enormous cartilaginous strength in the giant's torso. He managed to carry Joe a few steps, and Joe felt like he was riding one long smooth muscle, as if he'd jumped on a dolphin's back. The guy did not fall forward; he did not fall at all. With unearthly power he managed to twist, even as he began to stumble, and Joe felt himself slipping off the side of the giant's back, and the two men rolled down onto the pavement.

From behind, Joe immediately hooked his right arm around the giant's neck and locked it with his left. He squeezed. He meant to crush the man's Adam's apple in the crook of his right elbow. Choke him, whatever—just take the edge off this fucker, cuff him, and get the hell out of there.

But, incredibly, the guy was already prying Joe's arm away with his fingers. It was impossible. His fingers! What the fuck! Joe hauled with his opposite arm for leverage. It was no use. Those fingers pried their way under Joe's arm and levered it away.

Joe's shock—he could not remember ever being overpowered like this—gave way to panic. He looked around for help. No one. Empty alley, glimpse of an empty street.

And those hands! The strength in them was inhuman. They spread Joe's arms wide enough that the giant was able to roll over and face Joe like a lover. His hands found Joe's neck, encircled it. The thumbs met at the fleshy hollow below the Adam's apple, mashed around a bit as they sought out the windpipe where it was closest to the surface, just above the point where it disappeared into the rib cage, and when the hard pads of his two thumbs were settled on that exposed rubbery tube, he pressed.

A thrash of adrenaline convulsed Joe's body.

His head snapped forward instinctively to protect the vulnerable spot and, his hands caught uselessly behind the giant's head, his body beat itself forward and back.

Almost immediately—seconds—his mind began to unfocus, he felt himself beginning to lose consciousness. He looked into the face, inches away.

The giant leered back with those swollen bug-eyes. He seemed to sense there would only be this initial burst of resistance to overcome. He pressed his thumbs again. *Crush it, deform it.*

Joe struggled to free his arms. The pain was lessening slightly, losing its electric quality, its urgency. He found the guy's wrists, tried to rip them away, but Joe's own arms were stony and heavy. It felt as if both men were immovable, as if he and this fucking monster were petrifying into a sculpture. It was already too late. He was dying—actually dying. Could it happen this quickly? He had not expected—

There was a siren.

The pressure on Joe's neck lifted a little.

The siren was far off, maybe just a coincidence, city noise.

Then the pressure was back, harder than before, the thumbs crushing Joe's trachea, as if the giant meant to finish it quickly.

Joe thrashed again, readrenalized. Not dead.

He jerked his knee up into the giant's crotch—scratched at those bulgy eyes—

and it was over. Gone. No hands on his neck, no crushing pain in his throat.

The siren was close now, oscillating.

The man was running off. Joe heard his shoes brushing in the grit.

Joe dragged himself to his feet. He shuffled back up the alley to the girl. She lay in a curl with her back against the wall, knees up. Joe held out his hand to her. "Can you walk?"

"I don't think so."

"Are you hurt?"

"No. I don't think so."

"I'll get you out of here. It'll be okay."

Joe slid his arms under the girl and forked her up off the pavement. She was light as a child. Good-looking, maybe twenty-three, twenty-four. He wondered what it would be like to fuck her, what her body looked like, all automatic thoughts for Joe, but he could not work up any enthusiasm for the project, which he took as a worrisome sign that his encounter with the giant had left him unmanned somehow. The girl lay limp in his arms, her head against his chest, arms trailing down in her lap. Joe carried her out of the alley to the street, where he was startled by a blinding flash from a news photographer's camera.

13

"Vincent Gargano was in here looking for you."

The bartender had leaned over with his elbows on the bar to confide this news. He apparently expected Ricky to crap his pants when he heard it. When Ricky played it off, didn't even blink, the bartender straightened, relieved and disappointed.

"What about?"

"He didn't say. I didn't ask."

"When?"

"Couple nights ago."

"What'd you tell him?"

"That I haven't seen yuz."

"Thanks."

"What do I do if he comes back?"

"Just tell him the truth, Sull. Keep your nose out of it."

"Hey, maybe it's nothing, right?"

"Yeah. Just business."

"May be nothing."

"It *is* nothing. I just got through saying."

The bartender twisted a rag in his hands, anxious to change the subject. He gestured with his chin toward the evening *Globe* in front of Ricky.

COP FOILS STRANGLER ATTACK

Big photo of Joe with his grim scowl and mussed uniform, a damsel swooned in his arms. "What's with your brother? Can't keep his mug out of the papers lately."

"Who? You mean Elvis?"

"Yeah, Elvis Daley." The bartender snorted, but he was plainly worried. "Hey, Rick, no offense, but if you got trouble with Vincent Gargano, I'd just as soon you don't bring it in here, know what I mean?"

"It's no trouble. I told you."

"Just the same."

A look passed between them. Because of course it was trouble. Vincent "The Animal" Gargano was a stalker for Carlo Capobianco, the North End boss currently waging a campaign to consolidate the countless smalltime bookmaking operations in the city under his own control—a campaign that was building to its own bloody climax.

Until then, organized crime in Boston had never really deserved the name. No one had ever succeeded in organizing the city, or even tried. Boston had never produced an Al Capone or a Lucky Luciano, a Caesar to unite it. So the city's gangland remained fragmented and small-time. It was not even the seat of power for the Mafia in New England. That was Providence, where a heavily Italian population had created more favorable conditions for the Italian Mob than Irish-dominated Boston. It was from Providence that Raymond Patriarca governed New England beginning in the early 1950s, with the blessing of the Genovese and Colombo families in New York. Boston was a backwater. But now perhaps the city had found its Caesar after all, a cocky, pugnacious North Ender, the son of Italian immigrants, whose talent was perfectly aligned with the greatest opportunity: gambling.

Carlo "Charlie" Capobianco was a born bookie. He had got out of the Navy in 1947; just three years later he was running the bookmaking rackets of the North End consigliere Joe Lombardo. But this, Capobianco found, was no military operation. The bookies Capobianco saw were amateurs. They took bets on the numbers in the back of their groceries or barrooms. They treated the books almost as a secondary business. Most were independents: they paid a tribute to the Mafia in exchange for protection from the cops and from Mob shake-downs, and access to the race wire and lay-off bank. Nobody was monitoring them, nobody knew how much they were making or how much more they could afford to pay. It was a mess, run by old Mustache Petes like Lombardo who did not understand the numbers business or the potential of a properly managed, centralized gambling network.

Capobianco set out to take it over. From now on, there would be no more independents. Everyone worked for Capobianco and everyone paid. The bookies would render unto Caesar what was Caesar's. A tax on your take. A tax on your telephone—your lifeline, your link to the whole operation. A tax just for staying in the business. Charlie Capobianco wanted a piece of every nickel bet.

He was not interested in anything but bookmaking and the profits it threw off. He did not dabble in other Mob businesses—unions, dockworkers, truck hijacking, pornography, drug trafficking—because that was not where the big money was. Gambling, that was where the money was. Capobianco had grasped a simple truth: The Mafia was in the gambling business. Since the end of Prohibition, gambling had been far and away the Mafia's biggest source of income. The rest was a sideshow, for dumb-shit Irishmen and grabby New Yorkers. Capobianco meant to stick to his knitting.

He streamlined the whole operation. Business grew. In boiler rooms in the North End, phones rang off the hook. A dozen guys in each room to handle all the action. Horse races in the afternoon, dog races at night, numbers all day. In the horse room, Danny Capobianco, Charlie's little brother, carried a roll of half dollars to pay the phone operators, fifty cents a bet.

But alone, Capobianco could only go so far. He was not a made man. That meant he could not muscle in on crews that operated with Raymond Patriarca's blessing. He couldn't collect a debt if the deadbeat also owed Patriarca. He could not even protect himself from the other sharks in Boston's chaotic crimeworld. When they began to shake Capobianco down—when they taxed *him*—Capobianco did what he had to do.

He drove down to Providence to see The Man. Capobianco handed Ray Patriarca an envelope containing fifty thousand dollars cash and he offered the don a deal: fifty grand down and a guarantee of at least a hundred thousand a year in exchange for a monopoly on bookmaking in Boston. Patriarca accepted.

The deal changed everything. Capobianco moved in on the bookie rackets citywide, and in the early 1960s Boston got bloody.

Capobianco unleashed his stalkers, now augmented by a battalion of Mafia strongarm men, hundreds of them, with orders to bring the bookies to heel. The stalkers confiscated half the bookies' take—the tax. Bookmaking profits in turn fed a loan-sharking business, as sharks put that money back on the street at three or four percent *a week*. And that was the fatal formula: enforcers ordered to show no mercy in collecting debts; and debtors everywhere—bookies unable to keep up with the taxes, borrowers unable to keep up with the vig of three, even four hundred percent a year on sharked money. Bodies began to fall, particularly in the rundown South End. A New Boston indeed.

In the mayhem, a new generation of enforcers flourished. They were feral and vicious. Their violence was flamboyant. They cruised the city like sharks.

The apotheosis of this new breed was Vincent "The Animal" Gargano. And he was hunting for Ricky.

14

Amy had installed a new deadbolt on her apartment door, a monster of a lock that looked like it belonged on a bank vault. It quelled the unease she'd been feeling and it helped her sleep. She did not like to think of this foreboding as Strangler-anxiety; she did not see herself as the hysterical type. But it was getting hard to ignore the alarm on the street. Sometimes it seemed the Strangler was all people talked about.

In the beauty parlor, Amy had listened, captive, while a half dozen women debated the available tactics.

— —*I don't know what I should do when I get home. Maybe I should leave the door open and look around, so if the Strangler's inside I'm not locked in with him. But then I think, what if he's outside? Maybe I should lock the door as quick as I can.*

— —*Even when you're inside with the door locked, who says you're so safe? All these ladies he killed, even the young girls, he got in. He finds a way in, this guy.*

— —*When I go to bed, I set up soda bottles by the*

117

door, so in case he opens it during the night, I'll hear and maybe he'll get scared off.

— —He doesn't break in! They let him in! He talks his way in, he's a con man. So just don't answer the door . . .

On and on people talked. Nobody knew anything. Newspapers described the killer as a *phantom* and a *monster*, but they had no idea what he actually looked like. They hinted at *carnal sadism* or *ritualistic sexual deviancy* and suggested that the Strangler had *satisfied his unnatural appetites*. But the details were withheld; no one knew exactly what had happened to those thirteen women. Everyone was free to imagine the murders according to her own personal horrors. The victims, on the other hand, were absolutely real. In a city as small as Boston, it was not unusual to know someone who knew someone who knew one of the victims. Even if you could not find such a link, among thirteen victims, young and old, white and Negro, all nice girls, all grandmothers and college girls, it was not hard to find a victim who seemed familiar enough.

Far from distracting people from it, the Kennedy assassination fed the paranoia. It touched the same nerve. The Strangler too was an enemy within. The phantom fiend, they'd been told, probably looked just like them. If it turned out in the end that the city's resident monster was just another Oswald, well, they might be disappointed but they would not be surprised.

And so it went: Priests warned women from the pulpit to keep their doors locked. Jittery phonecallers flooded the police with warnings

118

about neighbors who were suspected of harboring fetishes, or men who tried to pick them up on the street, or mysterious hang-up calls. Single women felt their hearts quicken when they entered their darkened apartments. Strangler-anxiety became a fact of life.

Amy tried not to feel any of it. What the newspapers had said was true: Statistically, you were more likely to be killed by lightning than by the Strangler. Anyway, she had always felt strong, and feeling strong, she believed, made her so. Still, something was off. She wanted that big new lock. It helped her sleep.

Now she fiddled with the key, sawing in and out, searching for the proper fit as she clutched her purse and the mail and supported a bag of groceries precariously on one raised knee. Finally she was able to get the thing open. She stepped inside, snapped the light on—and screamed.

Ricky was in the armchair in the opposite corner.

"Jesus! Stop, doing, that!"

"I don't have a key."

"Exactly."

"I wanted to talk to you."

"So knock! Like a normal person!"

"Well, but you weren't home, see, so I just—"

She cut him off with a look, then lugged her groceries into the little galley kitchen.

Ricky followed her in and gave her a peck on the mouth.

"You've been drinking. Where were you? No, wait, let me guess. McGrail's."

"How'd you guess?"

"You're a creature of habit. You should have your mail delivered there."

"I've been banned."

"From McGrail's? They'll go broke without you."

"It's true."

"What'd you do, run out on a tab?"

"I consorted with the criminal element."

"You are the criminal element."

"I mean the real criminal element. This guy came to see me. That's what I need to talk to you about. I need to disappear for a while, take care of this thing."

"What guy?"

"Amy, really, you don't want to know."

"I do."

His face was blank. This was the infuriating thing about Ricky, the secrecy, the way he just disappeared into himself.

"What's going on, Ricky?"

He did not respond.

"Come on,"she teased."It's not so hard. It's what the little hole in your face is for; that's where words come out."

"Amy . . ."

"Fine, Ricky. That's just . . . fine."

"Amy, it's nothing. I'll take care of it. It's just better we don't talk about it. Trust me, I have reasons."

"What reasons? Tell me."

"Amy, please. Just let it go."

She studied him. She knew, oh, she knew what

Ricky did. But if he chose not to discuss it, then the subject was verboten. That was the unspoken rule. At times like this, though, it killed her to let it go, just killed her. Her temperament, her training, her every day was about finding things out. She was a born finder-out. But, good Lord, did she love that man! Everything about him. His face, his smell, his voice, his body. The more she looked at him, the more she feasted on him. It was just possible, too, that she loved Ricky the more for his tantalizing secrets. He was a story she could never quite get. In any event, there was no sense in pressing him for answers. He wouldn't talk anyway.

But in the next moment all that sighing, girlish acceptance was gone. How could you really know a man if you could not discuss his work? What kind of relationship was that? Where was it all headed? They'd been together all these years and still? . . . Oh, the hell with secrets! Were they a couple or not? Did he love her or not?

"Ricky, it's not fair. You can't just show up and tell me you're going to disappear for a while without even explaining what's going on. It's . . ."

"This again. It's what?"

"It's not fair."

"Not fair? How do you know that? How do you know I'm not doing this for your own good?"

"I think I can decide what's for my own good. I'm a big girl."

"Well, the answer is no. You don't get to know this time. It's *better* you don't know. You'll just have to trust me on that. Now, do you trust me or not?"

Her mouth fell open. Trust *him*? Ricky, you hypocrite! What balls! She raised her hand to slap him in the chest, not playfully but because there was nothing else to do, no other way to reach him.

Ricky snatched her wrist before she could strike him. He held it, and though his face showed nothing, he squeezed her arm hard. His message could not have been clearer: *Don't snoop.*

"Ow, Ricky, stop it, you're hurting me."

He released her, then shook his head, frustrated, inarticulate. "Sorry."

"You're hurting me."

15

Joe was the man of the moment. He had rescued the girl from the clutches of the Mad Strangler, wrestled with the very monster itself— and he'd had the extraordinary good fortune to be photographed in his hour of high heroism. (The incident took place a few blocks from Newspaper Row on Washington Street, where several papers maintained their city rooms.) There was still the matter of attaching a name to the suspect and then finding him, but at least the cops had a description now. Joe received a commendation from the commissioner. True, this was the same commissioner Joe had humiliated a few weeks before on national television, but to Joe the rescue erased everything that had gone before. He presumed he would be rehabilitated. He informed Brendan Conroy that his first choices for reassignment would be Homicide or maybe Alvan Byron's new Strangler Bureau. Neither would happen.

One night Conroy showed up at Station Sixteen before last half to tell Joe, "You've been resurrected." But the resurrection was incomplete.

Joe was restored to detective, but in Station One, in the North End. The precinct covered parts of downtown and the North and West Ends. But the West End had already been reduced to a construction site, for the most part. And the North End was small and insular; it tended to police itself, without interference from outsiders like the Boston PD. Joe told Conroy he did not want the assignment. It was a step backward. "Now, don't be stiff-necked, boyo," the old man advised. "It's a detective bureau. This is the way back. Take it."

And so Joe found himself in plain clothes again, standing before a narrow shopfront in the old West End, near North Station. The big plate glass window had been smashed, and the hole covered over with plywood sheets. Only a transom remained to identify the place, in gold lettering:

MORRIS WASSERMAN • 26 •
DELICATESSEN GROCERY

Moe Wasserman's little deli was on the ground floor of one of the few remaining tenements in the area, on one of the few remaining open streets, tethered to the city by a single road that led out to Causeway Street. Joe knew the place. He remembered that missing window. It had been decorated with gold lettering, too, in English and Jewish, and near the door cardboard signs had been taped to it advertising the lunch specials. Sometimes there would be a line out the door at lunchtime. But Joe did not know Jewish food, and what did he need it for anyway? He knew what he liked. Besides, he'd probably go in there and say the wrong thing. So he had never tried it. Ricky would have tried it. Ricky would have strolled in there and come out gibbering Jewish and munching on a kosher pickle and doing the hokeypokey and been elected mayor of Jerusalem, because that's how things went for Ricky. Not Joe. Joe had to work for things.

The shop was closed, permanently, and Moe Wasserman himself had to come unlock the door for Joe and show him in. Wasserman was thin and tired-looking, handsome but dingy, sixty-five or so. Joe liked him before he had even opened the door. He liked all Jews, he thought. Twenty years before, as a nineteen-year-old Marine, Joe had marched across France into Germany with the Fourth Armored Division and he had seen things. He had seen things. In France he thought he had seen it all in the fighting in the forest, nothing could shock him anymore. Then in Germany he saw what the Germans had been up to. He didn't like to think about it. Joe had figured out that every country needed its niggers and in Europe of necessity the niggers had been white. Growing up Daley, it had been an article of faith that the Irish were Englishmen's niggers. From that traditional ethnic underdogism, it had been a short leap to pro-Semitism. Even before the war, Joe's dad had openly admired Jewish boxers and gangsters, the local booze-runners like Charlie "King" Solomon and Louie Fox. Weren't the Jew-gangsters just looking out for their people the same way the Gustin Gang looked out for the Irish? And hadn't Hitler taught everyone, finally, the need for niggers everywhere to look out for themselves, to punch back? Joe was inclined to lend his muscle to the cause. His little brother Michael stirred the same feeling in Joe: There were people who just did not like to throw punches, and it was the duty of guys who did to punch back for them, because if you didn't, if you just stood by and let it happen, then you were guilty too. In a world that killed its niggers, you had to take a side. You had to stand up.

For his part, Moe Wasserman did not seem to care much what the hulking detective thought about Jews or the war or anything else. He let Joe in and shuffled around flicking the lights on, revealing the destruction in the shop. It was worse than Joe had expected. Everything smashed. The floor strewn with shards of glass, kitchen equipment, furniture. The old man, too: he had a bandage on his right cheekbone, a gauze patch held with white tape, and purplish bruises on his face. On the floor, someone had broomed open a path through the wreckage from the front door to a door at the back.

Wasserman saw the cop survey it all and he shrugged. "It hasn't been cleaned. I picked up the food, that's all. You don't wash a sock before you throw it out. So."

"Why don't you just tell me what went on here, the whole story, start to finish."

"The whole story? What story? This is the story. Look."

"Well, any information you can tell us, Mr. Wasserman."

"Eh, you won't catch them. Personally"—he made an apologetic gesture, a flip of the hand that said *Forgive me for saying so, but* . . . —"I'm surprised you're even here."

"Why's that?"

"You're not from the West End, are you, Detective . . . ?"

"Daley. Joe."

"Detective Daley. You're not from around here."

"I'm from Dorchester."

"You haven't been a policeman around here for long, either."

"I've been a cop fifteen years."

"But not here."

Joe frowned. This was echt Boston: *here* did not refer to the region or even the city; *here* meant this neighborhood, these few blocks. To a West Ender, Dorchester might as well have been Greenland. "No," Joe admitted, "not here."

"No. Because I would have seen you. Well, so let me be the one to fill you in, Detective. There haven't been cops here for a long time. Garbagemen neither; they let the garbage pile up in the street. Why? Because they want to say the West End was a ghetto, it was 'blighted.' So what did they do? They stopped cleaning it up, they pulled out the cops, they didn't fix the roads. That's how they put the rabbit in the hat, see? They make a ghetto, then they say, 'Look, a ghetto! Let's tear it down.' It's business. I understand. I'm in business too. But let's be honest in this here."

"I'm here now and I'm a cop."

"Yes. I suppose." The old man sighed dismissively. *You must be some boob of a cop to get sent here now.*

"Well, look, alls I can do is try. And I promise you I'll try. But I can't do anything if you won't even talk to me."

"An honest man, heh? Alright, my friend, we'll try. Here it is: Couple weeks ago, December two, I'm up in my apartment in bed. This is maybe eleven, midnight. I hear a car drive up. Everything's quiet around here now, it's empty at night, sounds carry. So, I hear a car."

"What kind of car?"

"Don't know. I was looking down at it from the window, my bedroom window upstairs. I got an apartment above the store. It was a four-door, dark color, maybe blue, maybe black, that's all I can see. Four guys get out, big guys with bats. I seen them come up the sidewalk and one of them takes his bat and he smashes my window."

"Did you call the cops?"

"Course I called the cops. What else am I gonna do? What difference does it make? The cops don't come; I told you. So these guys, they smash my window and they climb right in the front of the store and they just go through it with their bats and they break it all up. They broke everything. I mean, I got insurance, but what am I gonna . . . ? You know how long this place has been here? Thirty,

128

forty years. My father had it. So I get dressed and I go running down to the shop. I figure, if it's money they want, so what? I'll give it to them, at least they won't smash up the whole thing. Because there's nothing here to steal. What are they gonna take, a corned beef? I go down and I tell them, 'Just take the money, here it is, what else do you want?'. But they don't want the money. They just want to smash everything. So that's what they did. They smashed me, too—not with the bats, thank God. There was money right out on the floor; they smashed the cash drawer. They didn't even take it. All they had to do was bend down and pick it up. But no. They couldn't be bothered."

"Four guys?"

"Four guys."

"Can you describe them?"

"All the same, I guess. Big *shtarkers*, maybe not as big as you, shorter. But big, strong guys. One guy, the guy in charge, he might have been Italian, that one: dark skin, thick hair, scar on his face like this." He dragged a finger down his cheek. "Wolves."

"Wolves?"

"That's what they were. Wolves."

"They say anything?"

"Yeah, 'get out, get outta here.' Jew this, Jew that, Jew bastard, kike, that kind of stuff. Eh. But that was the main thing, just 'get out.' "

"You knew what that meant, 'get out'?"

"Of course I knew. You think these guys just took it upon themselves to come out and smash up an old man's little shop just for kicks? Think, my friend. Somebody paid 'em. Cheaper than a lawyer. Course they've got lawyers working on it, too."

"Who paid them, you think?"

"Farley Sonnenshein. The Redevelopment. The city. It's all the same. This is valuable real estate all of a sudden. Too valuable for a schnook like me. See, I own the building, so they can't move me out so easy. And I ain't giving it away for fifty cents on the dollar like the rest of them. I fight 'em. I'm a pain in the ass. That's what it comes down to, Detective. I'm what you call a pain in Farley Sonnenshein's ass, and he wants it to go away. But guess what? I'm not going away."

"What are you gonna do?"

"What am I gonna do? I'm gonna give him a pain in his ass like a hemorrhoid till the day he dies or he pays me what he owes me."

Joe walked through the empty West End toward Cambridge Street. He passed abandoned buildings for a block or two, then bare dirt blocks, then the streets themselves disappeared and there was only gritty hard mud. The air was warmer than usual, the second straight day of mild December weather. Demolition debris was everywhere, scraps of brick and steel and concrete. Wet slush. The melting made a soft trickling sound, audible beneath the city noise, like a faucet dripping in the next room.

Wolves, the old man had called them. Wolves.

Joe had seen wolves. In Germany there had been a camp— Ohrdruf—outside a town called Gotha, where Joe had stepped on something, a twig

130

maybe. He had looked down to see a human finger, shriveled, half buried by the weight of Joe's boot. He thought: They are wolves, all Germans, every last one of them. He would feel no mercy for them. He swore it.

Then Joe had gone on to Berlin, where he was stationed for several months before shipping out. He remembered the thousands of notices fluttering like bird feathers everywhere in the city, on buildings and trees, covering the enormous cylindrical pillars on street corners: messages for people who had vanished. He remembered the pipes and radiators clinging like vines to the walls of bombed-out buildings. He remembered a summer night with his pals outside a club called the Rio Rita, all of them drunk. Walking, they came upon a group of Russians, the squat brown Mongolian types with dirty smock-like uniforms, standing over a woman, waiting their turn while one of them raped her. On the ground, the woman had turned her head and, between the Russians' boots, she gazed out at the GI's. Her face was impassive, a mask which shook with the rhythmic jarring of her rapist's pumping hips. Joe took a step but his buddies held him back. *Leave it alone, Joe, not our fight, fucking bastards, too late, happens every day in this fucking place* . . . So they stood there. They let it happen. They were in the British sector, ducking the MP's outside a club that had been declared off limits; they didn't want trouble, not when they were so close to shipping out. Still, they could have stopped it. Maybe they figured there was a kind of justice in it—who were the wolves now and who the niggers? But Joe did not see it that way. He was still a cop's son, and he figured Berlin was where you glimpsed the truth of things, of life unpoliced, and all he wanted was to get the hell out.

Almost twenty years later, Joe could see that woman's face as clear as day and still feel ashamed.

"Hey, cop."

On a corner near Cambridge Street a half dozen kids loitered. A few city blocks still survived here, just north of the police station, the city reemerging, knitting itself back into existence after the void of the empty West End site.

Joe had been feeling addled by the morning's events, the smashed-up shop, the suggestion that cops had been complicit somehow in the West Enders' betrayal, and the fog of memories from the war. But those punks, those two words—"Hey, cop"—belted him back into the here and now.

"Who said that?" he demanded.

The kids smirked. They wore jeans and short jackets. A couple smoked.

"Who said it?"

"I did," one responded. He was the biggest of them. He had a swagger. "What, you can't even say hello to a cop anymore?"

"You the tough guy? Is that it?" Joe was bigger than any of these kids, but they seemed to feel there was safety in numbers. "All tough guys, huh?"

No answer.

"Who's the toughest guy here?"

After some wordless discussion, they nodded in unison toward the first kid.

"You?" Joe pulled out his pistol. He leveled it directly at the tip of the kid's nose. "Now I am."

The kid's eyes bulged.

"My name's not 'cop.' From now on you call me Detective Daley or Lieutenant Daley or Sir, you got that?"

Nod.

"Answer me."

"Yeah."

"You know that guy Moe Wasserman with the deli over near the Garden?"

"Yeah."

"He's a friend of mine. Somebody broke up his store. I want to know who."

The kid's eyes were slightly crossed from staring at the tip of the gun. "I, I don't know."

"Find out."

"Okay."

Joe put the gun away. "Give me your wallet."

The kid pulled a wallet out of his back pocket and handed it over. The wallet was warm and ass-shaped. Joe felt queer holding it. But he found the kid's license and confirmed the name, just in case.

"What's my name?"

"Daley."

There was an audible whish from the kid's lungs, and he doubled over onto Joe's fist, and Joe looked down at him with something like relief at having thrown a punch, finally. Joe kept him from falling, held him up with a fist still clutched under the kid's

133

belly. He could feel the lungs spasm. "Breathe," Joe counseled, "breathe." He held his right arm locked at a ninetydegree angle while the boy hung over his fist like a magician's cloth, to be whipped away revealing a bouquet or a rabbit.

"What's my name?"

"Detective Daley."

This was how you dealt with wolves.

16

Boston State Hospital, Mattapan.

Seated at his desk, the psychiatrist pondered a photograph. His index finger went to his upper lip and swept back and forth, back and forth, over a brushy mustache. "No," he decided. He set the photo aside and picked up the next one, another head-and-shoulders photo of an old woman.

His name was Dr. Mark Keating. He was chief of psychiatry at this public mental hospital, which was set in a sprawling woodsy campus in Boston. He had an air of slovenly cultivation: a froth of gray curls that still bore the impression of a hat, snaggled teeth, spectacles rotated a few degrees off horizontal. Michael equated that sort of Einsteinish sloppiness with purity of intellect, or of purpose, or courage or simple eccentricity, or all of these, because Michael knew full well that his own sensible, conformist appearance—the bag suit from Brooks, the brogans which he polished regularly with an old pair of underpants—signaled the opposite. The psychiatrist seemed to take Michael's visit in stride. He had been treating Arthur Nast

135

and talking to policemen about Arthur Nast for nearly ten years, on and off.

"This was the one, I think."

The doctor handed the photo across the desk to Michael.

"Helena Jalakian," Michael said. "She was fifty-six."

"She looks older."

"She lost her parents in the Armenian genocide. She was just a child, of course." Michael frowned. "She lived on Gainsborough Street in the Fenway, so she could walk to Symphony Hall and Jordan Hall. Classical music buff."

"This was the picture."

"I don't understand. She was the first victim. But you said you called the police on August"— Michael checked his notes—"twenty-third, in '62. There were already seven women dead by then."

"This picture was in the newspaper. Or a picture just like it, I don't know. But it was this woman. Until then I wasn't sure." He riffled through a bristling file folder, his head shaking. He came to a form with a photo paper-clipped at the corner. He tugged the picture free and laid it beside the first. "You see? This is Arthur Nast's mother."

Michael compared the two. The similarity was striking.

"And look," the doctor said. He arranged three more pictures from Michael's collection around the tiny shot of Nast's mother so they formed a cross.

Michael recited, "Ina Lanzmann, Mary Duffy, Jane Tibodeau. Look at that. Amazing."

"They are all, at least they appear to be, between fifty-five and seventy. Arthur's mother was fifty-eight when she died."

"So why did you wait so long to call the cops?"

"All I had was the resemblance of the pictures. I needed more. You understand, I'm bound by patient confidentiality. Generally, anything Arthur tells me, I'm forbidden to repeat. I could not come forward until I was convinced Arthur might really be murdering these women. Even then, many of my colleagues would not agree with my telling you these things. If it ever comes out that I revealed all this to you . . ."

His finger agitated the bristle-ends of his mustache again.

"Look, I've had my suspicions about Arthur for a long time. Arthur is not confined here. We do not have the resources to monitor his movements, and he has ground privileges, which means he can leave the campus almost any time he wants. So he has a history of wandering off. And of course he tends to get in trouble on these rambles. Arthur is rather odd looking and quite a large man; people tend to be alarmed when they find him rustling around in their backyards. He's been arrested several times for breaking and entering, trespassing, that sort of thing. Usually he's just broken into the basement of a building to sleep there or to take some little thing that's caught his eye, a bicycle or whatever. But sometimes he does more sinister things.

"After I saw the woman's photo, to satisfy my curiosity—to allay my fears, really—I checked the dates of Arthur's absences from the hospital against the dates of the first seven Strangler murders, in that summer of '62. The dates lined up perfectly."

"What about the other stranglings?"

"That's just it. If you remember, the first seven murders were all older women, all in a threemonth period from June through August 1962. Those are the warm months, when Arthur tends to wander. Then there were no murders for a while, until the winter, December, I think, and those next two victims were young girls in their twenties. I checked: Arthur was here on those dates. Which made perfect sense to me because Arthur's anger is not simply directed at all women. It is directed at one woman in particular: his mother."

"So Nast could not have done them all?"

"I know for a fact he didn't. It's the murders involving these old women that concern me. You see, Arthur despised his mother. He first came here in 1956. He'd already been in other institutions— Bridgewater, Tewksbury, the Shattuck. But I first met him in '56. He'd tried to kill his mother. Threw her down a flight of stairs. The judge pink-slipped him to us for the thirty-day competency evaluation. In the end it did not matter. The mother refused to testify; the case never went forward. But Arthur seemed to form some connection with me in those thirty days, and when the family ultimately decided he should be committed, in '59, he came back here. I've been treating him ever since."

"And?"

"Over the years he continued to abuse his mother. Punched her, kicked her, eventually he threw her down that flight of stairs. He would be arrested but the charges were never pursued. It's an awful thing to ask a mother to testify against her own son."

"What happened to her?"

"I can't prove it, of course, but it seems fairly obvious to me that he killed her, finally. This was in 1961. She was in the hospital, immobilized in bed, hooked up to an I.V. And then Arthur paid her a visit. Soon after he left, the old woman was found nearly dead on the floor beside her bed. The I.V. had been ripped out of her arm. The bed railing was still raised, so she could not have rolled off the bed. There were bruises on her neck. Arthur had choked her, obviously, ripped out the I.V., and tossed her on the floor. The mother died before she could ever tell what happened. The cause of death was heart attack induced by asphyxiation. So again, he was never prosecuted."

"Why did he hate her so much?"

"I don't know, not with any certainty. Look, I can't tell you everything Arthur has said about her; I do still have some obligation to maintain confidentiality. But I'm not sure it matters anyway. Arthur reports all sorts of abuse when he was a child, some pretty monstrous things, all of which may be gospel truth or, equally likely, all of it could be delusional. It was real enough to Arthur, that's the important thing. And of course the mother-hatred and the delusions feed on each other until Arthur can no longer see his mother as anything but a complete monster, one who persecutes him even from the grave. I will tell you that Arthur reports he still hears her voice. She berates him, accuses him, doubts him. On and on. So there was motive, if you can call it that."

"What's actually wrong with him?"

"A precise diagnosis in a case like Arthur's is very difficult. He's deeply disturbed. Likely schizophrenic. That's how he exhibits, anyway: delusional, with some pretty bizarre illusions; fractured speech and thought; occasional hallucinations; obsessive about certain things, his mother, women, sex. One problem in treating Arthur is that his intelligence is very limited, as is his ability to articulate his thoughts. At times he seems childish, almost autistic. So as a clinician you have this knot of problems: the storm of emotion whipping around inside him, the constellation of behaviors that may or may not signal schizophrenia or some other psychotic disorder, and all of it viewed through the fuzzy window of the man's limited intelligence and ability to communicate. And of course what makes this all so dangerous is that Arthur's mind is housed in this enormous, powerful body."

"Sounds like a real E-ticket ride."

"That wouldn't be the clinical term, but . . ."

"What about young women? When my brother found Nast in that alley, he was choking a college

140

girl, twenty-one years old, very pretty. She sure did not look like his mother."

"Yes. Well, Arthur's sexual . . . impulses are quite primitive and unrestrained. Now, to what extent that's rolled up with these feelings about his mother, I don't know. It's probably a reach to say his hatred for one woman has poisoned his perceptions of all women. In our conversations I have always had the sense that Arthur just does not have any feelings at all toward women except as sexual playthings. He does not empathize with them, he does not even perceive them as human. This is why I found it troubling that there have been old and young Strangler victims but none in between. Women interest Arthur either because they are old enough to be his mother or young enough to be objects of sexual desire. Women who fill neither role are of no interest. He does not see them."

"But you say he was here when the two young women were strangled, in December of '62?"

"That's right."

"So there's at least two stranglers?"

The psychiatrist shrugged. *Not my job.*

"Have you ever confronted him directly about the murders?"

"No. In clinical terms, that would be a very bad idea. He would never trust me again. But one day last year—and I did report this to the police—I found Arthur wandering in the hall in a doctors-only area of the hospital. He said, 'Dr. Keating, I need to talk to you.' I asked him what it was about. He said, 'The stranglings.' I took him to my office immediately. I was going to inject him with sodium pentothal and question him about the murders. But at just that moment I got an emergency call and I had to leave. I never got the chance to question Arthur directly. He never gave me another opportunity like that."

"Doctor, do you think Arthur Nast is the Strangler?"

"That's the sixty-four-thousand-dollar question, isn't it? Look, all I can tell you is I have a terrible, terrible feeling."

17

This broad was built like a brick shithouse. Packed into a blue dress pressurized across the bust and butt. Big vaulted Neapolitan nose, lacquered helmet of brown hair. Paula Something-or-other. Joe was partial to the brick-shithouse type, and when he had caught sight of this one progressing down Cambridge Street like a Zeppelin, he had thought she looked like Sophia Loren a little. He knew he could fuck her, he knew it the moment he saw her walking that stroppy walk. He brought her to Joe Tecce's for dinner, and now, halfway through her veal piccata with a side of pappardelle, this broad Paula was still hungry and Joe was feeling the familiar anticipation of a rich dessert.

When she excused herself to go to the "little girls' room," Joe sipped his wine and watched her ass, then he sipped his wine undistracted.

A man sat down in Paula's chair. "You know who I am?"

"No."

"Yeah you do."

Joe topped off his wineglass then offered the

bottle to the visitor. When a guy like Vincent Gargano shows up at your table, you make nice.

Gargano was short and doughy, a dark-complected guinea, with the sort of kissy Cupid's-bow mouth that belonged on an angel on a church ceiling. A street kid in a suit. He was not even gangstered up in the usual pinky ring and hockey-puck-sized watch. Maybe he was purposely guarding his reputation from any indication of softness. Or maybe he just didn't know any better. But intentional or not, Gargano's cheap suit and ringless fingers were like a friar's robe: they suggested a sort of incorruptibility. Vinnie The Animal was not violent for the money; he was just violent.

"You're Detective Daley, am I right? You just come over to Station One."

"That's right."

"That's some good-looking lady, your wife."

Joe glanced toward the ladies' room.

"You're a lucky guy."

"That's not my wife."

"Even luckier. *Hff*, that's some broad. Must be your sister."

"Something like that."

"She's somebody's sister. Not mine, lucky for you." Gargano grinned.This was charm,a pale version of it."Listen,I just come over to welcome you to the neighborhood, you know, let you know if there's ever anything I can do for you, help you out or whatever, something I can do . . . you know."

Joe nodded but did not reply.

"I'm offering you my friendship, see?"

"I see."

"I heard about that thing with The Monkey and that TV show, this whole . . . mixup. I liked the way you stood up on that. Never said nothin' about nothin'. You got a lot of fuckin' balls, Detective Daley, you don't mind my sayin' so. That's what I hear about you and that's what I think: this man's got balls like coconuts. Standup guy with two big fuckin' coconuts."

Joe nodded in a not unfriendly way. He figured Vinnie Gargano's head was filled with coconuts, but what could you say?

"I remember your old man Joe Daley. You look a little like him, only bigger."

"I've heard."

"Hey, can I ask you a favor?"

Joe shrugged.

"You don't mind? I mean, I don't wanna do anything . . ."

Another shrug.

"I got this cousin, he's a good kid, not like me. A little"—he pointed to his temple and made a face: *crazy*—"know what I mean, Joe? You got kids, right? So you know. So this kid, my cousin, he piled up all these parking tickets, with the construction and everything, and cuz he don't care, since we're just talkin' here. So he piles up all these parking tickets. End of the year, he goes down to the registry to renew his plates. Stands in a line around the block, the whole thing. And guess what? They turn him down. Just like that." He washed his hands together and showed Joe his palms. "I mean, whattaya . . . ? So I told him,'Hey, *stugatz*, just go pay the fuckin' tickets like Joe Citizen and take care of it.' But he don't listen. He's a fuckin' kid, am I right? Just screws the plates back on the fuckin' car and off he goes, like nothin'. So some cop over there in your station cites him for an unregistered motor vehicle. So now the kid can't drive. And if he can't drive, he can't work. You see the problem?"

Joe forked a piece of steak and showed it to Gargano. "You mind?"

"Go right ahead. While it's hot. Don't mind me. So the thing is, is I want to take care of this thing for this kid, my cousin. We all made mistakes when we were kids, right? So I seen you come in tonight and I figured, hey, that's Joe Daley's kid, why not reach out to him, see if he can help me take care of this thing. I mean, it iddn't like the kid robbed a bank. Am I right or am I right? I would be very grateful if you would do this thing for me. Very grateful. I would consider it a personal favor."

"Can't do it."

"I would consider it a personal favor."

"Can't help you. Sorry."

"If it's about the cost—"

"It's not about the cost."

Joe knew how it worked. He would do Gargano this small favor, then Gargano would slip him an envelope as a way of saying thank you, and that's how it would start. They would have their hooks in him. Charlie Capobianco's mob was famous for collecting cops. Their police pad was rumored to include the names of half the downtown cops, including captains and lieutenants in Homicide and Vice, even a special unit assigned to monitor organized crime. It was easy money, but the risk in getting tangled up with these North End guys was too high. Joe was determined to clean up his act. This bullshit with the bookies, and the money washing in and out—he'd had enough of the whole thing. As soon as he got back even, he was giving up the whole thing. Anyway, Capobianco hated cops almost as much as he hated Irishmen, and he harbored a special contempt for Irish cops. The last thing Joe needed was to crawl into bed with a guy like that.

"No offense," Joe offered.

"No, no. No offense." Gargano glanced around the restaurant. Joe Tecce's did a good business even midweek, and the tables were piled in close. "Anyway, like I said, if there's ever anything I can do for you."

"Alright."

"I hear you got a couple little tabs running, Detective." Gargano stared. The mask of solicitousness slipped just a little. "You hit a little cold streak?"

"Huh?"

"I hear you like the puppies. They don't like you so much though, lately."

"Something you can do about that?"

Gargano shook his head. "Can't help you there. No offense."

Joe's eyes fell. He cut his steak with affected concentration.

"Hey, that guy Rick Daley, that's your brother, iddn't he?"

"What about him?"

"Just askin' is all. I need to have a word with him, too. He's ducking me."

"Leave him out of it."

"It's got nothing to do with you, big brother. We got our own business to discuss, Rick and me."

Joe glared briefly, and foolishly, but then it is not always an asset to have balls like coconuts.

"Here comes your sister. Jeezus Christ, would you look at the tits on that broad." Gargano leered as she processed across the room. "Tits like that, they ought to strap her to the front of a ship, you know? Like one of those fuckin' statues with the big tits they put on the front of a ship there?"

Joe said nothing.

Gargano turned to him and smirked at his own joke, at Joe's abased silence. There could only be one alpha dog.

When the girl arrived, Gargano jumped to his feet, pushed in her chair for her, and wished them both a good meal.

"Friend of yours, Joe?"

"No. Come on, baby, let's get out of here."

"But I haven't finished my dinner."

"You'll finish it some other time."

18

Boston Homicide. BPD Headquarters, second floor. Friday, December 27, 1963, 10:30 A.M.

A dozen or so detectives clustered by the wall peering into a oneway mirror. The mirror looked into the Homicide commander's office, a small space—a desk, a few chairs, a low bookcase—where important interviews usually took place, since there was no formal interview room. Unfortunately the glass was only big enough for two or three guys to look through comfortably (inside the office, the window was disguised as a discreet little framed mirror). So the detectives had arranged themselves just so, craning, like kids watching a ball game through a hole in the fence. At the front of the crowd was Brendan Conroy's big slab of a face. Conroy was second in command at Boston Homicide. Michael Daley's face was there too, peering down a narrow sight path through the crowd, through the glass, to the back quarter of Arthur Nast's head. Next to Michael in the crowd was a Homicide detective named Tom Hart, who had been one of Joe Senior's favorites. Tom Hart was bald and puff-bellied and decent. There was an unmistakable significance, Michael thought, in the way Hart had positioned himself next to Michael. The implication was that Joe Senior's son could never really be an outsider here. Through the glass, inside the commander's office, seated at the desk, was George Wamsley.

They were all eager to know the same thing: Was it possible this bugeyed baldheaded towering mental case might actually be the Strangler?

Nast had managed to stay on the run for five days after the attack on the girl in the alley. He was discovered sleeping next to a furnace in the basement of an apartment building on Hemenway Street. The janitor who found Nast thought he might have been staying there awhile; he had made a bed out of oily rags and old blankets scrounged from the storage bins in the basement. He had also left an enormous turd on the floor. It reared up like a coiled cobra, which disturbed the janitor much more than the possibility that the Mad Strangler had nested in his building ("Who's gonna pick that thing up? I'm not gonna pick that thing up . . ."). When the cops came down into the basement, Nast blurted, "I know what this is about" and "It's about that girl." He gathered up a few of his things from the floor, crammed them into his pockets, and submitted to the handcuffs. He was taken straight to BPD Homicide.

Why George Wamsley decided to conduct the interrogation himself was a mystery to the assembled sergeants and detectives from Boston.

As far as anyone knew, Wamsley had never inter-rogated a suspect in a homicide or, for that matter, a jaywalking. It was arrogance, pure and simple, that was the consensus. Typical Wamsley. Typical of the whole farcical Strangler Bureau, which was dis-dained within Boston PD as a political stunt designed to turn Alvan Byron from politician to hero and thus to governor. Once the halo was fitted to Byron's nappy head, he would no doubt lose all interest in the city and its murders. Now, as Wamsley's interview stretched into its second in-effectual hour, there was a sinking feeling in the room that Wamsley would cost them their only chance to question Arthur Nast. From here Nast would be booked, then taken to the Boston Municipal Court to be arraigned on two life felonies—assault with intent to rape on the girl in the alley and assault with intent to murder on Joe—whereupon he would be appointed a lawyer. That, no doubt, would be the end of the interrogations. With each futile question from Wamsley, the cops' frustration grew.

Brendan Conroy groaned, sniffed, shook his head, rolled his eyes heavenward. *Lord, save us from amateurs.*

Wamsley: "The girl in the alley, where did you first see her?"

Nast: "I don't know."

"You don't know?"

Shrug.

"Was she walking?"

"I guess."

"And you thought she was attractive."

"Probably."

"Did you know her? Before that night, I mean."

"No."

"Well, how did you approach her, what did you say?"

"I didn't say nothing, I just . . ."

"You just what?"

"I don't know, I just— We were kissing."

"And you wanted to have . . . sexual relations with her?"

"I guess."

"Did she want to kiss you?"

"Yes."

"That's not the way she tells it."

Shrug. No answer. Nast bowed his head, waiting for the next question. He was no genius, but he had the sensible instinct to ball up like a sow bug until the danger passed.

"Did she like it when you put your hands on her neck?"

"I guess so. Ask her."

"I did. She said she was screaming."

"Was she?"

"Was she? A policeman heard her three blocks away!"

Shrug.

Wamsley massaged the back of his neck. "Arthur, have you heard of the Strangler?"

"No."

"Never?"

"No."

Wamsley said, a little helplessly, "Well, I find that hard to believe, Arthur."

Standing among the Homicide detectives, Michael felt his sympathies streaming toward them. Lord, save us from amateurs. But the sight of Brendan Conroy's massive Easter Island head, his back puffing with contemptuous sighs, jerked Michael back to Wamsley's side. What was Conroy up to? What possible advantage could there be in undermining Wamsley now? Michael tried to force his attention back to the interview, but he could not pull his eyes away from the silver back of Conroy's head, the plush of thick hair sheared close to the scalp, and he felt himself start to seethe. It was as if a key had been turned and a little engine inside him began to grumble. Michael had not always disliked Brendan Conroy. When Conroy and Joe Senior had been partners for years, Michael had regarded him as a sort of laughing rogue uncle, the guy you could count on to spill his drink on the tablecloth or tell a dirty joke to Aunt Theresa the nun. But now it was a struggle to control his distaste. True to his self-critical nature, Michael found a way to extract guilt and self-reproach from the situation; he rebuked himself for his lack of self-possession. But the thing was loose in him now, and working with Conroy only fed it.

So when Conroy snorted one time too many at the lack of progress, Michael snapped, "Give him a fucking chance."

The profanity gave away a little too much. The others turned to look.

"Just give him a chance," Michael repeated, more meekly.

Wamsley's mistake was in presuming that interrogation was a sort of debate, in which facts and logic count. Wamsley was clever and intelligent and correct, Nast was none of these; therefore, Wamsley must win. The A.G. was not prepared for a suspect who simply turtled, refusing to hear logic or acknowledge obvious facts, refusing to respond in any meaningful way. Unfortunately everyone on the opposite side of that mirror knew what Wamsley did not: a real-world interrogation was not a short, intense grilling that climaxed in a tearful confession to the crime; more often it was a very long conversation during which a wary, exhausted suspect let slip a single tiny clue. It was about noticing the seemingly insignificant detail—the fact a suspect should not have known, or the one he got wrong in some small, telling way, or the inconsistency between one statement and another. It was about the needle in the haystack. The best interrogator did not expect to walk out with a full confession. Murder confessions—common as pennies in movies and TV shows—never happened in real life. So the good interrogator just wanted the suspect to "give him something." By those standards, Wamsley's Q&A was painful to watch.

Wamsley hung in with Nast for another half hour or so. When he emerged, he had extracted some superfluous, arguably incriminating statements about the attack on the girl and on Joe—a bullet-proof case already, with two unimpeachable

154

victim-witnesses—but nothing on the Strangler murders. He was sheepish in front of the assembled cops, but buoyed to see Michael there.

"Well." Wamsley sighed toward Michael. "I guess that's it, then."

"George, come here, we need to talk."

Michael huddled with his boss at the opposite end of the long room, in which eight desks were arranged for the eight Homicide sergeants. Beside the two lawyers, a grinning cardboard Santa Claus was taped to the wall. On a chalkboard, the city's homicide victims were listed according to date of death. The list still included all the Strangler victims killed within city limits. Strangler Bureau or no Strangler Bureau, Boston Homicide was not ready to cede those cases just yet.

"He's lying," Michael said. "He told you he's never heard of the Strangler; his shrink says he specifically asked to talk about the Strangler. Didn't you know that?"

"No. I guess I—"

"Look, you can't keep challenging this guy, you can't keep cornering him. He's like a kid. He's scared. He's an idiot, but even he knows he's in deep shit. He feels like you're trying to trap him, so he's covering up. You have to talk with him, be his friend, be his daddy, win his trust."

Wamsley's protruding ears reddened. He rotated them toward the assembled detectives, who had turned to watch. "Keep your voice down, Michael."

"Never mind them, George. You hear me? You're going back in there and you're going to sit with him till he gives you something. That's how it works. That's how my dad and Conroy used to do it. Take Brendan in there. He'll make Nast think twice. Then you be on his side, George. Be his friend, get him to trust you—then fuck him."

"I don't know how to . . ."

"Just stop with the questions for a while. You go in there, the first thing you say is 'How you feeling, Arthur?' Ask him if he needs a break, if he needs to use the bathroom. Offer him something to eat, ask him if he wants a Coke. Then don't tell someone to get the Coke; go and get it yourself. And don't put it on the table; hand it to him. Uncuff him, then no questions. Just talk. Ask him about his shrink, Dr. Keating. Tell him Dr. Keating is a pal of yours."

"I don't know Dr. Keating."

"Lie."

A little smirk appeared on Wamsley's mouth. An idea. "You do it, Michael."

"No. It's a bad idea. My brother's a victim. I'm conflicted out."

"You're not conflicted out. Your brother is a cop, not an ordinary victim."

"Doesn't matter. It'd be a hell of a stink bomb for some defense lawyer to toss into the courtroom."

"Michael, why are you avoiding this? You know the file better than I do. And you seem to know what interrogation is all about. You must have heard your dad talk about it a thousand times."

"I'm not a cop."

"Well, neither am I. But it's our case now, not

theirs. The cops had their chance. They blew it."

"George, keep your voice down."

"Michael, just do it. Go in there and do it. That's an order."

So it was decided. Diplomatically, Michael asked the assembled cops if anyone objected. Tom Hart quickly spoke for the grumbling group: "No, it's a good idea. Michael's a smart kid. Give him a chance." Michael invited Conroy to join him, which fed Conroy's ego—the old cop swelled visibly at the invitation—and eased Michael's own sense of presumptuousness.

"Let's do this, son," Conroy said.

"Yeah, okay, Brendan. Look, I'm just going to keep him talking."

"And what am I going to do?"

"Just be yourself, Brendan. That'll scare the shit out of him."

A few cops sniggered.

Michael took off his coat, loosened his tie, and rolled up his sleeves.

He swept into the office and said to Nast, "Hey, Arthur. I'm Michael. How you feelin' today?"

No answer.

"Long day, huh?" Michael glanced at the desk but did not sit behind it. Instead he sat down in the chair next to Nast's. "You want a Coke or something? How about a spucky? You must be getting hungry. I'm going to have a Coke. You want one?"

"Sure."

Michael walked out, leaving the office door open so Nast could see the crowd of hostile faces outside

157

the room. Nast watched him walk the length of the narrow office, past the eight empty desks, and out into the hall. When Michael returned, Conroy had settled himself behind the desk, and Nast looked like a hopeless dog at the pound.

Michael handed him a Coke,sat beside him,and began to chat."I talked to Dr. Keating the other day."

"You know Dr. Mark?"

"Yeah. Dr. Mark's a friend of mine. He was asking about you. People are worried about you, Arthur. Would you like to talk to him?"

"Yeah."

"Alright, we'll see, Arthur. I'll try to call him for you."

At one o'clock that afternoon, more than three hours later, Michael showed Arthur Nast a snapshot of Joanne Feeney, the woman who had been strangled to Sibelius's Fifth Symphony. Nast smiled briefly: He recognized her. Michael said nothing when he denied it.

A little after three, Nast admitted that one summer he had done yard work for Mrs. Feeney at a summer cottage she had rented in Scituate. He had been living at a group home nearby. Once, she had even given him a ride back to Boston. "She was nice. She told me about music." Nast leaned toward Michael and confided, in a shy voice, "She was my friend."

Conroy shot a glance at the mirror, at the cops standing behind it. He gave away just the slightest grin. *Gotcha!*

19

In Harvard Square, on the sidewalk in front of the Harvard Coop, a strange man in costume—belted tunic over dingy jeans, authentic-looking sword dangling from a loop of string on his hip—declaimed from Shakespeare on the art of acting: "Nor do not saw the air too much with your hand, thus, but use all gently . . ." He had thinning, sandy hair and a slash of red on each cheek that resembled theatrical rouge. His skin was unlined and pinguid; he might have been anywhere from twenty to thirty-five years old. This actor had drawn a small crowd, largely by disregarding the advice he was delivering, but then it took some doing to stand out in bohemian Harvard Square and you could hardly blame him for hamming it up. Besides, he seemed to be in on the joke, an intelligent guy, probably some out-of-work Harvard grad—there were some who came to Harvard and simply never left; they just floated around the Square for years—or one of the legion of kooks and longhairs that called Cambridge home.

Ricky skirted the crowd. He slowed only enough to glance at the actor, not to listen.

He continued north on Mass. Ave. and was well out of the riot of the square when he became aware of a black finned Cadillac Fleetwood drifting alongside. Ricky turned quickly onto a side street. The Caddy moved with him, lurking behind the unbroken wall of cars parked at the curb.

A man's voice called from the car, "You Rick Daley?"

Ricky did not answer.

He had long expected this day would come. Capobianco's organization had never shaken him down before, but Ricky had figured the chaos would affect him somehow. There was only so much money Capobianco would be able to squeeze out of the bookies and deadbeats in the South End, and when he'd finished gorging himself there, he'd hunt around for new sources of income. It was only a matter of time before a stalker like Vinnie Gargano paid Ricky a visit. Try as he might to fly under the radar—Ricky never flashed a lot of cash, he lived modestly in a Cambridge apartment, dressed in jeans, drove a Ford Fairlane—word had got out that he was making a lot of dough. It was an occupational hazard; you could not do Ricky's job in perfect secrecy because you could not do it alone. The idea of paying Capobianco's tax was galling, of course. Ricky earned his money fair and square, with intelligence, creativity, skill, preparation, and hard work. If he was technically a criminal, he was a prince among criminals. His "crime" was victimless, unless you could consider fat-cat insurance companies victims. Not that it would matter to

Capobianco's men. They would shark him just as they sharked everyone else. And Ricky would swallow hard and pay, call it a cost of doing business. No sense getting killed when there was a deal to be cut.

"Are you Rick Daley?"

Ricky kept walking.

"Hey, you speak American? I asked you a question."

"Who wants to know?"

"Who wants to—? The fuck is this? Are you Rick Daley or not?"

"Yeah."

They were at a corner. The Cadillac eased to a stop in the crosswalk, blocking Ricky's path.

Ricky stood and waited. His eyes closed briefly, an involuntary wince. *Here we go.*

Vincent Gargano jumped out of the car, left the engine running, and stalked around it. "Hey, I want to talk to you." He stood chest to chest with Ricky, or, to be precise, chest to chin, since he was several inches taller. He wore a blue jacket over a deco-print shirt, both open at the chest despite the December cold. The exposed skin of his chest was lightly haired and a mustardy shade of tan. Gargano's face was pale and bloated. His eyes were heavily lidded, the irises cloudy like a man with cataracts or drugged.

Big as Gargano was, Ricky had expected more. A giant. He was actually disappointed at the pudgy, dissipated man before him. There were rumors Gargano was a heroin addict. Ricky could certainly have outrun him, but he had decided long before that he would submit, appease, pay the tax if that's what it took. Vinny Gargano's physical dissipation did not matter much anyway. He was not feared because he was strong; he was feared because he was ferocious.

"The fuck you so nervous about? I just want to talk to you."

"I'm not nervous."

"You're not fuckin' nervous? The fuck. You won't even fuckin' tell me your name, and you're not nervous? What, are you fuckin' deaf? Is that it? You fuckin' deaf, you didn't hear me?"

"No . . ."

"So, what? What do you got to be nervous about?"

"I told you, I'm not nervous."

"I just want to talk to ya, for Christ's sake. You know what I want to talk about?"

"No."

"You have no idea?"

"No."

"No fuckin' idea?"

"Sorry."

"You have absolutely no fuckin' idea?"

"No."

"How come you been duckin' me?"

"I haven't been ducking you."

Gargano scowled. He stepped back to light a cigarette.

Ricky thought his whole act—the movements, the affected Bowery accent, the bullying repetitions—owed quite a bit to the movies. Cagney, mostly. *Scarface* and *White Heat*. Ricky knew from experience, from his own family even, that actual cops imitate the makebelieve cops in movies and TV shows. He hadn't realized the phenomenon extended to gangsters as well. But here it was, a gangster imitating an actor imitating a gangster.

"I hear you're a thief."

"Where'd you hear that?"

"What is it with you? You don't know how to answer a question? Is this how you talk? Is that true, you're a thief?"

"No."

"You're lying. First question, already you're lying. You're a thief."

"I'm a burglar."

"The fuck's the difference?"

"I don't take things from people, only from buildings."

"So what? People live in buildings. Same thing."

"It's not the same."

"It's the same fuckin' thing. Take from buildings, take from people, stealing's stealing."

"I don't hurt anybody. I only take from empty rooms."

"They aren't empty until you get to 'em."

"That's right."

"You see what I'm saying?"

"Yeah, but—"

"You see?"

"Yes."

"You guys all know each other, you burglars?"

"Some."

"How about you?"

"I don't know any. I work alone."

"You hear anything about a job at the Copley Plaza a few weeks ago, some New York Jew? Somebody ripped off a bunch of diamonds?"

"I read about it in the paper."

"Yeah? You pull that job?"

"No."

"I'm gonna ask you again. You do that job?"

"No." Ricky took out a pack of cigarettes and lit up. He struggled to shield the match from the wind. "No."

"Who did?"

"No idea."

"What is this bullshit,'no idea'? You know who took those fuckin' stones."

"No."

"Yes, you do. Yes, you do. I hear you're the only guy that could've done it."

"Not true."

"You're supposed to be some hotshot thief."

"Burglar. Lots of guys could have done it."

"That's not what I heard."

"You heard wrong. It's a hotel room. It's nothing. I could show you how to get in there in ten seconds. Anybody could have 'loided that door with the 'Do Not Disturb' sign hanging right there on the doorknob."

"Yeah, but not anybody could fence that much. And not anybody'd know which room to rip off."

"Look, we don't have to do all this. If this is about the tax . . ."

"Who said anything about a tax? What fuckin' tax?"

"I just thought—"

"You know, you got a smart fuckin' mouth, you know that? You don't listen. Anybody ever tell you that?"

Ricky stayed quiet.

"That's some smart fuckin' mouth on you."

Ricky shrugged. About that, he thought, Gargano may have had a point.

"Now you listen to me, Mr. Smart-mouth-I-take-from-empty-rooms-dumb-paddy-mick-fuck. I know what you were thinking: some fatass New York Jew, who's gonna give a shit, right? Only this particular fatass New York Jew was under our protection. He paid good money. Know what that means? It means stealing from him's the same as stealing from us. See, that's how this works. If you're with us, you're with us. Not like you—this guy wasn't alone in the world. Now if we let someone just take from us and we don't do nothing about it, then how does that look? What kind of message does that send?"

Ricky waved his cigarette in a little circle. *I don't know.*

"Now I'm gonna ask you one more time. Who did that job?"

"I don't know."

"Did you do it?"

"No."

"Don't lie. Don't you ever lie to me. Did you do it?"

"No."

"Good. Cuz the guy who took those stones? He better be puttin' his affairs in order." Gargano stamped out his cigarette on the sidewalk. "You read me, shitforbrains? He better be puttin' his affairs in order."

"I read you."

"You read me?"

"I read you."

"Yeah, you read me alright. You know, I seen your brother the other night? Joe Daley. 'Nother dumb-fuck paddy-mick pig, that one. Joe Daley. You know how deep a hole that dumbfuck brother of yours is in? Kind of hole you don't climb out of."

"What does that mean?"

"It means your dumbfuck brother's not as good at betting as you are at stealing—excuse me, burglaring. He's in the kind of hole you get buried in. He's another smartmouth prick. How many of you fuckin' Daleys are there, anyway?"

"Two."

"Gonna be none before this is over."

Ricky smiled wanly.

"Maybe you'll wind up in the same hole, the two o' yuz."

The good news, Ricky thought, was that Gargano apparently did not intend to kill him then and there. Too much talking. Situation like this, you look at the bright side.

"You hear anything about those stones, you let me know, you got me?"

"How do I find you?"

"Ask your brother, Lucky Joe."

"How's he going to find you?"

"He don't have to find me. I'm gonna find him. Believe me."

Across Massachusetts Avenue, Amy watched the two men. She was not spying, she would have explained. She was reporting. If Ricky was in trouble, then she ought to know about it. She would have given her eyeteeth to hear what the men were saying. But even from this distance she could tell Ricky was in trouble. It was not so much that Gargano was doing anything overtly threatening, though he stabbed his finger toward Ricky several times. Nor did she recognize Gargano. Amy knew of Vinnie The Animal's reputation but had never seen him. It was Ricky. The way he submitted to the scolding. The way he slouched, the way he avoided the other man's eyes, the way he fussed with his cigarette. To be honest, Amy was not sure why everyone thought Ricky Daley was such a smooth character. She, at least, could always tell when he was lying.

20

Kat, in her slip and bra, rummaged in a jewelry box, lazily at first, then frantically. "Where is it?" she wondered aloud.

Joe lay on the bed with his eyes closed. He snuffled. His hands shifted. He clasped them over his belly, but that left his arms stretched, his elbows raised off the bed, so he allowed his joined hands to slide down the dome of his belly to the sternum. He sniffed again, peacefully.

"Joe, where is it?"

"Where is what?"

"The money. The cash that was in my jewelry box."

"It's wherever you left it."

"I left it in the jewelry box, Joe. Where I always leave it."

Joe made a show of rousing himself, with much emotive groaning and eye-rubbing.

"Joe?"

"I borrowed some. I needed some walking-around money. So shoot me."

"Some? There's nothing here."

"I needed cash."

"And where is it?"

"I spent it."

"On what?"

"On I don't know. I just spent it."

"Joe, no!"

"It's my money. I earned it."

"You gambled it."

"No."

"You gambled it!"

"It's my money! I can do what I want with it!"

"Joe, are you stupid? Do you know what that money was? Do you know what it was for?"

"I'm not stupid."

"It was for groceries, Joe. Did you think I was just keeping it for nothing? For myself? Now what do I do?"

"I'm not stupid."

"What am I supposed to do?"

"I'll go to the bank, in the morning."

"And do what, Joe? Rob it?"

He looked down at the blanket, burrowed his eyes into the mazy chenille pattern.

"We have no money, Joe!"

"I didn't . . ."

"Jesus, Joe, did you hear me? We have no money." She covered her face with both hands. "We have no money, we have no money."

"I'll fix it."

"How, Joe?"

"I'll take some details."

"You're already off working—or whatever—

169

twenty-four hours a day. When are you gonna work details? Tell me how you're going to fix it, Joe. Where's the money going to come from? A tree? We needed that money. For Christ's sake, Joe. We needed it."

"I'll figure something out."

"You'll figure something out." Kat's mouth contorted as the urge to cry began to get the better of her. She raised her hand to her eye, like a botched salute, and she held it there, fighting to hold herself together. "You can't keep doing this to us, Joe. You just can't."

"Kat, come on. So we're not rich. You knew that when you married me. I'm a cop."

"Oh, please, don't. Just don't. I don't see other cops starving."

"I don't see them getting rich either."

"Why do you do this, Joe? Don't you care? Is that it? You don't care about us?"

"No."

"Then why? I mean, what's going to happen here, Joe? What's next? Just tell me so I know what to expect. Are you going to start selling off the house? Am I going to come home one day and find the TV is gone? How about my ring? You want my ring? Sell it to some pawnshop for a few bucks so you can give it away to your bookie? You know what? I'm going to start sleeping in this ring, I'm not gonna take it off. I'm not gonna give you the chance. What's wrong with you, Joe? Jesus. You have a family. What's wrong with you?"

"Nothing's wrong with me. I told you, I'll fix it."

"Do you know you have a son?"

"Yes, I know I have a—"

"Little Joe's grandfather's still warm in the grave, and what are you doing? You're supposed to be a father, and what do you do? You disappear. You go off and you only come back long enough to steal from us, then you're off again. What are you thinking, Joe? You're stealing from us."

"I'm not. You're making a big deal. We're just a little short of cash. It happens."

"A little short of cash. A little short of cash. Well, at least you haven't lost your sense of humor. We're a little short of cash, Joe, that's true."

"I'll come up with something."

Kat sat down the edge of the bed.

Joe touched her lower back where a little roll of fat licked around her hip bone. "Come on, Kathleen, I told you I'll fix it. I don't want to talk about money."

"Get your hands off me."

"Come on."

"Joe, I swear, if any part of your body touches me, I'm gonna cut it off."

He pulled his hand away.

"You're killing us, Joe. You know that? You're killing us."

21

Bridgewater State Hospital.

A detective fiddled with the tape recorder, trying to load a new reel, and when he finally got it, he switched the machine on and gave Wamsley a thumbs-up.

The tape reels turned. They had all been here long enough—this was the second day of Albert DeSalvo's confession—that they had begun to watch the pattern of the reels, the way the unspooling reel would gradually pick up speed as it emptied. Each of the men dedicated a sliver of attention to monitoring the pattern as he stood listening.

"Alright, I'd like to talk about Joanne Feeney. Do you remember Joanne Feeney?"

"Sure."

"Alright then, Albert, just tell me everything you remember about that day."

Albert DeSalvo had a wide, thin-lipped, expressive mouth, and though his face was crowded with too-large features—a bulging, pendulous nose that hung a little offcenter, a head of thick dark hair swept back in a cheesy pompadour, a stubborn five o'clock shadow—it was his mouth that dominated. At rest the corners drooped, and his face was sniffy and sullen. But when he smiled, his face became, if not handsome, sunny and likable. At the moment, asked to recall the murder of Joanne Feeney, DeSalvo's mouth compressed into a frown, a little boy straining to remember where he left a favorite toy.

In a corner of the room Michael crossed his arms to ward off the chill, which might have been winter pressing through the shivering six-over-six windows, or it might have been the horror-movie atmosphere of this place. Bridgewater State was a hospital in name only. It was where Massachusetts sent the maddest of its madmen—including the "criminally insane" and "sexually dangerous"— who were not likely to find a cure anywhere, least of all here. Michael dreaded coming to Bridgewater. Craziness was in the air. There was a constant irrational noise, a rustle of shuffling feet and slamming doors, yips and shouts that echoed off the concrete floors and painted-brick walls. How could anyone take it, the doctors, the guards? To Michael, the place seemed to have floated out of some Victorian English fog like a ghost ship.

But here was Albert DeSalvo, the man who, improbably but enthusiastically, was claiming to be the Boston Strangler.

His lawyer was present as well, Leland Bloom, without doubt the best-known lawyer in Boston, maybe the best-known in the country. "The Perry

Mason of Boston," the newspapers called him. Bloom had won acquittals in a series of highly publicized cases, and been photographed for *The Saturday Evening Post* in the cockpit of his Lear jet and on the deck of his sloop. Bloom smoked a pipe while his client confessed to the murders. He seemed pleased. Bloom had negotiated an immunity agreement for DeSalvo. Nothing he said here could be used against him, nor anything the police found as a result of what he said here. And so his client was partaking of a time-honored tradition for men in his position: unburdening himself of every last detail, the better to wrap that immunity around him like a cloak. That, at least, was what everybody thought. But Bloom, with his pipe and his confident harrumphing, made them wonder. What was he up to? Bloom was an egomaniac and a self-promoter and a prodigal liar, but he was not stupid. So why was he letting his client do this? Who in his right mind would confess to being the Boston Strangler?

"I went over there—this is the one in the West End over there?"

Wamsley:"Right."

"I went over there, and this was on Grove Street, I think it was, over near the Mass. General. This was August, I believe."

Wamsley:"November."

"November. I confused her with the other one. I didn't know the names, you understand? This is the one the same time as Kennedy died, am I right?"

"That's right."

"A Friday, I think?"

"That's right."

"This is the one with the music? The—whattaya call it?—the longhair music. She had it on the hi-fi."

Wamsley: "That's the one. Go ahead."

"Okay. That day, I remember I was not planning on doing anything. I was just thinking, about Kennedy, this and that, I guess. I was on the main drag, just walking. And I felt the thing start building up in me, you understand what I mean? The sex thing, the image was building. And I was just walking around. I went up Grove there. It's a little hill. And the building, there was three or four steps up, then there was a buzzer-type door? And on the right there was a list of buttons. I just looked for a button with a woman's name on it. I don't even know why, I don't know exactly what I was thinking. So I go in and I start to go up the stairs—"

Wamsley: "What did the hallway look like, the stairs?"

"It was just a regular hallway. I'm not sure what you mean."

"Describe it."

"Describe it how? Cuz, I mean, I don't really see— If you tell me what you want to know, I'll describe it but, see, I don't really know, I don't understand what you're asking me."

There were two detectives from BPD Homicide in the room, Brendan Conroy and the Homicide Commander, John Maginnis. Both stared at DeSalvo skeptically.

175

"Just tell me what the hall looked like, the entryway."

"It was just a hall. You came in and the stairs were right there. You just went straight, I think, up the stairs."

"Straight? Or right?"

"Might have been right. Sort of straight right."

"Okay. What next?"

"I went up the stairs. Mrs. Feeney—I didn't know that was her name; I'm just saying this now, you understand—when I got up there Mrs. Feeney was standing out on the landing there, watching me come up."

"What did she look like?"

"She was old. See, that's what I mean. Like I was saying, this one I don't think it was about the sex. I mean, it was definitely about the sex. But she was an old lady and it, it was just different, you understand me?"

"I understand. What did she look like waiting on the landing?"

"She was old. She had kind of black hair."

"Black?"

"Kind of black and white. Like, I don't know how to say it."

"Salt and pepper?"

"Yeah, salt and pepper. And she was wearing a robe. I remember that. It was red with a kind of a pattern."

"What was it made of?"

"Cotton."

"Plain cotton?"

"No, it was a funny kind of—there was kind of a pattern in it."

"What kind of pattern?"

"Just like circles, in the cotton."

"Did it have a lining? What color was the lining?"

"It definitely had a lining. I know that. But I could not see the lining at that point. Just let me—"

"Alright, go ahead."

"I told her the super sent me to check the windows, and she said she did not hear nothing about it and she wasn't sure and all this, because of everything that was going on and everything. Everybody worried about the Strangler. So I said, 'Well, if you're not interested, if you don't want to have the work done, I don't care, it's all the same to me.' This is what I always say, you understand me, and this is where they always change their minds. I think maybe it's because when I say it, I really mean it, you understand? I really don't care if they let me in or not, at that moment. In fact part of me is kind of hoping they don't let me in so I don't do . . . these things. Like I said, this one, all these ones with the old ladies, it's not a sex thing. Not exactly."

"Then what is it, Albert? You do have sex with them."

"Yeah, but it's not—I don't know. I don't know. Anyways, she lets me in and I tell her the same thing. It doesn't matter what you say to them, see? I could have said 'check the pipes' or 'check the heat.' I say different things to them. But this one, I tell her the same thing: I need to see the windows in the bedroom and does she mind showing me where the bedroom is."

"So she let you in willingly?"

"Yeah. Showed me right in."

"What did the apartment look like when you went in?"

"It was just . . . There was like a hallway kind of in the center. And as you come in, I think you go, I think right, and there was a room there with chairs."

"What kind of chairs?"

"Just, I don't know, plain chairs."

"Straightback chairs, you mean."

"Yeah, straightback chairs. And a table. Kind of like a kitchen, like an eating room. And then down the hall, in the back, was the bedroom. So we get in there and she's kind of leaning over, clearing some things off the windowsill so I can get in there and do the work. And I saw the back of her head and that was when I did it. I hit her. There was a little, like a statue there. I hit her with that right here, behind the ear.

"So she just falls down. I think she was already dead, I'm not really sure. I got a pillowcase offa the bed and I tied it around her."

"Just a pillowcase?"

"Yeah. I tied it around her neck. She was lying there."

"What about the pillow? What did you do with it?"

"Oh, I put it under her, under her rear end. I tried

to turn off the music, but I could not figure out how to work the hifi set, there was something weird about it, so I just left it. Then, you know, I strangled her with the pillowcase. I pulled it tight, twisted it kind of."

"Did you have sex with her?"

"Yeah, there was sex."

"Describe it."

"Describe it? It was just sex. I put my . . . you know."

"You penetrated her?"

"Yes, there was definite penetration."

"In her vagina."

Pause. "Yes, in her vagina."

"Did you ejaculate?"

"Definitely."

"Inside her?"

"I think so. I might have pulled out, but I think it was inside her."

"You're sure?"

"No, not absolutely sure. I might have pulled out, you know, come on the floor."

"You ejaculated on the floor."

"Yes, I think so. I'm pretty sure of it."

"What next?"

"I left."

"Before you left?"

"Well, I put her, I kind of locked her feet in the chair."

"Why did you do that?"

"I don't—like I said, I don't know why I do these things. I don't like to talk about it because a—the whole thing—well, I gotta talk about it whether I like it or not, don't I? I don't know why I did it. I just did it."

"What did you do next?"

"I just left."

"You left quickly, you ran out? Or you looked around the apartment first, left it a mess?"

"No, I looked around the apartment. I didn't make a big mess of it or nothing, but I looked through some of the drawers and everything. She had a little cash there, just maybe five bucks or something, and I took that, but that was all I ever took. That's not what this was about, you understand? I took that and then I left."

There was quiet. The tape reels squeaked as they turned. Somewhere outside the room a guard laughed.

The detectives stared.

DeSalvo raised his right hand—later much would be made of the size of his hands, the strength they purportedly carried, but they did not seem exceptional at the time—and he held the hand up in the traditional pose that says *I swear*.

22

Ricky considered the little man at the door.

Stan Gedaminski wore a grubby wool overcoat that might once have been blue, and the sort of plain black shoes favored by beat cops and mailmen and other professional walkers. His hair was an unfortunate shade of yellow-gray that nearly matched the complexion of his face, so that his head seemed entirely of one color, a sickly shade of flax, like a photo blown out by too much flash.

"Hey, Stan. You got a warrant?"

"No."

"Alright. Come in, then."

For obvious reasons, Ricky did not disdain cops as most burglars did. He considered it a mark of his own professionalism that he was no more wary of policemen than any other citizen; it meant he had as little to fear from them. And why should he? A good burglar, happily, ought never to be caught. Prepare each job properly and avoid the cardinal sins of working too often and talking too much, and burglary was about as secure a profession as there was. This neutrality about cops allowed Ricky to maintain a cordial if wary relationship with some of them. Stan Gedaminski was one.

A detective in the BPD burglary unit, Gedaminski had an eerie instinct for the job. He would patrol in vulnerable areas—empty residential streets and apartment houses in midday, hotels in the evenings, businesses overnight—and accurately identify the man in the crowd who was a burglar about to strike. This talent revealed itself early, in Gedaminski's rookie year on the force. He was in uniform, walking a beat in the Back Bay on a busy afternoon. He saw a man, well dressed but nondescript, and decided to follow him. Later, Gedaminski would be asked what it was about this man that attracted his attention. He did not have an answer. Just a feeling. He followed the man to the Ritz-Carlton Hotel and immediately alerted the house detective of a burglary about to take place. Together they arrested this man in the empty room of a woman from Tulsa, where he was calmly pocketing her jewelry. Gedaminski's gift was a narrow one. He could not sniff out murderers or rapists the way he could burglars, nor did those other crimes interest him. He was content to work burglary cases, a futile specialty. In that, Ricky thought, he was the perfect Bostonian, contentious, rigid, parochial, and so contemptuous of ostentation that he would devote himself to the one crime in which the deck was stacked in the criminal's favor. You had to respect a guy like that, whether or not you liked him.

"Sorry to bother you, Rick."

Gedaminski watched as the great Ricky Daley shuffled inside, barefoot. It was nearly eleven A.M. but the guy had not showered yet. His hair was spiky, he needed a shave. The apartment was a mess. Some beatnik jazz record was playing.

"You just waking up?"

"Is there a law against it?"

"Out late? What were you up to?"

"Ever heard of Charlie Mingus?"

"No."

"Didn't think so."

Gedaminski had never been to Ricky's apartment before, and he made a survey of the living room. "Where's the Rembrandts?"

"Under the mattress." Ricky scratched. "What brings you out here, Stan? You're out of your jurisdiction."

"I caught this case. It used to be your brother's. I guess he got transferred out of Station Sixteen. They reassigned the case. Somebody took the little statue of Jesus out of the Nativity scene. You know, on the Common there."

"That's terrible. People."

"I need it back."

"What makes you think I had anything to do with it?"

"I got brothers, too."

"That's it? Guilt by association?"

"I just want the statue, is all."

"Way past Christmas, isn't it, Stan?"

"Christmas'll be back next year. Unless somebody steals it."

"Did you check the pawnshops?"

"Look, Rick, can we cut the shit? I'm not looking to make a big deal here. This isn't the Brinks job. I'm not looking to make a pinch. I don't really give a shit about the case. I just need that statue back, that's all. This is off the books. Just between you and me. If you could help me out on this one, I'd appreciate it. I got better things to do."

"I have your word? As an officer of the law and a Christian?"

"You have my word as whatever you want."

Ricky went to a cabinet, pulled out the statue, and handed it feet-first to the detective.

"Thank you."

"Well, some of us citizens like to help out our brave men in blue when we can."

"Jesus, this thing's heavy," Gedaminski said. "What do they make these out of, lead?"

"It's the weight of our sins. Haven't you heard?"

Gedaminski held the statue at his hip, like a book.

"Was there something else, Stan? You look like there's something else on your mind."

"I got this other case that's been bothering me. This hotel robbery at the Copley Plaza. Last November. Somebody took off a jeweler, maybe you heard about it."

"Of course I heard about it."

"Guy says he lost almost a million bucks. Diamonds."

"These guys all lie, Stan, you know that. Whatever they lose, they double it when they put in

184

the claim with the insurance company. It's a scam. You ought to be investigating those guys. Crooks."

"How much you figure the guy really lost?"

"Stan, come on. How would I know?"

"See, that's what I figured. It didn't look like you. The guy got in by smashing the window. Glass all over the room. I told them, 'That ain't Daley. Ricky Daley doesn't leave clues. He gets in and out without a trace, that's his M.O.' "

"Well, thanks. I guess."

"Big job, though, and nobody knows anything about it? So then I thought: if I was Ricky Daley, that's just what I'd do. Smash a window, make a mess. Change it up, you know?"

"I'd like to help you, Stan. I just don't know anything about it."

"Well, there's a lot of people from the hotel there, guests and whatever. Let's hope one of them remembers the guy."

"Let's."

Gedaminski held up the little statue. "Thanks for this. I won't forget it."

"Do me a favor: Forget it."

"Yeah, okay. Sorry about all this, you know, getting you out of bed before lunch."

Ricky showed him to the door. "Hey, Stan, can I ask you something? Why do you bother?"

"Bother with what?"

"There's all these serious things going on out there, women getting strangled and killed—for Christ's sake, the President just got killed. The whole world's going to hell, and you're wasting your time on pissant BandE cases. Who does it hurt, anyway? Some lady loses her earrings, so what? The insurance company pays her off, she gets a new pair better than what she lost. Who's the victim? The insurance company? Those are some of the most profitable corporations on earth. And burglars are the best thing that ever happened to the insurance companies; they convince people they need to keep buying insurance. These people, they're more likely to get hit by lightning than by a burglar. But every time somebody gets ripped off, ten idiots run out and buy insurance. It's a victimless crime. Besides, you can't stop it. Did you hear, last year Castro made burglary a capital crime in Cuba? Know what happened? The burglary rate went up—*up*. So what's the point? It's human nature. You can't stop it. I mean, I know somebody has to work these cases, somebody has to run around to the pawnshops and get back all the swag and make a pinch here or there to make it look good. But why you? You're a good cop, Stan, you got a good head. You could go out there and make a difference. Really. Go catch the Strangler. Stop bothering people."

Gedaminski's mouth opened a crack.

Ricky grinned. "Just kiddin', Stan. Hey, don't drop Jesus. He's fragile."

The detective sloped to the door. "They weight it down," he said.

"Excuse me?"

"The statue." He lifted the Nativity figure. "They put a weight inside so it won't blow away in the

186

wind, in winter, so it won't fall over and break."

"How do you know that?"

"I don't. It's a theory."

"See, that's why you're a good detective. I never could have figured that out."

"You're wrong, you know, all that crap you just said about burglary, about it's a victimless crime and nobody gets hurt and all that. A crime is a crime. It's all the same instinct. You look at any violent criminal, you open his probation file, you'll see old convictions for property crimes."

"Not quite the same instinct, though, is it?"

"This Strangler, what do they know about him? What's the same in every one of those cases? Two things: He gets in and out of these apartments without using force and without being seen. And when he's done with these ladies, what does he do before he leaves? He steals. Now what does that sound like to you?"

"You left out the third thing, Stan: He strangles women."

"I'll make you a bet: when they catch the guy, there'll be B-and-E's on his record."

"So you figure the Strangler is a burglar."

"It's a theory."

23

There was something about the rubble of the old West End that Joe liked. He could not begin to articulate this pleasure, but he enjoyed it just the same, as some dogs will thump their tails on the floor while listening to music. It made him happy. The demolition kicked up clouds of dust which the wind blew across town. Your eyes burned from it, and at the end of the day your shirt collar and the snot in your handkerchief were black from it. A church, St. Joseph's, stood alone in the dust bowl. Joe knew the West End mattered somehow, it signified, but signified what? His best guess: it was a reminder that under all this city was dirt, and maybe every once in a while, every century or so, a city needed a good knocking-down. A fresh start. A New Boston, and fuck the old one. Full of rot, the old one was. And wouldn't it be nice if you could tear yourself down and rebuild from scratch? A new Joe, new and improved. Didn't work that way. A city you could bulldoze; your past you were stuck with. Your debts, your mistakes, you were stuck with.

He made it a habit to swing by Wasserman's grocery every few days. The old Jew wasn't around much now. Joe worried that something might have happened to him. There were stories about old West Enders who had gone out for a cup of coffee and come home to find a padlock on the door. That was how the Renewal worked. Maybe they had figured out how to roust old Wasserman after all. But Joe doubted it. If the old man was not scared off by Sonnenshein's gorillas, he was not going to scare easy. Joe slipped notes into the mail slot asking Wasserman to call him at the station. Every time he delivered one of these notes, Joe heard the little mail door clack and knew the old man would never call. There was nothing a cop could do for him. It was too late for that.

During a midmorning visit to Wasserman's, Joe recognized a punk on the sidewalk nearby, the same kid Joe had introduced himself to a few weeks before by sticking his gun in the kid's face. Joe stayed in his car a moment, watching the kid slouch past. His movements were listless, tired. When Joe jumped out, the kid made no attempt to run.

"You remember me?"

"Yeah."

"You got something for me?"

"No."

Joe shoved him across the sidewalk. "What are you, fuckin' stupid? Are you stupid?" Joe saw the disdain on the kid's face. He'd heard the toughcop bullshit before and mostly he was just bored with it. Joe was bored with it, too, but it was the only flavor he had. "You said you'd find out who broke up the old man's shop. You gave me your word."

"I said I'd try."

"So?"

"I tried. Nobody knows anything."

"Well, somebody must know."

"No."

"Keep trying, kid—"

"No."

"Whattaya shaking your head? Keep asking around."

"No."

"What is that, 'no, no, no'? Why not?"

"Cuz it's stupid, alright? I already asked everyone who's left around here. Don't you get it? It's got nothing to do with us. There's none of us left here. Whoever did it, they came from somewhere else. Why would any West Ender want to help the Renewal? What do we get out of it? What do you give a shit, anyways? You think they're gonna hold this whole thing up because some old fart won't leave his place? Look around you, man."

24

February 13, 1964.

Early Thursday morning they met at the Strangler Bureau to discuss DeSalvo. The Homicide commander along with Brendan Conroy and Tom Hart from Boston Homicide. A few detectives from surrounding towns that had had Strangler murders. From the Bureau, George Wamsley and Michael Daley.

Wamsley was jubilant. It was evident from the first interviews at Bridgewater—from his manner and from the way he conducted the questioning—that he considered Albert DeSalvo the one true Strangler. In hour after hour of testimony, DeSalvo had provided many accurate details about the crime scenes. He knew at least something about all thirteen stranglings.

Wamsley reviewed all this in some detail before concluding, "It seems to me we've found our man."

The cops exchanged looks.

"Albert DeSalvo didn't kill anybody," Conroy announced. "He's full of shit."

"Excuse me?" Wamsley inquired.

"DeSalvo didn't kill those women."

"Lieutenant, who would claim to be the Boston Strangler who was not?"

"Someone who wants to be famous, who wants to be remembered. A con artist who thinks there's money in it. A movie deal for 'the true confessions of the mad strangler.' "

"You think he'd risk the electric chair for that?"

"Wamsley, he's in Bridgewater. It's a loony bin."

"He's in Bridgewater because he's sexually dangerous, not loony. They picked him up on a warrant out of Cambridge, for rape. Doesn't make him a liar."

"Doesn't help." Conroy snorted. "He conned you, boyo. Everything he told you, he got out of the newspapers."

"I don't believe that."

"The Feeney murder DeSalvo was going on about?" From a file folder, Conroy brought out an old copy of the *Observer* with a story under Amy Ryan's co-byline, "Two Girl Reporters Review Strangle Murders." "It's all here. The buzzer, the fact the apartment was on the top floor, the symphony music, the pillow. Even the bit about not being able to turn off the hi-fi: the victim's son had rigged up the record player to play through the radio somehow, so it didn't turn off the usual way. All DeSalvo did was study the newspaper. And I can prove it, 'cause there are mistakes in this article that DeSalvo went and repeated. Joanne Feeney's robe was not red. DeSalvo was confused by the description here. It says the robe was 'rose-colored.'

DeSalvo pictured a red rose. But the robe was pink. I saw it. And the rape: he claims he penetrated her vaginally and he may have ejaculated in her. But Joanne Feeney wasn't raped. Look at the autopsy report: no sperm in her vagina or her rectum, no injury to the external genitalia. DeSalvo was running a con. That's all it was."

"Well, I found him convincing."

"Wamsley, even he couldn't understand raping old ladies. You heard him. He's into sex with young girls. You could tell he did not do the old ladies. DeSalvo might rob an old woman, but rape her, kill her? Doesn't fit."

"Alright, okay, that's Boston Homicide's position."

"And Cambridge's," another detective interjected. "We've had Albert. He's been around here for years. He's not a killer. He's no saint, but he's not a killer."

Wamsley said, "We're going to have a hell of a time convicting anyone else if DeSalvo's already confessed. Anyway, I thought he was pretty convincing. Yes, he might have got some of it from the newspapers, but not all. There was just too much detail. No, I'm convinced. I'm convinced. So we're going to focus on DeSalvo for now. We've got a guy who's confessed to thirteen murders. We can't ignore that."

"He's the wrong guy," Conroy insisted.

"I don't think so," Wamsley said.

"Ask *him*." Conroy pointed at Michael. "What d'you think, college boy?"

Michael waited.

"What *do* you think, Michael?" Wamsley said.

Michael shook his head. "I think Brendan might be right. You've got the wrong guy."

"Well," Wamsley said, "someone has to decide. And that someone is me." His eyes swept around the table to see how the statement went over. "We go with DeSalvo."

25

Michael worked through the afternoon, through dinner, through most of the evening at the Strangler Bureau, which was located in the state capitol building on Beacon Hill. He had set himself the task of combing through the murder books again, for details that DeSalvo had got wrong in his confession. DeSalvo's confession was bogus. The more Michael thought about it, the more certain he became. It was not just that DeSalvo was wrong on the facts; his tone was wrong. Too eager, too quick to please. Too grandiose and expansive—the telltale exuberant falseness of a bullshitter. Wamsley had bought it, but maybe it was not too late. Maybe Michael could bring his boss around.

"Hey."

Michael looked up to see Amy standing in his office doorway. She was still wearing her work dress. Her coat was draped over her arms. She slipped the heel of her foot out of her shoe and back in— tired, achy feet after a long day.

"Don't you people lock your doors?"

"Don't have to. We're the cops. Who would steal

195

from the cops?"

"Me. Some of those files out there . . . Imagine the headline: 'From the Secret Files of the Strangler Bureau.' "

He groaned.

"No, no—'From the Desk of Top Cop Michael Daley.' " She laughed.

"Alright, alright, I'll lock the door. I didn't know I was alone."

"What are you working on?"

"I'd rather not say. You know, to a reporter."

"Ah. Sounds fascinating. Well, I'm not just a reporter. I'm family too, right?"

"You're shameless."

"Can't help it. It's a job requirement."

"Well, at the moment you can't be both. If you're a reporter, I have to keep my mouth shut." Michael dropped a stack of photos on the desk. "I wish I could talk, believe me."

"Okay, then. I'm not a reporter. What's wrong, Michael?" Amy had to remind herself over and over that Michael was different from his brothers, easier to read, more exposed than Ricky, easier to wound than Joe.

"Amy, if I knew something, something that could maybe be dangerous . . ."

"Knew what?"

"Never mind. Forget it."

"Tell me. What's the big secret?"

He dodged the question. "I don't know how you do this, look at this gore every day."

"You keep your distance."

196

"What if that doesn't work?"

"You make it work. Michael, what is it?"

He shook his head.

"Come on, how bad can it be?"

A beat.

He regarded her. "DeSalvo's not the Strangler."

Another beat.

She said, "How could you know that for sure?"

"The confession was a travesty. Wamsley practically fed him the answers, and he still got half his facts wrong. If you'd been there, you'd understand. DeSalvo isn't a murderer. He's got a short record. No prior history of rape or assault, barely any violence at all until these new charges in Cambridge. And there's no physical evidence linking him to any of the stranglings—blood, fingerprints, witnesses, nothing. I could make a stronger case against a half dozen other guys than I can against DeSalvo, confession or no confession."

"What about the other people there? Did they believe him?"

"Not the cops. Just Wamsley. Unfortunately it's his call to make. George has always thought there's only one strangler. Now he thinks he's found him. Probably he's scared shitless of not solving the case or of trying it to a notguilty. That'd be his epitaph, and he knows it: the man who let the Boston Strangler get away."

"Could be yours, too, if you're wrong."

"I'm not wrong."

Amy nodded.

"At least I don't think I'm wrong."

"So if DeSalvo's not the Strangler, who is?"

"Nast maybe. Maybe someone we've never heard of. I don't know."

"Jesus. So what do you do now?"

"I don't know."

"If you say nothing, and some other girl gets killed while DeSalvo is still locked up, then what? Could you live with yourself?"

"I don't know."

"That's a lot of I-don't-knows."

"I know."

Amy smiled. "You know what your dad said to me once? A cop with a bad conscience is the worst kind of cop, because he knows better."

"I don't have a bad conscience."

"Don't you?"

"No."

"Okay. Whatever you say."

"What do you think I should do, Amy?"

"You'll think I'm selfish."

"Probably."

"You have to tell. If the Strangler's really still out there, if you really believe that, then you have to let people know. Otherwise, what will you say to the next girl's mother when she asks why you knew about the danger but did nothing to stop it?"

"So who do I tell? The cops know already."

"Keep telling them, I guess."

"And what if no one listens?"

"Then what else can you do? Tell a reporter."

"Hm. If only I knew one."

"I could keep your name out of it. Call you a

'highly placed, reliable source,' something like that."

"They'd know. I already told Wamsley to his face. He knows how I feel."

"Well, you think about it, Michael. That's a hell of a secret to have to carry around. I couldn't do it."

"No? Will you keep it secret, Amy? You're not going to write this?"

She smiled again but did not answer. "Can I tell you something, Michael? Of the three of you boys, I like you best."

"That's not exactly what I asked you."

"I mean it. I like you best."

"Great. I'll be sure to tell Ricky."

"You're the best one. You'll make the right decision. I'm not so sure the other two would. But you? You're *good*."

"You're manipulating me."

"Maybe. But I'm not lying."

He thought it over. "Fuck it. Go ahead and write it. What the hell. I liked it better in Eminent Domain anyway."

"It's the right thing to do."

"We'll see."

"You know, there's something I need to talk about, too. A family thing."

"Ricky?"

"No. Brendan."

"I thought you said family."

Amy sat down. She put her coat aside, slid forward, and laid her forearm on the desk. "Michael, we've never really talked about this."

199

He avoided her eyes to muffle the little thrill of Amy, her directness, the outlandish possibility of a frank conversation about his family, the intimate pleasure of a shared confidence. She was so close. So close.

Amy wiggled further forward, to the very edge of her seat. "You don't like Brendan."

"No."

"Why?"

"Just don't."

"Why?"

He shrugged.

"Do you think Brendan did something wrong?"

"Wrong like what?"

"You know what I mean. Be honest."

"I just don't like him hanging around my mother, that's all."

"That's it?"

"That's enough."

"Michael, I need to tell you something. I see how you act around Brendan. I know how you feel; I don't like him either. I never trusted him, never wanted him around you three boys, and I certainly never wanted him anywhere near your mother. If he ever lifted a finger to her, I swear I'd kill him. Your dad had Brendan pegged."

"Pegged as what?"

"A cop with a bad conscience."

"So," he demanded, "what's the big secret about Brendan?" He imagined Amy had in mind some petty corruption Brendan might have indulged in. The sort of Boston mischief that only the newspapers cared about—and even they did not care much.

"Michael, what do you think about the way your father was killed?"

"I'm against it."

"I'm serious, dammit. Do you believe it happened the way Brendan says it did?"

"Why not?"

"Two experienced cops, Homicide detectives, go searching for a suspect. They go down to the docks in East Boston looking for a witness, some street kid who lives there, twelve, thirteen years old. They find the kid, he runs, they chase. Kid squirts down an alley, Joe Senior runs in after him while Brendan lags behind. Joe Senior turns the corner, kid shoots him once, in the chest—and Joe Senior is dead, bullet in the heart. Now Brendan hears the shot and, disregarding his own safety, he barrels around the corner, too, to help his partner. Kid shoots a second time, hits Brendan in the gut, and Brendan goes down, again with a single shot. Kid takes off."

"That's the story."

"Do you believe it?"

"It happens."

"Do you know how hard it is to kill a man with a handgun, with one shot, on the run? It's hard even to disable someone with one bullet. It's John Wayne stuff—bang, you're dead. Only in the movies. The fact is, to kill a man with one shot you need to be very lucky or very accurate. You have to hit the head or the heart. That's not easy when you're both running in a panic. But this young kid puts two cops down with just two shots, on the move, killing one? Doesn't sound right."

"So he got lucky."

"Twice?"

"It happens."

"Not like that. Once is lucky. Twice? Impossible." She looked Michael square in the eyes until he looked away.

"And another thing: why didn't Brendan get up and run after the kid? Why'd he let the kid get away?"

"Because he was shot. He nearly died in the hospital."

"That was later. Internal bleeding, then an infection. Those are complications. Neither was true when he was lying there, letting that kid run right past him.

"Then, when the Homicide guys interviewed Brendan in the hospital, he gives them nothing. Just a vague description: skinny, teenage, Negro. When in doubt, just say the magic word 'Negro' and the Boston PD goes running."

"They'd never seen the kid before. They were following a tip. What do you expect?"

"I expect an experienced cop like Brendan Conroy would have described the kid better. A cop is a professional witness. If it really went down the way Brendan says it did, he'd have done better than some faceless mystery Negro. Besides, how is it that no one else saw the kid? Come on—a Negro kid in that neighborhood would have stuck out like a raisin in a bowl of milk. So where is he? How come they never found him?"

"Okay, I give up. So who's the kid who shot him?"

Her response was a simple, level look.

"The Negro kid?"

"Michael. There is no kid."

"So who . . . ?"

"Brendan. It was Brendan."

"You sure it wasn't Oswald?"

"Michael, this didn't just come to me. I've been digging into it for a year."

"So where's the gun? If Brendan and my dad were alone in that alley, where's the gun? They never found it."

"Brendan could have dumped the gun anywhere. He had plenty of time."

"Okay, so if Brendan shot my dad, who shot Brendan?"

"Brendan shot your dad, then himself."

"Oh, come on!"

"Michael, did you know Brendan once shot a suspect in the side, right here"—she pointed to her side, just above the hip bone—"and the bullet passed right through, in and out, barely slowed the guy down at all. I have the file."

"But Brendan was shot right in the gut, here, not here."

"It's not so easy to shoot yourself accurately. Not if your goal is to survive. The bullet entered Brendan's body on a slightly downward trajectory, moving from his right to his left—just as it would if Brendan was holding the gun in his right hand. His shirt was singed by the discharge, he was shot at such close range. A few feet at the most. If Brendan weren't a cop, they'd have thrown out his whole story based on just the physical evidence."

"How about the motive? Brendan and my old man were best friends for twenty years. They were like brothers. Why would Brendan want to kill him? Lust for Margaret Daley? Greed for the Daley fortune?"

"I don't know. I haven't figured that out. Yet."

"Wow." Michael sighed.

"I know. Wow."

"No, I mean, 'Wow, you're a lunatic.' "

"It sounds crazy, I know. But look, you're the only one I can tell, Michael. Ricky would think I'm insane, and Joe would just kill Brendan with no questions asked. You're the only one I can talk to. Tell me you believe me. Tell me at least you'll think about it."

"I'll think about it."

"Okay. That's a start."

"So what'll you do next?"

"What would you do, Michael?"

"Tell, I guess. Tell Mum, at least. If she's climbing into bed every night with her husband's murderer . . ."

"She'll never believe it."

"No. She won't."

Amy smiled.

Oh, she was close!

"Look, Michael, I'm going to go write up that DeSalvo story, if you're still willing. It's not too late.

I'll get it in for tomorrow. We'll talk about this later?"

"Sure."

She got up to leave."You know, I meant what I said.You really are the good one."

He said nothing. Just looked at her.

"See you later, Michael."

The next morning's *Observer* blared "Tec in Strangle Probe Voices Doubt." Arthur Nast's grainy mug shot appeared on page one, right next to DeSalvo's. The story carried the familiar joint byline of Amy Ryan and Claire Downey. It was sourced to "a highly placed official speaking on condition of anonymity."

It was the last story Amy Ryan ever wrote.

26

There was a particular sort of hallucination Michael often experienced in a migraine aura. The effect was like a mosaic—as if the scene before him had been painted on a pane of glass, and the glass was then cracked. Seams and disjunctions threaded the image. The tiles shivered and slid across one another, misalignments were created and repaired. It was the world as Picasso painted it: fractured, tessellated, the solid surface of reality revealed as it really was, fissile and impossibly complex.

This was how Michael saw the scene of Amy Ryan's murder. His mind smashed the image.

Her red hair tousled, eyes closed, head slumped on a naked shoulder.

Arms spread, tied at either side of the headboard.

Two or three tan stockings braided into a single springy cord, wrapped around her neck so tightly that it was pinched into a distinct hourglass shape. Beneath her Adam's apple the stockings were tied off in a big drooping bow—the Strangler's signature.

Face mottled with bruises and blood.

A clear mucous fluid, probably semen, trailed from her mouth onto her bare chest.

Pale naked stomach, muscled, the taut skin creased where her body bent.

Auburn pubic hair, a broom handle rammed in her vagina, a delta of blood on the sheet between her bare legs.

Red-stained panties on the floor by the bed.

A small dining table overturned, papers spilled onto the floor.

A photo in a silver frame of Amy and Ricky kissing.

Michael stood in the doorway of the bedroom, dazed, frozen. Cops, a forensics technician, and a photographer bustled around him. Occasionally they moved him a step or two in this or that direction so he would not be in the way. "Oh my God," Michael whispered, "ohmyGodohmyGodohmyGod . . ." He covered his brow with one hand as if he were shielding his eyes from the sun.

"Somebody get this guy out of here," a testy voice said.

"Come on, Mikey, we got to go."

Michael felt the weight of Joe's arm on his back.

"Come on, little brother. Don't let 'em see you like this."

"I did this, Joe."

"The fuck are you talking about?"

"I told her about DeSalvo. She came to my office, we talked. I didn't think . . ."

"You didn't do nothin', Mikey, you hear me?"

"No, Joe, it's my fault."

"No, you listen. Whoever did this, we'll find him. When the time comes, we'll take care of it. We'll do what we've got to do when the time comes. But right now you've got to get a grip, Mikey, you've got to maintain—maintain. There's things we got to do right now."

"Jesus, Joe."

"You think you're the only one Amy ever got a tip from? She was doing her job, you were doing yours. That's all."

Michael stared at the body. Crucified, pornographic, obscene.

"Don't look, Mikey. Come on, we got to get out of here."

But Michael could not move. He slouched against Joe. It occurred to him that he had never been this close physically to his brother, except when they had fought, one of Joe's headlocks.

"Come on, stand up. We've got to find Ricky. We're gonna walk out of here now. Don't look at her, Mikey. Look the other way. Come on, you ready?" Joe laid a hand on his shoulder. He said, as much to himself as to Michael, "We've got to find Ricky."

They careened across Cambridge in Joe's Olds EightyEight. Michael was aware, remotely, that they were going too fast, that it was dangerous, but Joe's driving was part of the dream—of hurtling ahead barely under control, and at the same time of being at a still point in the center of all that motion, like John Glenn in his space capsule. And if Joe slipped, if the car crashed into a tree or an oncoming truck? Wouldn't matter, Michael thought. His head bobbled with the movement of the car. Back there, in front of Amy's tortured body, Michael had felt something trembling in that room, about to shiver through. An idea, a presence. A sense of understanding. But he could not quite pull in the signal. He could not understand it. And now whatever epiphany might have come was gone. Now the whole thing had no significance at all. It was stupid, pointless savagery, nothing more. He thought: *Go ahead, Joe, drive us into a tree. I'm curious.*

Ricky took the news like a punch. For a moment he questioned it. Maybe his brothers were playing some dumb, deeply unfunny joke. Or a mistake. They must have made some mistake. But after that he did not protest or wail or collapse. His body stiffened, then swayed on rubbery legs, like a heavyweight who has been socked on the chin and is momentarily unconscious on his feet.

Ricky retreated toward the back of his apartment, down a narrow hallway that connected the living room with the bedroom in back. He wore a pair of old khakis and a yellowed undershirt that hung off his shoulders. His hand trailed along the wall. All that loose-limbed athleticism, the dancer's litheness that had always marked Ricky's movements, was gone. Ricky disappeared into the back bedroom.

Joe called down the hall, "You alright, pal?"

"Yeah, yeah."

"We should all head over to Ma's."

Michael said, "Come on, grab your things, Ricky. You can stay with me a few days."

"Nah. No, thanks, Mike. I think I'll just . . ." Ricky wandered back into the living room. "You were in her place, Michael? You saw her?"

"Yeah."

Ricky searched the floor as if he'd dropped something.

"Jesus, I'm so sorry, Rick," Michael said, embarrassed to fall back on a cliché.

Ricky nodded. He went back down the hallway, and when he reemerged he was buttoning the last few buttons of an oxford shirt. "I gotta go," he mumbled in a distracted, unapologetic way. He grabbed a jacket from the couch and brushed past them toward the door.

Joe tried to grab his arm. "Hey—"

"Let me alone, Joe. I'll be back in a little while."

"We'll go with you," Joe said. "We'll all go."

"Nah. I'd rather just go myself."

"It's okay, Joe. Let him go," Michael said.

"We should stick together."

"We are."

When Ricky got back, he shambled into the living room, tossed away his jacket, and fell onto the couch beside Michael.

"Where's Joe?"

"He went to tell Mum."

Ricky nodded. "You know why they killed Kennedy?"

210

"No."

"Because they had to. He made too many enemies. Sicced his brother on the Mob, attacked the Cubans, pissed off the Russians, stirred up trouble with the Negroes in Alabama. So they had to get rid of him. See, Lyndon Johnson, he'll live to be a hundred. Because he's a compromiser. You don't need to kill a guy if you can cut a deal with him. You see what I mean?"

"No. Not really."

"That's why they killed Amy. It was the only way to shut the woman up."

"What about the Strangler?"

Ricky gave him a cutting look. "I think we've got our own strangler. I'm going to find out who did this."

"Did she ever tell you anything, a story she was worried about, a witness maybe?"

"No. She knew a lot of lowlifes; she wrote about them. But she wasn't worried about it. None of them ever did anything. At least she never talked about it."

"I was the one who gave her the DeSalvo story, you know. She came by."

"I know. It's alright, Mikey. If it wasn't you, it would have been someone else. She didn't take no for an answer. Besides, she probably had another source."

Michael made a face: *Bullshit*. He said, "I wish I hadn't seen her."

Ricky went into the kitchen and came back with a bottle of Jim Beam. "Here. There's nothing for

211

depression like a depressant." He handed his brother a glass.

"I'm supposed to be cheering you up."

"I'm never gonna cheer up, Mikey."

"Yeah, you will."

"Nah."

"You will. It takes time."

"No. Because I don't want to. I don't want to ever get over it. So let's just, you know, drink up."

Ricky took a drink then turned and stared off into space, and that was that. He was through discussing it.

To Michael, his little brother's face, in profile, looked weathered. At the corner of Ricky's eye, the first delicate wrinkles were branching. Ricky Daley was actually getting old. How remarkable. Michael had never noticed the changes. In his mind's eye, Ricky was always young, always smoothfaced, always the Ricky of his memory.

And the memory of Ricky was a potent one. When they had been kids, and Michael was first coming to realize that we are all trapped in the solitude of our own skins, he had nonetheless always felt linked to Ricky. Now it came home to Michael that both their skins had hardened, and he did not know Ricky at all anymore. More important, Ricky did not know *him*. Not the way he'd used to. So there it was, the human condition, and so what? What was the sense of worrying about it? People were consigned to interior space for a reason—for moments precisely like this one, when they were forced to give up people whom they would rather hang on to. We are built to withstand our losses. The Daleys would survive Amy's death. What else could they do? They were still alive.

Impulsively, Michael dropped his hand onto the back of Ricky's. Their stacked hands looked strange, like mating animals. Some old taboo, or a battalion of them, made Michael want to pull his hand away, but he left it there.

Ricky looked down at the two hands. A riffle of uncertainty crossed his face. But he left his hand there, too.

Part Two

Part Two

27

Michael opened his left eye—the good eye, free of the hydraulic pressure that swelled his right eyeball during a migraine. His eyelashes were crusted with mucus; he teased it away with his finger. The room was dark. He could make out the sloping surface of his pillow, the outline of the bedroom window. His head remained still. Behind him, his mother whispered rosaries. Her beads ticked softly as she worried them in her hand. Even then—with his brain pressing open the fissures of his skull, trying to blossom out of its thick bone case— he saw that it was funny. Margaret would treat his migraine with ancient cultic hocus-pocus. A half dozen norepinephrine tablets had not worked; maybe a dose of Jesus would do the trick. He had seen a cartoon in a magazine once: a witch doctor in a grass skirt dancing around a car with its hood raised. That was Margaret. The sound of her whispering infuriated him. Sibilant hisses, like mouse scratches. Why wouldn't she be quiet?

Michael thought he might vomit. He risked jostling his head to feel for the stainless steel mixing

217

bowl on the floor by his bed. His fingers found the bowl and he pulled it up onto the bed.

His mother whispered, "Michael?"

He let his eye close, let himself drift.

The attacks usually began on the right side, a ghost behind the right eyeball, and as the pressure intensified and expanded, the pain became increasingly physical, sensual. It invaded the bony and spongy and meaty parts all packed tight in his head, and the loose weave of capillaries that netted the whole thing and kept it drenched. At times it seemed that the interior of his skull was illuminated. He could visualize the smooth bowl of his eye socket, and the mounting pressure in his arteries, and the poisonous fluid accumulating between his skull and scalp. At its worst—when he wondered if someone observing his scalp might actually see it stretch—at these moments he was conscious of the weight of his brain lolling on its stem, this pulpy wet mass that contained his consciousness. His mind beheld his brain. It was an electrochemical engine, impossibly complex, and when it broke the doctors were at a loss to fix it. They understood the mechanisms of migrainous pain well enough. Michael understood them, too; he had studied the literature and even with his layman's knowledge he could follow the cascading failures—minute dilation of the arterioles feeding the brain, increased intracranial hydrostatic pressure, which in turn triggered the excruciating buildup of fluid in the subcutaneous tissue under the scalp, a drop in circulating serotonin, erratic electrical activity. The neurologists could explain how it all happened; what they could not explain was why. What triggered it? What was the First Cause? Somewhere in his brainstem was a flaw. The same sustained electrochemical reaction that produced Michael's mind was flawed.

In her shushy whisper, Margaret continued to page Dr. Jesus, who seemed not to hear the message, or was not inclined to answer it. But then, He had not interceded on Amy's behalf or on Joe Senior's either. How, after all that, could Margaret maintain her childish faith in the old Catholic fairy tales and trinkets? What made the Jesus myth any more credible than a thousand others that people had been chanting around campfires all over the world in Jesus's day? What distinguished Jesus from, say, the army of abandoned jesuses on Easter Island—except that Jesus had had the good fortune to be taken up by Europeans? Ah, it did no good to cross-examine her. Margaret's faith was its own answer. He took her religiousness as a sign—yet another sign—of her simplicity. A lifetime in the hermetic world of a housewife had left her dull.

He pushed his head down into the pillow. Sometimes he could mash the heel of his hand into his right eyeball and feel relief, or press on his neck at the carotid artery, or squeeze his entire head with two hands. But the relief came at a price: When the compression was released, the gush of pent-up fluid was excruciating. So, by experimentation, he had found a compromise in which he lay on his right side and pressed his head down into the pillow with light, steady pressure that could be maintained for long periods. This was the position he returned to now, out of habit. He thought the attack was beginning to crumble. The peak had been reached and passed, almost undetectably. The sensation of pain took on a slightly different tone— stale, stanched, like turbid standing water. The current was reversing. He could begin to imagine himself in control of his body again. The very profusion of all these thoughts was itself a sign of recovery; pain annihilated thought, but Michael was *thinking* now. He was coming back to himself. The rebound stage would progress relatively quickly. Still, still. Another hour or two.

In Michael's head was a film: His father, Joe Senior, not idealized but as he'd been in life, fifty-eight years old, thin and sinewy like Ricky, with a pair of reading glasses in his shirt pocket, in the same black windbreaker he always wore on the job. He was running. Fast. He could surprise you with his athleticism, even at fifty-eight. It was easy to forget Joe Senior had not always been old. The brothers always thought of their dad as an old man, decrepit from the booze and the long hours. When he ran, it was like a revelation—this, *this*, was the real Joe Senior, the young man inside the old one. The scene was a road, not a proper road but an access road along the water, bounded by red-brick buildings on the left and a molded-concrete seawall on the right. Ahead of Joe Senior a kid was scampering away. Probably just a reflex. See a cop—run. There were swarms of tough kids like this one scurrying around the East Boston wharfs. Wharf rats.

(In his confession at Bridgewater, as Michael listened, Albert DeSalvo had claimed he'd hung around the East Boston waterfront for a while as a kid. The waterfront had been his only escape from an abusive father, he had said. The wharfs had toughened him up. This was where DeSalvo learned he could take care of himself, that he had good fists. He did not hate cops—DeSalvo had hastened to point this out, always ingratiating—but the other wharf rats did. One of the beat cops here liked to blow the homeless boys who lived at the wharfs. He liked it when the boys ejaculated on his blue brass-buttoned tunic. The rats all hated that cop, but DeSalvo did not hate him, or any other cop. It was just a story, DeSalvo had said, a memory.

But Michael was conflating memories. When Joe Senior sprinted down that alley in 1962, no one had heard of Albert DeSalvo, or the Strangler, or Lee Harvey Oswald or any of the rest of it. This was Before. Michael depressed his head into the pillow again, tried to refocus. He had to slow his brain down to keep the movie running, to let the reel play out.)

The kid skittered around a corner with a neat pivot. He disappeared. He was there and then he was not. Black sneakers, blue jeans, white T-shirt, blue jacket—Joe Senior made his mental notes as he ran, he started writing his report. His feet tick-tick-ticked light on the gritty ground. Behind him were the heavier chunking footfalls of Brendan Conroy, his partner. Conroy chuffed loudly, struggled to keep up. "That's the kid!" Conroy shouted. "That's the kid!" Conroy and Daley had a tip on a homicide. They wanted to talk to this kid. When the kid vanished around that corner, Joe Senior seemed to accelerate. Something in him opened up and he found himself rushing ahead faster than he'd thought possible, lifted, flying. (Michael saw from his dad's point of view now, through the old man's eyes, heard the old man's breath in his own ears. He heard his dad say through Michael's own mouth, "Hold it! Police!") Joe Senior fixed on that corner, an alley between two buildings. He had to slow down to come around the corner. A good cop does not rush around a corner. But it was a kid. He was thirteen or fourteen years old, he was not a suspect, just a witness, a "person of interest." Joe Senior came around the corner a little off balance, turning left as his upper body pulled him right, momentum like an invisible string tugging his torso; he leaned right, put out his left hand to steady himself on the brick wall of the building. And here was the kid—

a moment's confusion—

no—

here was the kid with a snub-nose four-shot derringer, a punky toy thing—

wavering in the kid's hand—

and in the last moment the temptation was to stare at the gun but Dad looked up at the kid, caught his eye—

Joe Senior was going to say *No!*—

222

the tip of his tongue flattened against the roof of his mouth to sound the *N*.

And now beside Michael's bed, his mother was repeating and repeating those whispery rosaries imploring Jesus Christ and Saint fucking Anthony and God Himself to come down and heal the miscalibration in Michael's central nervous system, "grant him rest and relief"—this from the same Jesus who had not bestirred Himself to intervene on Amy Ryan's behalf as her blood soaked the bedsheets, nor to stop the bullet from a child's gun that drilled Joe Senior's chest—for that matter the same Jesus who coded the flaw into Michael's brainstem in the first place. Stupid woman. Stupid fucking woman.

"Get out!"

He spoke the words into his pillow and felt the muffled humidity of his own breath.

Margaret was silent.

He snapped his head around recklessly and the fluid swirled in his skull and phosphenes floated across his vision and he was dizzy and furious. He saw her face, wide-eyed, shocked, and knew how he must have looked to her. He did not care. His voice was low and raw. "Get! Out!"

28

The ball swung back and forth, back and forth, gathering its lazy momentum.

A small crowd stood on the sidewalk behind BPD sawhorses, heads tipped upward, slackfaced with fascination. A woman said, "Here it comes." The shopkeeper Moe Wasserman was in the crowd, at the front, watching his building come down. Joe Daley, too.

The ball entered the building easily, through the brick curtain, and nestled in a second-floor bedroom. Plaster dust filled the room and drifted out of the front of the building like smoke. The room was not quite empty of furniture. A bed remained, its mattress stripped, and a small bureau. There were other holes in the building, other three-walled rooms exposed to view. The crane operator tugged the ball, which snagged the bed as it dragged across the room.

The building came down. Thirty-five minutes. The cloud of plaster dust took longer to dissipate. It left ashy powder on the windshields of parked cars.

After, the crowd looked past the rubble pile,

across the newly opened air space to St. Joseph's Church a quarter mile away. The church sat like a fortress on the bare plain of the old West End site.

Joe tried to remember exactly what Moe Wasserman's building had looked like, but already it was hard to summon up a complete picture. There had been a pattern along the roofline, like steps. Hadn't there?

A few hours later—it was after sunset, beyond that it was hard to know; could have been six o'clock, could have been ten—Joe was at the Pompeii, a favorite joint near Haymarket Square. The owner had a special relationship with the Department, and the Pompeii stayed open till all hours. That was a handy thing. There were nights he didn't feel like going home after working last half, with his engine still revving and the house all dark and quiet, the kid asleep, wife asleep.

Joe lived on the hill in Brighton, in a little split-level ranch on a woodsy new street behind St. Sebastian's. The fancy house never suited him. This was not his neighborhood. He did not belong out here, pretending to live in the suburbs. When he thought of the house, he tended to picture Kat and Little Joe there, without him. Sometimes when company came, Joe felt like one of the guests. And at night—Christ. The street went black and the only noises were the bugs cricking and shrilling in the woods and the squawks of the city in the far distance.

So, late at night Joe took it someplace else to

work it off a little. That wasn't always easy. Some nights he never did run out of gas. The energy just seemed to feed on itself and Joe felt a tireless capacity for working, drinking, laughing, fucking, whatever came along. He could go all night. Tonight would not be one of those nights, though. An uncharacteristic weariness had settled over him since Amy's death. It felt like rot. His strong body was being pulped from the inside, like some massive blighted tree. Maybe this was what it felt like to get old. Your body rotted away with you in it. Age was a disease, a fatal one. The sight of that building under the wrecking ball seemed to fit the same pattern, though Joe could not quite articulate how.

Across the bar were rows of bottles like soldiers in formation, and behind them a mirrored wall in which Joe saw his own blockish face. At least his appearance gave nothing away, he thought. He still looked like the old Joe.

Also reflected in the mirror was the woman beside him at the bar, a big blowsy redhead with a lot of miles on the odometer but not a bad-looking broad once you looked past the wear and tear. The Pompeii-themed interior of the restaurant heightened the red in her hair. It was a brazenly false color for a gal her age, but rather than being put off by it, Joe understood. He saw the sassy natural redhead she'd once been and wanted to be still. With her right hand the woman held a cigarette wedged between her index and middle fingers while she made minute adjustments to the neck of her dress with the remaining three fingers.

Joe turned to his left to peek at her directly, and they exchanged faint, well-meaning smiles, signals of good intentions. Up close, she was even more ruddy and windblown than she had looked in the mirror. Too old for Joe, but there was something there. He liked the way she plumped on her stool like a hen brooding an egg underneath her.

"Hey," the woman offered.

"Hey," Joe said, and he faced forward and for the first time in weeks he felt happy. Diffuse, childish joy.

Jesus Lord, did Joe Daley love women! Not just fucking them, though fucking was certainly part of it. He enjoyed their company, he was happy in their presence. Their tricks, the smells and makeup and clothes. The power of their clothed bodies! The happy squeeze of cleavage, the rise of the hips under their dresses, the suggestion of nudity up an open skirt. He exulted in it. Joe was dumbfounded when people, especially men—baby brother Michael could be particularly preachy here— suggested there was anything low-down or girl-hating about Joe's womanizing. Joe couldn't imagine anyone loving women more or better than he did. How on earth could anyone take seriously the pretense of monogamy in marriage? Joe lumped it in with all the other crazy old relics of Catholicism, like Church Latin and celibate priests and Swiss Guards. What did Joe's appreciation of other broads have to do with his sincere love for Kat? It just didn't figure. One had nothing to do with the other. Maybe a smarter guy could understand it. Then again, if some smartass ever did figure it out, Joe hoped he would keep it to himself. He did not want any part of a world without women.

Joe raised his empty glass and shook the ice cubes. The bartender ignored him. Joe called him by name, but the bartender pretended not to hear as he hefted a rack of dirty glasses back into the kitchen.

"Wax in his ears." The redhead shrugged.

"I guess so."

When the bartender returned, Joe asked loudly for another bourbon rocks.

"Tab's getting pretty high, Joe."

"I haven't been here that long."

"Not just tonight."

"Just give me a drink. You're a bartender not a, a . . . accountant. Whattaya? What are you shaking your head? Just give me a drink."

"If it was up to me . . . It's not coming from me, Joe."

Joe gave him a vexed look, a first stirring of trouble.

"Hey, Joe, if it was up to me. I mean, what do I give a shit?"

"You're shitting me."

"Just throw in a few bucks, Joe. Make it look good."

"I don't have any cash, the banks are closed. What do you want me to do?"

The bartender shook his head. "Can't do it."

228

"Can't do it? The fuck is that, 'can't do it'? How long've I been coming here?"

"Long time."

"Long time is right. Is this how you treat a customer?"

"No offense, Joe, but if you were a regular customer, I'd have cut you off a long time ago. You're going to drink us out of business."

"You don't think I'm good for it?"

The bartender cleared away Joe's glass and slung the ice into a dump sink. Joe took the act as a provocation and he started to stand, and things might have got worse had the redhead not piped up with "I'll buy him a drink."

The bartender, though he was probably relieved to avoid a confrontation with Joe, gave her a look. "He's a cop, you know."

"So? I got nothing against cops."

After he had his drink, Joe lifted the glass toward her. "Thanks."

She said, "Never a cop when you need one."

"You need one?"

"Sure."

A few hours later Joe lay in this woman's bed. The pillow under his nose stank of her perfume. She was beside him, under a thin blanket, the cool skin of her bottom against his. She snored, fluttery tubercular snores.

The room was dimly lit with reflected street light.

Joe stared at the wallpaper by the bed, a faded flower print. The paper was peeling at the seams.

There must have been a room just like this one in Moe Wasserman's demolished building. Maybe it had flowery wallpaper, too. Probably there'd been lots and lots of rooms like this in the West End. People had lived in those rooms, those boxes, stood in them, slept in them, got born and died in them. Now they were all gone. The rooms didn't exist anymore except as boxes in the air. Pieces of sky. This room where Joe was lying—it had been a box in the air, too, thirty feet aboveground, until someone had come along and wrapped it in these four walls and floor and ceiling. He was lying in a bed thirty feet off the ground, in a box in the air. A city is a pile of such boxes.

And Amy's room was a box, splashed with her blood. By now the blood had been scrubbed off, probably. The walls had been repainted. They would re-rent the room as soon as everyone forgot what happened there. It wouldn't take people long to forget. Amy's death had meant nothing. The world still turned, people went about their business. Joe should not have been surprised. How many men had he killed in the war? Germans, Italians. Fifty, a hundred, who knew? Why bother to count? He did not give a shit about them. Not then, not now. He would happily have killed more if he'd had the chance. A person was nothing. A bag of bones. Joe Daley included.

29

The consensus among the Daleys was that Ricky, paradoxically, would be the one least devastated by Amy's murder. He was so deft with his emotions, or maybe just so secretive, that he would slink off like a cat and do whatever it was he did when he was hurt, but he would do it in private. Even to his brothers, Ricky's composure was a little eerie. He had stood at the wake for hours with a stone face, shaking hands. He had not shed a tear at the funeral or since. It seemed perfectly obvious he would get over Amy's death. He had loved her, yes, but in the end you did not have to worry about Ricky.

Kat never bought any of it, all the Daley admiration for Ricky, for the way he kept a cool head. She preferred the hotter emotionalism of Joe's temper or even Michael's brooding, which at least signaled a vivid interior life. You had to let off the pressure, wasn't that what Freud and all them had said? She thought there was something childish about Ricky's inexpressiveness, and she was determined that he would not go unmothered in his hour of need.

All this, at least, was the quick summary of things that Ricky formed when he opened his door to find Kat, all put together in her sweater set and space-helmet of black hair, holding a pan covered with tinfoil. Ricky, barefoot and wearing jeans and a T-shirt, unshowered for three days, felt strangely proud of his dishevelment. By comparison with his coiffed and scented sister-in-law, he was natural and unaffected. He was himself.

"I brought you dinner," Kat informed him.

"What is it?"

"What's the difference?"

"It's for me, isn't it?"

"Ricky, whatever I made, you'll eat." She bussed his cheek. "Ingrate."

Kat had never been to Ricky's apartment before and she paused by the door to survey it. Living room in front with a galley kitchen and a narrow hallway leading back to a bed- and bathroom. The living room was furnished with just a threadbare couch that might once have been saffron yellow but now was too dingy to be any color at all, and too assflattened to be comfortable. An unfinished bookcase held a hifi set, two long shelves of LP's, and books on the bottom shelves. Jazz music played. Kat bobbed her head to the strolling rhythm.

"You like it?"

"I don't know. Maybe."

"It's Miles Davis."

"I know who he is!" Kat's tone was surprised. She must have seen Miles Davis on a late-night show or Ed Sullivan or somewhere. She did not remember much except that he was bald and shuffled around the stage as he played.

"Here, take it." Ricky got the dust jacket and offered it to her. The record was *Kind of Blue*. "Keep it. It gets better the more you listen to it. I'll get another one."

"And play it with what? My finger?"

"You're kidding me. You don't have a record player?"

"Let's not talk about it."

"What are you—monks? Who doesn't have a record player?"

"I said I don't want to talk about it."

"I'll get you one."

"You will not. We don't need one. Joe wouldn't go for this longhair stuff anyways. Miles Davis." She sniffed. "How come you're giving away your records? You going someplace?"

"No. This one's getting scratchy. They're better when they're new."

"You buy records twice?"

"You buy milk twice?"

Kat snorted. *Yeah, okay, Ricky.* She went to the kitchen, slid the pan into the oven and turned it on, then came back out to clear a dirty dish and a beer bottle from the coffee table. "When was the last time you cleaned this place?"

"Hm, let's see, when did I move in . . . ?"

"Didn't Amy ever do it?"

"We tended to hang around at her place."

"Her choice?"

"Mine."

"No wonder." Kat looked around at the bare walls and bare floors. Dust balls gathered along the baseboards. "You think *I'm* a monk? You're just a monk with a record player. Look at this place."

Back in the kitchen Kat stacked the dirty dishes on one side of the sink and began scrubbing them. "So how you doing here, Rick, all by your lonesome?"

"Swell."

"Swell?"

"I'm fine. I mean, look, obviously it's, it's not— I'm fine. Really."

"You're fine. Well, that's just great. I'm not."

"No?" A ripple crossed Ricky's face. A confession of sentiment was coming, with the expectation that he would reciprocate. Kat had found his front door locked; now she would rattle the side door.

"I can't stop thinking about her. All day every day. Can't sleep, can't stop eating, I'm as big as a house. Look at me. I'm a wreck over here."

"Me, too."

"Yeah? You're a wreck?"

"Yes."

"I don't believe you. You don't say that like you mean it."

"Yeah, well, I don't say anything like I mean it. But I do mean it. I loved her. I just don't feel like coming all unglued. Doesn't mean I don't feel it."

She turned off the water and looked across her shoulder at him. She wasn't going to fall for one of Ricky's cons. "Can I ask you something? Did you really love her?"

"Of course."

"No, not 'of course.' I mean, did you really love her?"

"Yeah."

"Because I loved her and I want to know. Did you really love her, Ricky?"

"Yes."

"Because she loved you, you know."

"I know."

Kat stared a second more, and Ricky quickly inventoried his emotions as if he were checking his shirt for crumbs. He *had* loved Amy, in his way. Ricky wasn't much of a lover. He did not really have the knack for it; he tended to shy away from intense emotion of any kind. But he had loved her as much as he'd ever loved anyone. And if the whole relationship, in memory, felt like role-playing, with Ricky cast as the dutiful husband-to-be ... well, a lot of Ricky's emotions felt inauthentic that way. Ordinary experience always felt slightly counterfeit. It was only when he worked—when he actually was roleplaying—that he felt truly himself, that he seemed to fill his own skin. Anyway, people used the word *love* too freely. Who knew that love meant the same thing, felt the same way, to any two people?

"I was going to marry her."

"You were?"

"Mmhm."

"Since when?"

"Since I don't know."

"Did she know? Did you ever . . . ?"

"No. I was still, you know, getting ready."

"Hunh." Kat considered it. "Hunh."

Ricky wasn't sure why he'd said this. He had never actually decided to marry Amy. The words just felt right. They were the objective guarantee Kat was looking for, the currency she could accept. They made Kat feel better, so what was the harm? People wanted you to be something; you only had to intuit what that thing was, then be it, and they were pleased.

"Did you steal a ring for her yet?"

"Oh, that's funny, Kat."

She attempted another joke: "What would you do if she wanted to return it?" But her voice caught at the thought of a broken engagement.

The LP scratched in its catchgroove.

"Time to change the record." Ricky smiled. "See? Miles has good timing."

Ricky flipped the record with a practiced updown motion. Held between his palms, by its edges, the record was precisely the diameter of a basketball. He said, "Don't you have to get home for dinner?"

"I thought we'd eat together tonight."

"Joe's workin'?"

"No."

"He's just out?"

"No."

"Ah."

Ricky left it at that. Kat did not need much prodding; if she felt like talking, she'd talk. And talk and talk. It was probably nothing. A spat. Kat and Joe's marriage was a Ten Years' War anyway. It was hard to take every little skirmish seriously. Besides, Ricky and Kat had rarely been alone together. They had never spoken about things that mattered; they did not quite know how. They would have to rebuild their relationship now, without Amy to broker between them.

Dinner was a roast trimmed out with potatoes and carrots. By the end of it, Kat looked exhausted and teary. Her roast was consumed, and the money it had cost, and she was foggy with beer and the obscenity of Amy's murder and rape and mutilation and whatever else she had not been told about it. She hunched over her plate. To Ricky, the strain had sapped her of precisely the quality that made her attractive: her indomitable straight-backed strength.

He, on the other hand, felt his emotions streaming in the opposite direction, from resignation to resolve, from confusion to clarity. The meal—the food, the beer, the company—invigorated him. He thought he could answer Kat's earlier question, and he wished he could go back to it. Yes, he had "really loved" Amy. He loved her still. But love for Ricky was a behavior, a series of actions. The emotion itself was worthless, because it's internal and immaterial. Even at its intensest and most intoxicating—which, Ricky presumed, was what Kat meant by "real love"—it could only be enjoyed by the one who felt it, not by the partner who inspired it.

Ricky thought he could clarify that to his

sister-in-law, though the whole idea was not quite clear to him yet. It lurked in his mind, unresolved, just beyond articulation.

But Kat had moved on. She pushed the food around on her plate, distracted. "I made this whole dinner, I came over here to help you, so you wouldn't be lonely, that was the whole thing—now look at me." She brushed her finger under her eyes, though no tears had come yet.

"What's wrong? You thinking about Amy?"

"No. Maybe. It's everything, I guess. I just wish your brother, I wish he'd give me a break. I need his help now, you know? I need my husband. And what do I get?"

"What did he do, Kat?"

"Same thing Joe always does. He fucks around. He doesn't even bother to cover his tracks anymore. He comes home with it on his shirt, in his pockets, the stink of it, and he gives it all to me to wash for him."

"You want me to talk to him?"

"And say what?"

"'Keep it in your pants.'"

"He can't keep it in his pants. I know that. I knew it the day I married him."

"But you married him anyway."

"I was crazy about him."

"I could threaten to tell Mum."

"Oh, Ricky, you think she doesn't know? You three are such little boys."

"Not little enough, apparently."

"No."

"Can I ask you something? Why don't you just go cheat on him? Go jump the milkman, isn't that the way it works?"

"Ricky!"

"I'm serious."

"Because I don't want any dead milkmen, that's why. We've got enough trouble. Besides, we need the milk."

"Well, you've got nobody to blame but yourself, then. Trust me, you give Joe a dose of his own medicine, you'll get his attention."

"I can't."

"Why?"

"You really don't know?"

"No."

"Because I'm crazy about him." She shrugged. "He's just not crazy about me."

30

In the days and weeks after Amy's murder, Michael was trapped in a whirl of activity. There were the wake and the funeral to get through, and interminable condolence calls with Amy's family, which he took to be the Daleys' final earthly interactions with a clan that had never much liked them. The Ryans had hoped Amy would do better than Ricky, whose indefinite profession was always fishy. Ricky had told them he was a car salesman. They figured him for a charming loafer who might be on drugs. In the end, the Daleys mourned separately for Ricky's "wife." Well-meaning visitors loitered in Margaret Daley's living room, many of them virtual strangers. Their presence imposed on the entire family the role of hosts. There were multiple trips to the grocery store, the liquor store, to the corner Spar for ice and cigs, back and forth to the rear porch with overflowing garbage cans. The death ritual, Michael thought, was all about make-work. The busyness it created was its only purpose, a distraction, like a magician's handkerchief.

Only his migraines pulled him away from the

group-grieving. They came more frequently after the murder; stress was a trigger. Michael had been getting migraines since he was a teenager, but they had been rare then, once a year or so. In his twenties, the attacks came more frequently, but still only three or four a year. It was Joe Senior's death that made them a constant threat; now Amy's death set off a rolling series of attacks that never quite receded. The recurring pattern seemed to intensify the experience. Raw exposed nerves did not have time to heal and toughen between bouts. The onset of an attack, with its visual aura and incipient head-pain, meant he had to drop what he was doing and rush home, resting his forehead on the steering wheel at red lights or stumbling down crowded sidewalks. When he rejoined the mourners a day or two later, he would find the world subtly changed. The bustle would have subsided detectably. The ashtrays were less full; there were fewer empty glasses and beer bottles about; Amy's death had become remoter. Drained by the headache, Michael would slump in a living-room chair as strangers sat down opposite him and made expansive remarks about the inevitability of death and the importance of moving on. Over and over it was pointed out how unlucky the Daleys were—two family members murdered in the space of a year. Who would be next? A joke circulated: The Roman soldier who pierced Jesus's side must have been named Daley; now they were cursed forever. With the men, Michael chunked his beer can against theirs and drank. The women tended to flop a hand onto his knee or his wrist as they spoke, which distracted him from whatever bromides they may have been passing along. Why did they bother? Probably they mistook his exhaustion—after a migraine attack he tended to look sallow and hollow-eyed—for prostrate grief.

But Michael was not defeated so much as mortally distracted. He could not focus. The TV lured him. News shows, vapid comedies. He drank. He shuffled out for a pack of Larks only to forget half a block away what it was he had gone out for. The weeks after Amy's murder took on the feel of a dream.

One thing did hold Michael's attention: Brendan Conroy, who held court in Margaret Daley's house and draped his arm around her and pushed in her chair at the table. The more Conroy did, it seemed, the more he was beloved. Wasn't Margaret lucky to have him? Wasn't Brendan gracious to insert himself into the family this way? Wasn't Joe Senior smiling down on them now, seeing his old friend and his old wife together? Michael seethed. He could not take his eyes off this pink, insinuating, coarse intruder. The small scale of the house only exaggerated Conroy's bulk. Had Conroy murdered Joe Senior, as Amy thought? The suspicion possessed him. A spurious gravity attaches to the words of dead people, who cannot be cross-examined. Amy had known Conroy's secret, it seemed, and maybe Conroy had killed her too—then slid into Margaret Daley's bed with the residue of blood still on him. All wild blasphemies

Michael did not dare utter. He might simply be going crazy. Certainly he would sound crazy.

On Thursday afternoon, ten days after Amy Ryan's murder, George Wamsley appeared at the Daleys' home to pay his condolence call. Michael escorted him around the room making introductions, then they retired to the back porch for a private chat. It was the only place they could be alone, a narrow space crowded with garbage cans.

"So, Michael. What are your plans?"

"Plans. What, um, what plans do you mean, George, specifically? I don't think I have any."

"For work."

"Ah. That."

"Yes, that. You know there'll always be a place for you in the office, as long as Alvan is the A.G. You could just go back to Eminent Domain, if you like. Or the Civil Division. You're a natural litigator. It might be a good step, professionally. It's really up to you. We'd like to accommodate you if we can."

"But not the Strangler Bureau."

"Not the Strangler Bureau. You're conflicted out. I think you know that."

Michael searched Wamsley's placid equine face for a hint of something more, some hidden motive. Michael was the obvious source of the leak behind Amy Ryan's last story, which cast doubt on DeSalvo's confession—a leak that compromised the case against DeSalvo, in the public's mind at least. After that, it was unlikely Michael would be welcomed back to the Strangler Bureau, with or without a conflict of interest. He was not sure he wanted to work the Strangler case anyway. He could not tolerate the vision of Amy strung up on her bed, so he flicked it away, and flicked it away again. One reason Ricky had had an easier time of it, he thought, was that Ricky had not actually seen her. The fact made him jealous. Michael could never unsee what he'd seen. Still, he resented that the decision had been made for him, that he'd been talked about behind closed doors.

"What about Brendan?"

"What about him?"

"He's not conflicted out?"

"He doesn't work for me. I don't tell BPD what to do. Besides, Brendan's connection isn't as close as yours."

"It will be."

"Michael, a homicide investigation isn't a blood feud. Whatever problem you have with Brendan . . . Anyway, you don't belong there. The decision's made. Case closed."

"But the case isn't closed, George. Amy Ryan's murder can't be a Strangler case. Your man DeSalvo was already locked up in Bridgewater. The phantom fiend is caught, remember? Unless you have the wrong man."

"We're treating it as a strangling."

"Good idea. Keep it inhouse. Maybe DeSalvo will confess to it yet. By the time he's done, he'll be claiming he killed Kennedy, and the Tsar and Julius fucking Caesar."

"Are you through, Michael?"

"Apparently."

244

Wamsley went to the railing and looked out over the scrap of weedy grass that passed for a back-yard. He dug a pack of cigarettes out of his jacket and took a good long time lighting one.

"Is there a suspect, George?"

"Not an appropriate question."

"Sorry. Forgot my manners."

"Come on, Michael—"

"Must be something to do with seeing Amy Ryan strung up—"

"Alright! Alright, that's enough. What's got into you?"

"I've had a headache."

"You're giving *me* a headache."

"George, you have no idea."

"We're looking at this guy Kurt Lindstrom."

"The Shakespeare guy!"

Kurt Lindstrom had been among the earliest suspects the police had identified in the Strangler murders. Michael had urged him as one the Strangler Bureau should consider more closely, before Albert DeSalvo's out-of-left-field confession had essentially terminated the investigation. A 1954 graduate of Harvard, Lindstrom was from a small town in upstate New York. He spoke, or claimed to speak, eight languages. He was an accomplished classical organist who had appeared with the Boston Symphony. He had also been arrested for creating an LSD lab and experimenting with the drug, which was barely known to the cops at the time. Most memorable to Michael, though, was the fact that Lindstrom, an out-of-work actor, spent his days in full Shakespearian costume reciting speeches on street corners, usually in Harvard Square. Lindstrom claimed to have founded a theater troupe which he intended to relocate to New York City when the time was right. The Cambridge PD had picked him up on various trespass and suspicious-person charges. On one occasion he was asked by a bookish Cambridge detective how he managed to make such a convincing Othello. "I use Man Tan," Lindstrom said. Yes, but why, with the city in a panic over woman-killings, would he choose that role? "Because I understand him." Lindstrom certainly seemed to understand Othello's capacity for violence. His record was full of assault and indecent A&B charges, to go along with the raft of narcotics and vagrancy-type cases. If Arthur Nast had fulfilled one fantasy of the Mad Strangler, the Frankenstein monster of children's nightmares, it seemed to Michael that Kurt Lindstrom embodied an even more frightening alternative: the calculating Strangler smarter than the cops pursuing him, the faceless oddball standing next to you at the market.

"Hate to say I told you so, George."

"Then don't."

"And DeSalvo?"

"DeSalvo for all the others."

"You think that's gonna fly?"

"I think it's the truth. Whether it flies or not isn't my concern. It still makes more sense than a dozen stranglers running around in one city at one time."

"Does it? I'm not so sure. The more I see . . ."

"I can see how you would feel that way, after what's happened."

"It's not that, George. I'm more cynical than you give me credit for. What's Lindstrom's motive? Or is it just another mad strangler thing? He picked Amy Ryan by coincidence?"

"The theory is he murdered her because she wrote that story saying DeSalvo is the wrong man. He wanted to prove her right by demonstrating beyond a shadow of a doubt that the Strangler is still out there. Lindstrom wants DeSalvo cleared. He wants to be the Strangler. He wants to be remembered. If he can't be Macbeth, he'll be Jack the Ripper."

"That's the theory?"

"That's the theory."

"Well, I'll give you credit, George. It makes as much sense as anything else I've heard. Which is faint praise."

Wamsley tamped his cigarette on the railing and, when he was sure it was out, he dropped it into one of the trash cans. "You'll come back to Eminent Domain, Michael? Help build the New Boston and all that?"

"Sure. Why not."

"Okay, then. I'm sorry for your loss."

"Me, too. Say hello to my mother before you leave. She'll be honored you came. The man who caught the Boston Strangler."

"I'm surprised to hear you call me that."

"Eh, what do I care, right? I'm off the case."

31

Thirty-four steps. That was Michael's count. He had initially paced it off at a walk and reached a higher number. But his dad had been running and his stride would have lengthened. So Michael ran it, from the end of the access road to the alley, and he counted again, then ran it again and counted again. Thirty-four steps, about half that number of seconds. It had to be wrong. He was missing something. He assumed he was in the jigsawed world of the mystery novel; if the solution was right, the pieces would fit. They would slip together easily. They didn't.

He went to the alley, stood where the shooter had stood. The killer had beat Dad to this spot, waited for him to come skittering around that corner, and fired. So he had dashed around the corner ahead of Dad, pulled the gun, and was there ready-steady, waiting. A three-or four-second lapse, say.

Michael rehearsed the facts again. Dad and Conroy arrive in a cruiser at the Eastie waterfront, Dad driving. He parks with the driver's side of the car nearer the access road. Conroy, on the far side of

248

the car, sees the kid and shouts to him, across the roof of the car.

The kid, sitting with his back against a wall, looks up, registers cops!, and takes off. Then the thirty-four-steps, then the shot.

So how—if Amy was right—did a lardass like Brendan Conroy get into position to fire that shot in the alley? How could he possibly have beat Dad from the parked car to the alley?

Michael adjusted the facts to fit the movie in his head. Maybe Conroy had gone ahead earlier, before the sprint, or something had distracted Dad or drawn him away, giving Conroy a head start. Or maybe the car had been parked the other way (though it would have required backing in). Michael could have dreamt up a thousand scenarios to reach the desired climax. What he could not do was imagine a different climax.

He ran it again. He wanted to feel it, make the experience a physical reality. Thirty-four steps, *chick-chick-chick-chick-chick* ... Michael's head jostling. On his right the slate-blue emptiness of Boston Harbor. The water was choppy and white-capped, the colors of a chalky blackboard in school. It made an oceany whishing sound. Beyond the harbor the city rose up on its little hill a mile away, still a nineteenth-century skyline, ten stories tall, a mean little port city without a skyscraper, an American Marseilles. *Chick-chick-chick*, thirty-two, -three, -four, and the corner. Turn. Gun. Shooter. Bang.

Again. Slow it down.

Turn.

Little four-shot derringer.

Pan up to the shooter's face—Brendan Conroy's face. Flushed, maybe a little grimace at having to perform this necessary, distasteful task. Did he say anything first? "Sorry, Joe, hope you understand"?

Dad's tongue flattens itself against the roof of his mouth, readying to say *No!*

Bang.

32

Joe hated working details, but there was no way around it. He needed the money. Of course, what he earned on a detail was peanuts. At $3.50 an hour, he would be lucky to walk away with twenty-five bucks. His bookie debt, by contrast, was now an outlandish twenty thousand dollars or so—twice what Joe made in a year. He was not quite sure of the total debt. It was divvied up among a half dozen bookies, mostly in the South End, all charging different rates, rolling the vig back into the Big Number, pulling figures out of a hat, moving their lips and rolling their eyes toward the ceiling as they did the math, then writing it all down in Chinese in their little notebooks. By the time they'd finished figuring, Joe had no idea what the true number was. So what could you do but take their word for it? If they said you owed, you owed.

His luck was bound to turn, and soon enough he would have plenty of cash to pay the whole thing off, whatever The Number was. He would make everyone happy, even Kat. All he had to do was keep playing, stay in the game long enough for things to even out. It had to happen: bad luck must be balanced by good, ten coinflips that come up tails must be followed by ten that come up heads. One man simply could not keep losing forever. In fact the longer he kept losing, the more he felt he could not walk away. All the money he had lost was an investment in future good luck. With every lost bet, he figured, the odds shifted a little further in his favor—"flip a coin a hundred times . . ." The trick was to keep the wolves at bay long enough to ride out the cold streak and reap the reward.

For a long time Joe believed he could do just that. He was able to keep the faith. Oh, it would take a little belt-tightening, he would have to deny himself a few things—not his strong point—and he would have to work a lot of details. But with the hundred bucks a week he got on the sleeve, he could make his nut every week, just about. He needed about six hundred a week to keep up with the vig. Some weeks he had found a way to get it, or to get close enough for a cop. Of course he saw the futility in using his padmoney to pay the bookies. Those dollars came from the North End and, like homing pigeons, they circled right back to the North End. One of Capobianco's lieutenants paid off a sergeant at Station One; the sergeant paid Joe; Joe then made his rounds through the South End paying off the bookies; and a few days later those same bills were back where they started, all sorted and banded in one of Capobianco's counting rooms. Charlie Capobianco had set up a vast bucket brigade to move cash, spilling just enough dollars along the away to keep everyone at it. Of course many weeks—most weeks—Joe had been short, sometimes a lot short, and he'd had to bluster and bargain his way through. But it had never been a problem. Cop privilege, Joe figured—his shield was just that, a shield. With it, he'd pull through, somehow.

But now he knew: He wasn't going to get out of it, ever. He'd been fooling himself. The hole he was standing in was the hole he'd be buried in. Maybe it had been Amy's dying. Or the fact that he'd turned to a shylock for the first time, to borrow cash to patch the hole—a fatal mistake, one that inevitably brought out the wolves to surround the wounded limping animal. Maybe it was the new ferocity in the city's crime world. Maybe it was all these things. A gloomy paranoia infected the city after so many murders, high and low.

Charlie Capobianco's campaign to take over the bookmaking rackets had unleashed a frenzy of killing as surrounding gangs felt the squeeze. The period would later come to be known as the Irish Gang War, but it was nothing as noble or purposeful as war. The Winter Hill crew was systematically exterminating the rival McLaughlin gang, in Charlestown, but most of the violence was just small-timers sharking each other. A gang war, it turned out, was an opportune moment to settle any old score. So the bodies started to turn up. They slumped in abandoned cars . . . three suitcases were left in an alley beside a hotel downtown, emitting an eggy stench . . . a headless corpse lay in an unlocked apartment, its windpipe gaping in the neckhole ... a mysterious dark syrup leaked from the trunk of a car parked in the hot sun, and people complained of the stink. ... By now there were nearly twenty dead, most of them shot, two strangled, one throat slit, one beheaded, one drowned. The preferred method was the double-cross—the bullet usually entered the back of the head. Beware the smiling pal who invites you on a job, or stands back to let you walk through a door first, or offers you the front passenger seat while he sits behind.

Meanwhile Capobianco was tightening the screws not just on the books and shylocks who put his money on the street, but on the suckers who took it. A new policy was now in force: The clock never stopped. A deadbeat was never allowed to pay only principal, even if he'd been bled dry. It was a senseless policy unknown in New York or Chicago, for the obvious reason that the Mob could no longer extract money from a deadbeat once it killed him. But that sort of nuance was lost on Charlie Capobianco. He wanted his money, all of it, right now. In Boston the clock ran until you made your final payment, one way or the other.

So here was Joe, in his too tight uniform pants and too small policeman's cap, standing in the Greyhound bus terminal at one in the morning, wondering whether he could afford the price of new uniform pants, having long ago spent the two-hundred-dollar clothing allowance the department gave out each year. The bus station was, to

Joe, the absolute worst detail there was. Some guys got the details at Symphony Hall—Joe got the bus station. It figured. But the bus station was the only detail that hired seven days a week, it was indoors, and it fit Joe's schedule. He could work a "first half" till midnight, then the detail from midnight till six or seven the next morning. So he took it. Interminable nights of waking up bums with his nightstick and breaking up blowjobs in the men's room and, mostly, doing nothing at all, and for what? So he could hand over what little he earned to the greaseballs. He had at least figured out that he could park his car nearby and go sleep in it. If he wandered through the bus station once an hour to make it look good, that was enough.

Around one, the place was completely abandoned and Joe was dazed with boredom when the fin of a black Cadillac glided into frame in one of the big windows. Not the sort of car that belonged here at this hour, or any hour. Joe went to the window and watched Vinnie Gargano get out of the car. Gargano stood there, looking around. He shrugged his shoulders and waggled his head like a boxer getting loose before a fight. It was remarkable how these guys appeared at your most vulnerable moment. Joe—who had been turning over in his mind thoughts of Kat and twenty thousand dollars— quickly tried to work up a little of the old confidence. He sucked in his gut and buttoned his pants, which he had opened so he could breathe easier, and tried to find his old chesty GI posture. But his body had lost its memory. When

Gargano wandered in through the steel-and-glass doors, Joe was still trying to arrange his shoulders and chest properly.

"Hey," Gargano said. "When's the next bus to Poughkeepsie?"

Joe forced the corners of his mouth into a weak smile.

Gargano strolled around the waiting room. The banks of molded-plastic seats were empty, the ticket windows closed. No buses left at this time of night. The station stayed open overnight just to receive the occasional arrival from God-knew-where—a handful of exhausted, bedraggled passengers would shuffle through, like immigrants from some faraway country, then silence again.

"The fuck you doin' here?" Gargano asked.

"My job."

"I thought you were some detective. Big shot."

"What's it to you?"

"I got a right to know how my taxes are gettin' spent."

"You pay your taxes?"

"No."

"Alright, then." In Joe's head, the sentence ran on with its natural momentum: *Alright, then, go fuck yourself.*

Gargano strolled around the circumference of the waiting room with the distracted manner of one lost in thought. From the side—which was Joe's angle of view as he turned slowly on his heels to keep Gargano from moving behind him—Gargano had an unmistakable simian look. His arms hung to his midthighs, a beard of fat rounded his face into a snout. The rumor was that Vinnie Gargano had packed that man into three suitcases, even taken care to place the head face-up to greet the cops.

"They told me down the station I'd find you here."

"Yeah? Who told you that?"

"Some cop, whoever picked up the phone."

"I'll have to talk with them about that."

"Whattaya gonna, 'I'll have to talk with them'? You know, this is what I hear about you, over and over again, same fuckin' thing: You're some tough prick, nobody wants to deal with you. You know that? Pain in the ass. You go looking for trouble."

"You heard wrong. I don't look for trouble."

"No? Trouble finds you, then."

"Seems like that."

"Yeah, seems like that." Gargano pushed open each bathroom door and poked his head in to confirm it was empty. "So what are we gonna do?"

"About what?"

"About what. Funny guy, 'about what.' Listen, shit-for-brains, I know what kind of trouble you're in. Maybe you can fool a bunch of dumbfuck cops and these broads you run around with, and maybe you can fool that dumb-fuck brother of yours, the thief/burglar/whatever-the-fuck-he-is. But you don't fool me. You don't fool me. I seen guys like you. I see guys like you every fuckin' day. You don't fool me."

"I'm not trying to fool you."

Gargano paused, mollified by the note of servility in Joe's answer.

"I'm not trying to fool nobody," Joe said, modulating his position. A little wince showed on his face: all balls, no brains, and he knew it.

Gargano ignored it. "What are we gonna do, Joe?"

No answer.

"This is a problem. You got a big tab here, Joe, big tab." He wagged his finger. "It's not good. This is a real problem. We got a real fuckin' problem, you and me."

"I've been paying."

"No, Joe. See, if you were paying and doing the right thing, see, I wouldn't be here, would I? I wouldn't even know your name. You'd be just some dumb cop."

Gargano moved toward the middle of the room and settled into a seat. "When are you gonna get this money, Joe?"

"Soon."

"No. I said *when*. You tell me exactly when you're gonna get it. Monday, Tuesday, Thursday, what?"

No answer.

"I'm guessing you don't have the money."

"Not right now."

"Not right now."

"Not right now."

"So what are you giving me this bullshit about 'soon'?"

"I could get some of it."

"Some of it?"

"Yeah."

"How much?"

"I don't, I don't exactly—"

"*How much?* How fuckin' much, Joe?"

"I don't know. Couple thousand."

"A couple thousand? Is that a joke? You think this is some kind of fuckin' joke, you make fuckin' jokes with me? Are you being funny? Tell him a couple thousand and that's the end of it, like this is some joke. Is that it? You think this is a joke?"

"No."

"No what?"

"No, it's not a joke."

"Fuckin' right it's not a joke. You know, I heard you weren't the sharpest fuckin' guy." He shook his head. "So what are we gonna do?"

"I don't know."

"Where are you gonna get this kind of money?"

"I don't know."

" 'I don't know, I don't know.' You don't know much." Gargano had gradually moved to the edge of his chair, leaning far forward with his hands on his knees, and now he slouched back. "I ain't leavin' here till I know where you're gonna get this money."

No response.

"How about your brother the thief?"

"Let's leave him out of it."

"Why?"

"Because it's my problem, I'll fix it."

"He's got money."

"Not this kind of money."

"You hear about that Copley job? He's got plenty of money, that one."

Joe was not sure what Ricky was calling himself these days—a car dealer or a realtor or a club owner—but he knew it was not wise to reveal anything to a guy like Vinnie Gargano. Joe didn't know what he didn't know, sometimes he didn't know what he *did* know, and so when it came to Ricky he made it a policy to know nothing at all. Saying too much could get Ricky killed. "My brother doesn't have that kind of money and he isn't a thief."

Gargano grinned. "Jesus, you really are dumber than a box of rocks."

Joe shrugged. He felt at once defeated and oddly relieved. Gargano's appearance here felt like a culmination—as if Vinnie The Animal had come into that bus station bodying forth all the bad luck and all the defeats Joe had been enduring, and now at last it might all come to an end somehow. Probably badly, it was true, but any sort of end would be better than this slow slide. Gargano was right, after all: Joe had passed the point where he could hope to pay off the debt. From here the vig would bury him, fast. He had no way to stop the clock, and so time itself had become a burden, the passing of an hour was a reason to suffer. He wanted it to stop.

"So how are you gonna get this money? You got a nice house. I seen it."

"It's mortgaged."

"So sell something. What do you got to sell?"

"*Pfft*. Nothing."

"You know what I usually say in this situation? I tell the guy, 'Look, you owe ten grand, fifty grand, whatever it is. You only got one thing that's worth fifty grand. I'll buy it from you. You know what it is?' " He paused.

"No," Joe said. "What is it?"

"It's your head. I tell him, 'Sell me your fuckin' head for fifty grand and we'll call it even. I'll take it right now. You want, I'll even cut it off for you.' Then I show him the knife." He reached inside his leather coat and produced a small knife.

"What if the guy really doesn't have fifty grand?"

"They tend to find it."

Joe's eyes closed.

"Relax. Your fuckin' head isn't worth fifty cents. Let me tell you what you're gonna do. You're gonna come work for me."

"That won't— I can't do that."

"Please. I seen Nicky Capobianco's police pad." Nicky Capobianco was Charlie's brother, fixer, and money man. "The morning after the prom is a little late to be calling yourself a virgin. You've been taking the money. Now you can earn it."

"Earn it how?"

"Just help us out. If you hear anything we should know about, you tell us, that's all. If there's gonna be a raid, we need to know that. If there's a bug somewhere, obviously we need to know that. You're a cop, you hear things."

"I don't hear much. You're gonna be disappointed."

"There's other things you can do. Errands. We got a lot of work. You're a big guy; we'll find jobs for you."

Joe bowed his head.

"Relax. It's not so bad. Alls I'm asking is just help out a little, pitch in. It's the least you can do. I mean that."

33

With a machine-like shuffle, Fish counted tens and twenties from a roll. At one hundred dollars, he would shift the pile to one side, moisten the pad of his thumb with his tongue, and riffle out another. His dexterity was surprising. Fish looked old and gristly. The skin on his hands was spotted parchment. His fingernails were overgrown to the point of dangerousness. But there was something magical in the way those hands spun out bills into ten neat piles, recombined them, and handed the stack to Joe Daley.

"Thank you."

"Hope your new boss chokes on it. That's between you and me." Fish watched the money disappear into Joe's pants pocket and made a sour little frown. "Make sure it gets where it's going."

"How about I do my job, you do yours?"

"I'm just sayin'. Remember whose money that is in your pocket."

"Pretty strange, huh? You putting money in my pocket for a change."

"I seen stranger."

"Well, it's strange to me."

"You'll get used to it. You're a natural."

"Hey, why are you always breaking my balls? What'd I ever—?"

"You just took my hard-earned money. You want I should thank you?"

"Come on, Fish, this is just business. I don't like it any more than you do."

"You like it fine."

"Oh, you know this."

"I got eyes, I can see."

"Well, you're wrong."

"I been doing this a long time," Fish shrugged, "but . . ." *Whatever you say.*

"Anyways, this isn't about me. If it wasn't me sitting here, it'd be somebody else."

"But it *is* you sitting here. That's the point."

"That's right, it's me sitting here, so how about you just treat me like a professional and we'll get this over with. Unbelievable. Like I don't have enough on my mind without this shit from you. Jesus, as if I haven't given you enough money all these years. That doesn't count for nothing?"

"You think I keep all that? I don't keep it. You people bet against each other—the losers pay the winners. That's the way it works. I'm just the matchmaker. You want to know where your money went, go find somebody who won that day. I don't have it. Alls I keep is the juice. It's nothing, crumbs."

"Charlie Capobianco does okay with crumbs."

"Volume."

"Well, anyways, you took a lot of crumbs off of me."

"So now you get to take some back. Funny, huh, Detective?"

"I said, that's enough with that, Fish. I didn't tell you to go get in this business."

"I was going to say the same thing to you."

"Yeah, well, I don't have a whole lot of choice."

"Whatever you say, boss."

"There's things you don't know, Fish."

"You'd be surprised. Hey, you are what you are, is all I'm saying. Your father must be spinning in his grave."

"Watch your fuckin' mouth." Joe reached across the table and tamped his finger against Fish's chest as if he were pushing a stubborn button there. "I'm not gonna tell you again. It's enough with that. Am I going to have to hear this crap every week?"

"No. Guess I said my piece."

34

Seagulls had nested on the roof of Station One. They came and went from the yellowbrick parapet, landed, squawked, fretted, flew off again. Three dun, speckled eggs lay unprotected in a nest of twigs. A fat furry chick bumbled around the edge of the roof, following the high yellow-brick wall. It was the same speckled gray-brown color as the eggs. The chick paused here and there to inspect bits of garbage collected in the stones that covered the rooftop, cigarette butts, beer cans, Christmas lights. When the chick reached an enormous pair of black shoes, it tried to hop up toward the laces.

"Beat it," Joe Daley said.

He shifted his feet and the little bird waddled off. Joe returned his attention to the view from the parapet, rooftops bristling with antennae, Beacon Hill and the waste field of the West End at dusk. Below, cars emerged from the Sumner Tunnel and disappeared again into the city.

A voice behind him: "Jesus, Joe. What, are you hiding up here?" Brendan Conroy negotiated the roof door, the raised threshold, the steel bar that propped the door open. He was awkward in the topheavy way that big old men are. To Joe he looked like a moose crossing a stream, from stone to stone. "I've been all over this fucking place looking for you. Three flights of stairs, *pshh*. The hell are you doing up here?"

Joe removed a cigarette from his lips and showed it.

"Ah. Why didn't you tell the lieutenant? What if they needed to find you?"

"I'm off."

"Go home, then. You've got a family, young fella."

"What's on your mind, Brendan? You must have climbed those stairs for a reason."

Conroy came over. He was not tall enough to look out over the parapet, so he scanned the rooftop. Three chimney stacks, an air shaft, those filthy goddamn birds screeching and flapping. The one finished feature was a cupola complete with Palladian windows, gold dome, and pineapple finial. Conroy was in full uniform, gold chevrons on his arm. "You know, I've never been up here."

"Only place you can be alone around here."

"Go home, Joe. It's time to go home."

"That's what you come up here to tell me?"

"Your mother's worried about you."

"And she sent you."

"If your dad was still around . . . Joe, you can't blame the woman for worrying about her son. What's wrong with you?"

"You don't want to know, Bren. Trust me."

"Come on. Can't be that bad, boyo."

"It is."

"Maybe I can help." Conroy waited but got no response. "You remember the time you got pinched for that thing in Dearborn Square, looking for trouble? 'Member? Who'd you call when you were too scared to tell your old man?"

"I was a kid. This one's tougher to fix."

"Maybe."

"Trust me. Ol' Uncle Brendan can't fix this one."

"Whatever it is, boyo, it's just you and me here. You and me and the pigeons."

"Those are seagulls."

"Okay, seagulls, whatever."

Joe smirked. No doubt Conroy meant well, but even if Joe had wanted to confide what he was feeling, he could not have named it. It was not fear. On the contrary he felt safer now than he had in a long time. He might even have been clever. By playing both sides of the fence, he had appeased the enemy without paying or promising anything. Nor had he actually done anything he felt ashamed of. The work was nothing. There were occasional mid-morning calls to transport a suitcase to the North End. And occasional rounds of hole-in-the-wall shops that did a small book—smoke shops, groceries, a shoe-repair joint—to collect the tax. Far from a villain, Joe felt like a functionary in an ancient and very large organization. He was just an errand boy, for now. And Fish had been the exception; the people Joe had called on thus far had not resisted or even resented paying. Capobianco's tax was just ordinary overhead. It seemed to Joe that The Catastrophe had occurred without fanfare, so maybe—just maybe—it had not been a catastrophe at all. And yet, and yet . . . he could not shake this feeling. He did not feel comfortable around cops. He had a shameful secret. He was a spy among them. And stripped of his cophood, he did not feel quite like Joe Daley anymore. Maybe he never would.

"I took a wrong turn, Bren, that's all."

"What did you do?"

Joe hesitated. Well, what the hell. Might as well tell somebody. "I got in a hole. Betting."

"Betting on what?"

"Numbers, sports, horses, name it."

"And?"

"I have to—I kind of have to work it off. They've got me running errands. That's it so far. I'm sure it'll be more."

"Who's they?"

"Capobianco's crew. It was Vincent Gargano came to me."

"Ah. And how big a hole are we talking about?"

"Too big. More than I have."

"I can get you the money."

"I don't think that's going to be enough now. I don't know that I can just walk away."

Conroy nodded. "Who knows about this?"

"No one."

"Not even Kat?"

"If Kat knew, my mother would know. If my mother knew . . . I kind of wanted to handle it my own way."

"Of course, of course. Alright, keep it to yourself, then. Let me see what I can find out. Maybe there's something we can do."

"I appreciate that."

"You're not alone in this, boyo. You know that, don't you?"

"Okay, sure."

"Anyway, it sounds like you didn't have much choice. Did you have a choice?"

"Yeah, a bullet in the hat."

"Alright, then. So don't grind yourself up over it. You do what you have to do, Joe, understand? Just don't go too far. Run a few errands or whatever, just remember you're still a cop. If you go too far, no one will know you."

"Okay."

"We'll take care of it. You stay cool. You have a family, son. You have a son of your own. You have a responsibility to them. No one can say you did the wrong thing till they walk in your shoes."

"Thanks, Bren. I'm glad my dad's not around for this."

"Let me tell you somethin': Your dad was no saint, God rest his soul. Sometimes he did what he had to do, too."

"Yeah? Like what?"

"Like I'm not going to say. He's passed away and he was a friend of mine and he loved you boys something awful. If there were things he did not want to tell you, then that was his decision and it's not my place to do any different. No father tells his son everything, Joe. No father does and no father should. A son never really knows his father. There's too many years in between. But I knew him. I knew him like a brother. Like a goddamn brother, your dad, and he was a good, clean, honest cop. He never did anything—anything—you boys should be the least bit ashamed of. So don't misunderstand me. But just the same, he was a man, same as you, and he lived in the world, same as you, and that's all I'm gonna say about it. I don't want you coming up here on the roof mooning over 'what would dear ol' Da think?' Because I'll tell you: He'd understand and he'd back you up, same as I'm going to back you up. That's what we do. We do what we do, and we don't apologize. That's how a family works."

"Alright. Okay." Joe wasn't sure whether Conroy was referring to the Daley family or the police family. He suspected there was not much distinction, to Conroy at least. "What are you going to tell my mother?"

"What am I going to tell her? The truth: this young fella's been working his fingers to the bone and he's tired, and she and Kat and the rest of the ladies' sewing circle should just leave yuz alone for a while, let us work it all out."

35

Symphony Hall. Wednesday, three-thirty P.M., final closed rehearsal before the weekend's performances.

Something was happening inside the music, something was stirring. The musicians seemed to sense it. During a rest they inhaled deeply, as if to fill their lungs with it. The orchestra had been augmented with freelancers to play the piece—Respighi's *Pines of Rome*—and the stage was crowded with players and instruments, extra brass, an organist. Some of the horns were stationed in the balconies around the hall, where they stood at attention behind the gilded latticework railing. The conductor was a trim, bald man in a snug black cardigan, like a midshipman's jacket. His upper body jerked with the movement of his arms. He barked curt German-accented instructions and expressive grunts: *Hup! Tick! Ta!*

At the back of the hall, Ricky lurked in the shadow of a doorway. Up to this point, he had not liked the piece very much. The earlier movements had reminded him of the corny orchestral music in

Disney movies, bright and brassy in some places, self-consciously solemn in others. Probably classical music just wasn't for him. But around the three-minute mark of the fourth and final movement, he felt it too.

The music unclogged. Out of a stagnant, reedy pianissimo passage, the horns stepped forward and began to blast away. The unstable B-flat opened out onto a major key—"Hah!" the conductor exclaimed—and the brass pulled the entire orchestra into a cycling crescendo that lasted two thrilling minutes, with the horns in the balconies blaring back over the empty hall and the conductor calling for "More!"

At the rear of the stage, the organist tipped his head back, his mouth yawned open, and he played in a sort of ecstasy or sustained orgasm. This was Kurt Lindstrom.

After the rehearsal Lindstrom emerged from the stage door with a couple of older musicians. The threesome stood chatting a moment. One of the men said something at which Lindstrom laughed too loudly, then he left them. He walked away on St. Stephen Street, bouncing on the balls of his feet, chest thrust forward.

Across the street and half a block behind, Ricky walked too. He had tracked any number of suckers with an eye toward taking them off, and he was meticulous about this aspect of his job. He was confident—over-confident—in his ability to size people up. He figured that any semi-intelligent thief could acquire the few basic facts needed to pull off a burglary: the victim's daily routine, the sort of locks on the door, the jewelry or other things to be taken. What set Ricky apart, he believed, was that his empathy was more acute than that. He thought he understood something about the people he ripped off. When circumstances allowed, he lingered in their rooms, inspected their bookshelves, LP's, medicine cabinets, and refrigerators, to confirm his impressions. He had a thief's haughty scorn for his victims, who must be less clever or careful or nimble than he was, otherwise they would not be such easy prey. At the same time, he disapproved of the low-rent burglars—the stepover men and window smashers, opportunists and drug addicts, most of them—who ignored the human aspect of the job. They did not bother to research their victims, let alone study the finer points, lock-picking and the rest of it. They did not prepare, and so they were forced into unnecessary risks. Fools. Between the rich fools Ricky victimized and the poor fools who occupied the bottom rungs of his own profession, it was hard to say whom Ricky disdained more.

The rich ones, probably. As a student of the behavior of rich people—who, after all, had what Ricky wanted—he was stupefied by the mediocrity of the city's upper classes. To anyone who preached the old fairy tale of America as a meritocracy, Ricky might have invited them to view the wealthy as a burglar would. Was there a more foolish, careless class than these rich old Yankees? They left their

274

inherited jewelry lying around in dresser drawers and strolled out of the house with their doors unlocked, or badly locked—then they stiffed the waitress at lunch on a nickel or dime tip. If this was the ruling class, then it was about time the Kennedys of the world took over. A government run by thieves would, as the saying went, make the trains run on time.

Now here went Kurt Lindstrom loping down St. Stephen Street like some cartoon aristocrat. Something in the young man's springy walk—like some flightless, fast-running bird—and the stubborn lick of blond hair on his forehead, and the FDR tilt to his chin, signified to Ricky a Yankee jackass of a certain type: foppish, effeminate. It was impossible to accept that this man might have murdered Amy. A musician and out-of-work actor whose only dramatic performances were the Shakespearian speeches he delivered on the sidewalks of Harvard Square, his old college haunt. Amy could have broken this guy in half. But brother Michael believed it, and the cops believed it, so Ricky had set out to prove it.

Lindstrom turned right on Symphony Road and entered number 50, two blocks down. The building was a four-story walk-up. Most of the buildings on the street were of the same type: simple red-brick bowfronts, unadorned except for rough-hewn granite pediments above the doors and windows. This was mostly a student area, and the street had a scruffy look. The bricks needed pointing, the little front yards needed weeding. But there was a genteel Victorian appearance, too, in the uniformity of the buildings, the low scale, the repeating curves of the street wall formed by those bow windows.

Ricky stood across the street and watched the light come on in Lindstrom's apartment window. After a few minutes he climbed the stoop and noted the apartment number on the entry buzzer.

But he did not immediately leave. He went behind the building, inspected the rear entrance, the garbage cans, noted the cars parked there.

An alley, which was wide enough for a truck to pass through, ran down the center of the block, behind the rows of apartment buildings. About a block down this alley, on the opposite side, was the back of 77 Gainsborough Street, a redbrick bowfront very much like the one Lindstrom lived in. Helena Jalakian—the very first Strangler victim—had lived in a small apartment at 77 Gainsborough Street. She had been murdered there on June 14, 1962, the start of that terrifying summer.

Helena was fifty-six, a seamstress, first-generation Armenian immigrant, and classical music buff. She had taken the apartment in part because it was such an easy walk to Symphony Hall. She had attended the BSO open rehearsals and stood in line for rush tickets. She liked Brahms, disliked Mahler, disliked the new little German conductor who was not warm enough for her taste. She luxuriated in Symphony Hall; the opulence of it would once have seemed unimaginable to her. Had Helena met the young musician who lived nearby, who walked home along the same streets? Had she seen him on stage? Had they chatted by the stage door one day? Would she have opened the door for him willingly, eagerly? Would she have turned away from him to go change out of her housecoat, maybe then to offer him tea and cookies? Helena Jalakian had been clubbed on the back of the head, raped vaginally, apparently with an object (no semen was found; the object was never identified or recovered), beaten, and strangled with the cord of her housecoat, which was tied off in a bow—the first occurrence of that signature knot.

Returning to his own apartment, Ricky found the door smashed, the doorknob dislodged. He eased the door half open with one fingertip, but it caught on something and he had to shove harder.

Inside, the destruction was so complete that the apartment barely resembled the one Ricky had left a few hours before. Drawers were dumped on the floor. The sofa had been stripped down to the frame. The cushions had been sliced open, the cotton batting pulled out and tossed on the floor. The bookcase that had held the hifi and the records lay splintered on the floor. Most of the discs were shattered. Ricky would miss them most of all. He had built his LP collection over the course of several years, and sorted it with loving care, alphabetically within jazz genres. What a waste. Leave it to Gargano and his goons—for no burglar would risk making the sort of racket these guys must have made, and no cop would work this hard. They had smashed up a magnificent collection, and for no good reason. Ricky had already told him he did not have the missing stones.

36

"Mikey, let me have those."

Ricky indicated with his chin that he meant the rolls, and Michael passed the dish.

They ate quietly again. Forks and knives clinked, mouths mashed. No one spoke.

At Sunday dinner, the family felt particularly decimated. During the week it was easier to forget how devastated they had been. Not here. With Joe absent—he was out working another detail—each couple at the table had been halved. There was too much room between the chairs, too much empty space on the table. Kat, Ricky, and Mother Margaret all seemed diminished by the absence of their voluble partners. They were not used to carrying the weight of a conversation. Over the years, they had gotten used to the attacking, serve-and-volley style of their mates. They preferred to respond—to quip, to reply, a withering sentence or two and then shut up. This table had never been the place for long speeches anyway. The words flew too fast, everyone talked over everyone else, babbled, blurted, shouted, insulted, teased. Short, loud, and sarcastic, that was the Daley style. There was only one blusterer left, Brendan Conroy, and his gaseousness was particularly off-key tonight. Between Michael and Ricky there were affronted scowls—that this hammy buffoon was poking their mother seemed outrageous, still—and soon enough Conroy grew quiet, too. Even Kat, armor-plated as a battleship, was lost in her own thoughts.

Dinner lasted twenty minutes. It felt like an hour.

After dinner Michael sprawled on the couch, dazed in front of the television.

One by one the family drifted away. Kat helped with the dishes, then stamped a kiss onto Michael's forehead before leaving. Little Joe waved dutifully, "Bye, Uncle Michael." Ricky lay draped across the armchair, then abruptly he got up and went home, too. He chucked Michael once on the shoulder on the way past: "See ya, Mike." Margaret went upstairs to read and fall asleep.

The sudden turn of the ebb tide left Michael beached on that couch, alone with Brendan Conroy, to their mutual discomfort. Michael would have taken off, but a stubborn sense of turf kept him there. This was still his home, Michael's and his brothers', though soon Brendan would displace them. He would roll that big pink body into Joe Senior's bed, as he had already enthroned himself in the father's seat at the dinner table and his armchair in the living room. But for now, as long as Michael remained on the couch, he could stave all that off. He could exercise a child's life tenancy in his mother's home, and there was nothing Conroy could say or do to dislodge him. Maybe he would even fuck with Conroy by staying long enough that Conroy would go home to his own bed instead of climbing the stairs to sleep next to Margaret.

If Conroy was troubled by any of this, he was not letting on. He watched the TV through a pair of black-framed reading glasses that rested on his mug awkwardly, like a costume. When he pried the shoes off his feet with much struggle and shoe-scraping, Michael said, "Make yourself at home, Brendan."

At nine o'clock, Michael insisted on watching *The Judy Garland Show* instead of *Bonanza*.

"*Bonanza* is in color."

"I know." Michael would rather have watched *Bonanza*, too, but he could not help himself.

"You're a pisser, there, boyo."

Michael did not respond. He lay on his back, head propped on the armrest, one arm curled around his head. He knew how it must look to Conroy: a fruity pose, Byron come to Dorchester. Fuck 'm. Michael would lie there any way he damn well pleased. It was his couch. He'd lie there all night just for spite. The little fuckyous are the sweetest.

"How long are you going to keep this up?"

"Keep what up, Brendan?"

"Moping."

"The word is mourning."

"Mourning, is it? How long will you be doing it?"

"Amy's only dead a few weeks. You in a hurry?"

"Oh, come on. You've been at it longer than a few weeks, boyo."

"Have I? Must have lost track of time. Been having too much fun, I guess."

"You're mourning your dad."

"Well, he'd do the same for me."

"Not this long, he wouldn't. You know, there comes a time, Michael. You don't mourn forever. Life is for the living."

"Hm. I thought it was for the dentist's office. Now, Time, that's for the living. But Dad does not get Time anymore. Or Life. He got thrown out of the TimeLife Building, the poor bastard."

"I'm trying to talk to you here, seriously, man to man, and you're making jokes. I don't get you, Michael."

"I know you don't. Isn't that always the way with families? Fathers and sons, you know."

"You blame me for your old man dying, is that it?"

"Should I?"

"Of course not."

"Then why do you ask?"

"Because something about me pisses you off, and for the life of me I can't figure out what the hell it is."

"We're just oil and water, Brendan. Irish salad dressing. Don't let it bother you."

"Doesn't bother me. Doesn't bother me one bit."

"No, it doesn't seem to."

"Doesn't bother me a bit."

"Alright, Brendan, let's just be quiet now and watch Judy Garland."

"Fuck Judy Garland."

Michael dilated his eyes in mock horror. *Fuck Judy Garland?*

"If you've got something to say to me, say it. Cut with the jokes and the snide remarks, you and Ricky both, couple of little kids. Be a man, for Christ's sake, would you?"

"I'm trying. For Christ's sake."

"Aiyiyi, to get a straight answer out of you . . . You think your dad dying is my fault?"

Shrug.

"Answer me, Michael, yes or no: Do you think your dad dying is somehow my fault?"

"Yes."

"Yes?"

"Affirmative. Roger. Ten-four. Aye-aye."

"How?"

"I don't know."

"He doesn't know. Well, you've got some nerve, boy, I tell ya. I love these armchair quarterbacks. What more should I have done, Michael?"

"Run faster."

"Run faster?"

"Run faster."

"And what would that have done? You mean so I could get shot instead of him? Maybe you forget, I did get shot. I've got a hole in my gut to prove it. I nearly died. Do you know I still get blood in my shit?"

"No. Didn't know that."

"Well, I do. I shit blood. What do you have to say about that?"

"You should watch what you eat."

"Go ahead, make jokes. You like to forget little things like me getting shot because you're so busy feeling sorry for yourself."

"It's a full-time job."

"Let me ask you something: If I did die, would that have been enough?"

"Would have been a start."

"Well, that's just fine. I'm a little dense, I guess, I'm just a thickheaded old Irishman, but I get it. I'm done with this. You hear me? You want it to be like this forever? Fine. But just so's you know, I understand what this is really about. Couldn't be more obvious. Poor little boy doesn't like to see his mommy with anyone but daddy, so you blame me for anything and everything. What a, a—"

"Cliché?"

"Yes. And for what it's worth, you're wrong. Your father's dying broke my heart. I'd do anything to find the kid that did it."

"Would you? So what have you done to find him? Tell me, what have you done? Where's that kid, Brendan?"

"How the fuck should I know? If I knew, don't you think I'd move heaven and earth to find him?"

"I don't see you moving heaven or earth."

"What do you recommend?"

Michael shrugged. "I'm not a cop. Neither was Amy."

"That's not an answer. Tell me, boyo, what should I do? What would satisfy you?"

Another voice intervened: "That's enough."

Michael twisted to see his mother standing on the bottom stair in her pale blue housecoat, arms folded across her belly. He sat up.

"You two are going to have to learn to live with each other. That's all I'm going to say. Michael, you show a little respect. Brendan, time for bed."

"Time for bed, Brendan," Michael mocked.

Conroy gathered up his shoes and padded across the room to the foot of the stairs. Margaret stood aside to let him pass on the narrow stairs. Even so, there was barely room for the two of them. As he climbed past her, Conroy's hand lifted the little wood ball out of the newel post at the bottom of the stairs. That wood ball, the size of a large orange, had been loose for almost thirty years. Conroy seemed surprised to see it in his hand, as if it had adhered there. He fitted it back on the post then continued up the stairs unembarrassed. His hand curled over the wobbly banister, incongruously massive on the handrail burnished smooth by children's palms.

Michael could feel that banister passing under his own hand, the narrow rounded top, a hairline joint that scratched across the palm halfway up, a scabrous patch where the wood grain roughed your thumb pad, the upturn that signaled the top of the staircase.

"You go home too, mister." Margaret sighed. "Work in the morning." She did not wait for a response but turned and trudged up the stairs.

37

Parts of the West End construction site were surrounded by an eight-foot plywood wall. Here and there the wall was decorated with propagandistic posters: "Coming Soon: A New Boston" and "The Future Is Now . . . Here!" Bostonians took these promises with a grain of salt. Politicians and other gasbags had been talking about a "new Boston" long enough that they wondered where the hell it was, just as Old Englanders once upon a time must have wondered where the New one was. So the wall was defaced in predictable ways, lewd and anti-authoritarian. One sign was somehow graffiti-proof, though. It was enameled steel, very large, and it hung at the corner of Cambridge and Charles Streets, near the jail. The sign showed an architect's pen-and-pastel sketch of those four white towers in a grassy park—dreamlike, impossibly modern. There were no cars in the drawing; the buildings apparently would be accessed by spaceships. Pedestrians tended to pause before this picture, stumped, awed by it. Buildings like these simply did not exist in Boston.

They were too good for Boston, too good for the likes of us. The image arrested everyone who passed, thin-lipped women with shopping bags and gray men in blue suits with brown shoes. They tended to stand there and shake their heads with schoolmarmish disapproval: the ostentation of it all, the naked, gaudy ambition. To the side of the picture was the opportunistic name of the project, JFK PARK, and a long list of credits like the roll call at the end of a movie:

A SONNENSHEIN DEVELOPMENT • CITY OF BOSTON • MAYOR JOHN COLLINS • BOSTON REDEVELOPMENT AUTHORITY • URBAN RENEWAL ADMINISTRATION • SONNENSHEIN CONSTRUCTION CO. • FIRST NATIONAL BANK OF BOSTON • THE NEW BOSTON TRUST

Moe Wasserman arranged to meet Joe near this sign. It was an unseasonably warm day in early April, an early intimation of spring. Wasserman was agitated. When Joe showed up, Wasserman blurted, "He's here! Come see!" The old man hustled Joe down Charles Street, along the perimeter of the site, to a chainlink gate where a dozen men loafed around a cafeteria truck. A small army of construction workers swarmed over the site, which occupied about a quarter of the old West End footprint, but somehow Wasserman had found his man.

"There!"

"Which one?"

"In the red jacket. Drinking his coffee like he don't know I'm lookin' at him. He was there. Not the one in charge, but he was there."

"You're sure?"

"Course I'm sure."

"How sure?"

"Listen to this guy, 'how sure?' If I wasn't sure, I wouldn't have brung you."

"Alright. I've got to be sure is all."

"Detective, I'm not asking you to shoot him, just talk to him. How sure do you got to be?"

Joe walked onto the construction site with the happy sense of trespassing.

The man looked up. Early twenties. A sleek, dense mat of hair opalescent with Brylcreem. Slit eyes. He was squat and thick-bodied. A white tank top showed off his inflated shoulders and arms. On his right biceps was a tattoo of a red devil wearing boxing gloves above the initials U.S.M.C. Seeing Joe, the kid put down his coffee so his hands would be empty.

"I want to talk to you," Joe said.

"Yeah? Who the fuck are you?"

Joe wavered, as if the kid's words had blown him back. He tried to recalibrate his approach. Joe firmly believed in the streetfighter's code: In a fighting situation, the only strategy is attack, attack, attack— stick out your chest and tell 'em "fuck you," be ready to hit first, and stay on your feet at all costs. He knew the game. Now this kid was eyeing Joe, watching his reaction. His mouth puckered up in a defiant, kissy pout. The proper response would be a show of overwhelming force. Joe tried to stimulate the necessary resources to match this wop dago fire hydrant, this, this Golden Gloves Guido greaseball gangster punk fuck . . . ah, but it was no use. He was exhausted and unprepared. He did not have the energy. He took out his badge-wallet and showed the kid his shield. "Watch your language," he instructed in a stern-fatherly way.

The kid sensed his victory. "Sorry, Officer," he said, still wearing that lippy little moue. "I didn't know. You coulda been anybody."

They retreated to a corner of the dusty rubblefield, where the kid took care to strut his insubordination. Holding his coffee cup, he flexed his right arm so the little red devil quivered on his biceps. Joe had a similar tattoo, a boxing leprechaun, in the identical spot. The coincidence reinforced his sense of failure.

"Where were you the night of January ten, around eleven, midnight?"

"No fuckin' idea. Where were you?"

"Watch your mouth."

"Sorry. I don't remember. Why? What happened?"

"There was a shop over near the Gahden that got broke into."

"You came out here to hassle me over some diddlyshit B-and-E?"

"Language."

"Sorry. It's just . . . *pfft*. You got nothing better to do?"

"This is all I have to do, all day. You got a car?"

"Why?"

"Who's got the black sedan?"

"What black sedan?"

"Four guys showed up with baseball bats in a big black sedan and broke the place up."

"What four guys? What the fu— What are you talking about? You have absolutely no idea, do you?"

"I've got an idea. I've got a pretty good idea. I've got a witness who IDs you as one of the four apes that did it."

The kid stiffened at the word *apes*. "Who? That fuckin' geezer you showed up here with? Half blind . . ."

"That half-blind geezer picked you out of all the guys working on this site. Tell you what: I bet he'd pick you out of a lineup ten times out of ten. Put him in front of a jury and I'll take my chances."

"So arrest me. Go ahead."

"Not today."

"No, not today. Didn't think so. You got nothing and you know it."

"What's your name?"

"Paul."

"Paul what?"

"Marolla."

"Give me your license. Where do you live, Paul Marolla?"

"Lynn."

"Figures."

Joe took down the guy's name, address, and

D.O.B., and handed his license back to him. "Nice talking to you."

"Fuck you."

"We'll talk again."

"Fuck you."

"You want to come down the station and cool off awhile?"

"For what?"

"Suspicious person. Disorderly. I'll think of something."

"Fuck you."

Joe shook his head. Somehow, unwittingly he had played the cool hand. He felt smart—at least he felt he looked smart. He had not said a wrong word, and rather than risk spoiling this little miracle of nonviolent interrogation, he decided to walk away, though he was not sure quite what he had, what good this man's name would do.

"Watch your language."

"Fuck.You."

38

They were like vampires, these Mob guys. They came out at night. Lunch was breakfast, supper was lunch, the workday ended anytime before sunrise. The big boss, Charlie Capobianco, would drive himself into the city from his sprawling oceanfront house in Swampscott after noontime. His workday began at the "clubhouse" on Thatcher Street. Around seven he might sweep into a favored restaurant with his retinue, like a feudal lord paying a call on a vassal. Then it was on to C.C.'s, a bar he owned in the Combat Zone where he kept an office. Sometime around two or three in the morning Capobianco would drive himself home. Hardly anyone knew when he left; hardly anyone was still around.

BPD Station Number One was in the same North End neighborhood, a couple of blocks off Hanover Street, the main drag. It was not unusual for Joe to recognize these guys on the street, big shots like the Capobianco brothers or Vinnie Gargano, or schools of bottom-feeding plug-uglies that cruised the area. Some he knew by name, many more by face. Long before Joe had enlisted in—or been impressed into—the Capobianco organization, he had made it a point to ignore them. Most cops did the same. Leave the gangbuster crap to the movies. In real life, there was only danger for a cop in tangling with these guys. Better to keep a respectful distance. And now that he was lugging around his Big Secret, Joe avoided the North End altogether, lest a wave or a nod betray him.

A shit-cloud had settled over Joe. Every day, bad luck all around. Every fucking day, more trouble. It was all around him, it was inside him, this fucking Trouble, like a virus, and now he would have to ride out the illness right to the end. He was so damn tired. He needed a good long sleep was what he needed. If he could just sleep, then—*then*— maybe he could think this thing through.

After working a last-half, around one in the morning, Joe guided his big Olds Eighty-Eight to a stop behind a fancier black Cadillac on Mass. Ave., across the river in Cambridge. He turned off the ignition. Nearly a full minute passed. Inside the Cadillac the dim silhouette of Vinnie Gargano threw up his hands, and Joe figured he had better get going. He slipped into the passenger seat of Gargano's Caddy.

"What was that with the sitting? What, are you listening to the radio?"

"No. I was making sure nobody was going to see."

"Who the fuck's going to see?"

"I don't know. People."

"What people? I got things to do. I'm sitting here thinking, What's with this guy? Is he waiting for me to come to him or what? This is some crazy fucking cop I found!"

Joe shifted in his seat.

But Gargano was in a lighthearted mood. "If I was that broad from Joe Tecce's with the tits out to here and the hair out to here, you wouldn't be able to get in the car fast enough. You'd'a jumped through the window, *pshoo*, with your pants around your ankles."

"I took care of that thing."

"Listen to you, 'I took care of that thing.' "

"I took care of that thing you asked me."

Gargano gave Joe a disappointed look. All business. This big, dumb mick was rejecting his friendship. Again. So be it.

"I talked to the prosecutor at the BMC. He's going to file a nol pros."

"Speak English."

"He's going to shitcan the case."

"What else?"

"What else what?"

"What else do you want to tell me?"

"Nothing." Joe puzzled over what Gargano might be fishing for. What the hell was Joe doing here with Vinnie The Animal Gargano? Why would Gargano take the time to oversee Joe's case personally? There were bigger tabs to collect. There were also better ears to occupy Gargano the spymaster. As a fixer or an ear, Joe Daley was not worth the trouble.

Gargano handed him an envelope. "A little walking-around money."

Joe checked inside. Two hundred. Two or three days' vig. Walking-around money was all it was. Then again, why would Gargano help Joe out of the hole he had dug? *You're a dummy*, the little voice said. Taking the money would do nothing but seal Joe in further. He took it anyway. He needed it. *Dummy*.

"I got something else for you. You know about that Copley job? Half million in diamonds."

"Read about it in the papers."

"I need those stones. They belong to a friend of mine."

"Diamonds? What do I know—? I don't know dust from diamonds."

"I said they belong to a friend of mine."

"I don't know about that kind of stuff."

"I thought you were a detective."

"Not that kind."

"The fuck's the difference? You're a detective—detect."

"It's just, I can't promise . . . I don't know how, where to start."

"You don't know where to start? Here, let me give you a fuckin' clue. Start with your fuckup of a brother."

"My brother?" Joe tried to deliver the line in a natural way.

" 'Oh, my brother!' Yeah, the thief. Something gets stolen, you start with the thief. Whattaya think?"

"But—"

"Just get the stones, Joe. Your brother didn't do it, fine, I don't give a shit. I really don't. Just get the stones, that's all I care."

"You want me to squeeze my own brother? I can't do that."

"You can. You will."

"Give me something else. Anything else."

"They figured you'd say that."

"Well, they figured right. I'm not gonna do it."

"They also give me this." He dug in his jacket pocket for a folded piece of paper and laid it on the dash in front of Joe.

The paper listed Kat and Little Joe's names, the family's home address, and Little Joe's school, all in neat Palmer Method handwriting.

"Let me tell you something about how this thing works. Don't ever tell me no. You got me? I don't ever want to hear that word out of you. Just get those stones."

39

Two policemen at the door. The taller one was Buczynski (he pronounced it buzzINski) from the Manhattan Burglary Squad. He was average height and thin, and he might have been handsome if only he were better dressed and took all those things—pens, scraps of paper—out of his shirt pocket, and learned not to wear short-sleeve shirts with neckties, and stood up straight, and learned to shave properly and not drench himself so in aftershave. Buczynski did look like a policeman, at least, which was more than you could say for his partner.

This was a little pale-yellow lump of a man with another of those names, Gedaminski—the name rumbled on and on like a freight train behind that G—and no amount of cleaning up was going to salvage him. This man Gedaminski did not seem the police type. He was small, doughy, and rather anemic-looking. What chance would he stand against a respectable criminal? One wanted to put him under a warming lamp like a jaundiced baby. He had come all the way from Boston, driven, he said, though one got the sense he would have walked if necessary. He did have a beady little attentiveness about him. Otherwise, nothing. A complete disappointment.

Anyway, it seemed like great fun to talk to policemen. A lark. It would make a marvelous story. To meet them she had dressed simply, in a dove-gray sweater and pants, no jewelry except a watch and very plain stud earrings. She wanted to project that she was more than she seemed—she was the sort of girl who, under different circumstances, would have thrived as a burglary detective, perceptive and ready for action as she was. She did not like that they would make assumptions about her. They would presume. They would dismiss her with two words: Park Avenue. So she was inordinately hospitable. She put out coffee and muffins, the sort of food she imagined policemen enjoyed. She was eager to help.

But really, what could she tell this Gedaminski that she hadn't already told him on the phone? He had come an awfully long way just to confirm a very simple story.

Gedaminski handed her a photo.

"Yes!" she said. "That's him." She was surprised to remember the man so clearly. But he had been handsome. There had been a presence about him. She had thought, upon seeing this man, *He is just like me somehow.* "Tell me his name. Is that alright? Am I allowed to know his name?"

"Richard Daley."

"Are you sure he's the one? It seems like a mistake."

"Why don't you just tell me the story again."

"Alright. Well, it's just what I told you. Does your friend know the story already?"

Buczynski had agreed to drive his counterpart from Boston as a courtesy. They had worked together before. Gedaminski had been to New York chasing this or that suspect, usually Daley. A real pro, a *good thief*, often worked out of town, the better to go unrecognized. Gedaminski had long suspected that Ricky Daley had paid a few visits to Manhattan to steal and not be bothered. Gedaminski knew, too, that Ricky worked with the same fences over and over, a trusted few, and none of them were in Boston. There was no better place to fence jewelry than New York. There it could be quickly broken up and moved. Often the only way to catch a good thief was to follow the swag. It was very easy to steal, but very hard to dispose of stolen things once you'd got them. Most thieves had to settle for twenty or thirty cents on the dollar from a fence. Good thieves did better; there was less risk in dealing with them. Burglary detectives spent much of their time trolling pawnshops and jewelers, tracking the swag. Gedaminski would have given his left nut to know where Ricky Daley fenced his stuff. He and Buczynski had canvassed the usual layoffs in New York several times, with no luck. Gedaminski got along fine with Al Buczynski, though Buczynski talked too much, and the Old Spice he wore gave the Bostonian a roaring headache and made him suspicious of the entire NYPD, since perfume on a man was a sort of subterfuge, and perfume on a cop smelled like corruption.

"Well,"the woman said,"it's just like everybody says:Where were you when you heard Kennedy was shot? I was in Boston. The Harvard-Yale game was that weekend. We were supposed to stay the whole weekend but we didn't. They wound up postponing the game, anyway. We were staying at the Copley, my husband and I. We sat in front of the TV all afternoon, it seemed like. We were with friends in the Back Bay. And I was drained and just, just exhausted, I suppose. I just couldn't bear to watch the TV anymore—they were saying the same things over and over again, hour after hour, I couldn't stand it. So I went back to the hotel, to the room, while my husband stayed to watch.

"When I got back to my floor, I came off the elevator and I was walking down the corridor, getting my room key out and so forth, and there was this sound, not like a gunshot but like a firecracker or a pop, just *crack*. Well, I was spooked already from that whole day, so it frightened me and I kind of stopped there in the hall a moment. When I got to the door of my room, I was fumbling with the key. My hand was trembling. I was—well, I wasn't crying exactly, but tears were coming out, you know?—and I was just anxious to get into my room and lie down. So while I'm trying to open my door, a few doors down the hall a door opens and out comes this man—this Richard Daley. He looked much nicer than he does in that picture. He was wearing a very nice suit and he had no luggage. I noticed he did not have a room key, he was not locking the door behind him. He just pulled the door shut.

"He came walking down the hall toward the elevators. He saw me struggling with my door and as he went by me he said, 'Are you okay?' I told him my hand was shaking and I could not seem to get my door open. He said, 'Here, let me help you. I'm good with locks.'

I gave him the key and he put it in my lock and opened my door for me. That was it. He said, 'It'll be okay,' and he smiled and he turned to go.

"He was really very nice. Very nice. You know, something in his face made me think, you know, just for a moment, *maybe it really will be okay*. I said to him—not that it mattered, but I just wanted him to stay there for another minute, I don't know why; I liked him, and it was such a crazy day—I said to him, 'Hey, you forgot to lock your door.' So he stops and he kind of looks at the door, and he says, 'It's not my room. I just checked in and they gave me the wrong room. I asked for a suite. That room is a single.' So I said something about 'Well, it's a horrible day and you can't really blame the fellow at the front desk for making a mistake.' And he smiles—not a happy smile, I mean just a reassuring kind of smile—and he says, 'No. It's just a mistake. I'll go right down and straighten it out.' And that was it. He went down the hall, and I went into my room, and I never thought anything of it. I never even heard about the robbery in that

301

room. We checked out an hour later and came right home. We didn't want to be away."

"You're sure it's him?"

She picked up the picture and looked at it again. She was absolutely certain and yet she could not quite hold both facts in her head at once—this was the nice, handsome man she had met in the hotel corridor, and this man was a thief. That he would rob someone during the chaos of That Day, well, it was particularly profane and opportunistic, and it added to her confusion.

"I'm sure," she said. "Richard Daley. But he wasn't, he didn't seem . . . I just—"

"You're sure it's him?"

"Yes, it's the same man but . . . he was just in the wrong room."

"Trust me, lady, he's always in the wrong room."

40

Ricky was in the wrong room.

With the lights still off, he worked his hands into a pair of leather driving gloves. These were tan calf-skin, very thin. He liked them because the thin leather permitted him to feel, they were not too hot to wear nor too bulky to fit in a coat pocket, and they were stylish. He took pride in the hidden aspects of his craft, just as a master cabinet-maker takes pride in perfect dovetails at the backs of drawers. This was what it meant to have an avocation, a calling. That his life's work would take place entirely in the shadows, unwitnessed, was precisely the reason to do it perfectly. He was a member of a secret guild, and he felt a little thrill of professionalism when he worked his hands into those gloves, flexing and unflexing his fingers, packing the leather down into the crotches between his fingers. He was at work and happy.

Ricky turned on one light, then lowered all the shades. He made a mental note of where each shade had been.

This would be a leisurely job. He had clocked it

only a couple of days—criminal negligence by Ricky's standards—but Kurt Lindstrom's one-week engagement with the BSO was a bit of good luck he did not want to miss. Tonight Lindstrom would be in Symphony Hall performing the *Pines of Rome*, as he had done the two previous nights. The piece was scheduled after the intermission; there was no way Lindstrom would be back before ten.

Ricky searched the front room methodically. He did not touch anything unless it was necessary to see behind or under it, and he meticulously replaced everything.

There was an upright piano in a corner with stacks of sheet music. On the fold-down music shelf of the piano was a handwritten arrangement Lindstrom apparently was working on. Ricky did not read music but he studied the pages anyway. It was written in pencil with a sure hand and no eraser marks or cross-outs. Each line spanned eight full staffs. It looked impossibly complex, coded, mad. Above the piano was a reproduction engraving of a scowling Beethoven.

One wall was lined with bookcases, some improvised from boards and cinder blocks. The books overflowed them and were stacked on the floor in haphazard piles. But there was nothing haphazard about the shelving. In one area were crime novels, everything from Dreiser's *An American Tragedy* and volumes of Dostoevsky to pulps—but mostly pulps. This was a well-thumbed library. More than half were paperbacks, their spines cracked and concave. Lindstrom was a reader and, apparently, a rereader. Ricky rather admired Lindstrom's library, which was heavy in California noir, Hammett and Chandler of course, but also included a lot of Jim Thompson and Patricia Highsmith and Chester Himes, all filed by the author's name. There were a few mildly risqué titles too, *Gang Girl* and *Hitch-Hike Hussy* and that sort of thing. Ricky tipped these out of the line and smirked at the lurid covers: scarlet women in various stages of undress, leering fedora'd men with oversized handguns.

Lindstrom maintained a separate three-foot shelf for his pornographic magazines. They were arranged vertically with spines flush, just as good suburban families arranged their *National Geographics* in neat yellow ranks in the den. Ricky realized the danger of rifling through this shelf—no doubt it was a portion of the library Lindstrom visited again and again—so he removed the magazines one at a time and replaced them with precision. Ricky was not immune to the fascination of pornography and he was no prude, but Lindstrom's magazines shocked him. Not the garden-variety pornography, of which there was quite a lot, with an emphasis on bondage and a separate subsection with names like *Hellcat Grannies* and *Gray Foxes*. And not the ordinary soft-core girlie mags, *Black Velvet* and *Busty* and *Wicked*, the type that included cocktail recipes between the pinups. What jarred Ricky were the others. They were graphically sadistic. It crossed his mind that it might have been illegal merely to possess them. These magazines were printed on cheap newsprint.

That the photos were in black and white and poorly shot, underlit, sometimes not even focused, somehow added to their authenticity. Women trussed in contorted positions, with baroque leather strapwork or artlessly calf-roped. Their breasts were clamped or stretched. They were raped, both with objects and by naked, black-hooded, potbellied, small-bottomed men whose penises were not shown. These women winced or stared boggle-eyed at their torturers. In one photo a woman lay dead—playacting, presumably—and bleeding. In another shot, a woman slouched from a whipping post, as if lynched, her arms pulled up behind her at an unnatural, unfakeable angle. Some showed women's faces badly beaten.

Ricky's mouth fell open. For a few minutes he forgot the need to sweep the apartment quickly and efficiently then get out. The magazines seemed the opposite of pornography, which existed to stimulate. He could not imagine more dick-shriveling images than these. He stared, transfixed.

Then he saw it.

The images, in a magazine called *Bound*, might have been crime-scene photos from one of the Boston stranglings—except that the magazine was dated July 1958. The "victim" in the photos was a woman in her fifties, wearing a housecoat and girdle. The "strangler" was dressed, ridiculously, in a thievish cap and mask and hepcat jacket, all of which he wore in every photo. In the first shot he wore black pachuco pants; in the rest, no pants or underpants at all. The victim was bound and "raped," then "strangled" with a garrote of braided sheets and nylons, which was tied off in a bow in the final photo.

Ricky knew.

Something collapsed inside him. The hidden reserve of strength that had carried him through the night of Amy's murder and the funeral and the long weeks afterward—in an instant, it crumbled. He replaced the magazine precisely, and moved to inspect the rest of the apartment. But his eyes watered. He wiped them with his upper arm. Thoughts of suffering led immediately to Amy. Only a few, Joe and Michael among them, knew the details of the murder. The rest did not want to know. They did not want to dwell on the fact that a family member had been murdered. They were embarrassed by it. In some obscure way, they felt tainted by their association with murder, however blameless the victim. They did not want the sort of negative celebrity that attaches to a murder survivor: *Did you know his daughter/wife/mother was killed by the Strangler?* They did not want to be perceived as carriers of murder, or of whatever trait had attracted it, weakness, bad luck, fate, sin. The sexual nature of the crime only doubled their shame. So they pretended the murder never happened. They acted, all except maybe Michael, as if Amy had died of cancer or in a car accident or in some other non-sensational, non-violent way. Ricky had done it, too. Maybe having known Amy so intimately, having known her body, he was the one who most needed to block out the details of her murder.

But it was impossible to maintain the fiction here, in the room where the Strangler lived, where he had first formed the idea, where he had retreated after the crime. Here it was all too clear. Amy had not died instantly. Her dying had been a process, a long, excruciating, bloody process. To turn away from that fact, to pretend it had not happened—as if she had passed into fiction, a book we could safely put back on the shelf because the subject did not suit us—was not polite or discreet. It was cowardly. Amy had suffered.

He thought, *Monstrous, monstrous.*

More quickly than before, Ricky scanned some of the other shelves. And here was another impossible juxtaposition: Lindstrom's psychopathic sexual deviance occupied the same mind as an elaborate intellect. His shelves were crowded with Hobbes, Locke, Hume, Rousseau, Kant, *Leviathan*, the *Principia Ethica, The Critique of Pure Reason*.Most were paperbacks; all were broken-backed and grungy with fingering. Ricky did not know what linked these books, whether they shared a central concern or not. He opened one book, Hobbes's *Leviathan.It* was full of scribbles, little stars, underlinings, brackets, annotations—the leavings of a ravenous mind that had passed this way.

In the bedroom, in a top drawer where Lindstrom kept his own underwear, he found a pair of women's panties. Ricky nudged them open with his gloved finger. They were large and made of an elastic rubbery material, like a girdle. They were certainly not Amy's. They were torn at the waistband and flyspecked with a brown liquid that might have been blood. They were a souvenir of a murder, and Ricky was tempted to take them. But he could not take them without betraying that he had been there. Lindstrom did not know he was being watched and certainly did not know he had been found out; Ricky wanted to preserve that advantage. So he balled up the enormous panties and replaced them in the drawer just as he had found them.

He retraced his steps, raising the shades to their original height, turned off the lights, and let himself out. And here was a final glitch, an unprofessional stumble for which Ricky would reproach himself later.

The door had two locks which had to be relocked. The first, in the knob, was simple enough; it locked merely by closing the door. But above it was a drop lock, an old Schlage, one that should not have given Ricky any trouble. This type of lock was very slightly more difficult to pick because of the added weight of the bolt mechanism, which resisted the rotation of the cylinder. The added resistance required a lock picker to secure the cylinder with enough torque that he could overcome the resistance of that weight and turn the lock, yet not so much torque that the pins misset as the pick lifted them. It was a matter of touch—a very, very simple thing, especially for an accomplished pick man like Ricky who took pride in his skill and practiced constantly. But he fumbled with the lock. When he tried to rotate the cylinder, it jammed—the pins were misset—and he had to start again. Another misset, and he had to repeat the process a third time. The whole episode took just seconds. But it was a fumble, and he might have been put in a bad position if someone had come along. No one did come, luckily, and Ricky did manage to relock the door. But the lapse troubled him. It was not a clean job.

41

Margaret Daley emerged from the bathroom after showering. She scrubbed her hair dry with a hand towel while simultaneously pinning her elbows against her side to secure the bath towel wrapped around her. When she had finished, she stood before a mirror. There was a man in the doorway. Her body jerked and she yelped, "Michael!"

He slouched against the doorpost in his courtroom suit. On his way to work, presumably. He had lost weight. His eyes were baggy with exhaustion.

"What are you doing here? How did you get in?"

"Your boyfriend left the door unlocked on his way out."

"My boyfriend? Michael, are you mental? What's wrong with you?"

"He's not your boyfriend?"

"I'm a little old for boyfriends. It's none of your business anyways what he is."

"Do you love him?"

"Oh my Lord, Michael, it's too early to have this conversation. I'm not even dressed yet." She minced into the bathroom—a big woman

311

simulating a dainty woman's walk; Michael was not sure whether she walked this way out of habit or because she was selfconscious about her body being so exposed—and she came back out wearing a frayed terry bathrobe. "Is that what you're so upset about, that I'm with Brendan now?"

"Do you love him?"

"Michael, I'm not going to answer questions like that. It's absolutely none of your business. Are you crazy, showing up like this in the morning? What did you do, lurk around outside till you saw Brendan go?"

"Yes."

"You couldn't have called?"

"I thought we should talk face-to-face."

"Michael, sit down." She flung the blanket over the unmade bed and sat down on the edge. "Sit down."

He frowned at the bed. "I'd rather stand."

"Michael, do you feel alright? You know, everybody thinks you're going mental with this thing."

"I feel fine."

"Are you drinking?"

"No."

"Are you . . . on drugs?"

"Not yet."

"Then what is this? You're like a crazy man already. What's going on with you?"

"I just don't like your boyfriend, that's all."

"Stop calling him my boyfriend. You sound ridiculous."

"What should I call him? 'Daddy'?"

"You call him Brendan. That's his name, it's what you've been calling him for thirty years. And you better watch your tone with me, young man. I'm still entitled to a little respect even if your father's not here to keep you three in line."

"Well, I wouldn't worry too much. We have Brendan to keep us in line now."

"Michael, come here. Sit down here now."

He sat beside her on the bed. The adjacent night table, Joe Senior's night table, was littered with trash, crumpled tissues, a paperback novel thick as a beefsteak, a nearly empty water glass.

"Michael, you have to stop this. Whatever it is you have against Brendan, it's time to put it away, you hear me? I can't stand this. I don't recognize you anymore. It's like you're another person. Where's my Michael, hm?"

"Do you love him?"

"What difference does it make?"

"It makes all the difference. It makes all the difference."

"Why? I don't get you. Why?"

"Because you had a husband."

"Had. He's dead, Michael. I'm not. Did you want me to jump into the box with him and the both of us get buried?"

"I want you to act—I want you to act like you respect him."

"Of course I respect him. I was married to him for thirty-three years. How could I not respect him?"

"Then what are you doing with this . . . pig?"

"Pig! Michael!"

"You're right. That's not fair. There are plenty of perfectly respectable pigs out there."

"Michael, where is all this coming from? This . . . hate? You've known Brendan your whole life. Your father—who you seem to think was some kind of saint—"

"I didn't say that. Not a saint. Not a saint. Just a decent guy. Showed up for work every day, never cheated, did right by his family, that's all I'm saying. And after that, after forty years almost of being with a good guy, you settle for this? Brendan Conroy isn't worth the half of my father and you know it. You can't even compare the two. It's like apples and . . . a pig."

"Brendan is a good man."

"Oh, stop. He's an obnoxious blowhard. And worse, Ma, believe me. Much worse."

"Worse?"

"There's things you don't know."

"Oh, *pssh*. Now you really do sound like a mental case."

"Doesn't it bother you that Brendan was there the day Dad died?"

"No."

"That the man you crawl into bed with, who puts his hands on you, who touches you, is the last man who saw your husband alive?"

"Michael, stop this!"

"Then he told some cock-and-bull story about a kid they never found? Your husband was murdered and Brendan was there and they never found the guy. That doesn't bother you?"

Michael shuffled to the bureau. His fingers sought out the small items she had collected there on a painted tin tray: a Hummel figurine, hair clips, her rosary, coins. In the top middle drawer, which was open, the brown handle of Joe Senior's service pistol was half buried among the stockings and girdles. He looked back at his mother sitting on the bed. The sheets were mussed. She had twisted to face him. On a wall in the corner was a photo of the three boys when they were fifteen, thirteen, and nine respectively. Nearby was a picture of Jesus with his long hands pressed together in prayer. The picture reminded him of the church, and the church reminded him:

"Do you . . . ? The two of you . . ."

"Do we what?"

". . . use . . . birth control?"

"Oh my God! Michael! How dare you? That's it! This conversation is over! *He's* a pig?"

"Alright, alright!"

"You're the pig! Pig! Pig!" She shook herself, like a dog shaking water out of its fur. "Oh!"

He said nothing.

"Oh!" she blurted again.

"There are things about Brendan you don't know, Ma. I don't think you should see him."

"Oh, you don't? Well, that's just too bad. I'm a big girl. I'll decide who I see and who I don't see."

"This is serious. There's things Amy knew."

"Things like what, Michael? What on earth are you talking about?"

"Amy thought—" He checked himself. She

315

would think he was insane even if he credited the story to Amy. She would think he was insane just for believing it. So he hedged. He did not accuse Brendan Conroy, quite. "Brendan knows more about Dad's murder than he lets on. That's what Amy thought."

"Amy thought that, huh?"

"That's right."

"You know, this isn't the first I've heard this. Brendan told me what you said the other night. He thinks you're a nutcase, too, you know. I defended you, but you know what? I think maybe Brendan was right. You might really need help, Michael."

"Then help me."

"How? Take you to McLean's, put you in a padded room?"

"Don't see him, just for a while. For me. Do it for me."

"I can't do that. You know I'm not going to do that."

"Why not? Tell him you're sick, tell him you need time to think, it's moving too fast, you have cancer, whatever. Mum, trust me, women say these things to me all the time. He'll get the message."

"But I don't want to not see him."

"You do love him."

She groaned, exasperated. "What is this love-him, not-love-him? Why do I have to love him or not love him? I don't even know what that means. Do I love him like I loved your father? No, because I'm not eighteen anymore and neither is Brendan. So what is it supposed to feel like, Michael, for me?

Why can't *I* decide? Why can't I just be with someone? It's no sin to want to be with someone, you know. Is it such a sin to not want to be alone?"

"No, it's no sin. Just a mistake."

42

Claire Downey's desk at the *Observer* was in a corner of the newsroom, where the racket of clacking wire-service teletypes joined the general clamor of the room—the arrhythmic *whack*-[pause]-*whack-whack* of typewriters, the men in rumpled white shirts speaking in raised voices like a ship's crew shouting into the wind. At the center of Claire's desk was a big Royal typewriter. The logo on it had been written over with a marker: "Royal" had been altered to "Goya-KOD." Surrounding the typewriter were papers, a wire basket, folded newspapers, a Kent cigarette carton converted into a pencil tray, an ominous-looking spike to impale papers. All these things seemed to have collected at random, as if blown onto the desk by a swirling breeze.

Michael hovered near the desk until a woman approached. She wore a plain gray skirt with a white blouse. Her face was broad and square, pretty in a girlish, quick-smiling way. It was framed by brown hair, which she parted on one side of her forehead and pinned on the other, like a bobby-soxer. Michael was disappointed. He'd been expecting Katharine Hepburn.

"Are you Claire?"

"Yes."

"I'm Michael Daley. My brother Rick and Amy Ryan—"

"Of course."

"She and Rick . . ."

She smiled. "I know who you are, Michael. Amy talked about you. I saw you at the funeral, from a distance."

"You have a minute to talk?"

She glanced up at the clock: two-fifteen. "A minute, not much more. I'm on a deadline. The evening edition."

"I just have a few questions about Amy."

"Fifty-five seconds."

"Okay. You worked with Amy on the Strangler story?"

"Yes."

"You shared a byline. Did that mean you worked together on all those stories?"

"For the most part. We did our own reporting. We wrote together."

"Why did you stop tracking the story?"

"We didn't. The story stopped moving. DeSalvo confessed, and the investigation stopped. The story now is the trial. When the trial starts, we'll cover it—I'll cover it."

"What about the murders themselves?"

"Our reporting was mostly about the police work. Amy and I weren't investigating the

319

murders; we were investigating the investigation."

"So you never checked into other suspects? Arthur Nast? Kurt Lindstrom? Never contacted either of them? Never interviewed them?"

"No. We weren't crazy. Well, Amy might have been crazy. I wasn't."

"So Nast or Lindstrom never threatened her, never had a grudge?"

"As far as I know, she never spoke to them."

"Was she having trouble with anyone else? Threats?"

"No."

"Did she ever talk about Brendan Conroy?"

"Brendan Conroy? In what way?"

"As someone she was investigating?"

"No. Brendan Conroy was someone she used as a source."

"On the Strangler stories?"

"On all sorts of stories."

"What about my father's murder? Did she ever talk about it?"

"Not with me."

"She *never* talked about how Conroy's partner got killed?"

"It was a big case; Amy may have talked about it. But I don't remember anything specific." She laid her left hand on Michael's arm. "I'm sorry about your father, of course."

Michael noted the wedding band on her finger.

"So what was Amy working on, then?"

"As far as I know, she was preoccupied with two stories: the Strangler and the rats in the West End."

"Rats in the West End? That's not a crime story."

"Two-legged rats."

"Ah. What about them?"

"I don't know. But I can guess. There's a lot of money to be made on that project. That's the kind of cheese those rats like. Money. You want to figure out what the story was? Find the cheese."

"How?"

She pointed at the graffiti on her typewriter. "Know what this means? Amy wrote that. It was her little joke. Goyakod. It means: Get Off Your Ass, Knock On Doors. That's what we do here. That's all there is to it. Go to the West End and start knocking on doors."

"But there aren't any doors in the West End anymore."

"See? This job isn't as easy as it looks. Your minute's up." She sat down, sandwiched a piece of carbon paper between two sheets, and rolled them into the typewriter platen. "Go. If you find anything, let me know. Now go. Good luck."

Michael did go, but he paused to watch her from the doorway. Across the room, she sat with her shoulders erect, touch-typing quickly, eyes on her notes. She was the only woman in the room, and easily the best typist. The men tended to tamp the keys with their two index fingers. They held pencils clenched in their teeth or wedged behind an ear and forgotten there. They glanced up nervously at the clock on the wall.

Then and there Michael fell for Claire a little, despite the wedding ring, or because of it. He had always been prone to these little swoons. He could not help it. He found women irresistibly affecting, and there was an onanistic promiscuity in the way he developed and abandoned crushes. But they came less often now. Love is a sort of hope, and Michael was not feeling much of that lately.

43

Seated in a Barcelona chair that forced him into a reclining position just a foot or so off the floor, Joe eyed the receptionist behind the desk, this blonde broad with a swirl of hair like whipped cream whom Joe would have liked to bend over the desk right then and there. He tried to haul himself up out of the chair, but it would not let him go. The seat cushions were tipped backward, and the chair was so low he could not get his legs underneath him. The effect was like tossing a sandbag onto Joe's lap. He could not get up.

The receptionist smiled agreeably.

Rather than struggle like an overturned beetle, Joe decided to wait until she looked away. He occupied himself by imagining her naked. He considered the cost of liberating her from her clothes, the time, the money, the risk that this chick would be the one that finally snapped Kat's patience. The receptionist was probably worth all that, depending on her ass, which Joe still had not seen and which could change the whole calculation. Probably it was a big, majestic thing, like an enormous cleaved peach, which was Joe's type. But what if her ass turned out to be one of those no-ass asses that left the back of a skirt to droop, or an overripe ass that slumped like rotten fruit? So much depended on the ass.

The receptionist busied herself with papers on her desk. The phone in front of her was a sleek white plastic thing that resembled a sleeping cat, and Joe admired it. It looked expensive. It rang and she answered it briskly, "Sonnenshein Development, Mr. Sonnenshein's office, this is Ingrid."

How would it feel to lay that phone against his own ear? It must be light, lighter than the prewar models at the station made of heavy black Bakelite, their cords wrapped in gutta-percha. And of course it would still carry the intimate warmth of Ingrid's ear.

In order to fuck her and do it the right way, he would have to take her out, and that would cost money, which he did not have. Then there was the time it would take sitting in a restaurant or a bar, time he did not have because he had to work details and work off the money he owed. Also, he never saw his kid anymore. He would have to make that up to Little Joe as well, after everything else. The whole thing did not make sense. But there she was, and with an addict's logic he rationalized, *If I was hungry, I'd eat, so . . .*

"You ever sit in these things?" Joe said.

"No."

"This has gotta be the most uncomfortable chair on earth. You should try it."

"Why would I want to sit in the most uncomfortable chair on earth?"

"Because it's the most of something."

"Mm, the most of a bad thing."

"Yeah, well, I know, but most is most."

Joe rolled out of the chair as if he were falling out of a hammock. On his feet again, he had a look down at the receptionist, who looked right back, and there was a little stir in Joe's groin, the machinery twitching awake. "You like this job, workin' here, answering the phone?"

"Sure."

"Must meet some interesting people. Big shots."

"Some, I guess."

He handed her a business card. "You ever need anything, help with any kind of trouble, you give me a call. Sometimes it helps to have a friend."

She dangled the card by a corner as if it were dripping wet. "A friend?"

"That's right. Everybody can use a friend."

"To help me out of trouble."

"Out, in, whatever."

Something passed between them, a look, which Joe took to be an agreement of some kind.

Then there was the sound of footsteps and a change in the atmosphere of the room, like the drop in barometric pressure that precedes a storm, and Farley Sonnenshein came out of his office with his hand extended. "Detective. I'm sorry I kept you."

"Thank you for seeing me, sir."

"Come in, come in. Coffee? Did Ingrid already offer?"

"She did. I'm all set."

"A cop who doesn't drink coffee? I better watch myself."

Sonnenshein was tall, six-two or six-three, and handsome in an agreeable, unpretty way. He was nearly bald. What little hair he had was cut very short, which made it hard to determine his precise age. He might have been anywhere from fifty to sixty-five.

He led Joe into his office, which continued the spare steel-and-blond-wood scheme of the reception area. There were trophies on the shelves and walls: shovels from ground-breaking ceremonies, hard hats, architectural drawings, photos including one of Sonnenshein with President Kennedy.

The developer directed Joe to a little seating area where they could face each other without a desk in between. Joe sat down and crossed his legs, left ankle on right knee. Sonnenshein crossed his legs, too, but in a more elegant way, knee on knee. Joe tried to imitate this position, but his thighs were too big to do it right and squeezing them together compressed his testicles painfully, so after a graceless attempt he reverted to his original pose.

Sonnenshein was Jewish but looked like a Mayflower Yankee, which made him doubly foreign to Joe, a member of two exotic tribes. Three, if you counted the rich as a distinct supra-ethnicity, as Joe certainly did. Guys like Farley Sonnenshein had been stepping on Irishmen the better part of a hundred years now. The hell with that picture of

Sonnenshein and JFK, the Irish martyr. Joe knew full well how rich Yankees and rich Jews saw Kennedy: The president had molted off his Irishness and evolved into a virtual Yankee, a male Grace Kelly. And Joe knew how the rich still perceived guys like Joe Daley: Dorchester micks, common as dirt. It was all Joe would ever be. Queasy with deference and resentment, he was anxious to leave before he'd asked his first question.

"Well," Sonnenshein said, "what can I do to help you?" He seemed to feel no apprehension about a visit from the police.

Joe reviewed the facts of the B-and-E at Moe Wasserman's grocery, the four apes in a dark-colored sedan with baseball bats, their lack of interest in the cash that was in the register, and Wasserman's subsequent identification of one of the thugs working construction on the West End site.

"I see," Sonnenshein said. "So you want to know whether I sent that gang to roust the old man from his—what was it, a grocery store? The answer is no."

"So how does this guy Paul Marolla find his way onto your construction crew?"

"I have no idea. I certainly don't keep track of individual laborers. On a project of this scale we use so many subcontractors, I rather doubt this Marolla works for us anyway. Most of the crews on the site are subs. Have you ever worked construction, Detective?"

"Yes."

"Then you know how it works. I have my own crews, but I'm also a broker. I bring together the people needed to make the project happen."

"And the shopkeeper? What do you remember about that building, the little old man who refused to sell?"

"Well, I know you read the newspapers, Joe— may I call you Joe?—so you realize there have been a lot of cases like that in the West End. Lots of little old ladies and little old men. You remember Mrs. Blood? She became something of a *cause célèbre*. And of course I was cast as the villain. No matter. I take my lumps. So be it. If your question is 'Do I remember the little old grocer near North Station?' then my answer is no. If you're asking me whether I remember the *building* near North Station that delayed a portion of this project, then the answer is yes, I most certainly do. Of course.

"But this is nothing personal, Joe. I don't know what that man may have told you, and I'm certain he feels abused—how else could he feel?—but this is just business. More important, this is about a project that's vital to our city, Joe. Absolutely vital to our future. We can't forget: For every old man or old woman who is inconvenienced, there will be a hundred or a thousand who benefit, directly or indirectly. You know, Jack Kennedy had a saying, 'to govern is to choose.' Choices sometimes have to be made. Nobody enjoys making them, I assure you. There are no bad guys here, Joe."

"Somebody broke up this guy's store—"

"You're a determined man, Joe, a real detective, I appreciate that. But I'm asking you to expand your focus just for a moment, see the big picture. Did you know that at the end of World War One Boston was the fourth-largest city in the country? Do you know what it is now, Joe? Thirteenth, and still falling. In the last twenty years, while the whole country has been booming, only one major city actually lost population: Boston. You see what I'm getting at, Joe? We can feel sorry for the little guys who get hurt, but this city is fighting for its life. I'm sorry for Moe What's-his-name and his shop, but what I'm really worried about here is: Will this city live or will it die?"

"Hey, alls I'm asking is who smashed up that shop?"

"I don't know."

"No offense, but the one with the motive is you."

"I had no motive to do that, Joe. We obtain these properties through perfectly legal means. The city and state take them through eminent domain. Why would we ever want to get involved in that bully-boy stuff? We don't operate that way. We don't have to."

"Mr. Wasserman says you won't pay him what the building's worth. Says you two are in a beef over it."

"What's any building worth? Whatever the seller decides?" Sonnenshein smiled, taking Joe into his confidence. "There is a charming local custom in this town, Joe: A covered wagon comes through, and everyone tries to rob it. It's one reason so little gets done. After a while, the covered wagons decide to go elsewhere."

"I don't follow you."

"No, I imagine you don't." Sonnenshein nodded. "Let me assure you, I have no information about your shopkeeper being roughed up. I don't know anything about it. I would never do anything that would endanger the success of a project like this one. There's just too much at stake. I think that answers all your questions. Now, was there anything else, Detective?"

"Um, no, I guess that's it." Joe nodded, defeated. "I'm sorry to bother you. If I think of anything else—"

"It's no bother. No bother at all. You think of anything else, you go right ahead and call me, Joe. I don't like the idea that people are out doing these things to make me out like a thug."

44

Ricky had been lingering at the back of the gallery when it struck him, when the connection came clear. He slid along the wall to the edge of the front row, where the newspapermen cocked their heads and scratched in their notebooks, and the only two women in the audience clutched their purses in their laps. Ricky tried to catch a glimpse of DeSalvo in quarter profile at the defense table watching his lawyer deliver his closing argument to a jury of men. Albert DeSalvo had not shrunk from attention during his eight-day trial. He had not testified, of course—the con he was running would not have survived a competent cross—so he'd had to make the most of his entrances and exits, and in between he had emoted sympathetically from his chair. But even in this straitened role, DeSalvo had managed to project his likable grandiosity. He was satisfied with the work they were all doing together in that room. He was here to settle accounts, a standup guy, not the sort to deny the obvious, not a bad guy at all really. Ricky watched DeSalvo watch his lawyer. (The lawyer Leland Bloom was a famous closer and he was just beginning to find his voice now, the bombastic high gear that could elate a jury as it did Bloom himself: "If this is not a case of not guilty by reason of insanity, then there is no such thing. Let's just wipe it off the books because the words themselves will be rendered meaningless. Let's tear it up . . .") Ricky studied DeSalvo's features, the melted-wax nose and the brilliantined pompadour and five-o'clock shadow, and he thought: *Oswald*. The similarity was not physical. In the few photographs that recurred in the news-papers, especially the grainy old snapshot of Oswald with his rifle propped on his hip—the image already had become iconic, the trope by which we knew Oswald, knew everything we needed to know about him; we assumed that rifle on his hip was the famous 6.5-millimeter Mannlicher-Carcano carbine he'd brought to the sixth-floor window of the Texas School Book Depository— Oswald seemed a wispier, more delicate type than DeSalvo. What was it, then? Ricky studied him.

DeSalvo turned, perhaps detecting the heat of Ricky's stare or simply noticing that a man had moved forward out of the crowd. There had been death threats, even one against the defense lawyer that had shut down the trial for an afternoon. DeSalvo's face tightened with a moment's concern, then relaxed again, satisfied that Ricky was no threat, just another civilian drawn to the spectacle of History Being Made. He gave Ricky a little nod, then turned back to listen to his lawyer pronounce him the one true Boston Strangler.

"Hey, slim, you gonna stand there all day?"

Ricky glanced back. "Sorry."

The courtroom was jammed. The Middlesex Superior Courthouse was a steep redbrick mausoleum. The courtrooms were not big enough for a crowd this large. Albert DeSalvo's trial had consumed the city. Reporters arrived early to secure the best positions. Extra court officers were detailed to the courtroom, and Cambridge cops stood guard in the hallways and outside on the sidewalks. Alvan Byron came and went from the gallery, Wamsley too. Mayor Collins was said to receive briefings every afternoon. The glamorous B-list singer Connie Francis, who was appearing at Blinstrub's in town, showed up one day to watch. But the focus was on DeSalvo and his rogue-elephant lawyer and the resolution of the Strangler drama, the other story from that horrible, stultifying year of 1963 that still needed wrapping up.

Except this trial did not feel like a wrapping-up. DeSalvo was not even being tried for the stranglings. His entire marathon confession to thirteen killings could not be used against him; it had been given under a grant of immunity. And there was not a scrap of evidence linking DeSalvo to any of the stranglings. In fact, whether Albert DeSalvo was actually the Strangler was still a matter of debate among cops and prosecutors. The problem was DeSalvo himself. He kept insisting he was.

So DeSalvo was on trial for the so-called Green

Man attacks, four cases in which an intruder had broken into women's apartments and assaulted them. (The cases were named for a "Green Man" because, for weeks before the Boston attacks, the police teletype had been reporting a vaguely similar series of incidents in Connecticut in which the suspect had worn a green shirt and pants, presumably some sort of work uniform.) But the Green Man attacks were not stranglings. They were not even murders. In one case, there had been a garden-variety rape—the attacker had forced a woman to fellate him—but the rest were aborted, inconclusive attacks in which the Green Man had tied women up and groped them, only to abandon the attack in remorse or skittishness. ("Don't tell my mother," he told his last victim as he ran off.) The charges were a lumpy mess of lawyerspeak: B-and-E with intent to commit a felony, unnatural and lascivious acts, ABDW. This was not the operatic, macabre horror of the Strangler murders. It was the sort of low-rent trial that usually goes unreported, the kind that assistant D.A.'s bide their time with while waiting for Something Big.

So why was Albert DeSalvo copping to the stranglings in an unrelated, smalltime case? According to Leland Bloom, the reason was simple: DeSalvo actually was the Boston Strangler and therefore must be insane; so by proving he was the Strangler, DeSalvo would prove himself not guilty by reason of insanity in the Green Man cases or, by extension, in any criminal case. Besides, Bloom calculated, his client was looking at life in prison anyway for the Green Man cases, so what was there to lose? It was such a daffy legal strategy, no one would have taken it seriously but for one fact: this was Lee Bloom, the Perry Mason of Boston, the Learjet lawyer who had won acquittals in places more glamorous than his rundown hometown. He was the swashbuckling native son who was too big for Boston but had stayed here anyway. So nobody mentioned the fact that there was no way in hell the Green Man was going to do life without parole on these chickenshit charges. Twenty, twenty-five years max, parole in ten— even that would be a stretch. More important, if DeSalvo actually succeeded in convincing a jury he was the Boston Strangler, they were never going to acquit him whether he was insane or not. What juror would want to go home to explain to his wife or daughter that he had released the Strangler on a technicality? It was legal hara-kiri. Of course there were lots of theories to explain DeSalvo's ardor to confess to the stranglings. He wanted money, it was said, both the reward offered by the governor and the profits from book and movie deals. He was a pathological liar; he had confessed not just to the thirteen known stranglings but to a couple more besides, and according to Bloom the orgy of selfincrimination had not stopped there— DeSalvo claimed to have committed two thousand rapes and attacks over a period of eight or nine years. To the cops and lawyers and shrinks who knew DeSalvo it was even simpler: Albert DeSalvo wanted to be someone. He wanted to be famous.

But these were inconvenient facts. Alvan Byron had his eye on the governor's office, and Leland Bloom would forever be the lawyer who represented the Boston Strangler. And the city could sleep at night, finally. It did not matter that the end would be inconclusive. That, too, suited the city's mood. Jack Ruby had already ensured an inconclusive end to the JFK murder; here was the local analogue, the smaller, cruder bookend to the national drama. It was as if the men and women of Boston had had enough. They were glad to have the Strangler ordeal behind them. They agreed on a resolution. They wrote their own ending. It was even tacitly assumed that Bloom, by allowing his client to admit to the stranglings, was doing a civic service. He was manipulating the process to the right outcome. Besides, even the Perry Mason of Boston could not exonerate a man who would not stop confessing. DeSalvo was the Strangler—so be it.

Ricky did not buy it. He retreated to the back of the courtroom more convinced than ever that Albert DeSalvo was no more the Strangler than Oswald was a lone crank with a rifle. It was an old story that always worked: History caroms off the unpredictable acts of misfits like DeSalvo and Oswald. We liked to believe it because it was simple, it made the mysterious and incomprehensible seem suddenly very small and manageable. *All that worry and all along it had only been an isolated crackpot.* Ricky knew better. The night Amy was murdered, after all, Albert DeSalvo had been locked up tight at Bridgewater. What if Michael had been right? What if there was not one strangler but several, not one monster but monsters all around? And what if the city was right, too— that there are some facts just too frightening to live with? You could not worry about stranglers forever.

To no one's surprise, the jury did not stay out long. Three hours and forty-five minutes. They came back at five-fifteen, a home-for-dinner verdict. Guilty on all counts. The judge immediately sentenced DeSalvo to life in prison for the simple reason, he explained from the bench, that DeSalvo was the Boston Strangler, *de facto* if not *de jure*. The next morning's *Observer* screamed "DESALVO IS THE STRANGLER," and so it was true, DeSalvo became the Strangler, and the next morning it seemed truer, and the next and the next until no one remembered to question it anymore.

45

The door was heavy steel, ugly, painted black.
Graffiti was etched top to bottom in the black like a
scratchboard, using whatever stylus came to hand,
a key, bottle cap, knife, whatever you had in your
pocket or could pick up off the sidewalk. Whose
marks were they? There were a lot of tenants with
"behavior problems" living here at the Cathedral
Project, people who were hard to place in housing
projects but had to be put somewhere; it was part of
the Housing Authority's mandate. And of course
there were plenty of "behavior problems" in the
neighborhood, too, slouching loiterers with slidy
eyes on every street corner; maybe it had been them
scrabbling against the door after dark, when the
project was locked. Most of the marks were just
strikes lashed in the paint.

Michael pushed against the door, then rattled it,
and finally had to shoulder the thing to get
it squealing open. How, he wondered, did the old
folks who lived here ever get the door open?

Inside he was confronted with a long bank of
battered mailboxes. The Cathedral Project, a

338

yellow-brick monolith between Harrison Avenue and Washington Street near Franklin Square, housed some two thousand low-income tenants. Michael scanned the mailboxes looking for the name and apartment number. Outside, trains clattered by on the elevated line, which straddled Washington Street on paired legs like an enormous centipede, and the mailboxes shivered. He found one with a handwritten card taped to it with foreign-looking numbers. Presumably this was how Europeans wrote their numerals, with a horizontal strike across the middle of the 7 and fishhook tail on the 9. He wandered into the wrong wing of the project looking for number seventy-nine. It took him ten minutes to find the right apartment.

A woman answered through the closed apartment door, "Who is it?"

"Mrs. Cavalcante, it's Michael Daley. I don't know if you remember me."

"You from the Renewal?"

"No. I was the lawyer in your trial, when they took your apartment in the West End. I'm a lawyer. You remember?"

"From the Renewal?"

"No, Mrs. Cavalcante. I'm with the Attorney General's office. I just have a few questions. It's not—you're not in any trouble. Just questions."

Michael could barely remember the old woman. She and her husband were both short and slight, he recalled, and during the brief hearing they had spoken mainly to each other.

339

"I don't want no questions."

"It's about what you said that day, Mrs. Cavalcante. In court. What you said. You said something about gangsters had come to your apartment. *Dinquenti, cinquenti,* something. I'm sorry, I don't speak Italian—I don't remember the word."

A chain rattled, then two locks, and the door opened a crack. An eye peered out, with a dull yellow sclera but alert, flicking up and down, nervous. "*Delinquenti.*"

"*Delinquenti,* yes. *Si.*"

"I remember you." She opened the door now and glared. "I remember you." Propping herself with a cane, she gimped back into the apartment on one dead leg, which she urged forward with a roll of her right hip. "I remember you."

"Did you hurt your leg, Mrs. Cavalcante?"

"My hip. I broke my hip."

"I'm sorry to hear that."

Pssh, she said.

"Should you be walking on it?"

"What else should I do?"

"Rest."

"I already rest. Three weeks I'm in the hospital with all old, sick . . ."

"I'm sorry," Michael said again.

Pssh, she said again.

"Is your husband home?"

"No. He'll be back. What do you want from us now?"

Michael closed the door behind him. "Look, I know how you must feel, Mrs. Cavalcante. I know how it must have looked to you. But there was another side. I had a job to do."

"What do you want from us?"

"Mrs. Cavalcante . . ."

She stared. The old couple had both been small but, Michael recalled, there had been an erect, peasant sturdiness about them. Two tough little brown nuts from some Umbrian hillside. No longer. Whether it was the injury to her hip or the effort of moving, only a few months later Mrs. Cavalcante looked withered, humpbacked.

"I wanted to ask you— I got to thinking about what you said that day, about men coming to your apartment?"

"Do you know what they did, the Renewal? When I was in the hospital with this hip, and the doctors were telling me I would never walk again, I should just stay in bed, do you know what they did? They sent in the movers and they took away my things. Pictures my dead son, dead from twenty years, they take away and they throw them in the trash like nothing. They wait until my husband comes to visit me in the hospital and they do this, they sneak. This is the kind of people. All my dishes, my blankets, my clothes, everything gone. Just like that they come, they take it all. I come home and my apartment is empty. My home twenty years." She stood waiting for an answer from Michael, a confession of remorse. She had checkmated him and an apology was her due.

Michael regarded her—she looked like a comma, standing there with her hump, a curlicue of hard gristle left over from what must once have been a fuller, softer woman—and he knew he could not say what both of them surely realized: that it did not matter, nobody cared. The Cavalcantes had been in the way, and so they had been swept aside and it was done now. There was no point in analyzing the right and wrong of it. Right and wrong had nothing to do with it. It was quaint even to think in terms of the old virtues. You would think she would have learned by now.

"So then I come home," the woman continued, reciting a familiar litany, "and one day while we're asleep they boarded up the building! With us inside! We had to shout out the window till somebody heard and the cops come get us out. We could've been killed in there, they could have knocked down the whole thing and buried us.

"Then they send us up to Lenox Street, this tiny little apartment where you can't even turn around. And you can't go out at night. It's all colored, drinkin' and hollerin' all night and day. Knives—they'd soon as slit your throat. We didn't even open the door. They had guys there would knock on your door and push their way right in if you opened it. We didn't like to get killed, so we just sat inside like two crazy people not answering the bell. The social worker had to put her card under the door before we'd even open it. Finally we made a stink about my hip and I can't walk up the stairs, till finally they give us this place. Only forty-seven bucks a month, and that's with the light and gas included."

"It's very nice."

"Not like what we had, though."

"No. I suppose not."

"We're all alone here. Never see the old crowd anymore. They're all out in Medford, South Boston, different projects all over. Most of them went to Medford." She pronounced it *MED-fid*. "Unless they had family somewheres would take them in, they all went to Medford, flew away like birds." She waved her hand. "What am I gonna go to Medford?"

"Mrs. Cavalcante, about that day in court. What did you mean when you said the *delinquenti* had been bothering you back in the West End?"

"Eh,these guys,they come around and say, 'You have to go, everybody has to move out. If you don't move, we'll throw you out.' "

"Who were they?"

"Big guys."

"Did you know any of them?"

"No. I seen 'em around, some of 'em, but I didn't know them."

"You saw them around in the West End?"

"Some, I said. Most we didn't know." She moved to a chair with that oscillating step-lurch and sat down slowly. Michael made tentative gestures to indicate a willingness to help, but she ignored him. She said, "They come at night, they bang on the door, say they got a message for us: 'What do you think you're doing? How come you don't move out like the rest?' They think we're gonna get scared and just go. Where were we gonna go? Huh?

Sometimes there'd even be cops come around, knock-knock-knock, 'Hey, Mrs. C, hey, you should move out someplace else. Hey, it's not safe for you here no more, all these empty buildings, this construction.' "

"What cops?"

"Cops, I don't know."

"Were they in uniform? How do you know they were cops?"

"Because I know! Some was uniform, some wasn't uniform. They were cops."

"Did you know them?"

"Only some. The ones we had in the neighborhood."

"Maybe they were just looking out for you, like they said."

"Like you were looking out for me when you threw me out on the street? I guess I should be lucky—everybody's so busy looking out for me, like a princess."

"The others, the bad guys, did they threaten you?"

"Yeah, they said, 'You gotta go, you gotta go.' It was all the same: 'It's not safe for you here no more.' "

"Did they do anything to frighten you?"

"Sometimes they called on the phone. 'If you don't get out, we're gonna shoot you, hey, we're gonna burn down your building.' One of them told my husband he should watch out, he could fall down the stairs in the building and nobody'd ever find him."

"In court that day, you called them gangsters. Did you mean real gangsters?"

"I said *delinquenti*—criminals. I don't know from gangsters. What, you don't think a cop can be a bad guy? You should see. How come you're so concerned all of a sudden?"

"Because somebody got hurt."

"Somebody who?"

My father, Michael thought but did not say. When he had been a kid, the Daleys received threatening phone calls too, usually at dinnertime, from cons Joe Senior had put away. The calls would come from Walpole or Deer Island. Michael or one of his brothers would answer the phone to a grinding voice, *I'm gonna burn down your fuckin' house, I'm gonna fuck your wife, I'm gonna cut up your kids, I'm gonna shoot you in the fuckin' head*. The calls continued all the years Joe Senior was in various detective bureaus and Homicide. Michael hung up the phone as soon as he heard the first bad words, just as he had been told to do, but he could not un-hear them. How had his father, a gentle man who submitted himself to be pig-piled and horse-ridden and smart-alecked by his sons, mastered these killers? "Don't you worry, Mike," his dad used to say. "Big man hiding behind a phone." But his dad did worry, and Michael worried too. One of these men might escape his cage and come find Michael and mutilate him. Would Michael sacrifice one of his brothers to save himself? It would be best, he understood, if the animal ate Joe and let Ricky and Michael run away. But in a pinch it was clear

Michael would have to let himself be devoured to save Ricky, who must be saved. Would he have the courage to surrender to it? What would it feel like when adult hands engaged Michael's body and cracked it, or a knife unzipped his skin, or a spinning bullet drilled into him? When he was five or six, Michael had been shocked when his dad took him fishing at Jamaica Pond and blithely yanked the hooks from the sunfish they caught, tearing ragged holes in their jaws, cheeks, and eye sockets as the fish arched their bodies in agony. Michael had told him to stop. His dad had tried to appease him, first by saying that the fish could not feel pain because their brains were too small, then that the wounds would heal after they were flipped back into the water. Neither was plausible, and Michael decided not to fish anymore, ever. "What a pussy," Joe had said, and no one argued the point. After that, Dad had taken Joe and Ricky fishing in Jamaica Pond, and none of them seemed troubled by the suffering of the fishes. So maybe it just did not matter.

"A cop got hurt, Mrs. Cavalcante."

"*Pssh*. A cop gets hurt and everyone comes running."

"This one was a good guy. Not a *delinquenti*."

46

"The fuck is this, Rick?"

"Edith Piaf."

"Edith Piaf. Fuckin' Cambridge."

"She's French."

"Well, I know she's French. That's not my point."

"You know Edith Piaf?"

"No, dummy, I can hear. She's singing French. I've been to France, remember? She'd be singin' German if it wasn't for me."

"Good thing you went, then."

"What kind of place puts Edith Piaf on the fuckin' jukebox?"

"The customers must like it."

"Exactly. That's my point. What kind of people come to a place like this?"

"Me."

"See, there you go."

"You said pick a place you wouldn't see anyone you know. Trust me, no one you know comes here."

"Why would they?" Joe looked around the place, a scruffy basement bar called the Casablanca—the Casa B, everyone called it—on

347

Brattle Street in Harvard Square. He snorted. What a scene. Couple of boho hippy poets needing a bath and a haircut. Skinny Harvard rich kids needing a wising-up before they went off and became stockbrokers. Dumpy Cambridge broads looking like washerwomen."Jesus, Rick, I could see Michael hanging around a place like this. I figured you knew better."

"Sorry to let you down."

"What are you doing out here anyway? Who would want to live in Cambridge?"

"It's better not to live where you work."

"Yeah? Why's that?"

"I cross that river, I'm in Middlesex County. Different cops, different D.A.'s. Nobody knows me here, no hassles."

Joe nodded. He scraped his beer bottle with a thumbnail, distracted.

"Relax, Joe. I just told you, you're out of your jurisdiction."

"I don't give a shit. Do whatever you want. What, you think I'm gonna arrest you?" But Joe's disdain seemed to have exhausted itself on Edith Piaf and the Cambridge hippy scene, and he fell quiet.

Ricky did not know exactly what to make of it. What was Joe up to? What was going on in that massive head of his? Ricky always went a little crazy with Joe. All that firstborn's confidence and facile conservatism, the dense, bullying, confrontational manner, the reflexive, arrogant, empty-headed, aggressive xenophobia . . . Joe was

Ricky's negative image. If they had not been brothers, Ricky was sure, they would never have been friends. As it was, they needed Michael as a middleman. Alone, there was a relentless fractious undercurrent to their conversations, as if their thirty-year relationship had been a single ongoing argument. But, in the way of brothers, Ricky could not completely escape admiring Joe, who had, after all, willingly accepted the weight of their patrimony. Fatherhood, husbandhood, cophood— all the things Ricky did not want and doubted he could sustain, Joe took on his shoulders and dead-lifted every day. You had to see Joe the way Kat saw him, Ricky figured: firm, not stubborn; doggishly loyal, not just a company man. Still, Ricky was never sure how to reach Joe.

Chuck Berry came on the jukebox, "Sweet Little Rock 'n' Roller."

Joe dipped his head in a stiff, rheumatic way to the beat. Not exactly his style, but getting there.

"Well, come on, Joe," Ricky said, "you sat through Edith Piaf. Whatever it was you had to say, you might as well get it off your chest."

"I'm supposed to give you a message."

"From who?"

"Gargano."

Ricky felt a freeze. It began between his shoulder blades and washed up the back of his neck. He smothered it as best he could, permitting himself just the slightest rustle of his shoulders, as if he were resettling a jacket that had begun to slip off.

"It's about that Copley thing. They think you've

got the stones. They want the stones, is all. He says they just want the stones back and that's all it is. That'll be the end of it."

"You believe that, Joe?"

"I don't know, Rick. These guys . . ."

"Yeah."

"If you've got the stones, just give them up. Don't fool around with this. I don't care how much they're worth."

"It's not about that. If those guys think I did that job, I'm dead. Whether they get the stones or not."

"Did you do it?"

"Joe, I can't— You really want to know? You can't tell them anything you don't know. And they're gonna ask you."

"They won't believe me anyways, whatever I say."

"Still."

Joe nodded.

"Gargano told me you got yourself in a hole, Joe."

"When was that?"

"Few months ago. He came looking for me about this. He mentioned you."

"Yeah, well, it's a bigger hole now."

"How big?"

"Big."

"I can get you the cash."

"It's a lot of cash, Rick."

"I can get anything you need."

Joe shook his head.

"Anything."

"Doesn't matter. They're not gonna let me out. I'm a witness now. If I go to the feds, I could have Gargano locked up by suppertime. They aren't gonna let me just walk away from this."

"Fuck, Joe, why didn't you come to me? I've got money."

"We never— I don't know, Rick. It was like, I had it under control. That was the thing. I did. It's not like I never got in a little hole before. That's how the thing works: you go up, you go down, it's all part of it. You can't let it bother you. I kept figuring it'd turn around. Only this time I just kept going down and down and down. But I had it under control. It was like, it happened real slow and then real fast. Real fast."

Ricky massaged his eyes with the fingertips of one hand.

"Ricky, I'd just as soon Kat doesn't know about this. We got enough trouble already, alright?"

"She's gonna find out eventually, one way or the other."

"Let's make it 'the other,' okay?"

"Okay. How about Michael?"

"Let's just keep it you and me for now."

Ricky made a disapproving face but said nothing.

"What do you want me to tell them about the stones, Rick?"

"Tell them I don't know anything about it."

"It's not gonna be the end of it."

"I know."

"So what are you gonna do?"

"Don't know yet. What are you gonna do?"

"Don't know yet."

"Is this all they've got you doing, squeezing poor guys like me?"

"No. I do some other stuff, too."

"Kind of stuff?"

"I'd rather not talk about it.'If you don't know anything,'like you said."

"Maybe we should go away somewhere for a while."

"We could go to Ireland. Always wanted to go to Ireland."

"That's an idea. We'd fit right in."

"You could go to France. Fag."

"You know, what if I walk out of here and these guys shoot me?

That's gonna be the last thing you ever said to me, calling me a fag. You're gonna feel like shit."

"I'll get over it. I'll listen to a little Edith Peeaff. That'll make me feel better."

"I'm serious, Joe. If I go somewhere, to France or whatever, you want to come? They won't find you."

"France?"

"It's better since the Germans left. Trust me."

"What happened to Ireland?"

"Alright, Ireland."

"I can't. I got a family."

"Bring 'em."

"What'll we do there?"

"I told you, I've got cash. We won't have to do anything. We'll sit under a shamrock tree all day."

"What about Little Joe?"

"They've got kids over there. He'll make friends."

"For how long?"

"Till it blows over."

Joe frowned.

Ricky's eyes fell.

It was never going to blow over. These guys were not going to forget, much less forgive. If the brothers left, it would be forever.

"Can't do it, Ricky. This is where I live. Imagine me in Paris."

"Think about it."

"Yeah, okay, right. I'll think about it."

"Maybe one day you'll wake up and I'll be gone, y'know?"

" 'Kay." Joe studied the tabletop. He refused to lift his eyes.

"Not tomorrow, Joe. I'm not going anywhere tomorrow."

"Good."

47

At mid-morning, Michael stood in the doorway of
the BPD Homicide office at Berkeley Street. He did
not like coming here, where Joe Senior had worked
and where his murder had been investigated,
inconclusively. To Michael, this was still his father's
office. Two long rectangular rooms side by side,
sergeants on one side, detectives on the other. In
the detectives' room, second from the end, was the
desk that had been Joe Senior's. It reminded
Michael, yet again, of the awesome moment when
his father had ribboned down to the ground and for
the Daleys everything went to shit.

So he paused at the threshold and forced himself
to see the place in perspective, to realize that it was
just a room after all. Empty but for a single
detective, Tom Hart, who studied a pile of papers.
On the wall opposite, the row of windows faced the
Hancock building, each at a slightly different angle,
like frames in a film strip. The overhead lights were
off, and the shadow of an ailanthus tree outside
dappled the wall.

Tom Hart had not been a friend of Joe Senior's

the way Brendan Conroy had been. The two had never played handball at the Y or drunk after work or visited on Christmas. Hart had been a protégé. Once upon a time, Joe Senior had taught him how to work a homicide case, and forever after, Tom Hart's view of the elder Daley was tinged with the sort of schoolboy admiration younger men often form for older ones. Balding as a forty-year-old when he first came to Homicide, now at fifty Hart was just plain bald. He brushed his remaining gray hairs straight back and out of the way, and meeting him, you saw his handsome, ram-jawed, granitic head as a single piece rather than an assemblage of parts, like a bust carved from a single block of stone. He was the ranking detective in the squad, number three in terms of seniority behind the commander and Conroy, but probably higher in the eyes of his peers who saw him as a "good cop" in every sense of the adjective.

Hart noticed Michael and greeted him warmly. He escorted Michael to a chair with one arm crooked in the air a foot or so above Michael's shoulders, protectively, as if he were shepherding an invalid or an idiot to a wheelchair.

"Where is everybody?" Michael asked.

Hart's eyes swept across the empty room. The office was lightly staffed: eight detectives and eight sergeants for an entire city, working staggered shifts, with cases assigned to whoever happened to be working when the call came in. It was not a job for deskmen. "Out working," Hart said, "what do you think?"

"We alone here?"

"For the moment."

"Well, maybe we could go somewhere? In private. There's something I need to talk to you about."

"Something wrong?"

"No, no. Never better. I have some information. I'd rather not be attached to it."

"So why'd you call me? You've got a houseful of cops over there. I thought Brendan Conroy was . . . well, whatever."

"There's all different kinds of cops, Tom. Brendan's not the kind I need right now. You are."

"What kind is that?"

"Kind I can trust. Tom, you knew my dad. I need someone who'll handle things the way he would if he was here, for me and my brothers."

A little riffle stirred Hart's features. "Alright, come on."

They shut themselves in the commander's office at the end of the room. It was the same office where, months before, Michael himself had interrogated the giant, Arthur Nast, and linked him at the least to one of the Strangler murders. Behind the little mirror on the wall was a peephole, Michael recalled. The intimacy of a sub rosa meeting in here was, or might be, an illusion. But what could you do? You had to trust someone, and Tom Hart was as good as a priest. Better, actually: a priest with a size-thirteen boot and a nine-millimeter in his desk, both of which might come in handy if it turned out God was otherwise occupied at a prayerful moment.

"Alright, then. So what was so important?"

"It's about the Strangler."

"Not our case. You know that. Take it to Wamsley."

"This is a case he doesn't know what to do with: Amy Ryan. All Wamsley has is DeSalvo. And even DeSalvo can't figure out a way to confess to it; he was in Bridgewater when it happened."

"Well, it's still the A.G.'s case until I hear different."

"It's an unsolved murder in the city of Boston, Tom. You want to leave it to that fruitcake so he can call in a psychic to solve it for him?"

The fruitcake in question, of course, was Wamsley, who had in fact hired a psychic to fly into Boston early in the Strangler investigation. It had fallen to Tom Hart to escort this man discreetly around the city, even bunk with him at a hotel in Lexington. The whole thing had made Wamsley a laughingstock among cops, who had more colorful names for George Wamsley than fruitcake.

"Alright, Michael. No harm in listening, I guess."

"I have a friend with an interest in the case. Someone who's completely trustworthy."

"Who? I need a name."

"This is in confidence. It's someone close to me."

"I still need the name. You can trust me, you know that."

"My friend can open doors."

"Ah. That one."

"You remember Kurt Lindstrom? He was a suspect in some of the stranglings."

357

"The Symphony guy. Othello."

"Right. Well, my friend has, by ... um ... arguably extralegal means, he got into Lindstrom's apartment. He wants you to know what he found there. He says Lindstrom has bloodstained panties. At least it looked like blood. He says the panties are big, like a girdle, like the kind an old woman would wear. And there's magazines, porno but not the regular stuff—women getting raped and killed."

"So? The guy likes porn. So do I. So do you."

"It's not just that. My friend says there's pictures there that look like they come straight from the Strangler murders: women tied, tortured, strangled with ropes tied off in a bow. Lindstrom lives on Symphony Road, right around the corner from Helena Jalelian, the first victim."

"Jalakian."

"Jalakian. She was a Symphony fan, remember? She must have seen him at some point. She probably would have let him in. And the alley behind her apartment goes right down to Lindstrom's building. He could have strangled her and got home without ever showing his face on the street."

"And what do you—what does your friend—suggest we do?"

"Get a warrant, today. Put all this in an affidavit, get a warrant, and get in there."

"Get a warrant for a murder DeSalvo's already confessed to?"

"Confessed isn't convicted. Come on, Tom, you see where this is headed. There isn't going to be a trial. Wamsley doesn't have a case. There's no evidence against DeSalvo. The confession's not admissible. Even if it were, it's not enough to convict. The guy was in a mental hospital when he confessed. So Wamsley'll let it drop, DeSalvo'll rot in Walpole, and everybody goes home happy. Meanwhile Lindstrom is still out on the street. Are you going to leave him out there, when I've just told you he has Helena Jalakian's bloody girdle in his sock drawer?"

"You don't know either that it's Helena's or that it's bloody."

"How much proof do you need, Tom, before you *start* investigating?"

"Michael. No judge is going to open up those Strangler cases without Wamsley's sayso. There hasn't been a strangling in nearly six months, since Amy Ryan. I know DeSalvo was in custody when Amy was killed. Still, it's been a long quiet period. Now, if you could link this guy to Amy somehow, we might have something. Otherwise, I'll never get a warrant with just that tip; your 'friend' is a thief."

"Who among us is without sin?"

"Not him, certainly."

"Look, Tom, he asked me to give you the information. You do what you think is right with it. It's up to you."

"Tell you what: I'll look into it, see if I can get the Strangler Bureau people to reconsider at least that Jalakian case. But I wouldn't hold my breath. Nobody wants to talk about this anymore. The Amy Ryan case, obviously that's a different thing. But you haven't made that link yet."

"Alright. I'll tell him. And you'll keep my friend out of it, right, Tom?"

"I'll keep him out of it. Tell him, from now on leave the police work to the police."

48

The view from Kurt Lindstrom's bay window at mid-afternoon:

A half block away, on the opposite side of Hemenway Street, people clustered at a bus stop. There were eight of them, four young women, apparently students; one young man in a beatnik-style hooded overshirt and floppy-brimmed leather hat; one man in a business suit; a heavyset Negro woman with a shopping bag from Jordan Marsh; and a thin man in a navy Boston Edison repairman's uniform. A bus arrived from the right. It filled the view, a wall of sooty fluted steel and parallelogram windows. After a few seconds the air brakes sighed and the bus pulled away, sliding out of the left side of the window frame, and revealing the sidewalk empty again, empty except for the Edison repairman, who stood alone. After a time, he was joined by a woman. She faced left to watch for the next bus. The Edison man stared straight ahead, though, across the street, apparently to this very window. He was Ricky Daley.

49

Sap gloves were leather gloves with powdered shot sewn into the knuckles. The shot, seven or eight ounces of steel or lead, was ground fine enough that it would form to the knuckles. For a hundred years, they were the copper's secret weapon when wading into a bar brawl or street riot or other slurry of blood. Joe's pair was well worn. When he laid them down the fingers curled exactly as his own fingers would, and when he glimpsed them at rest in his locker or glove compartment, palm to palm like praying hands, they stirred an emotion in him that was very like love. We adore certain objects because they are in one way or another extensions of our own egos, and so it was with Joe's sap gloves. He did not consider them weapons because, unlike a gun or a knife, they did not endow him with an ability he did not already have; they simply improved his own nature, like eyeglasses. On his hands, they became part of him. The weapon was still the punch. But with the sap gloves, a good hard punch became a stunner, and a stunning punch became a knockout. What a high, to throw a fist so enhanced, so weighted and unbreakable—to spread your legs and get a good base under you, and with your own thighs, hips, back, and shoulders to whirl up such bone-crushing power. And all with no change in your appearance except those ordinary-looking black gloves.

"Finish it," Gargano said.

Joe was panting and sweaty.

At his feet a man lay balled on the concrete floor. The man's filthy raincoat trailed away behind him, like a sleeping child's tossed-off blanket.

"Come on, stand up."

"No."

"Get up, asshole!"

"No!"

Gargano intervened. He said in low voice, "Stand the fuck up, you piece of shit, or you'll never get off that floor."

The guy's name was Slots. He booked out of a bar called Chiambi's, a bucket of blood near the corner of Bennington and Brooks in East Boston. He was a numbers guy but had also been a roughneck in his day and he was slow to accept the new order. For a while he had refused to pay any tribute at all to Charlie Capobianco, which had earned him an educational beating. Then his payments had slipped again and The Office had noticed because Capobianco always noticed when money went missing. The boss's first impulse was to squash the guy out, but someone in The Office had intervened on behalf of Slots, some friend of a friend of Nicky Capobianco, another North End book named Gerry

Angiulo—Joe could never keep it all straight, all the crazy dago names and shifting alliances. Alls he knew was that by some shadowy miracle Slots—whose nickname referred to the fact that he had lost an arm in the Pacific twenty years before and was said to resemble a right-armed slot machine—was not scheduled to check out on this night, although he might have wished otherwise by the end. A couple of Gargano's men had driven Slots to a bar up on Blue Hill Avenue. The place was owned by Gargano. Its basement, mildewy and cluttered with beer cases, was the last thing a lot of guys ever saw.

"Shoulda stuck him in a chair." Gargano sighed ruefully. He turned to his guys. "Get him up."

Slots was yanked to his feet.

"Go ahead, Joe, we don't got all night," Gargano said.

Slots gave Joe a bleary smile, which Joe admired. The guy had balls. Already he looked pretty bad. His face was beef red. His right eye had swelled nearly shut.

Joe hefted his gloved fist, cocked it by his ear, and fired it at the corner of the man's left eye, where the heavy bones of the skull thinned into the more delicate orbital bones of the eye. Through the steel on his knuckles he felt the side of the face give way, the skin, the bony substructure, the mush behind it all.

Slots's head snapped back and his knees gave way simultaneously. He arched down and backward like a dancer, already unconscious, hung there, then collapsed.

"Alright, go clean yourself up, Joe."

Joe stared at the sprawled body. Blood was smeared on the floor and on the man's clothes. Joe searched his head for a thought, a reaction, but there was nothing, not remorse or pity, not even a practical concern for his own situation (a clean shirt, a ride home). The nullity was not unpleasant. Just a white, open space to drift in.

"There's a sink right over there."

"I know where it is."

"Don't put your shirt back on. First take off that undershirt, leave it here."

"Alright."

"Hell of a fuckin' shot you got there." Gargano snorted to the other two, "D'you see that? Jesus Christ, that was fuckin' beautiful, man. Fuckin' A. Just fuckin' beautiful."

Joe shuffled between the stacks of cardboard liquor cases. The sink was on the opposite side of the basement. He did not like to think about what might have been rinsed down the drain of that sink over the years. Not just beer, certainly. He heard his own panting, felt the weight of the gloves dangling from his arms. He paused to look back down the aisle between the boxes.

Gargano took off his jacket and laid it aside. He wore a scarlet pimp shirt, slim black slacks, and mod ankle boots with a big finger-loop in the back. His gut bulked against the shirt fabric. Gargano looked down at the unconscious body and sighed again. A single red brick lay on the floor nearby, tossed away by someone, misplaced— the building was wood with a poured concrete foundation, not a brick in it except this one. Gargano picked the brick up, raised the right leg of the body, and slid the brick under the knee so that the joint was flexed a few inches off the concrete floor. He stood, raised his own leg up like a drum major, then stomped down on the man's shin, just below the knee. The tibia dislocated with a *snick*. Gargano slipped the brick out, came around the body, and propped the other leg the same way. He stomped again, just once, like a good carpenter driving a nail with one slap of his hammer.

50

Ricky stepped through the window out onto the fire escape and he smiled. It was laughably easy—like some low-rent junkie step-over artist, the bums who made a living out of climbing fire escapes and literally stepping over the side to enter apartments through open windows or reaching in and grabbing whatever they could. Imagine, taking that sort of chance! If it weren't so stupid, Ricky might have admired the courage of these idiots. He lowered the window behind him, checked up and down the alley, then smashed the single big pane with a jab of his foot. The shattering glass made a cymbal-crash. Gingerly he raised the window sash again. Was that the way they did it? He guessed so. It certainly looked messy enough. He descended the stairs like a debutante and rode the drop-ladder down to the sidewalk.

A block away, at the corner of Hemenway and Westland Avenue, he called the police from a phone booth.

"Station Sixteen."

"Yes, I'd like to report a burglary."

"What is your name, sir?"

"I'd rather not get involved. I'm just a concerned citizen. The address is fifty Symphony Road, apartment seven."

"Alright, we'll send someone right over."

"Okay, and listen, can you do me a favor? I think you better call Tom Hart in Homicide and tell him Kurt Lindstrom's apartment just got broken into and there'll be cops inside there."

"Excuse me?"

An hour later, the Daley brothers waited together on Symphony Road, across the street from number fifty. In the dim New England light—like a bulb burning out—the three of them appeared to smolder in hues of dull gray. Michael stood front and center, arms folded, watching patiently. Joe hulked behind, at Michael's shoulder. Some part of Joe was always in motion: a hand explored a pocket, his head cricked this way or that, his foot pawed the sidewalk. Ricky had retreated to a stoop to smoke a butt. He alone seemed to realize the process would take a while.

A black-and-white cruiser and an unmarked car were double-parked in front of number fifty.

At length, Tom Hart came out of the building. He wore a crumpled fedora on his bald head. He made his way around the unmarked car to the driver's door, which brought him within a dozen feet of the brothers. He caught Michael's eye and shook his head with a little frown. Nothing. They had found nothing.

51

At McGrail's, in a corner booth, his back against the wall and one foot up on the bench, Ricky smoked a butt and watched the door. Between drags his hand, with the cigarette angled outward like a dislocated sixth finger, sought out the ashtray and rotated it on the table. Ricky liked bars in mid-afternoon, when they were empty or nearly so. The bready smell of stale beer. The damp stink of twice-breathed air. It was three o'clock. Shafts of weak sunlight angled from high transom windows, flecked with dust motes that densified and textured the light, and created the illusion that the shafts were things you could touch. The light reminded him of empty churches. It had the captured quality of church light, of daylight diffused through stained glass, a perpetual late-afternoon of empty pews and cool stone walls.

Stan Gedaminski came in and stood by the door, turning a scally cap in his hands, sniffing the air. Apparently he did not like what he saw. The bartender was missing. Three barflies slumped on nonadjacent stools. One of these men, sensing a policeman in the environment, sloped off hastily to the bathroom.

Ricky waved with his cigarette hand, and Gedaminski slid onto the bench opposite him.

"You want something to drink, Stan?"

"I'm working."

Ricky shrugged.

"Jesus, Rick. What are you doin' here, a grown man, on a weekday? It's the middle of the afternoon, for Christ's sake. Like a bum."

"When should I come?"

"After work."

"I got the day off."

"Then go do something useful. It's not right."

Ricky doodled with his cigarette ash in the ashtray, shaping it into a cone. He smiled wryly. Something about Stan Gedaminski he liked. "What's on your mind, Stan, besides my bad habits?"

"I thought you might want to make a statement about that Copley thing. The diamonds."

"I told you, I don't know nuthin' about nuthin'."

"You may want to think about that. I got a witness from the hotel, a lady in the room across the hall. She puts you coming out of that room around the time of the robbery."

"She's got it wrong. Whoever she is."

"She says you helped unlock her door for her. Remembers you clear as day."

Ricky made a face: *So what do you want me to do?*

"I could arrest you now. I've got P.C."

"So do it."

"Just, if I was you, I wouldn't leave home without my toothbrush from now on, just in case. Now's I got a witness, I figured you'd be smart enough to tell me what the hell you were doing in that hotel if you weren't there to steal."

"Is that what you figured? Or did you figure you still don't have enough?"

No response.

"Something you should know, Stan: I've got an alibi. I was right here. Bartender'll vouch for me. Anyway, you don't have the stones. The grand jury's gonna want to know: If I took all those diamonds, where are they? Where's the evidence—where's the money, where're the stones? I don't have it, Stan. You know why? Because I didn't do it."

"We're still running down the fences."

"Can I tell you something, Stan, off the record?"

"Depends what it is. I'll decide what's off the record."

"There's a rumor going around, those stones belonged to Charlie Capobianco. The jeweler was a protected guy. Now Capobianco's got his stalkers out looking for who did it."

"I heard that."

"All I'm sayin' is, if you're gonna charge somebody, Stan, just make sure you get the right guy. And don't run around saying you *think* this guy or that guy did the job, alright? 'Cause there's not gonna be a trial. Whoever you charge, he'll go into Charles Street and he won't come out, and you know it." Charles Street Jail was where defendants were held pretrial. "Vinnie Gargano'll reach him there same as on the street. He's got more guys in that place than you do."

Gedaminski nodded.

"If you want to arrest me, fine. You got a job to do. There's no hard feelings. But if you can't make the case, Stan—*Stan*—if you can't make the case, you keep my name out of it. Don't just nod, Stan, say it. Tell me I have your word. This is serious. This is my life we're talking about here. Tell me I have your word."

"Alright. You have my word."

"Okay. That's good enough for me."

"You know, I got a call a few days ago about a B-and-E on Symphony Road."

"Yeah?"

"Some guy picked the lock, walked in the front door, then for some reason he broke the back window from the outside. Just like the Copley job. Nice, clean job on the lock, too. Good burglar."

"*Pfft*, people. Can't be too careful these days."

"Funny, those two jobs looking so much alike, isn't it? Guy like you wouldn't fall into a pattern like that, though, would ya? Too smart. The great Rick Daley."

"I don't know what you're talking about, Stan. I don't know why any burglar'd be working in that neighborhood anyway. Nothing worth taking. Sounds like an amateur. Some junkie."

Gedaminski snorted. "Hey, what do I give a shit? 'Tween you and me, if that Lindstrom character had something to do with your girlfriend there, then

372

fuck 'm. You three can do whatever the hell you want. This Copley thing, though, I'm not gonna stop. I'm gonna check every fence, every jeweler, I'm gonna dig up your front yard if I have to. If I find those stones, even one of 'em—if I find those stones, there'll be no free pass on that one, Capobianco or no Capobianco. I like you, Rick. But I don't like you that much."

52

"Can I help you with those?"

Margaret Daley hefted a brown paper bag from the trunk of her car, a corner of the bag bunched in her fist. But at the sound of the voice she relaxed the bag back down onto the floor of the trunk and turned. The young man on the sidewalk had an amiable appearance, a full-moon face, his cheeks pinked by the cool spring air, a tousle of dirty-blond hair. She guessed he was thirty, maybe a little older. He wore a white oxford shirt and khakis, all very wrinkled—the Brooks Brothers uniform of Michael's Harvard pals. Is that what he was, a Harvard rich boy? There was a boyish quality to him, certainly. Probably one of those men who retain a childish aspect right into old age, a boy in a man's body. Or maybe, unconsciously, she was just lumping him in with Joe, Michael, and Ricky, who were roughly this young man's age and whom she could not help regarding as eternal children, and so she saw the kid in him. There was something familiar about the boy on the sidewalk, but she could not place it. Maybe she had met and forgotten him. A friend of Michael's maybe. She tended to forget. For all these reasons, and out of a reflexive old habit too, she called him *dear*. She said, "No, dear. I can manage."

"You sure? They look heavy."

"They are heavy."

"Then let me help you! Don't be silly!" He loped forward and, by hugging the grocery bags against his chest, managed to lift them all at once. "Where to?" he asked.

"I— Are you sure you can carry all that?"

"Of course. 'Screw your courage to the sticking place, and we'll not fail.' "

Margaret searched his face. "You're not from around here. I'd know you."

"No. But I'm happy to help."

"Well," Margaret said, relenting, warming, "aren't you the gentleman." She pulled her keys out of her pocketbook and led the young man up the front stairs.

"I like the basketball net out front," he said in his affable way. His eyes were on her ankles.

"Yes. My children."

"I'm something of a basketball aficionado myself."

"Are you?"

"Not a very good player, I'm afraid. More of a fan. But I do love it. That's the thing, don't you think? To love whatever you do."

"I suppose."

"The people who excel in life, who really leave their mark, that's what they have that ordinary people don't: enthusiasm."

"I guess. I didn't catch your name."

"It's Kurt."

"Kurt what?"

"Lindstrom."

"What kind of name is that, dear? German?"

"Swedish."

"I never met anyone Swedish."

"Well, my great-grandfather was Swedish, but I'm not. I'm a mutt." He smiled.

"We're all mutts. Lord only knows where half the people around here come from."

"Lord only knows."

She unlocked the door and swung it open. Not long before, she would not have let a stranger into her house. But now DeSalvo was behind bars. Life had begun to return to normal. She said, "Kitchen's straight through there, in the back."

The young man beetled through the living room under the load of grocery bags, eyes flicking left and right, at the living-room sofa, the fireplace, the television, the stairs. In the kitchen he put the bags on the counter and took a moment to scan that room as well.

Margaret,at the kitchen door,said, "Thank you.A true gentleman."

"May I have a glass of water, please?"

"Sure."

She indicated with a gesture that he was blocking the cabinet where the drinking glasses were kept, and he stepped aside. She got a glass down for him and filled it from the tap. She felt, or thought she felt, his eyes on her. Her left hand moved to the

side of her neck and covered it, a gesture she disguised by pretending to straighten the hair behind
her ear. She handed him the glass then moved to
the counter opposite, to create a space between
them.

"This is a lovely old house," he said.

"Nothing fancy."

"Doesn't have to be fancy to be lovely. How old
is it?"

"I don't know, really."

"I never got your name."

"Margaret Daley."

"Margaret. Lovely. Like the princess." He sipped.
His eyes darted around the room, ticking off the
toaster, a heavy cutting board on the counter, a cut-
glass vase in the window above the sink. He went
to a picture on the wall. "Is this your family?"

"Yes."

"Three sons?"

"Yes."

"Very handsome. And this is your husband?"

"Yes. That's Joe."

"And where is he?"

"He's passed away."

"Oh, I'm so sorry, Margaret."

Tsk, she said, shrugging the subject away. "Well,
thank you for lugging those groceries. I don't know
what I would've done."

His eyes returned to her face then drifted downward so that, by the time he spoke, they seemed to
have settled around her chest. "It's nothing." He
flipped a lock of hair off his forehead. "Anything

else I can do? Anything need fixing? Old houses like these, things fall apart. I'm pretty handy."

"No. Nothing needs fixing."

"Shall I take a look around, just to be sure?"

"No. It's alright."

"Well, then." He came toward her, reached out, and placed his half-empty glass on the counter beside her, then moved back again. "I guess that's it, then."

"I'll show you out."

"Alright." He waved his arm, inviting her to lead him through the kitchen door.

"No, no, please. After you."

She had stepped closer now, within arm's length—the kitchen was small—and again he reached out toward her. "This is lovely." He lifted the pendant of a necklace she wore, a gold crucifix with ornate scrollwork. She felt his hand at the open neck of her dress. The edges of his fingernails scratched across her skin, then the coarse crusted skin of his knuckles came to rest on her collarbone, dry and cool at the hollow of her throat. "Where did you get this?"

She leaned back a little but decided that the boy was just being inappropriate, not threatening. It would be a relief to have him out of the house but, projecting herself a few seconds into the future, she did not want to remember his visit as frightening in any way. He had done nothing to alarm her, and so her apprehensiveness seemed to be just old-age anxiety. She shooed it out of her mind. She was not old. Not some vulnerable, helpless, brittle old woman. There was also, of course, the hint of a sexual offer in his touch, but she was too old for that, and he was rather effeminate, probably a homo. She could hear her three sons ridiculing her for even suggesting a much younger man had made a pass at her. So she consciously decided not to be put off by his gesture, but to ignore it. She lifted the pendant out of his hand and slipped away from him, through the kitchen door. "Never mind where I got it," she said. "I don't remember anyways."

"Too bad. I thought my mother might like one just like it."

"I don't remember where I got it."

She reached the front door and held it open for him. She was relieved to have the open door beside her, the street noise, daylight.

They were not quite so alone now.

"I'm sorry, Margaret. Did I say something wrong?"

"No."

"You seem upset."

"I just have things to do."

"Alright, then." He extended his hand, with the pink palm turned halfway up,for her to shake."It was very nice meeting you.Maybe I'll see you again somewhere. Around the neighborhood, maybe."

She regarded his hand a moment before shaking it once, curtly. Its warmth surprised her. "Maybe."

He made another of his amiable grins and went off down the stairs with that queer loping stride of his.

She closed the door and, quietly, lest he hear, she slid the chainlock into its groove.

Margaret tended to see in her three sons very specific aspects of her husband, so that, like a triptych or a tailor's three-sided mirror, together the boys formed a picture of their father. Joe's temper and Ricky's sneakiness—both qualities were inherited from her husband, though in him they had been just facets. Michael's melancholy had been his father's, too, though again Joe Senior had managed it better. Fully expressed in Michael, Margaret did not know quite how to respond to it. She had a tin ear for that sort of thing, and she knew it. But she could not help seeing how attractive Michael's involution was. It was the Irishest thing about him, that melancholy, maybe the only genuinely Irish thing—though he was vindictive, too, which she also admired—and she felt that even when he made good—when he finally got married and moved to the suburbs and "passed" for a Harvard Yankee the way some coloreds passed as white—he would still have that Irish fatalism in him, that little bit of unsmiling Dorchester to stain him forever.

It was to Michael that she confided her unease about that odd boy Kurt Lindstrom. She waited till evening to phone him, and she related the story in an offhand way—". . . oh, the strangest thing, dear . . ."—which was her habit. Fortress Margaret did not betray her upset; even her husband's sudden death had been endured without keening or self-pity. But in her indirect way, she signaled something was not right. Michael's reaction surprised her. He ordered his mother to go next door immediately and call Joe to come get her. Michael was going to speak with Lindstrom himself, to set him straight. Maybe he would bring Ricky along, too. The decisions and the tone were so far out of character, Margaret did not know what to make of it. In their brief conversation, Michael never did inform her who on earth this Kurt Lindstrom was.

That she followed his orders anyway, without question, and that Joe then did the same, seemed momentous to Margaret. Without discussion, the captaincy of the family was passing to diffident, moody Michael, who wanted it least and who, Margaret had always assumed, was the least fit for it. She remembered him at four years old when he had got sick with spinal meningitis. The doctor had set his chances at fifty-fifty. She could still picture Michael in his hospital bed, arching his back in agony like a small animal. He had survived, of course, which his father interpreted as a sign of the little boy's strength. Margaret read it the other way: her middle son was fragile, weakened. The runt of the litter, bracketed by her two indestructible mastiffs. Now Michael was the one issuing orders to her.

And Margaret herself? She was not old, not yet, but she was—what? Obsolescent. Irrelevant. Her sons did not come to her for advice anymore; they did not want her opinions. If Joe Senior had been alive . . . well, no sense in thinking that way. *What if* did not matter, only *what is*. So the time had come to start taking orders from her boys. Okay, then. Alright. So be it. But she meant to share this thought with Brendan sometime: It was murderous, ruthless, the way younger generations rose up to displace older ones.

53

Once he'd decided on the crime, he was no longer one of them.

They crowded past on the sidewalk. Raucous college girls with pale necks and arms, laughing, stumbling arm in arm, celebrating the first summery evening of spring. An old couple shuffling toward Symphony Hall. Negroes traipsing back to the Mass. Ave. bridge, to the South End, completing their daily migration. They did not know that tonight was special, tonight there would be violence.

Michael knew.

In the pocket of his Baracuta jacket, clasped in his right fist, was a rock. At least it had looked like a rock when he'd first picked it up; on closer inspection it had turned out to be a chunk of concrete. It was heavy, roughly the shape of an egg, fractionally larger than his own fist. Pebbles were embedded in its stippled surface. This concrete egg fit his hand and had a pleasing heft like a wellmade tool. And like a wellmade tool it had an inviting quality: To hold it was to want to use it.

Ricky sat nearby, on a stoop, smoking a butt. "Sit down, Mikey. Don't make a fuss."

"Don't feel like sitting down."

"You're making a fuss."

"I'm not making a fuss. I just don't feel like sitting down, alright?"

"Alright. So stand. I'm just sayin', you're gonna call attention."

"I'm just standing here. What am I gonna call attention?"

"Alright. I'm just sayin'."

That rock in Michael's pocket felt like a mistake, and he seemed to see himself walking away, down Symphony Road toward St. Stephen Street, innocent, empty-handed.

But he could see the appeal of it, too, of lashing out. Armed, ready for action, he no longer felt quite as powerless against the accumulating anxiety. The city and the country beset by enemies. DeSalvo behind bars, but not the Strangler, not Amy's killer certainly. And now the newspapers were speculating that Khrushchev had been behind the Kennedy assassination, still intent on establishing missiles in Cuba to menace us. Meanwhile, the city government had announced the demolition of yet another neighborhood, Barry's Corner in Brighton, triggering a small revolt. Enemies without, conspiracies within. Hidden forces at work. Certainly the Daleys were acquainted with this mood, schooled as they were in the whole impacted Irish thing—a half millennium of impotent, irredentist, mythologized victimhood. At some point wasn't it easier just to pick up a rock?

At last, Lindstrom rounded the corner from Hemenway Street with that jangling looselimbed walk.

"That's him," Ricky said.

Michael glanced up and down the block, and saw no pedestrians, which he took to be a sign that his project was blessed, inevitable. Fate would not grant him a nosy old woman or an alert cop, a prudent excuse to abandon his duty. He started across the street.

"Kurt Lindstrom?"

Lindstrom's face grew puzzled. "Yeah?"

Michael drew the rock out of his pocket. He meant to raise it above his shoulder, to smash it down on the crown of Lindstrom's head. But he did not. He thought of Lindstrom in Margaret's kitchen. He thought of Amy Ryan. His right arm felt paralyzed.

Lindstrom eyed the rock. He took a cautious half-step into the alley, away from Michael. "Yeah?" he repeated.

Michael stepped toward him, but already he knew he would not attack. Already he was asking himself, How far did he intend to take this? If he started, where would he stop? He stood there.

"You stay away from Margaret Daley," Michael said.

"Margaret? You mean the lovely woman with the groceries?"

"Just stay away." Michael let go of the rock. It clattered on the pavement.

385

"Is it a crime to help a woman with her groceries?"

There was a sound. Michael turned to see Ricky coming to join them. Ricky's face registered nothing. Michael was about to tell him it was all over, that he'd said his piece, there was no need for anything more, but Ricky did not stop to listen, did not acknowledge his brother at all.

Ricky picked up the rock at Michael's feet, and in three quick stabbing gestures he smashed the butt end of the rock down on Lindstrom's head. There were two hollow-sounding knocks, the rock striking the helmet of bone under a thin layer of hair and tissue. The third blow made no sound.

With each strike, Lindstrom crumbled a little further until he was kneeling on the pavement, hands pressed to the sides of his head. His blond hair was speckled with red. On his knees, forehead nearly touching the ground, Lindstrom's shirt went snug against his back, revealing a thin torso scooped along the sides like a woman's. The spine rose up in the center, a ridge of peaked bones.

Ricky smashed that ridge, and Lindstrom cried out.

"Michael," Ricky ordered, "stay here. Don't let anyone come back here."

Ricky dragged Lindstrom down the alley, behind the building.

The next minute lasted a year. Michael heard the sounds of his brother beating Lindstrom. The rock made a wet slap as it struck. Lindstrom barked out for help twice. Ricky grunted with effort.

When Michael finally went back there, he found Ricky splashed with blood. His right hand, which held the rock, was literally red. It looked painted. A spatterline of blood droplets was stitched across his face.

Lindstrom lay on his side, covering his head. Tentatively he lowered his arms and his head lolled back.

Ricky stood over him. He seemed to target the broad bone of Lindstrom's exposed forehead. He flipped the rock in his hand so that the narrower tip was exposed at the bottom of his fist—a more concentrated blow to punch a hammerhole in that shell, to shatter it.

"Ricky," Michael said. "Stop."

54

Station One.

Joe pushed into the lobby from the wagon house, into a whirl of coming and going, cops drifting in like a rising tide for the shift change. He meant to get up the stairs to his locker, grab his things, get his car, which was double-parked, run out to the house for supper with Kat and Little Joe, then bolt back into town for a detail at Hayes-Bickford's which he needed because they paid cash on the spot, no waiting, and he needed to turn that cash around to make his nut with Gargano, who cut him no slack for all the work he was doing, all the risks he was taking. Joe always rushed through the stationhouse now. He could not bear to linger. Discreet as he had been about moonlighting as a strong-arm, among cops a taint had attached to him. No one ever said anything. He could not even be sure it was really there. But he seemed to hear disdain in their voices. He thought they swerved to avoid him in the hallway, as if he stank. They fell silent when he entered the locker room. It was not simply that he was crooked, even outstandingly so.

No one knew the true extent of it, Joe was sure, and anyway the rule among cops was "see no evil, speak no evil." The cops who were not on the sleeve, roughly half the force, even if they did begrudge the others their little envelopes of cash, kept their mouths resolutely shut. No, in Joe's case the real problem was that he had managed the whole business so badly. He'd been a fool. He was marked for a bad end, and no one wanted to be standing nearby when it arrived.

The lieutenant on the desk was a hump named Walsh. Big-bodied, dough-faced loudmouth hump with gray hair spit-combed back over his scalp, and a pencil-line smirk. Kind of guy who always had something to say. Walsh called to Joe, "Hey, Detective"—a message in the formality, a jab— "Conroy wants to see you. He's in the pool room."

"What's he want?"

"To give you a medal. The hell do I know?"

"Well, what did he—? Never mind."

Joe cast a yearning look toward the stairs. This was the contingency he could not afford, the surprise that disrupted the whole schedule. Already he began to imagine the complications rippling through the rest of the night: the chilly phone call to Kat to say he would have to skip dinner again, the empty promises he would utter about making it up sometime, and his own sour mood as he loafed around Hayes-Bick's all night. Fuck, he thought. Fuck fuck fuck fuck fuck.

There was a pool table in a room on the first floor of Station One. No one was sure why it was there, who had put it there, or how long it had been there. Certainly no one played much pool. There seemed to be a lot of miles on it, though. The baize had gone milk-white and bald in places, particularly where the balls were racked and where the cue ball was spotted.

Joe found Brendan Conroy alone in this room, contentedly maneuvering his way through a solitary game. Conroy's bulk tended to shrink the table by comparison. In his hands the cue seemed foreshortened, child-sized. But his game was surprisingly delicate and artful. As Joe entered, Conroy neatly pocketed a ball in the corner and drew the cue ball back toward the center of the table with biting backspin.

"You a pool shark, Brendan?"

"How much you got in your pocket?"

"Nothin'. Some gum maybe."

"Guess you won't find out, then."

Conroy surveyed the table. He leaned over the end—stiffly, impeded by his belly—and tapped a deft little touch shot in which the cue ball dawdled from the center of the table to the rail, shouldering the seven ball into the side pocket as it passed. He came around to the side of the table to smack the next ball home along the rail with a happy clack.

"You come here to play pool? 'Cause I got to go. Kat's waiting. She'll have my balls in a vise."

"Let her wait. It'll be good for her."

"Jesus, Bren, you don't know. I got enough trouble."

390

"That's why I'm here. To ease your trouble. You're moving."

"Yeah? Where now?"

"Vice and Narcotics."

"You're shittin' me."

Conroy lowered his eyes to the level of the table, seeking a clear path for the cue ball. "I shit . . . you . . . not."

"You want me to chase hookers around all day?"

"Somebody's got to do it." Conroy boxed the cue ball into a muddle at the far end of the table where it bumbled around without purpose. "Now look what you made me do."

"Brendan, if it's all the same to you, I'd just assume stay where I am. I've got some things workin' here."

"It's not all the same to me. I extended myself on your behalf, boyo."

"I know. It's just—"

"I extended myself and now I expect you to say thank you and listen to sense. You may not think much of Vice and Narcotics, but it's a step up. More money. No victims, no pressure. You want to make captain someday? You've got to learn every aspect of the business. Learn your trade. A good detective can go anywhere, Homicide, Burglary, Vice and Narcotics, doesn't matter."

"I'm no detective, Bren. We both know that."

"You're a good police, Joe."

Joe did not answer.

"You're a good police, and Vice and Narcotics is where you're needed at the moment. And it will

391

serve your purpose as well. Two birds with one stone. Take you away from the North End for a while. Get you over to Berkeley Street; time you started meeting some people who matter, and stop pissing people off."

"What's that mean?"

"This is a small town, boyo."

"And?"

"Little birdie tells me you paid a visit to Farley Sonnenshein."

Joe said nothing.

"Now, why would you go and bother a man like that?"

"I was working a case."

"A B-and-E."

"It's not just a B-and-E."

"No? What is it, then? A few broken windows. They didn't even take anything. What've you got? Trespassing, malicious destruction—misdemeanors. And for that you barge in on a man like Sonnenshein? Foolish."

"B-and-E in the night-time isn't a misdemeanor."

"Don't smart-mouth me, boyo. I don't need a law lesson from you."

"The case won't go down, Brendan."

"It'll go down. They all do. Someone else'll make it go down."

"It's my case. I want to close it."

"Good for you. That's admirable. Now forget it. Go chase hookers and stay out of trouble. Someday you'll thank me. And let's leave Sonnenshein alone. They're the chosen people, Joe. Who are we to

bother 'em? Lord knows, He didn't choose us."
Conroy's pale blue eyes fixed on Joe until the
matter was settled. He then produced an envelope
from an inside coat pocket, laid it on the side of the
table, and went back to his game.

"What's that?"

"Going-away present."

"From who?"

"So many questions, Joe."

"It's from Sonnenshein, isn't it?"

"It's from a general fund."

"Well, I don't want it."

"Oh, don't get your shorts all in a bunch, Joe.
Every cop gets a little something when he leaves
this station, every cop who's willing. It's their way
of saying thank you."

"I've been thanked enough."

"Suit yourself."

Conroy returned his attention to the table. He
frowned.

Joe turned to go, but that envelope jerked his
leash. He came to the table reluctantly, against
his own will, and peeked inside it. He put the envelope down and turned for the door again.

Conroy's frown deepened. The cue ball was
hemmed in. It had been a bad break. There was one
shot, perhaps: the ten ball to a corner pocket. But
the three ball obstructed the path just enough to
spoil the shot. Conroy considered. He extended the
cue and nudged the offending ball a half rotation
aside.

Joe left the room and closed the door behind him.

Conroy clacked the ten ball home. He sighed, *ahh*.

Joe opened the door again, marched to the table, grabbed the envelope, and left.

55

Boston State Hospital—formerly the Boston
Lunatic Hospital— occupied a two-hundred-acre
campus in Mattapan, most of which was a virgin
wood. A wrought-iron fence enclosed the entire
circumference of the property. The few scattered
buildings were red brick, vaguely federalist, with
shallow roofs and white moldings and trim. The
bigger buildings looked like old industrial mills.
The smaller ones might have been little school-
houses or private homes.

The administration building to which Ricky was
directed was one of these, a three-story brick house
with a white portico. The forest seemed to be
closing around this structure. Trees overhung it,
vines crawled over its surface, the grass out front
was high and weedy.

Like a lot of city boys, Ricky had no real feeling
for nature. The work of men was done in cities, and
what lay between cities was best hopped over in a
plane or sped through on a highway. When circumstances compelled him to the beach or out into the
woods, he was uneasy. And in town, where nature

erupted out of the concrete, as in this forest in the middle of Mattapan, it was the forest that seemed artificial—a big green obstruction to be got around on the way to where you were going. A big green pain in the ass.

But these woods were not so benign. There were no people around despite the warm weather. When Ricky had been a kid—the Daleys' house in Savin Hill was just a few miles away—there had been more than three thousand patients here. Now a policy of "de-institutionalization" had nearly emptied the hospital. Only a few hundred souls remained. The grounds were shabby and dilapidated, almost ghostly. Soon these buildings would be abandoned altogether, the forest would close around them, and that would be that.

Why did all that bother Ricky? A few old buildings moldering in the woods, an old insane asylum being decommissioned—what was the big deal?

But Ricky's mood remained stubbornly shadowed. He was not so good at playacting anymore. He was no longer a ventriloquist's dummy; he was too much himself. Amy would have gotten a kick out of that, of course. The thing she had most wished for—Ricky's genuine presence, his new capacity to feel deeply, to ache—had come about only as a product of her dying. It was a joke she would have appreciated.

Would it be profane of Ricky to enjoy what he was doing, tracking down Amy's killer? He thought it was precisely what Amy would have wanted. She certainly appreciated the pleasures of sleuthing, of following the clues, feeling the knot relax and come undone in your hand. More important, Amy knew the consolation of hard work. She knew it was all essentially a distraction. The dailyness and busyness of work obscured the bleak realities—that life was short and pointless and precarious and so on and so on. Why think about it? Better to keep your head down, keep on working. Finding Amy's killer was more productive than grieving. Maybe it was grieving.

At the administration building, a nurse escorted Ricky to the office of Dr. Mark Keating. The title *Chief of Psychiatry* was stenciled on the frosted glass in the office door.

Inside, the doctor hunched over his desk. His elbows rested on the desktop. The fingers of his right hand picked at his scalp. Dr. Keating hoisted up his head, as if its weight was becoming too much for his neck. "Mr. Daley?" he said, puzzled.

"Yes."

"I'm sorry. You're not the one I spoke to."

"That was my brother Michael. He gave me your name. It's about your patient, Arthur Nast."

"Former patient." The doctor gestured toward the chair in front of his desk."I think I told your brother when we spoke: I'm bound by confidentiality. There's not much I can tell you."

Ricky sat. "I just have one question."

The doctor grunted, skeptical. He plowed his fingers into his hair and left them there, with hair kinking out between them. To Ricky, he resembled an old baboon, with his shoulders hunched and his baggy face and electrified hair.

Ricky had a copy of the morning's *Traveler*, quarter-folded. He laid the newspaper on the desk. On page one, below the fold, a headline read,

FORMER STRANGLER SUSPECT FOUND DEAD

A small photo showed Arthur Nast, gaunt, bug-eyed. The photo was misleading. It did not suggest Nast's inhuman qualities, his gigantic size and strength, his Martian, distorted features. He looked merely like a thug.

The doctor glanced at the story and sighed.

"This didn't happen, did it?" Ricky picked up the paper and read aloud, " 'Arthur Nast, once a leading suspect in the Boston Strangler murders, was found dead early last evening in his locked cell at Bridgewater State Hospital, a secure mental facility. Nast apparently swallowed a fatal dose of an anti-depressant medication which he was supposed to take regularly but which he hoarded instead, apparently for the purpose of suicide.' Now, that didn't happen, did it?"

"Does it matter?"

"Very much."

"To who? Nobody cared about him when he was alive."

"Nobody cares about him now, including me. It matters because the truth matters. So, do you believe Arthur Nast killed himself?"

"I think you'd better tell me who you are."

"My friend was Amy Ryan, the last girl who got strangled."

"Ah. And you think Arthur did it?"

"No. Arthur was in Bridgewater when it happened."

"Why the interest, then? Why not let Arthur have some peace in death, finally?"

"Because I want my peace now."

"I see. You're not a policeman, are you?"

Ricky shook his head.

"No, you don't sound like one. Well, look, there's not a lot I can tell you. I wasn't there. I haven't seen Arthur in several months."

"You knew him as well as anyone."

"Alright, then, to be frank, no, I rather doubt that Arthur killed himself. Certainly he did not have the intelligence or the technical knowledge to do it that way—to form the plan, to determine what a fatal dose would be, to hide the pills until he'd accumulated enough. That's all well beyond Arthur's capacity. I doubt Arthur would ever have considered suicide in the first place. I don't think it was in his makeup. He never voiced any inclination toward suicide. He was never depressed, to my knowledge. Of course I can't rule it out, but it strikes me as very, very unlikely. On the other hand, I can't imagine who would want to kill Arthur, either."

"I can."

"Arthur had no enemies in Bridgewater."

"He did. He just didn't know it. Someone did not

want him to confess to any of the Strangler murders. Someone didn't want to see DeSalvo cleared. If Arthur Nast talked, if he laid claim to the murders and described them convincingly—even more convincingly than DeSalvo, which would not be hard to do—then the whole thing would start to fall apart, wouldn't it? How could people go on thinking DeSalvo was the Strangler if another, better suspect started confessing to the same crimes?"

"Who are you accusing, then? The docs? The guards? The prisoners?"

"I don't know. I don't know who put those pills in Nast's hand, but I know why they did it: They're covering up."

"May I ask you a question, Mr. Daley?" A skeptical, honeyed tone came into the doctor's voice. It became the voice of a therapist. The shrink apparently thought Ricky himself was a little crazy, a little griefsick, delusional, conspiracy-minded. "If you prove all this, a cover-up, if you do find the 'real Strangler' who killed your friend Miss . . ."

"Ryan."

"Miss Ryan—what then?"

"Then I'll see that justice is done."

"How?"

"I'll see him go to prison. He'll know he didn't get away with it."

"What then?"

"I don't understand."

"You said what you want is peace. Will you have it? What then?"

Ricky blinked. His mouth drooped open as if he were about to respond. But his mind, the thought-stream so hard to silence earlier, had gone utterly quiet. *What then?*

56

Sunday Mass at St. Margaret's.

Frozen in time, Michael thought.

Same harp parish. Father Farrell still at the altar.
Whitehaired heads in the pews, all those Sullys and
Murphs and Flynns and Flahertys—except that the
white heads now belonged to the parents, not the
grandparents, of Michael's generation. Here were
the same kids he and Ricky and Joe had grown up
with, all looking a little flabbier than their fathers
had at this age. Same brick cathedral named for a
Scottish queen, Saint Margaret. It was Margaret's
husband, Malcolm III, who murdered Macbeth,
and Michael always figured they should have
called this place St. Malcolm's—but they didn't
make saints out of guys like that.

Anyway, this parish already had a Margaret:
Daley. In her customary seat, front and center.

And beside her, Brendan Conroy, in the aisle seat,
where every time he lowered his bulk down onto
the kneeler, his own fat knees squashed out the
narrow ruts dug there Sunday after Sunday by Joe
Daley, Sr.

And beside them was Joe, drenched in worry. Kat, wearing a matching blue coat and hat. And Little Joe, in a clip-on tie.

No Ricky. Ricky did not bother. Did not care what his mother said. Ricky was blithely agnostic about the Lord, and he was not about to fall for Margaret's tail-chasing argument that doubting is a necessary part of faith. God or the God-shaped hole simply held no interest. What difference did it make? How would you live your life any differently, God or no God? Forget it, pal. Not a useful way to spend your time. Sunday mornings Ricky slept in.

So the last seat in the Daleys' row was taken by Michael. Michael who did not believe in God or Church, and who had not been to Mass in years. And yet, he figured, if he could just swallow the placebo—if he could trick his brain into giving his heart a rest— maybe there would be some relief here. Praying to a nonexistent God would be every bit as effective, in psychological terms, as praying to a real one, the whole thing being an exercise in talk therapy and blissful submission. And he could not deny that the placebo worked for billions of people. Why not for Michael, then? Wasn't it at the darkest moments that grace was supposed to descend? To wish for the thing, to crave it, was to make it so. But to Michael, the Mass—every aspect of it, the tortured Christ above the altar, the dull expressions of the parishioners' faces, the familiar musty smell of the church— seemed puny and desperate and exhausted. He had been a fool to come back here. As the Mass progressed, Michael's disappointment quickened into anger, which he flung out at the entire parish for their collusion, for taking Conroy in. They saw Conroy walk in with Margaret on Sunday morning, they saw him cup his hand under her stout elbow as she shuffled out into the aisle for Communion, saw the two of them march around here with imperious nonchalance. Nothing went unnoticed here—over the years Michael had heard his mother condemn virtually everyone in this parish for one indiscretion or another—and yet no one raised an eyebrow. They pretended not to notice. Had they forgotten Joe Senior already?

At Communion, Michael followed the rest of them out of the pew to line up two abreast. It did not even cross his mind not to take Communion. People would gossip, his mother would grind him for embarrassing her.

The man beside Michael in line whispered, "Hey."

Michael turned to see Kurt Lindstrom. His face was mottled with blue and yellow bruises, and one eye bulged, but he was still smirky and undaunted, like a rich cousin.

"Didn't expect to see you here, Michael. Should you be in this line?"

"Shh."

"Have you confessed?"

Michael did not respond.

"Have you confessed?" Lindstrom whispered. "For what you did to me?"

404

The line inched forward one step.

"It's alright, Michael. I forgive you."

A step. Another step. "Michael, who's that with your mother?"

The line stopped.

Lindstrom, imitating the others, stood with his hands clasped at his belly. "She looks lovely today. Saint Margaret. Did they name the church after her?"

"Shut up," Michael whispered.

"Such a lovely woman."

"Shut up."

When they reached the front, Michael knelt on the red-carpeted stair. Lindstrom knelt beside him.

The priest worked his way efficiently across the row of communicants. When he reached Lindstrom, the priest hesitated, distracted by the bruises. Lindstrom opened his mouth and extended his tongue too far. Again there was a pause. The priest seemed unsure whether he was being mocked. He laid the wafer on that too-long tongue, and Lindstrom retracted it slowly.

The priest hesitated at Michael, too, and gave a bent little smile. Long time since he'd seen Michael Daley at Mass. He placed the wafer on Michael's tongue, then moved on to Little Joe.

Michael circled around to the outer aisle to return to his seat. Turning, craning his neck, he could not see Lindstrom anywhere.

57

Vinnie Gargano had an idea: "You wanna know what you do? You do like the Romans used to. Get yourself a cross, a few hundred crosses, whatever, you set 'em up where everyone can see, up nice and high, like on the Common or someplace, and you fuckin' nail these fucks up and leave 'em there a couple of weeks. Let the birds eat 'em. That's the Roman way, see, that's the Italian way. None of this take the guy in some little closet in Walpole and fry him up where no one can see. The whole point is people gotta see. They gotta see! I mean, that's the whole fuckin' point, am I right? Now I guess they ahn't even gonna do that anymore. They're just gonna stick 'em in a cell and leave 'em there. The fuck good does that do?"

He scanned the table for an answer. Gargano's features were scumbled in the dim light. His eyes in particular had a hooded, drowsy menace.

But the three mooks at the table were mushing crab Rangoon and sub gum chow mein in their mouths and could not do much more than nod and make humming sounds to signal their agreement.

But agree they did. They always agreed with Vinnie The Animal, even in his drunken expansive moods.

Gargano loved going out for chink, and this was his favorite afterhours stomp in Chinatown, Bob Lee's Lantern House. They took care of a guy here. Gave him an upstairs room. Gave him mai tais and Blue Whatevers with the little pussy maraschino cherry wrapped in an orange slice and speared with a little plastic sword—drinks that, despite appearances, could knock Sonny Liston on his ass. Plenty of cooze at the bar. No bosses; the bosses stuck to the tomato-sauce joints in the North End or the basement office at C.C.'s Lounge over to Tremont Street. And the cops did not even know Chinatown was part of the city. The only cop Vinnie The Animal was likely to see in Bob Lee's Lantern House was the one he brought with him.

"What about you, cop? What do you say? What good does it do?"

"Whaddaya askin' me? Fuck do I know?"

"I just figured you're a cop, you see this shit every day."

Joe shrugged. He did not like Vinnie The Animal. He was not charmed or frightened by him. He was too tired and too drunk to feel anything. "I don't see nothing, Vin."

"The fuck you do. You pop some fuckin' guy, he's out the next day. Or maybe he does a little time and he's out in a month or whatever. You know what I'm sayin'. Doesn't make any sense, keep arresting the same guys. It's got to bother you, don't it?"

"Not really."

"It should."

"It's the system."

"It's a shitty system, then."

"I'm over it."

"That's the problem. That's why you cops never get anywhere. Put me in charge for a day."

"And what? You'd crucify everyone? That's your big idea? Round up all the jaywalkers and the hookers and crucify 'em? That's a great plan, Vin."

"Not hookers. Who said anything about hookers? That iddn't even really a crime. I'm talking about murderers here. I'm talkin' about the way you need to do things if you really want to get the thing done. You think they had a lot of murders in Rome?"

"Sure."

"No way."

"How do you know?"

"I just know. 'Cause they understood. People want to see this stuff. That's why they put up all those crosses. That's why they built the Colosseum, so people could go see the fights and see people dyin' and whatnot, and they're happy. People need to work it off a little. You gotta let 'em. You gotta do that. For the people."

"They can go to the movies and see all that."

One of the mooks chimed in, "Like *Ben-Hur*. You see that one?"

"The fuck are you talkin' about, *Ben-Hur*?"

"It's a movie."

"I know it's a movie. *Stugatz*."

"I'm just sayin', Vin. You were talkin' about goin'

408

to the Colosseum and see people gettin' killed, and then Joe here said they could see all that shit at the movies, so I said they can go see *Ben-Hur* and see people gettin' killed—at the Colosseum. It's all in there. That's what I'm sayin'."

"And I'm sayin' it's a fuckin' movie."

"So what, it's a movie?"

"So it's make-believe."

"*Ben-Hur?* I thought it was nonfiction."

"That's *Spartacus*."

"They're both nonfiction, *Spartacus* and *Ben-Hur*."

"Would you guys shut the fuck up. I'm not talkin' about fuckin' movies. I'm bein' serious here. Jamokes. Listen, the Romans lasted a thousand years. Or whatever. You know why? 'Cause they didn't fuck around. That's my point. Jesus comes along and tells 'em, 'I'm God' or whatever, and they say, 'Too fuckin' bad, get up on the cross.' They didn't give a shit, these guys."

"Yeah," Joe said, "but Jesus won."

"How did he win?"

"Vatican's in Rome."

"How does that help Jesus? He was dead."

"I don't think you really get the whole Jesus thing, Vin."

"No, you're the one who doesn't fuckin' get it. What I'm sayin' is, there's a proper use. There's a proper use. Hitler, same thing. If they'd a killed Hitler back when he started making trouble, they'd a had no problems, none whatsoever. Instead we had to go send millions of guys over there. And what'd we tell 'em? 'Go kill as many of these fucks as you can.' That's what I'm talking about. A proper use."

"Hitler? What are you talking about Hitler?"

"I'm sayin' a guy like that you got to take care of. You can't just look the other way, even on the small stuff."

"That was a war. It's different."

"It's not different. Same rules. It's always war."

"You're crazy, Vince."

"Yeah? If I'm so crazy, how come you work for me?"

"Because I'm stupid."

"And these guys? They stupid, too?"

"Is that a real question?"

They laughed, Gargano, the mooks, everyone but Joe.

"Here's what I'm sayin'. Bein' a cop and all, you know I'm right. I'll make you a bet: The guy that killed that what's-her-name, the girl you know that got strangled, the reporter . . ."

"Amy Ryan."

"Amy Ryan. I'll make you a bet: That wasn't the first one he did. That's a guy with a history. He's been in the can, too, I betcha. They had him and they let him out so he could do that there."

"So?"

"So she was a good girl, wasn't she, this Amy? Didn't deserve what she got?"

Joe did not answer.

"So if they'd a taken care of him the first time he did it, like they should have—"

"You don't know what a guy's gonna do. In the future."

"Trust me, sometimes you know." Gargano gave him a look.

The mooks hummed and nodded some more. Vinnie The Animal, after all, did have some expertise in this area.

58

Kat at Ricky's door again. Defeated.

"What's wrong, Kat? What happened?"

"I don't know. I just don't know what to do. I'm just . . ."

"Jesus, come in."

Ricky attempted a series of solicitous little gestures, a palm laid on Kat's shoulder, an arm outstretched toward the couch, a reach to relieve her of her purse. The resulting display was a little ridiculous, like a sailor semaphoring, and Ricky wondered again at his new awkwardness. It was a new role, Ricky After, and he had not learned to play it yet. Ricky Before—detached, irresponsible, bored, charismatic—had been a closer fit. But Kat's very presence here seemed to confirm the change in Ricky, or at least the change in the family's perception of him. He had never been the type that weeping women turned to. He had not, for that matter, been in very direct touch with the female side of the family at all. For years Amy had represented him among the women. She had explained him to Margaret and Kat and the various aunts and

412

cousins who materialized at family functions. But now Kat was here, and Ricky wanted to be what she needed.

Kat, though, seemed to gather strength as she came into the apartment and observed the mess there. She regarded Ricky's apartment as if it were a direct reflection of his interior life, and she seemed to calculate that, whatever problems she might have, Ricky might actually be worse off.

"Where's your record player? And all those records?"

"Somebody broke in."

"Somebody what!?"

"You heard me."

"Sorry, Ricky. It's just . . ." She snorted. "Can't trust anyone these days."

"I can give you back that Miles Davis record."

"No, you keep it."

"New couch?"

"Yeah."

"Thief took the old one?"

"Sure."

"That's weird, thief taking an old couch like that."

"Long story."

"I bet."

Kat sat on the new couch and ran her palm over the cushion.

It had been eleven weeks since Gargano's goons turned Ricky's place upside down looking for the stones. In that time Ricky had bought a used couch and coffee table and a new hifi, but that was it. He did not feel the same connection to the place. He thought he might move. He had no idea where. Someplace far away.

"You got to help Joe."

"Help him how?"

Kat lowered her face into her hands.

"What, is he catting around again?"

"No, it's not that. I think he's in trouble. He's betting. And we're broke. I mean literally broke. You know? We have no money, Ricky. I don't even—I have nothing to give them for dinner tonight."

"Jesus, Kat, why didn't you say so? I have plenty of cash. It's no problem."

"It is a problem. He's not acting right. I think he's in trouble."

Ricky fished some cash out of his pocket. He peeled off two twenties and a ten, and handed it to Kat.

She gawped at the bills in her hand. "This is—I can't take this.It's too much."

"Take it. I'll get you more."

Kat kept a twenty-dollar bill and put the rest down on the coffee table. "Thank you. We'll pay you back, Ricky, I promise."

"You don't have to pay me back, Kat. It's for you."

"Ricky, do you know what's going on with Joe? You do know, don't you?"

"I— He told me a few things. Not the whole story."

"What did he tell you?"

"Nothing, Kat. Really. It's nothing you need to worry about."

"Ricky, you gotta tell me."

"I really don't know the whole thing. Joe and I don't talk much, you know that. All I know is what you know: He likes to bet, he got himself into a hole, he's a little short of cash right now. It's not so bad."

"Not so bad? He steals from us! He steals—from us! We have bills. You can't imagine the bills."

"Give them to me. I'll pay them."

"I can't do that. He'd kill me."

"So don't tell him. Just put them all in a paper bag and give them to me."

Kat rubbed her eyes. Her hand was jittery, with fatigue or strain Ricky could not tell. "Ricky, you won't let anything happen to him, will you?"

"He's a big boy. He doesn't need my help."

"Ricky, you look at me and you promise you won't let anything happen to him. He's your brother."

"You overestimate me, Kat."

"Promise me."

"I promise."

"Look me in the eye."

"Alright, alright. I promise."

Kat exhaled a long sigh, as if the thing was agreed: No harm would come to her Joe. The twenty was still in her hand—that made two prayers answered. She folded the bill in half, then folded it again, so those magical digits, 20, showed in the corners. This piece of paper would change her life, it would stave off catastrophe. Kat had never thought much about money until the last year. Now she thought about little else. She opened her pocketbook and got out her wallet to put it away carefully. On twenty bucks she could feed her family for a week, maybe more.

Ricky retrieved her coat, which she had dropped on a chair. On the pretext of holding it open for her, he slipped the other thirty into her coat pocket.

59

Margaret answered the door looking bulletproof in a wool twinset and skirt. "Michael," she said. "What are you doing here? No work today?"

"No."

"Are you all right?"

"No. All wrong, actually."

"What does that mean? Did you call in sick?"

"No."

"Don't you think you should? What if someone's looking for you?"

Michael hunched past her, as a porcupine trundles across a road with its load of erect quills.

"I really think you should," Margaret repeated. "What if they're looking for you, Michael? Why don't you go use the phone in the kitchen? It's the responsible thing, dear. It'll just take a second."

Michael stood in the center of the small living room. One of Conroy's Mickey Spillane novels lay on the table by the big saffron chair.

"I need to ask you about Dad."

"Okay."

"Did you ever ask Conroy about him? Since we talked that morning?"

"I wouldn't insult him."

"You wouldn't insult him? So you insult Dad instead?"

"You take that back, Michael."

"Well, you have to insult one or the other. It's awkward that way."

She pulled her cardigan tight around her and crossed her arms. "Why do you say these things?"

"Tell me what happened with Dad."

"I don't know what you mean."

"Those last few months, something was wrong. Dad was upset about something. Moping around, drinking too much, smoking like a chimney."

"Your father had a stressful job. I'd think you'd know that. He had ups and downs, same as everyone else, same as you. There was nothing unusual about your dad taking a drink, either. He was not Superman."

"That's what I figured, too. He was not Superman, so what? So maybe he took a pop at night, who cares? Happens to everyone. Only then he got killed. Now, that doesn't happen to everyone, does it?"

"He got killed on the job. What did smoking and drinking have to do with it? He was in good shape. He was always in good shape, your father."

An image flickered in Michael's mind: Dad on the beach, not muscular but sinewy and lean.

"Help me, Mum. I need to know. There was one night at supper, a few months before, and Joe was saying how great it was to be a cop and all that, and Dad said something like 'It's not as great as it used to be.' "

"Oh, he said that all the time. Your father was getting old. He was tired. You try working those hours someday. You'd be tired, too."

"No. He didn't say he was tired, he said he was tired of it. He loved being a cop. So what was he tired of?"

"Tired is tired. He worked hard."

Michael frowned. "You know what's funny? When Joe got into trouble—that business with the bookie—we all knew just who to turn to: good old Uncle Brendan."

"I don't see what one has to do with the other."

"Well, it's just, if Dad was in trouble . . . All those years he and Brendan were partners."

"And?"

"And Brendan isn't exactly the kind of cop Dad was, now, is he?"

"I don't like being cross-examined, Michael. This is not a court. Anyway, you seem to think you have all the answers. Why don't you just say what's on your mind."

"Two murders in one family in the same year. That's a hell of a coincidence. And no answers. No help from the cops—everything stays unsolved, unsolved, unsolved."

"Michael, you have to let go of it—"

"No. I don't want to let go of it. I went to see Amy's friend at the newspaper. You remember Claire Downey?"

"I remember the name in the paper next to Amy's."

"Well, I asked Claire what she knew about it. Why would Amy think Conroy would ever want to harm my dad? I mean, even if Conroy is crooked, what would the motive be? Turns out, according to Claire, Amy was looking into the West End—two-legged rats in the West End.

"So then I went and talked to an old friend. Well, not a friend exactly. She thinks I'm the devil on earth—and I am—because I got her thrown out of her apartment so the tenement could come down so Farley Sonnenshein could put up one of his new buildings and make a few million more than he already has—all for the betterment of our fair city, of course. Mrs. Cavalcante, her name is. Nice little Italian lady. She told me there were bad guys— *delinquenti*—threatening her, trying to scare her out of her building so they could get in there and build those new apartments. Nothing too surprising there, right? A lot of money at stake, a guy like Sonnenshein probably isn't above playing hardball. But get this: Mrs. Cavalcante says some of the *delinquenti* were cops."

"Michael, you're not suggesting your father was one of them!"

"No. Don't be ridiculous. Dad might not have been Superman but he sure as hell was a Boy Scout, next to your boyfriend anyway."

"Oh, Michael, you're not turning into one of those conspiracy nuts."

"Not a conspiracy. I'm talking about business

as usual. Just a few cops on the take."

"Business as usual is a couple of bucks here and there."

"That's right. And as long as it's business as usual, the good cops like Dad are willing to look the other way. That's how it works, right? The whole department isn't crooked. Only half. But the good half has to shut its eyes—or at least its mouth—while the crooked half runs around with their hands out. But what if something changed? What if Dad started seeing things that weren't business as usual, even for Boston, and he couldn't look the other way anymore?"

"Good Lord, Michael, what does any of this have to do with Brendan?"

"Brendan would do things Dad would never do."

"Michael, I don't know what's going on between you and Brendan, but I want you to understand something. Whatever Brendan did, whatever he might have got up to, your father did too. They weren't just partners, those two, they were friends. They were Ike and Mike. You talk like it's all good Joe, bad Brendan. It just wasn't that way. It wasn't that way at all."

"Amy thought different."

Margaret shrugged. "Then she was wrong. Bless her heart, she was a living angel, but she was not perfect, either. Now, I know how you felt about Amy. Sometimes we see with our hearts, Michael. Let me ask you something. How do you think your father put you through Harvard on a cop's salary?"

"I worked my way through."

"Yes, you worked, more power to you. But you had plenty of help. How do you think your father did that for you? How many other cops' kids were there at Harvard with you? We're not the Kennedys, Michael."

"Well, that's for sure."

"Your father had three children. Sometimes he did what he had to. He didn't invent the system."

"I'd have no problem believing that except for one thing: In the end, when Dad died, the only other man in that alley was Brendan Conroy. If Dad decided he couldn't just look the other way, if Brendan had gone too far and Dad was getting ready to blow the whistle— well, look, I can explain why Brendan might be in that alley with a gun. What's your explanation, Ma?"

"I don't need an explanation."

"When you crawl into bed with him tonight, you might feel different."

She slapped him. "I'm still your mother. Whatever you might think of me."

60

Joe, big dismissive smirk: "What are you, crazy?"

Michael shrugged.

"What about you, Rick? You believe this shit?"

"If Mikey says it . . ."

"If Mikey said the sky was green?"

"I'd go have a look."

Joe mopped his hand across his mouth. "No way. There's just no way."

Ricky swigged his beer and lounged back in his chair. They were at a place in the Fenway called Herbie's Cactus Room, around the corner from McGrail's and with fewer ears. Of course Ricky might have rejected the idea out of hand, too, but Amy had believed it and that changed everything. For her sake, he had to consider it, at least. And the more he considered, the more the audacity of the idea— Brendan Conroy killed Joe Senior— argued in its favor. A lot of people, no doubt, slept a little more soundly the night Amy Ryan died and took her headful of secrets with her. Maybe Conroy had been one of them.

Joe was having none of it. "I know Brendan. I

know him way better than you two clowns. Way better. There's no way. I just can't, I just can't . . . Okay, okay, okay. Michael's got a hair across his ass about Brendan. That's fine, that's your business, Mike. But this is nuts. You don't go around accusing people like that."

"I'm not accusing. I'm just saying there's enough there we ought to look into it."

"Who are we? What are we gonna look into it? That's the police's job."

"You think the cops are gonna investigate Conroy? He's in Homicide."

Ricky smirked bitterly. "Wouldn't be the first case he didn't solve."

"It's not our job, Mike."

"I didn't choose it, Joe. I was just living my life, having an ordinary day, and then the phone rang and Dad was dead and suddenly we were all about dying. We've never been the same since. At eleven fifty-nine we were a regular family, at twelve-oh-one suddenly we were the family that had a murder. I didn't choose this job, 'son of a dead guy.' I'd give it back if I could."

"The fuck are you talking about?"

"Can I ask you something, Joe? If you found the guy that killed Dad, and there was no doubt about it, you knew he was guilty, and it looked like he was going to get away with it—"

"If, if, if."

"That's right, if, if, if—what would you do?"

"That's not what this is."

"I know. I'm just saying, what if? If you knew who did it?"

"I don't know. Kill him."

"Kill him," Michael repeated evenly. "Kill him."

"I don't know. I guess."

"I agree."

Joe shook his head. "What are you talking about, 'you agree'? You don't even know anything yet, and already you're ready to kill him? You ahn't exactly the type, Michael. Tough guy."

"I meant, I agree it would be the right thing to do."

"I think he just called you a fag, Mike. What does that mean, he's not the type?"

"Means he's a fag."

"Say it to his face."

"You're a fag, Mike."

"Well, he said it to your face, Michael. Give him credit."

"Okay, I'm a fag."

"I knew it!" Ricky grinned. "Pickle sniffer."

But Michael was grim. "I think we have to think about it."

Joe: "Again with this. Would you shut the fuck up? No one's killing anyone."

"We have to think about what we're going to do if it's true."

"It's not true. Would you just get that? It's not true."

"Joe, he didn't say it was true. He said if."

"I know what he said, Rick. He keeps sayin' it without sayin' it."

"All I'm saying is we have to consider it. Because that's where we're headed."

"Mike, do you know this is already a felony? It's called conspiracy to murder."

"We're just having a philosophical discussion, Joe."

"Oh, is that what we're doing?"

"Come on, if they arrested everybody who ever talked about murder, or thought about it or read about it . . ."

"Well, I'm not thinking about it. I'm out."

"All right. You're out. How about you, Ricky?"

"Is this a conspiracy or still just a philosophical discussion?"

"Just talking."

"You hear that, Mr. Cop?"

"Joe knows. We're just talking. In the abstract. What do we do, Rick?"

"We do nothing. If we have evidence, we pass it to the cops. Give them a chance. If they do nothing, we take it to the feds."

"And if the feds do nothing?"

"If the *federales* do nothing, then . . . we think of something else."

"That's all I've been doing is thinking, Ricky."

"I know it. Maybe you should shut it off awhile, Mikey. You're making yourself crazy."

"I think maybe everyone else is crazy."

"All crazy people think that."

"I think if Conroy is the one and we don't do anything about it . . ." Michael shook his head as he searched for the end of his sentence. ". . . then shame on us."

"Mikey, are you being serious?"

He pondered before answering."I don't know,Rick.To be perfectly honest."

"Look, you know when the chips are down, we're with you, right?"

"Except Joe, of course."

"Joe's with you too. When the chips are down." Ricky gave Joe a hard look.

Joe declined to offer any confirmation. Just sat there.

"Well, that's comforting. Guess it's me and you, Ricky. The Two Musketeers. Doesn't have the same ring, does it?"

Joe said, "You got enough trouble already, Ricky."

"What's that mean, Rick?"

"Tell him. Go ahead. Tell him what it means."

"Doesn't mean anything. It means Joe's got a big mouth."

"Tell him what it means, why don't you?"

"The point is, he'd be there for you. Isn't that right, Joe?"

"Yeah, whatever. Crazy fag running around like Sherlock fuckin' Holmes."

"Mikey, though . . . you're not gonna do anything crazy, right?"

"I told you, everyone else is crazy. I'm the only sane one."

61

Joe found him in one of the "social clubs" in the South End. This one was called the Top Hat, though you were more likely to see a flatbrim fedora here on one of the old Mustache Petes. It occupied the bottom two floors of a tenement. Here the oldtimers mixed with the younger generation of kill-crazy grunts like Vinnie The Animal, and all the gangsters, young and old, mingled with the plain civilians, to drink and play poker or barbooth, with no trouble from the cops who were either bought and paid for or simply knew better. You could get a watered-down beer for a dime while you dropped a fifty at the tables, and out of that fifty bucks, one and a quarter—the magical two and a half per-cent—would be passed from hand to hand to hand to Charlie Capobianco's counting room. When Joe walked into this place—the Top Hat was members-only but the thing had been arranged, as everything was always arranged, somewhere outside Joe's hearing—he knew something had changed. Here, finally, was the step too far. He had the sense of the floor moving beneath his feet, as if he had stepped onto a boat as it left the shore, the black water opening up behind him. But Joe's unease was a wordless, formless thing, and he barred it from the front of his mind where it might coalesce into an idea, a clear reason not to go ahead with it. This was the soldier's way of completing a mission. Don't think. Don't question your orders. Just execute. Accomplish the objective. But the sub-thought persisted, even gained strength and shape: Don't do this.

Paul Marolla lurked at the periphery of a bar-booth game with a drink in one hand and a cigarette in the other, pimped out in a puce polyester shirt that showed off his bodybuilder's physique. His hair was slicked and opalescent. The backs of the men watching the game were too tall for Marolla to see over, a fact he finessed by affecting a honed indifference. Here was a man content with a beer and a smoke and a view of taller men's backsides.

Joe moved through the crowd toward him. The people seemed to part for Joe, which added to the static in his head, the sense of stoptime. He did not know why they opened a path for him, whether they made him for a cop or a troublemaker or were just being prudent, giving a big man a wide berth. Maybe it was not happening at all, just Joe's mind playing tricks.

Marolla spotted him and his face churned as he placed Joe. It had been weeks since this hulking cop had questioned him at the construction site. The connection made, his face relaxed into a smirk.

"I need to talk to you," Joe said.

"What about?"

"Never mind what about. I need to talk to you."

"So talk. The fuck?"

"Here?"

"Why not?"

"You want everyone to see you talking to me? Maybe I should flash my badge."

Marolla considered.

"I'll see you out front," Joe said. "Alone."

"When I finish my drink."

Joe looked at the half-empty glass. It crossed his mind to snatch Marolla's lit cigarette from his fingers and drop it into the drink. But Marolla was in for a hard night. What harm in granting a reprieve? Joe left him there, and with that little act of gallantry and knowingness he felt himself rise above the Top Hat and its greaseball clientele. He was an insider.

Joe waited at the curb until, five minutes or so later, Marolla came out of the front door. Marolla glanced to his left, at a bigshouldered curlyhaired dago leaning by the doorway, waiting for someone. This dago wore a wool sportcoat with natural shoulders and a thin tie. He had a horizontal lightningbolt scar on the left side of his head which showed as a jagged part in his hair, though a little lower than a proper hairpart. The two exchanged nods, and Marolla turned toward Joe. He made it three steps.

Behind him, in one motion the scarhead dago produced a baseball bat from the shadows which he swung with one hand, his right, the blow sprung with such whippy quickness that Joe was startled even though he knew it was coming. It struck the right side of Marolla's head, above the ear; maybe Scarhead was trying to create a false hairpart like his own. Marolla's eyes closed and he sprawled down to the sidewalk, and Scarhead stumbled over him, and Joe was left staring at the unmarked door of the Top Hat for a moment.

Car doors opened behind him. Scuffling.

There were seven other guys besides Joe and Scarhead, soldiers, most of them young and feral. They stood around the body—Marolla lay on the pavement with one arm and one leg crooked at right angles like a sleeping child—and it seemed inevitable that one of them would stomp on a finger or a cheekbone just for the hell of it.

Vinnie Gargano jostled the body with the bottom of his shoe. No reaction. "Okay, let's get going. Good job, cop.That's some strong little fuck. No sense wrestling him out of there." Gargano seemed proud to have deployed his new weapon so artfully. His reputation had not been built on clever tradecraft. He had proved it wrong.

Four men, one at each corner, lifted Marolla by his hands and feet and spilled him into the trunk of Gargano's Caddy. The trunk was big and empty and perfectly clean. Marolla's body curled up inside it like a cat. A ball of twine was unwrapped, new from the hardware store, still banded in cellophane, and Scarhead hogtied the body. While an assistant pinned Marolla's arms together at the

small of the back, Scarhead wound the string
around the wrists several times then cinched the
loop tight with a belt of string between the wrists.
He tied Marolla's ankles the same way, then connected the wrists and ankles with a long tie-line.
This step caused a momentary frustration.
Pinioning Marolla's wrists together had locked his
body in its fetal curl, so that when Scarhead pulled
the wrists and ankles together the body squatted in
a ball rather than arching backward. Annoyed,
Scarhead had to loosen the drawstring, roll the
body onto its stomach, then flex it backward into
the proper archer's-bow position. Someone urged
Scarhead to hurry. He responded in a pissy voice,
"Fuckin' thing won't bend. Muscleman." He
checked his ropework carefully, pulled the long tie-
line to test it, and gave a satisfied grunt.

The trunk was slammed shut and the men got
into two cars. Joe was in the back of the lead car,
Gargano's Cadillac.

But they did not head for any of the usual desti-
nations. Not west to Blue Hill Avenue where
Gargano had his bar. Not south to the deeper
recesses of the South End or the waterfront. They
went right past the North End, too. North, over the
bridge, and Joe knew—it was over for Paul Marolla.
He was already dead. There was no reason to take
him out of town just to put a beating on him. You
took a guy out of town to dump him, ideally inside
the borders of a rival mob. True, with the so-called
Irish Gang Wars still raging, murder was becoming
a more brazen and haphazard business, often done

on the spur of the moment wherever the victim happened to be. A Charlestown mug named Connie Hughes bought it right on this bridge, victim number thirty—a Winter Hill crew in two cars trailed Hughes up onto the bridge, through the tollbooth, then dawdled up alongside his Chevy and unloaded sixty rounds from M1 carbines into it. Still, it was not the right way to do things. So Joe was aware that the point of this trip was to throw off the cops. That he was here, that none of the others cared to hide any of this from him, was a final defeat.

In the car, no one spoke.

Joe listened for sounds from the trunk. Marolla lay just a couple of feet away, behind Joe's back. But Joe heard nothing. Just the engine hum and the road rattle. Was Marolla still unconscious? Or awake, thinking, ransacking his thoughts for a way out? Marolla had to know, even in the dark of the trunk, that the ride was taking too long. By now he must have realized the fix he was in. How did it feel back there, in the blackness and cold, suffocating, muscles aching from the rope and the tortured posture? Joe forced his attention outward, out the window at the city lights, the outer boroughs where city blocks gave way to strips of businesses set back behind aprons of parking lot.

"Where are we going?" he said.

"Revere," Gargano answered.

Revere. Made sense. No one would look for the hand of Carlo Capobianco in a murder there. Even Capobianco could not crack Revere, the perfect

Mobtown. Bostonians tended to talk about Revere as "Dodge City": violent, anarchic, isolated, irredeemably rotten. But the comparison was not entirely fair to Dodge City, which at least had a lawandorder sheriff. Revere had no such advantage. In fact, when the old bookie who ran the Revere rackets died in 1963, it was the deputy chief of police, Phil Gallo, who took over as Mob underboss. The two great powers in the city, the government and the Mob, finally merged in the person of Deputy Chief Gallo. It was not as shocking as all that. Revere had been a mobocracy long before Gallo's coronation made it official. The old joke was that even the dogcatchers in Revere were on the sleeve. Jewish bookies and Italian strong-arms had flourished there for half a century. But Charlie Capobianco had perceived an opportunity in the leadership change, a hint of weakness. He had moved on the city's bookmaking rackets, and Gallo had hit back. One morning Gallo went so far as to shoot up Capobianco's Cadillac while it was parked on Huntington Avenue outside his girlfriend's place. It soon became apparent that Charlie Capobianco's offensive was doomed. Gallo had a direct line to the superboss in Providence, Raymond Patriarca, and Patriarca was not going to let Capobianco take the city. Revere would survive as an independent principality within Capobianco's empire, and Revere's gangsters would remain stubbornly ungovernable, like Basques. It must have pissed off Capobianco no end. Maybe dumping poor dumb Paul Marolla's body in Gallo's backyard would give the new boss a pain in the ass, at least. Certainly it would point the cops away from the North End.

Joe didn't give a shit about tectonic shifts in the Mob landscape. Bunch of mooks killing each other. None would be missed. What bothered him was the thought he could not stave off: victim number thirty-one, the next to go, lay in the trunk two feet from where Joe sat. Joe could imagine himself coffined back there. He could feel it. The metal frame of the trunk, the whoosh of the road a foot below his ear. Empathy, of course, was an un-helpful instinct in this situation. Marolla was already dead in all but the biological sense. No sense investing your emotions in a corpse. Joe would picture him only in wide frame. No human-izing closeups; those were reserved for the living, who were worthy of sympathy. But even the long view—from high above, two cars progressing down a two-lane highway, visible only as dim cones of light thrown by their headlights in the dark, and as we zoom in, a cutaway view into the sealed trunk, this insignificant curled little animal—the long view was worse. Joe felt a panic of claustrophobia. He shook it away, forced himself to relax.

This was the way they would come for Joe, too, someday. They would not come heavy, they would not send a soldier. They would use someone he trusted, an old friend, someone he felt safe with. Joe's murderer would come wearing a smile, bearing a shiny gift—an offer, an invitation—he might even be a cop. No frontal assault, no spray of machinegun fire, no "you dirty rat." The blow would come from behind, a sucker punch, the Beantown special. Joe would never see it coming.

In Revere they came to a motel called The Hideaway. Cinderblock construction, neon sign out front. A high picket fence bordered the parking lot. It blocked the view of the industrial plants on either side, though both were marked in threefoot lettering visible above the fence, REVERE MARINE ENGINE CO. on one side, INDUSTRIAL HEAT TREATING on the other.

Gargano nosed the Caddy into a parking space next to a white '63 Impala. The second car parked on the opposite side of the Impala.

The men got out, stiff-limbed, stretching, shaking off the ride. They gathered around Gargano's trunk.

Inside, Marolla was awake. He pulled in a deep oxygen-rich breath, blinked up at them—and launched into his defense. "Vince. I didn't do anything. I swear. I don't know what they told you but I swear to God, Vince, IsweartoGodonmymother'sgrave, whatever they told you I did I didn't do it."

Gargano said, "You don't even know what the fuck you did, but you didn't do it?"

The men laughed.

Marolla did not laugh. "Sorry, Vince. Sorry. Tell me. I can explain."

"You skimmed."

"No!"

"You skimmed."

"No! I did not! I swear! You gotta listen. It's a mistake. I'm tellin' you."

"No mistake." Gargano said to no one in particular, "Get him into the other car."

The trunk of the Impala was opened with a key. With a grunt, a couple of guys lifted Marolla and heaved him into the trunk of the Impala. The car kneeled under the weight. "Sleep tight," one of them said.

Joe stood among them. He was not sure how to handle himself, whether to assert his loyalty to the group with some sort of wiseacre remark or just keep quiet and let them speculate that he might, in the end, be a real cop. The fact was, Joe had no intention of being a real cop. He knew the rules. You talk, you die. Maybe you die after you talk to the D.A., maybe you die after you talk to the grand jury. But cop or no cop, you talk, you die. Everyone could be reached. Besides, how would he explain his own role in tricking Marolla out of the Top Hat? He was already an accessory. Who would believe, or care, that Joe had thought Marolla was only going to be roughed up and released? Anyway, it was already too late. Seven of them, one of him. Joe had no choice. No choice but to let it happen. Soon it would be over anyway. Marolla would get the traditional two in the hat and the trunk would be closed and they could go home. Joe lowered his eyes. Out of habit he noted the license number of the car, for the report he would never write: Rhode Island plates, PM 387. No doubt the plates and the car had been stolen separately. Probably the Impala had been left here a few days before so its arrival would not attract attention the morning after the murder. Rhode Island, PM 387—Joe wished he could write it down in his notebook. That was proper procedure. He did not trust his memory. Did not trust his own mind. He had seen death before. He'd killed guys before, Germans. He could do this.

The Impala had a long, low trunk. With the lid raised, it looked spacious enough.

Marolla was trying to jerk himself up onto the side wall of the trunk so he could face them from a semisitting position.

"Gimme that string," Gargano said.

"No! Vince! Don't! It's a mistake. Listen to me, just one second—"

" 'Ooh-ooh, it's a mistake!' Tell me how it's a fuckin' mistake? Huh? Tell me. Tell me how it's a fuckin' mistake, you fuck. Go on, I'm listenin'."

"It just is. I didn't do it, Vin, I swear. You gotta believe me. I know everybody says that, but I'm telling you the truth. Please."

"You must think I'm fuckin' stupid. Do you think I'm stupid?"

"No. Vin, no. I don't think that."

"Do I *look* stupid to you?"

"No."

"Then what are you talking to me like I'm fuckin' stupid, telling me it's a mistake? How can it be a mistake?" Gargano was handed the ball of twine and he began to unwind it. As he worked, he explained himself, like a father explaining the

438

punishment he was about to dish out. "They know how much you got. You think they don't know these things, they don't count it first? Money can just disappear and nobody's gonna notice? Your job was to take that money and deliver it. And you were short. Not once, not twice, over and over. They were watching you, you dumb shit. They always watch the fuckin' money. Don't you know that? The fuck did you think, nobody was gonna care? You could just help yourself, like that money was yours? Is that what you thought?"

"I can pay it back."

"I thought you didn't do it."

"I didn't. But I mean, if it's missing then it must be my mistake. My mistake, see? *My* mistake. I'll pay it back. Plus the juice, whatever you say it is."

"Just stop talkin', a'right? Fuckin' embarrass yourself. Shit your pants." To no one he said, "Let's do this already."

"No! Stop!"

Marolla scanned the faces and, desperate, he locked on Joe: "Hey, cop, help me out."

Joe shook his head.

"Cop. C'mon, help me out. You're a cop. You gotta. Help me out."

Joe felt the eyes of the group shift toward him. He shook his head again. "Nothin' I can do, pal."

Lying on his side Marolla managed to lift his shoulders a few inches off the floor of the trunk. "I can te— I can tell you what you want to know. Those questions."

"I don't have any questions."

"You do you do you do. We talked, remember? We did, we talked." Marolla's voice was skittery-frantic-breathless. But he was still negotiating, still talking. He seemed to think if he could just keep someone engaged, he could buy himself a little more time. A little more time."We talked once, we talked. The West End, remember? The grocery store, that whole thing? You wanna know what happened? You wanna know? Huh? You wanna know? I can tell you. I can tell you. I'll tell you the whole thing, the whole thing, I'll give it to you, the whole thing. Forget that guy, the grocery, that's just one building. That's nothing. I can give you the whole thing."

Gargano said, "Shut the fuck up."

"These guys—"

"I said shut the fuck up."

"These—"

"Jesus!" Gargano collared Marolla's neck with two hands and hammered the man's head against the lip of the trunk three times. A frenzy, then over.

"Hey, cop." A spreading, woozy smile. "Hey, cop, I know who killed your old man. I know who you are. I can tell you." Marolla knew he was doomed. He seemed finally to accept it. It gave him false courage. "Wanna know who killed your old man? That's what you really want to know, isn't it?"

Gargano gave the man's head a final crack against the car, like a fisherman gaffing a stubborn flapping fish, and Marolla slithered down inside the trunk. His face lolled on the floor.

Gargano leaned over to add his own ropework, but the body was too far away."Get over here,"he growled.He dragged the body closer, then began to wind the twine around Marolla's neck.

Marolla bucked. He tossed his head back and forth to avoid the string. "No! Don't don't don't! Please. Please don't, please don't, please don't!"

One of the mooks stepped forward to hold him still. Gargano pulled the string taut around the neck, then ran several long loops connecting the neck-rope to the ankles. He jacked Marolla's feet up a little to create slack, and shortened this segment until the weight of the feet and legs tensioned the string. Then he released Marolla's feet, and their weight pulled back on the noose.

Immediately Marolla began to choke. His head jerked from side to side. He gasped. After a moment he figured out that his arms had been tied to his feet by Scarhead, and by pulling this segment of the harness he could lift his own feet upward and relieve the pressure on his neck, and he inhaled deeply several times.

"Please. Don't do this. Please. Please. I'll get the money. I'll get it. I'll get it. Please, Vin. *Please*. Please."

Gargano took out a knife. Joe thought he might slice off an ear or finger as a trophy. Instead, Gargano sawed through the safety line that linked Marolla's hands and ankles.

Unsupported, the legs tugged the rope down and Marolla began to strangle again. He curved his back and legs as far back as possible to create some slack. But he would not be able to hold this position, bent backward to the limit of his spine's flexion, neck and ankles joined by strings like an archer's bow. He would tire, his legs would straighten, and he would be strangled.

Gargano said, "Hey, cop, come here."

Joe stood by the open trunk.

Marolla's body quivered.

Gargano said to the man in the trunk, "Hey, you got anything to say to the cop now? No? Didn't think so." He hawked, rolled his jaw as he organized the mucus in his mouth, then spat it on Marolla's face.

Joe stared at the spit. It was beneath the sideburn, at the hinge of the jawbone. A gob of phlegm, vaguely peanut-shaped, in a puddle of spittle. It repeated the shape of the adjacent earhole. It was a fetus. It metastasized into something more articulated and spiny, maybe a seahorse, the tail of which seeped into Marolla's eye and, unable to wipe or shake it out, he squinched the eye shut, then a blanket was thrown over him and the whole image was gone, lost beneath the folds of the blanket that shifted with the man's infinitesimal movements. The blanket was to muffle the sound.

Gargano slammed the trunk shut, and the Impala bobbed down and up.

As Joe stared, the car seemed to jiggle, though maybe it was his eyes playing tricks again.

Part Three

Lock-picking takes place in a tiny space, the keyway. If it were magnified, the keyway would resemble a narrow corridor with a smooth steel floor and sawtoothed ceiling. Set into that ceiling are four pins (or more, depending on the lock), each of which travels up and down inside a cylinder. When each pin is raised to its proper height, the lock opens. The jagged edge of a key lifts all the pins at once to their assigned heights. The lock picker's task, simply put, is to raise those pins one by one.

It was a matter of feel, of course. When a pin reached its release point and set properly, Ricky could sense—through the pick in his fingertips, through his ears, his eyes, through no specific sense at all—a little give in the lock, an infinitesimal release like a sigh. But for Ricky lock picking was first and foremost an act of imagination. A good pick like Ricky could visualize the interior of that keyway. He could blow it up to the size of a cathedral and wander inside it and look up at the round bottoms of those pins hanging from the ceiling. He thought that if he were ever locked up in a prison cell, he would spend his days with his eyes shut imagining the insides of locks, impossibly complex locks with baroque devices designed to defeat him, mechanical marvels as yet undreamt by lock makers, and he would pick them for the sheer insolence of it. He would open them pin by pin just as, in dreams, other prisoners would open women's blouses button by button.

And pin by pin was the proper way to pick a lock, Ricky believed, the only way. There were quicker, dirtier ways, of course, and in practice the need for speed sometimes required a shortcut or two. The most common technique was "scrubbing," which meant scratching the pick quickly over the pinheads, knocking the pins upward. While scrubbing back and forth with the pick, the lock picker would apply enough torque to the cylinder that the pins would be trapped in their "unlock" positions before they rebounded and zinged back down. But scrubbing had a critical drawback: it scratched the pins and the keyway, and it sprayed metal dust inside the lock—which is to say, it left evidence that the lock had been picked. That sort of sloppiness was anathema to Ricky. A good pick left no trace. And of course, every burglar knew that the best way to open a lock was not to pick it at all but to get the key somehow. Alas, stealing or conning a key to duplicate it—or "smoke" it, in the argot of thieves—was risky as well. It generally required the thief to "show face," a cardinal sin.

So Ricky became expert at pin-by-pin picking. He crafted his own picks, which were roughly L-shaped, a design lock pickers called a "rake." The long arm of the L, the handle, was five or six inches long. It was tuned to be flexy enough to provide feedback to the fingertips yet stiff enough to push hard on a pin. The proper stiffness was a matter of endless experimentation. The short arm of the L was dished at the tip so it would seat properly on each pinhead. On big jobs—and at this point big jobs were all that interested him—he researched the locks he would encounter ahead of time, and he made picks customized to those models. The net result of all this effort was that Ricky worked very fast and very clean. To stand behind him while he picked a lock was to watch a man open a door with a slightly sticky key.

Which is why, when Ricky unlocked the door to Carlo Capobianco's headquarters on Thatcher Street in the North End, the event looked entirely unremarkable. A man walked up to the door, jiggled a key in the lock (or seemed to), and let himself in.

Ricky himself was surprised by the ease of it. The door had a single lock, a simple Yale deadbolt with a beveled keyhole. You could find it at any hardware store. Ricky could disassemble and reassemble that lock in the dark, as a soldier could disassemble and reassemble his machine gun.

But of course it was not the lock that Charlie Capobianco relied on for security. It was the North End itself. Boston's Little Italy. Insular, watchful, all eyes and ears. Not so much a neighborhood as a village within the city. Capobianco had grown up here on Thatcher Street. The road was barely two cars wide curb to curb, walled in by redbrick tenements. Residents easily carried on conversations from open windows on opposite sides of the street. Capobianco knew that a non–North Ender skulking around or breaking into buildings around here would be noticed. He knew it would get back to him. Then, too, maybe he did not need a lock on the door at all, because who would be foolish enough to break into Charlie Capobianco's office?

Ricky slid those four tiny pins up and felt the cylinder turn. He eased inside and locked the door behind him. It was three.A.M.. He had clocked the job for a couple of weeks and determined that this was the ideal time, the quiet Sunday-to-Monday overnight, after the Capobiancos' nocturnal business had been done and before the city began to stir, which happened around five in this blue-collar neighborhood. The office was on the ground floor. Charlie Capobianco's mother and one of his brothers were asleep in apartments upstairs.

Ricky stood stock-still, listening, allowing his eyes to adjust to the darkness. Which was not quite darkness but a dim stony blue-gray light, fed by the ambient street light, and as Ricky's eyes adjusted a long room was exposed. Thirty feet deep. A round Formica dining table with four cheapo vinyl chairs around it. A couch and two upholstered chairs, which might have been secondhand. A small desk in the far corner. A kitchenette. No carpet. Everything crummy and used. No evidence of the Capobiancos' power. None of the equipment you would expect to find in the executive office of a big business—no filing cabinets, no adding machines, just a single telephone—though the Capobianco gambling business was already grossing several million a year, virtually all of it in cash, a torrent of cash that had to be invested or put back out on the street.

Ricky traversed the room slowly. With each step the floor creaked—the ancient floorboards seemed to bend as they accepted his weight—and each noise forced Ricky to freeze again until he was sure no one had heard. His nose wrinkled; the room reeked of garlic.

In the desk he found a few papers, but just a few, and his heart sank. There was a broad clothbound ledger book, rectangular and flat. The binding was held together by two little wing nuts on bolts.

Ricky brought the ledger into the kitchenette. Around a corner was a small sink, the only interior space in the office, shielded from the windows, and here he risked turning on a tiny flashlight, the size of a finger.

Under the flashlight the book was dented and frayed. The cloth cover had faded to a pale green that matched the ledger sheets inside. Long ranks of digits, apparently unlabeled, though Ricky presumed the labels were encoded. Maybe the labels were just numeric as well, as if the accountant who had assembled these ledgers could comprehend only mathematical language—the instinctive language of the Capobiancos. Ricky's eyes skimmed the arrays of digits. He understood only that this was the wash of money through the system, streaming in from card and crap and bar-booth games in the backs of taverns, from bets taken by bookies, and recirculated to the street to be sharked or to cover overhead. Page after page, the digits metering the flow. He came to a page where letters did appear, foreign bodies, like stones in a stream. Names. Names. And one he recognized. His eyes widened.

"What's Capobianco pay you for?"

"Capobianco? Who Capobianco?"

"I just want to know: What does a mobster get for his money?"

"If I were you, boyo, I'd watch my mouth."

"It's a simple question, Brendan."

"Simple question? You should be embarrassed for even asking me such a thing. All three o' yuz, you should be embarrassed. That's all I'm gonna say." Conroy's right hand wrung the skin of his cheek. He looked from Michael to Ricky to Joe, his favorite. "You in on this, Joe?"

"It's like Michael said, Bren: simple question."

"I didn't ask what Michael said. I can handle Michael. I'm asking you. Does he talk for you now?"

"Yeah. He does." Joe's lips went on moving, as if he had intended to say more but no sound came. The ghost words would have been an apology.

"Big happy family, you three."

Michael said, "Not so happy."

"No. I suppose not. You want to tell me what this is about, Michael? You've got all the answers. What's on your mind, Harvard boy?"

"You're on Capobianco's pad."

"Says who?"

"Capobianco."

"Bullshit."

"Look, Brendan, why don't we skip this part, alright? You're offended, okay, I got that. What we want to know is what he pays you for. What do you do for him?"

"You know, I don't get you, Michael. I always treated you like a son. Go ahead, make faces. But I was like a father for you, and you know it."

"Two fathers, then. Lucky me."

"Lucky you is right, boyo."

"Two is one too many. Maybe I'm just old-fashioned."

Ricky smirked.

"Well," Michael said, "good thing we had a spare, eh, Brendan? Where would we be now? Fatherless. Orphans. And who would adopt *us*? Especially Joe."

Conroy squinted, bewildered. He wore plain clothes, a coat and tie that did not sit properly on his cambered chest, and the whole of his torso heaved one time—inhale, exhale. Then—too suddenly for Michael to react—too quick even to register the snap in the old man's mood—Conroy bolted forward—"You fuckin' little shit"—at

451

almost the same instant Joe charged toward Conroy to intercept him—

Michael had a flashing image of two long freight trains on transverse tracks, night trains barreling toward the intersection—

Conroy hit Michael, gathered two fistfuls of his coat, drove him back—

at the same moment Joe's shoulder punched into Conroy's side—

air chuffed out of Conroy's mouth, next to Michael's ear—

and then Michael was on the floor, the small of his back against the baseboard.

He heard Joe's voice, low and lethal: "Try that again, Brendan, and I'll fuckin' kill you." Michael blinked up to see Joe kneeling over Conroy with his rockfist cocked. "I mean it. I'll fuckin' kill you."

"Joe!"

"Joe!"

Joe's head inclined toward his brothers' voices, but he did not release Conroy and he did not unclench his fist.

"Joe," Conroy soothed, "what are you talking about, kill who? Who do you think you're talking to? Let me go, boyo, come on. This is ridiculous. Let me up, son."

Joe remained frozen, his left arm locked on Conroy's shirtfront, right arm cranked back. For a long moment it seemed that he would launch that fist straight down into Conroy's face and straight through it to the floor. But Joe's expression faltered and became poignant, and his fist relaxed perceptibly.

"That's right, Joe. Let me up." Conroy tapped Joe's wrist.

The contact seemed to jolt Joe back from his thoughts. Reinvigorated, he agitated Conroy's shirt and pressed him down into the floor more firmly. He straightened his fingers and balled them again to harden his fist.

Conroy made a short-armed gesture of surrender, palms up.

Michael said, "Joe? You okay?"

"What's he been telling you, Joe?" Conroy nodded toward Michael. "He's been filling your head up, hasn't he?"

Joe shook his head slowly, but the questions diverted him, complicated everything, flooded him with facts and speculations and unknowns, all Michael's and Ricky's theories which Joe half understood for a moment only to lose them again. "What about me, Brendan? Did you treat me like a son, too?"

"You know I did."

Joe shook his head again. He yearned for the words. It was an affliction, this constant clutching for words. It felt as if he had been excluded from a conversation. Intuitions murmured past, thoughts that could not be condensed into language, and were lost before Joe could hear them. He imagined there was more to himself, a secret unrealized Joe hidden in all those mutterings, a Joe that would never be accessed. Now, what did he want to say to

Conroy? The simple truth—*I loved you, you broke my heart*—was unsayable, and was not the whole story anyway. But no other words were available.

Joe said, "You're not my friend."

Immediately he was embarrassed. What a childish, stupid thing to say. He wished he had not said anything at all. He wished he could go back ten seconds into the past, before he had exposed himself as a dumbshit. But the declaration mesmerized Conroy and Joe's brothers too, and seeing its impact Joe began to feel he had stumbled onto the right formulation almost by accident, as if he had sat down at a piano and banged the keys and somehow a song had emerged, a miraculous perfect little song. He let go of Conroy's shirt.

Joe said, "I'm through with you, Bren. Just answer Mike's question."

"What's he been telling you, Joe?"

"Just answer him."

Conroy labored to his feet. He retreated to the opposite side of the room.

Ricky came over to offer Michael a hand up. "You alright, Mikey?"

"Yeah."

"You and your new daddy seem to be hitting it off pretty good."

"Yeah, I think he's warming up to me."

Conroy tugged his clothes straight. "You boys act like you've discovered some original sin. Well, I'm not very original, I hate to tell you. It's the way things work."

Michael said, "Oh Christ, Brendan, nobody gives

a shit you were on the sleeve. But from Capobianco? The guy's a murderer, for Christ's sake."

"So what, I took from Capobianco? You think your old man was too good to take Capobianco's money?"

"Yes."

Conroy shook his head. "Just let it go, Michael. You don't know your ass from a hole in the ground, alright? You hear me? You don't know from Capobianco, you don't know what it means to be a cop, you don't know shit from Shinola, and I'm telling you, as a friend: Just let it alone. The hell do you care about Capobianco, anyways?"

"I'll tell you what I care. Turns out your boss Capobianco killed my father—I mean my real father, Brendan, the first one, remember him?"

"Wha . . . ? How do you know that?"

"A little bird."

"What little bird?"

"Goombah named Paul Marolla."

"Who the hell is Paul Marolla?"

"What's the difference?"

"Well, according to you, he's a witness in a murder. I'm in Homicide. I want to talk to him."

"That's not going to be so easy. He's tied up."

"The fuck does that mean?"

"He's in the trunk of a car in Revere somewhere. They'll probably find him in June or July, first good heat wave. The way I heard the story is Marolla took some of Charlie Capobianco's money and Charlie was not willing to just let it go. So Marolla goes into the trunk and on the way out he starts blabbing: He knows about the West End, he knows about my dad. So you see where this is headed, Brendan: You worked for Capobianco; you were there when Joe Daley died—maybe Capobianco wanted Joe Daley dead. A plus B equals C. But what am I telling *you*? You're a homicide detective, you know how this works."

"You got it wrong."

"So enlighten me. Just answer the fucking question! What did you do for Capobianco?"

"Same as your old man did! Same as half the department does for someone or other! Capobianco runs bookie joints. It's not like we don't know where they are. I didn't bother with them. That's it. We let him operate."

"He pays you too much for just that. I heard you're one of the highest-paid guys he's got."

"He pays me more because I have stripes on my sleeve. Doesn't mean I do a goddamn thing for him. I worked my way up, same as everyone else. Besides, most of what he gives me is for other people. I'm a middleman. It's part of my job."

"Come on, Brendan. I always thought a crooked cop—"

"You righteous little pri—"

"—I always thought a crooked cop had to do a little more and a little more, know what I mean? You fix a ticket, then you fix a little case in the BMC, then maybe you make some evidence disappear, then someday you find yourself picking up the phone if there's going to be a raid and Mr.

Capobianco might want a little fair warning. Work your way up, like you said."

"What does that have to do with murder?"

"How far up did you work, Brendan?"

"Now that's enough. This conversation is over."

Joe parallel-parked his grumbling Eighty-Eight in front of the old house, under the basketball hoop.

In the front passenger seat, Michael realized that, for the first time, he felt no connection to this house. Just a pile of boards, barely distinguishable from the other double-and triple-deckers lining the street, all of them peeling brown and white, and tilting slightly on sunk foundations like uneven teeth. Had he really grown up here? It felt like a hundred years ago. Maybe he would try to convince his mother to sell this old dump, go somewhere nice, maybe near the water, maybe the Cape. She never would, of course. She planned to live here. With Conroy.

Margaret appeared at the top of the stairs before they even got out of the car. The sleeves of her sweater, a fuchsia cardigan, were pushed up to her elbows. Her hair was held back by a headband, a girlish detail, but she did not look young. Her face looked pale. Her thin, lipsticked mouth stood out like a red incision in her porcelain face.

Old women had to be careful about lipstick, Michael thought. They could look so red-mouthed and smeary and ridiculous.

"What are you three up to?" Without unfolding her arms, Margaret glanced at her watch and frowned. They should be at work now. Honest people were all at work now.

Michael said, "We need to talk to you, Ma."

"Talk," Ricky advised, "or Joe'll beat the crap out of you."

Each of the boys bent to bump-kiss her cheek as they passed. She received these kisses impassively, arms still folded, with a swivel of her head to offer up her cheek.

Michael thought she gave him a particularly cool look, but he could not be sure and in any case he did not, for once, feel quite as vulnerable to her. He felt, vaingloriously, like a prince sweeping past with his retinue.

It was Michael, after all, whom Joe had sought out to confide what had happened up in Revere and to share the tip that the mob had some kind of role in Joe Senior's murder. It was Michael who had counseled his brothers to solve the mystery together, not so much to pool their various talents but because the outsiders whose job it was to find Senior's killer had failed and, worse, seemed to have given up. And it was Michael who had directed Ricky to break into Capobianco's head-quarters—though his goal had been to corroborate Marolla's tip, to find some scrap of evidence that would link the Capobiancos to the murder. The dis-covery of Conroy's name in the ledger had been a surprise. Maybe it should not have been.

The Daleys sat in the kitchen, at the little break-fast table. This table had just four seats, so it had been used when Joe Senior was at work during mealtimes. But then, Joe Senior had been at work during most mealtimes. A detective's work schedule did not have much to do with the ordinary nine-to-five workday. Homicide had been the worst; he would disappear for days at a time, working a case while it was hot. The boys had come to think of this table as theirs—the place where they could laugh out loud and stick green beans in their noses and fight over the sports page. It had an avocado Formica top flecked with little gold asterisks and a scalloped aluminum band around the sides, like you would see in a diner.

When the situation was explained to Margaret, minus a few gruesome or worrisome details, she did not seem to find anything especially new in it. Her husband was still dead, under mysterious circumstances. And Brendan Conroy was still what he was: a bit of a blustery politician but a good man and an old friend. She did not believe Brendan was corrupt, merely that he lived in a turbid atmosphere—you could hardly walk around in this city without it leaving a little grime on your nose. So her boys had scratched up a couple of new details. What had changed, really? Nothing. Michael did not like Brendan—that was what it all boiled down to. Well, those two were just oil and water, and they would have to find a way to get along. That was Michael's problem, not Brendan's, and certainly not hers.

But now there was something new. It was not just Michael anymore. Now he had Joe believing it, too, that Brendan was some kind of villain. And Ricky!

Joe had always been a get-along go-along sort of boy, an easy mark. But Ricky? God bless 'm, he was a living saint—but Ricky looked out for Ricky. Ricky was the kid who stole the quarters Michael collected to send to the pagan babies in Biafra. Yet here were all three of them, her all-grown-up children, ganging up on her.

Michael said, "I don't think he should be here anymore."

"Oh, good Lord, Michael, haven't we been all through this?"

"Just till we know."

"I already know. I know Brendan. It's enough for me."

"He can't stay here anymore. When this is over, if I'm wrong, I'll set it straight with him. But for now it's better he gets out."

"Why, Michael? Because some gangster knows Brendan's name?"

"Yes."

"Ma," Joe said, "just do what he says."

She flicked a withering glance at Joe. Who asked him? "He's still Brendan. He's been our friend a long time, Michael, longer than you've been alive. You don't just turn your back like that."

"Look, you tell him anything you want. Blame it on me. Tell him I'm crazy. But I don't want him around here, I don't want him around you. Just till we get this straightened out."

She shook her head in a noncommittal way.

"Did Dad ever talk to you about Capobianco?"

"No. He never talked about work. He went off to

460

work and he came home. He was never much of a talker, you know that."

"You ever hear him mention that name? Capobianco?"

"Not to me. He and Amy used to talk about it."

"Amy?" Michael's head wavered, as if knocked back.

"You know how Amy was. If she wanted to know something, she wasn't afraid to ask."

"What did she ask him about?"

"Well, she was always after your dad for stories. Dope about the police department, about whatever she was working on. It was not a big deal. They were family. They chatted."

"He was the source."

"Well, I wouldn't call him a *source*—"

Michael shook his head. His right hand went to his brow, smoothing the eyebrows with two fingers absently—

and he sensed somewhere in his skull, afloat behind the thick bonewall of his forehead, the first dim presence of pain, like a ghost.

He saw the two women.

Claire, the career-girl newspaper reporter. *Two-legged rats in the West End. Lots of money to be made there. That's the kind of cheese those rats like. Find the cheese.*

And of course he saw Amy, too, the night before she was killed. Why would Brendan Conroy kill Joe Senior? What motive? *I have an idea.* A wiseacre smirk. *I have an idea.* And of course she did have an idea: because Senior had been spilling what was

461

going on in the West End. The West End had to be cleared. The New Boston had to come.

The pain hovered in his skull, settling now behind the right eyeball. A tumorous weight leaned against the back of the eyeball. An ache. It draped itself over the ocular nerve like a boa on a tree branch. Still faint.

He tried to empty his head of thought, of stress. He was not his body; he was *in* his body, and he could control it. Maybe the storm would pass him by, blow out harmlessly to sea.

"You alright, Mikey?"

"Yeah. I'm okay."

"You don't look okay."

"We got to go. There's something—"

The three of them stood to leave. Michael put his hand on the table to steady himself.

Ricky grabbed his arm. "Sure you're okay?"

"Yeah."

Michael let his eyes close.

He was not his body. He was *in* his body. Empty the mind. Release the pressure.

But it was already too late. The thing was inside him. The anxiety of the last few days. Plunging from one lead to the next, feeling the solution closer and closer. He wished he was not there. He wished he was at home. He did not like people to see him when the migraines came. It was a weakness, this inability to regulate one's own body.

"You know what?" he said. "Maybe I better just—"

There had been no aura this time. No illusions—

no melting surfaces or mosaic vision, no sense of wonder. The aura did not always come. Sometimes it was just pain.

"Mike," he heard Joe say, "want me to drive you home?"

"No. I'm just gonna go lie down for a while. I'll catch up with you guys later. Sorry. I hate this." He shuffled toward the kitchen door. "I hate this."

Later. An hour, several hours.

There was a sound in the dark, in the deep space: a ticking like the tip of a tree branch tapping a windowpane.

Near its peak, Michael thought. Had to be. It squeezed his head like a helmet. In the interior of his skull there was throbbing, synchronized to his pulse. He felt, or imagined he felt, the beating of vascular arteries as they piped the toxic fluids into his head, the rhythmic earthwormy bunching-and-stretching of peristalsis.

Again, he caught that sound in the darkness. Less faint. Rhythmic. Approaching. Chink-chink-chink. More insistent now, like a child's finger tapping on the window, demanding to be let in. *Chink-chink-chink*.

He lay on his side, utterly still, and searched for the sound, but the signal was weak.

Chick-chick-chick-chick.

There it was! Footsteps.

The pain subsided momentarily.

Chick-chick-*BANG!* As if a door had slammed open and the sound that was distant and external

463

was now inside his head, chick-chick-chick-chick-chick-chick.

He saw feet running, close up, black patrolman's shoes in a dead sprint, soles scratching the sandy pavement.

Joe Daley, Sr., so vivid! So thrillingly close! His cheeks jounced with each step. His nylon windbreaker luffed and crinkled as the wind filled it. He held one hand over his heart to keep his junk—reading glasses, notebook, smokes—from jumping out of his shirt pocket.

Michael could reach out and touch him. Inches away. Touch his father's face.

But Joe Senior pulled away. Michael was behind him now. Saw his legkick as he ran. Eastie warehouses to the left, harbor to the right.

Farther behind Joe Senior—well behind—was Conroy. He chugged along slowly, then jogged, then stopped altogether. He grimaced. What had he done? What had he done to his friend?

Joe Senior seemed to sense his partner had dropped away. At the corner of one of the big red-brick buildings, he turned around and spread his hands: *The hell are you doing, Brendan?*

"You go," Conroy wheezed. "I'll catch up."

Joe Senior shook his head. Conroy was a character. How they had lasted this long together he would never know.

Senior disappeared around the corner of the building into the alley.

Enough!

Michael had seen enough. He turned off the

464

movie. He knew how it ended. He knew how to make the pieces fit. There would be time to confirm it later. For now, sleep.

Margaret opened the door and the young man swept in with it, as leaves that have accumulated in a doorway will be pulled inside when the door is opened. He did not step all the way into the house. He stopped directly in front of her.

"Hello, Margaret."

There was a delay, a fraction of a second, during which Margaret placed him—there were bruises on Kurt Lindstrom's face, one of his hands was bandaged—then she slammed the door against him with a yelp of surprise and fear. He warded off the door, pressed it open again. Margaret continued to push for a moment but realized she would not be able to force him out, so she stepped back. She behaved as if she had invited him in, as if she was not distressed by his presence. What choice was there? She retreated to the living room.

"Oh, come on, Margaret. What are you so afraid of?"

"I'm not afraid."

"No. No reason to be."

"I'm not."

"Course you're not. Nothing to be afraid of."

"My sons will be home soon."

"Will they?" He checked his watch. "It's late."

"What are you doing here?"

"Visiting."

465

He ambled into the small room. His posture was lazy and pliant, like a teenager's.

She got out a cigarette from a pack on the coffee table and lighted it in an actressy way. They were talking, at least. That seemed to matter, to suggest that she had a say in what might happen here. She could engage him, steer him.

"What happened to your hand?"

Lindstrom looked at the hand. "Your son."

She presumed he meant Joe. "I'm sorry."

"Oh, I don't blame you. Why don't you offer me a drink?"

"A drink?"

"Yes, a drink. What kind of hostess are you?"

"I don't—what, what would you like to drink?"

"What do you have, Margaret?"

"There's some beer, I think."

"No, not beer. How about Scotch. Do you have Scotch?"

"I'll go see."

"Why don't I come along? Maybe you'll have one, too."

She led him into the kitchen. She walked with her arms stiff at her sides.

The booze was in a cabinet at eye level. She raised her arm to open it, self-conscious of how the gesture tautened her clothes against her back and shoulder. Should she scream? Run for the door? She doubted she would make it to the door before him, even allowing for the advantage of surprise. A scream, she thought, would alarm him, set him off. As long as they were talking, maintaining the pretense of civility, there was hope.

She said, facing the cabinet still, "How do you want it?"

"Neat. Make one for yourself too, Margaret."

"I don't drink it."

"Alright, then. You don't have to do anything you don't want to do."

She poured his drink and handed it to him. Should she have thrown it in his eyes? Would it have worked?

"What do you want, Margaret?"

"I'm not thirsty."

He laughed. "No, not to drink. What do you want, right now?"

"I want you to leave."

"But I just got here."

"It's late. I want to go to bed."

"Will you have me back another time?"

"Yes."

"Now, why don't I believe you?"

She started to say something, a lie to reassure him. She felt her lips move but no sound came. He had no weapon. At least he did not seem to. She could not be sure. In most of the Strangler cases there had been no weapon. The Strangler had used whatever heavy object came to hand to bash his victims, then improvised a garrotte from whatever he had found in their apartments—nylons, bathrobe sashes, scarves, sheets. But in a few of the cases there had been knife wounds, mutilation . . .

"Margaret?"

"It's true. Another time you can come. It's late."

He turned his bruised face forty-five degrees and looked at her from an angle, skeptically. "What has Michael told you about me?"

"Michael?"

"Yes, Michael Daley. Your son."

"Nothing."

"Nothing about the Strangler?"

The air went out of her. The subject had now been introduced and would have to be addressed, finessed, if she was going to maneuver out of the situation. "No."

Lindstrom offered no response, but something in his posture, a tensioning along his elastic spine, suggested he knew she was lying. They were on different terms now.

"He says," Margaret elaborated, "there's more than one strangler."

"Yes, but one for the old ladies, isn't that right?"

"I don't, I don't know. Most of them, yes, I suppose."

"Not DeSalvo."

"No."

"Me."

She did not answer.

"Oh, come on, Mrs. Daley. He's told me as much."

"I don't know. I just . . ."

Lindstrom nodded. He already knew all the answers, knew she was lying, knew *why* she was lying. None of it mattered at this point. What would happen, would happen. "May I ask you something, Margaret? A personal question?"

Her eyes went to the floor. Sheet linoleum in a pebble pattern of browns and ochers, dull with age.

"Have you ever had it in the ass?"

Her rectum and buttocks contracted. The rest of her, shoulders, neck, backbone, all went slack. She was not really there—this simply could not be happening.

"Have you ever had it in the ass?"

"Oh my God," she murmured.

"Have you?"

"Oh my God."

"Well, either you have or you haven't. It's a yes-or-no question."

Her head was bowed. She managed to rustle it back and forth: no.

"Why don't you get those clothes off?"

"No . . . no . . ."

"It's not so hard."

"I can't."

"You want me to do it?" He put down his glass. "Come over there and do it for you?"

"No."

"What do you want, then?"

"Want?"

"That's right. We're just a couple of old friends here having a chat. You can tell me anything."

"Oh my God."

"Just tell me, Margaret. Anything you desire."

"I want you to please leave."

"Leave? Just like that?"

"I won't tell anyone."

"You mean, you know who the Strangler is, the

Boston Strangler, but you'll keep it to yourself? You, a policeman's wife?"

"I don't know anything. Some mixed-up kid in some kind of beef with one of my sons . . ."

He picked up the glass, sipped, and his mouth made a series of puckers as he considered. "Alright, then."

"You'll go?"

"On one condition: you tell your son Michael I came around to say goodbye."

"Where are you going?"

"Parts unknown."

"Okay. I'll tell him."

"One more thing and then I'll go. I'd like a kiss."

Her head craned forward slightly, as if she had not heard.

"That's all. Just a kiss goodbye. Then I'll go."

She shook her head.

"Well, then it looks like I'm here for the duration. Shall we get back to our conversation?"

"Just a kiss?"

"A kiss and I'll go."

"I have your word?"

"Scout's honor."

"One kiss and you'll go."

"That's right."

She moved in front of him. Lindstrom was younger than Ricky, her youngest, by several years. Maybe it was just his appearance, smooth-skinned, ruddy. He might be half her age. Or less. He smelled of Scotch. She closed her eyes and tipped her head.

"No-no, you kiss me, Margaret. For a count of ten, let's say. Get my money's worth."

She could knee him in the crotch, or run, or search for a weapon. But she would not. She knew she would not do any of those clever, resourceful things people did in movies. It was only a kiss.

She placed her closed lips against Lindstrom's. One, two, three . . .

His hand went to the back of her head. His tongue emerged from his lips, thick and eely; it penetrated her mouth. A muffled squeal. He pressed her face against his. The tongue was of a grotesque length. Its surface had a fine nubby grain. The tip of it did something fancy against the roof of her mouth then circled around nearer the gumline. The broad fleshy body of it flattened itself against her and wiped back and forth, luxuriating.

He let go of her, and she fell back. She thought she might vomit.

He sighed contentedly. "Wasn't so bad, was it?"

She gave no response.

"Mmmm. Thank you, Margaret."

"You said you'd go."

"And so I will."

They moved toward the kitchen door. He gestured for her to go first. She did not like the thought of him being behind her, but the door was just a few feet away, the whole incident nearly over—she could already see herself ten seconds ahead, relieved, unhurt—and she felt the lure of that so-near moment. It occurred to her, too, that he had gestured her forward exactly the same way in

471

exactly the same spot when he had come to the house the first time.

She went ahead, arms folded. Her tongue mopped the roof of her mouth to scrub away the taste-memory of him. She was disgusted with her body. The filth of him, his spit, his taste, would be piped down her throat into her guts. She would absorb it. But she had to be strong for only a few more seconds, a few more steps.

There was a flash and a hollow sound.

Nothing. An empty moment.

Then she was aware of being on the floor. The hall floor. On her back. She could see up the stairs.

His hands were under her skirt. He was stripping off her nylon stockings. She heard a groggy voice say, "Don't rip my stockin's," and it was a moment before she quite knew that the voice was her own. He tugged the stockings down over her calves, over her heels. Somehow her shoes had already come off.

She screamed.

He punched her face twice. "Don't scream."

He sat down heavily on her stomach. She felt the weight of his body oscillate on her stomach as he wound up the stockings together.

Her head was jostled roughly then dropped back down on the floor, hard. She wanted to reach for the back of her head, but he had pinned her arms with his legs.

She felt the nylon rope pull up against the back of her neck as he made the first simple overunder knot, then the rope zipped down tight, it cut into her neck, cinched it shut, and she could not breathe or stand the rocketing pain of it. She thrashed, panicked, and even as she did so she felt him completing the knot, securing the noose.

His weight lifted off her.

She continued to thrash until she could pry her fingers under the nylon and open a little space to gasp a stingy little breath, but already she felt herself being lifted by her hair and pulled up the stairs and she had to kick with her feet to keep her body moving so the top of her head did not get yanked right off.

"Come on, you."

The stairs banged against her back and her bare heels and she was actually relieved when they reached the smooth upstairs hallway. She kept her legs crabwalking as best she could as she felt her skirt being lowered by the friction of her back and butt against the floor, she felt her shirt untuck and the floor scrape against the bare skin of her lower back.

"Where's the bedroom!"

He released her hair and she dropped painfully on her shoulder. Her scalp ached. She wondered if the skin that tightly bagged the skull could be separated from it somehow, lifted away from that ball of bone, and whether the two could ever be rejoined as they were before.

She heard the bedroom door open.

Lindstrom made a sound—"Heh"—whose meaning she could not guess and before she could parse that syllable—

there was an explosion and Lindstrom staggered back against the wall before her.

She scanned up from his oxblood-red loafers to his khakis where, above the right knee, a red stain had blossomed.

She turned her head, painfully—the nylons—and saw in the darkness of her bedroom, underlighted from the hallway, Michael with his father's gun. He was ghastly pale, white as marble, as he always was during a migraine attack. In the dim light, shoeless and crazyhaired and wearing his undershirt, he looked like a ghost of himself. Behind him the drawer where the gun was kept was still open, her lingerie spilling out. (It occurred to her that, in Joe Senior's twenty-three-and-a-half years on the force, it was the first time the gun had ever been fired outside the practice range.) Michael held the gun in one hand, but the weight of it seemed too much for him. It threatened to topple him forward.

Above her, Lindstrom encircled the stain with the fingers of both hands, as if he meant to choke it. But the blossom of red continued to deepen and evolve as he, and she, watched it.

Michael took two unsteady slide-steps toward the bedroom door.

Lindstrom looked from his wound to Michael to Margaret to the gun. He darted off.

Margaret and Michael heard him stomp down the stairs and out the door and away down the street.

Michael took one more slow-motion step in the

direction of Margaret before his head rolled to one side and he seemed to glance upward and his body ribboned down to the floor.

Charging up the stairs with Joe, looking up at him from a few steps below with the foreshortened perspective that angle imposes, it occurred to Ricky what an awesome creature Joe really was, a centaur with massive haunches above oddly dainty ankles. He would hardly have been surprised if one of Joe's sneakers slipped off to reveal a black hoof. Joe had come here to kill Lindstrom. Ricky had no doubt he meant to do it. He had his service pistol with him. If Lindstrom was lucky, Joe would use the gun. For his part, Ricky still was not sure, halfway up the stairs, whether he would help with the killing or prevent it. *If* he could prevent it, that is, once Joe got started.

Joe kicked in Lindstrom's door with a single stomp by the door handle. He stood in the doorway panting.

The apartment was empty. All that remained was an old Westinghouse electric fan, unplugged, and a few loose papers on the floor. Kurt Lindstrom was gone.

He would never be seen in Boston again.

Walking on a warm night made Joe think of dying—not afraid, just aware that there could only be so many nights like this, strolling in shirtsleeves, in any one lifespan. So, when he felt a hand grab his upper arm, he was already in a waning mood, prepared, philosophically at least, for the possibility of some Very Bad Thing. And yet he was misled momentarily by the busyness of his surroundings—Boylston Street at Park Square, where a new Playboy Club was under construction— and by the intimacy of the touch—an insinuating wiggle of four fat fingers in the crevice of his armpit—so that when he turned, he was wearing a bemused smile. He was expecting to see a friend.

Instead he found himself face-to-face with one of Gargano's apes. Joe knew this man. His name was like a birdcall, Chico Tirico. A typical street-soldier type, a slab-faced guinea wiseguy. Tirico was fitter than most of them, though. He had been a heavyweight boxer and stayed in shape. No incipient double chin, no bowling-ball belly dropping out of his shirt. (Gargano himself had been a fighter, too, once upon a time. It was not an unusual background among mob stalkers. The neighborhood boxing gyms were like stud farms. A Golden Gloves kid could always have a muscle job if he wanted it.)

"Hey, cop," Tirico said.

Joe slapped the guy's hand away indignantly. He did not like the way it looked, the suggestion that some mook could place him under arrest. He was still a cop, despite everything.

There were three other goons alongside. Alerted by Joe's gesture, they drew closer.

"Take it easy," Tirico cooed.

They drew back again, and Gargano came into view. He looked sallow and drugged. Word was

476

that Gargano had been doing heroin for years now, and his habit was getting out of control. His face seemed out of focus; Joe glanced away from him to the grid of red bricks on a wall to be sure his vision was still sharp—that the blurring was indeed in Gargano's face and not Joe's eyes.

Gargano said, "Somebody wants to talk to you."

"Who?"

"The big boss."

"Wants to talk to me?"

"That's right."

"Bullshit." Joe gestured with his eyes at the four apes. "Why all the muscle if alls we're gonna do is talk?"

"It's just talk, Joe. You have my word."

"Where?"

"C.C.'s Lounge, right around the corner. You'll be back in a minute, like nothing ever happened."

Joe calculated. It was reckless of Gargano to approach him in such a public place, even after dark—a gangster grabbing a cop off a busy downtown street. Joe took it as another sign of his own diminishing life expectancy; Gargano would not risk burning a valuable source if he meant to keep him around much longer. Then again, in a heroin haze Gargano's erratic behavior might not signal anything at all except his own unraveling. Vinnie The Animal was following a wellworn Mob career path: He would go out in a blaze of glory someday, done in by the very wildness that had made him, like Paul Muni in *Scarface*. But if The Animal had intended to kill Joe, he would not have pulled a stunt like this one. In any case, Gargano had too much muscle on his side. Joe opted for a tactical retreat.

"Alright," he said. "I'll meet you there."

"No. Come on, come with us in the car."

"Pretty crowded car. What, am I gonna ride in the trunk?"

"For fuck's sake, Joe, I already told you, it's not like that. I swear."

"Just the same. Nice night for a stroll."

Gargano shook his head. People were so mistrustful. "Alright, you stroll, then."

Chico Tirico gave him a shove. "Stroll, motherfucker."

Joe let it go.

He walked three blocks through the Combat Zone to C.C.'s Lounge, on Tremont, as Gargano's blackfinned Caddy lurked alongside, tactlessly.

Reassembled there, the group marched through the bar. The early-evening drinkers all turned their heads in silence to watch them pass, the prisoner and his escort.

Down an ancient staircase to a basement office. Grimy, small, windowless. A few chairs, a desk.

Two men waited inside.

Gargano gestured for Joe to go inside, and he did.

The smaller of the two men stood facing him. He was slim and tall, thought not as tall as Joe. Mid-fifties, Italian, with dark thick hair going gray at the sides and in a patch above his forehead. He stood in a theatrically defiant way: arms folded, head tipped back, offering his chin and a Mussolini frown.

"You're Daley?" the man said.

"Yeah."

"You know who I am?"

"No."

"I'm Carlo Capobianco. This is my brother Niccolo."

Joe had heard of Charlie and Nicky Capobianco. Tonight they were Carlo and Niccolo. They were Italian and Joe was not. At the moment this fact seemed to be all that mattered.

"This is the last time you disrespect me. You hear me? Last fuckin' time. Your whole fuckin' family. Your brother the thief steals from me, now you make trouble for me, what am I supposed to do?" He glowered.

"Is this about money?"

"Is this about money?" Capobianco's face tensed.

" 'Cause I can get the money up. I swear."

Capobianco came forward, suddenly and inexplicably pissed off. He stopped a few steps from Joe so that the disparity in their heights would not be so apparent, and he stood with his chest out and chin up like a gamecock. He spoke fast and loud: "Are you fuckin' stupid? These Irish fuckin' cops— what, do you got fuckin' rocks in your head? Answer me, you got rocks in your head? Or *potatuhs*? Look at 'm: nine feet tall and nothing but *potatuhs* in his head. This is what we got, a whole police department full of these backward fuckin' Paddys. How the fuck do you guys ever fuckin' catch anyone? You walk around with your hand out and your head up your ass—what I want to know is, how the fuck do you ever catch anyone? Huh? Let me ask you something. How is it when the Italians already ruled the fuckin' world, a thousand years ago or whatever, you fuckin' Paddys were still running around in the woods like fuckin' cavemen, digging in the dirt for something to eat?"

"I don't know."

"You don't know? You fuckin' stupid?"

"No."

"No? No? I hear you're a fuckin' idiot. I hear you're about the stupidest Paddy cocksucker on the police force. And that's saying something."

It occurred to Joe that, all things being equal, he could break this greaseball guido midget in half with one hand. But all things were not equal.

Capobianco wiped a curl of spittle at the corner of his mouth. "This is the last time you disrespect me."

"Charlie." Nick smiled in a way calculated to soothe both men. He was older and coolerheaded than his brother. He wiggled his finger: *Let's get on with it*.

Charlie Capobianco said, "You been told to stay out of the West End?"

Joe was thrown. He was prepared to talk about money. Capobianco would threaten him about his spiraling debt, demand he pay it off or else, and Joe in turn would offer whatever empty promises came to mind. It was an exchange he and Gargano had rehearsed many times already. It was supposed to be about money, not the West End.

"You were told, stay out of there, let it alone."

"Yeah."

"Then you get moved out of Station One and they tell you again: Stay out of the West End. And still I got to hear about this dumb fuckin' Paddy cop running around over there. You take my money? Like the rest of the pig cops in Station One, you take my fuckin' money?"

"I guess so."

"So how come when I ask you for something you don't do it?"

"I don't understand. You asked me for something?"

"Jesus, you are a dumb fuck. I told you to stay out of the West End. You stupid fuck."

Joe's thoughts snagged on the word *stupid* every time it was repeated. He had to force himself to hear the rest. He rotated his head so that one ear was aimed at Capobianco, to be sure he caught it all and could repeat the remainder of the sentence in his mind minus that word. What the hell was Capobianco ranting about?

"What," Joe said simply, "do you care about the West End?"

"Never mind what I care. Your job isn't to think. You're not smart enough to think. Your job is to fuckin' do what you're told." Charlie Capobianco wandered away from Joe, deeper into the small office. "Just do what you're told or you're gonna wind up like your thief brother."

"What's this got do with my brother? This has got nothing to do with my brother."

"No. He's got enough trouble."

"He didn't do nothin'."

"No? Well, just the same, I wouldn't stand too close to him. Be a shame to lose the both o' yuz."

"You stay the fuck away from my brother."

"What?" Capobianco was livid again, the switch was thrown. "What did you say to me?"

But Joe was too far gone. Fuck Capobianco. Fuck this whole thing. "I said, stay the fuck away from my brother." He saw Capobianco's expression coil again, and knew he had fucked up. But it was too late.

Charlie Capobianco said to his brother, "Get this fuckin' guy out of here. Get him out." Then to Joe: "I'm through with you, cop. You understand me? Do you know who I am? You better learn your fuckin' place. Learn your fuckin' place. This is the last time you'll disrespect me. You know what a contract is?"

"Yes."

"Then don't stand too close to your brother."

Joe absorbed the warning slowly.

"And stay the fuck out of the West End. This is your last warning. You cost me enough money already. And to answer your other question: it's always about money. Dumb fuck, what'd you think it was about?"

Joe tended to sleep in short snatches of two or three hours. When he had worked nights, years before, his body had become accustomed to the inside-out schedule: first halfs alternating with second halfs— a six-to-midnight shift one night, midnight to eight A.M. the next—six nights a week, or three cycles. "Short days" and "long days," cops called them. Sleep no longer correlated to night. You slept when you could for as long as you could, but always too little. Joe's work schedule had improved after he made detective, but by then he seemed to have lost the ability to sleep deeply. At best, he drifted just beneath the surface of waking. As a result, he thought, he tended not to dream, at least he did not remember his dreams. Dreaming occurred during deep sleep; Joe could not submerge that far.

But tonight he did dream. He dreamed he was climbing into the back seat of a car. A coupe of some kind with a tomato-red interior. He thought it might be the new Bel Air by the way the roofline curved downward to enwrap the backseat passengers. Someone was holding the driver's seat forward for him; he could not see who. Joe did not want to be in this car. He could not straighten his neck, the roof was too low. He tried to tip his head but his hair rubbed against the headliner, so he slouched down on the bench seat, only to see the roof drop down even farther. He panicked. He knew that if he stayed in the car, coffined in the back seat, he would die there. He struggled to climb out.

And then he was awake, in his body in his bed in his room, with the window open. No longer afraid. The bedroom was cool. A bluish light from the street illuminated everything, as it always did.

"Jesus," he whispered. He reached behind him and his hand found Kat's substantial rump.

She had been a nurse when he met her, a big square-jawed girl with a sense of command about her. That was what had first attracted him, not her looks but that air of mastery. She was the kind of girl who got things done, who managed. Joe had always known he was just a knockaround guy, but when he was with her he had felt a little of her competence and gravity. He figured maybe he could manage, too. Not anymore, of course. As Joe had dashed himself against the rocks, his wife's sensibility had only made him feel the more out of control. But once . . . once.

He rolled onto his back, ran his hand down the slope of her hip. Her nightgown was cool. She did not stir.

He thought of Capobianco's words, *This is the last time you'll disrespect me*, and wondered whether they were meant as an order (*Don't disrespect me again*) or a threat (*You won't get another chance to disrespect me*). It was ridiculous, even funny, that he might die without ever realizing he had been warned—like a cow he would be herded into the slaughterhouse, unknowing right to the end. It seemed significant that Capobianco had chosen such ambiguous words. He had left room for interpretation. Also, it did not make sense that Capobianco would arrange a personal audience just to inform Joe he would be killed. Clearly his intention was to bar Joe from the West End, just as Capobianco had said. Yes, Joe had fucked up by backtalking, but volatile guys like Capobianco forgot such things as soon as they calmed down, or were swept up by the next outrage. Yes, Capobianco would get around to killing Joe someday, when he had extracted all the cash and advantage he could extract. But not soon. For now, the one in immediate peril was Ricky. *Do you know what a contract is?*

Through the open window Joe heard the sounds of the city. Kat stirred under his hand. He waited to see if she would roll away to go on sleeping or roll toward him for warmth. She came to him, lifted her head and laid it on his chest. He squeezed her back, her arm, her tit in an experimental way, reminding himself. She was not what she had used to be. Her strong body was now padded with a quilty layer of fat. But she was still herself, and he was reminded that her bigness had been part of the attraction in the first place. She was built, if not to the scale of his own body, then at least to grander specifications than the perfumed broads he usually chased around, who tottered around on spindly heels to raise themselves up. He felt himself begin to get hard, and it occurred to him that all his "cheating" had actually enhanced his appreciation for Kat, and he congratulated himself on his open-mindedness with regard to women. Sampling other women only made him appreciate his wife all the more. What could be more destructive to a marriage than monogamy? You simply had to handle the issue with discretion, as Joe always had. What Kat didn't know would never hurt her.

"You awake?" he whispered.

"No."

"I am."

She felt him. "Jesus, Joe, you've got to be kidding. Now? All this time . . ."

"Lie back," he said.

Under his hands she lay half sleeping, and even when she lifted her nightgown over her head he thought she might be sleeping. Her arms were clumsy. Maybe to Kat this was a dream.

It was when he was inside her, surrounded by her body's warmth, that Joe saw this house without him in it. Kat, Little Joe—dying would mean saying goodbye to them, and they would go on living. Would Kat marry someone else? Where would she live? Would she be happy? And Little Joe. He was nearly fourteen now. What would he remember of his old man ten years on, or twenty? Would he think of his dad every day or not at all? Would thinking of Joe make them happy or sad? Who would they go to when they were in trouble? Margaret, Michael? Joe's dying would be one last thing he would steal from them.

He faltered, felt himself soften.

"You okay, Joe?"

"Yeah."

"What's wrong?"

"Nothing. Sorry."

Kat held his face in her two hands and studied him. "What is it, Joe?"

"Just tired."

"*Now* you're tired?"

He grinned, expelling air from his nostrils.

"Wakes me up in the middle of the night and then he says he's tired."

Joe decided to purge his mind of everything that was outside the four corners of the bed. They were two bodies, one partially inside the other, and there was no need to hump the whole thing up with any more significance than that. There was no need to think at all. Animals died by the millions every day. It meant nothing. Why think about it?

A warm night in June.

There were a half dozen women at the corner of Washington and LaGrange. They reposed against the facade of the adjacent building, or smoked, or drifted to the curb and slugged one hip out toward the street, waiting for a car to ease alongside or a pedestrian to make eye contact.

To Joe, some of them weren't bad-looking broads, and he wondered what grim secret biography could explain this or that one's becoming a streetwalker. Certainly there were a couple he would consider giving a poke, under different circumstances. Joe was seated in his car farther down Washington Street, a half block from them. He dragged on a cigarette; it tasted like nothing, as if they had stuffed it with straw instead of tobacco. He had no interest in leaving the car to disperse the hookers, let alone arrest them. Didn't give a shit. Hookers. Waste of time, the whole thing, Vice. Even the name—Vice. What a fuckin' joke.

One girl, with a very pale and painted face, came

to the corner to glare at Joe and flick her cigarette butt in his direction, then she returned to the wall and resumed the group's attitude of boredom and insolence.

Joe let his head tip forward. Maybe he would sleep. Five, ten minutes of shuteye was all he needed, and no sooner had he decided to nap than his mind switched itself off. That was how it had been lately: He was always on the verge of sleeping, he could give in to it at any moment. He snapped awake once, but he was too heavy-headed to resist it and he closed his eyes again. The air was cool, the windows open. It was nearly nine but not quite dark in the car; he had parked by a streetlight, some of which light illuminated his eyelids. No matter. He could still doze awhile.

He heard street sounds. Snippets of conversation came in clearly, then dopplered away. Cars grumbled past, each one creating a whisk of warm wind in the open window as it went by. Somewhere a man laughed loudly, "That's right! You gut me! You gut me!" Joe relaxed but did not sleep.

At some point the ambient noise became muffled, blocked. There was an adjustment in the atmosphere, a drop in pressure.

He opened his eyes.

The street scene in his windshield was essentially unchanged. But no pedestrians were nearby. The hookers had drifted around the corner up LaGrange, toward Good Time Charlie's, out of view.

There was a car parked beside Joe's. He was

aware of it before he actually turned to see it, a long blackhooded car.

A voice: "Hey, cop."

Joe looked to his right across the passenger seat to see Vinnie Gargano doubleparked beside him, so close, the car doors nearly touching, just a few inches between the windowsills. At the same time Gargano seemed far away, in a separate space, tanked inside his own car. Gun.

N—

Gargano hesitated, perplexed, as if he did not understand what his eyes had just told him: big Joe Daley's expression had not changed, but a neat dark circle had winked open on his forehead. It appeared so suddenly and—the bullet's flight being unobservable—inexplicably that for a moment it seemed like a magic trick. The hole seemed to have come from inside him. Daley's body slumped back, and the hole filled with blood which ran out thick and gleaming as poured paint. Gargano recovered himself, remembered he had work to do—his jobs had become increasingly sloppy and frenzied, the trigger-hysteria getting the better of him—and he emptied his clip into Daley's body and sped off.

Long day. Michael leaned back, eyes shut, one toe poised on the ledge of an open drawer. The chair reclined with little metallic ticks, his weight transferred from his buttocks to the wings of his back, vertebrae popped into line with agreeable thumps, and when he had found the right balance he removed his foot from the desk and lay there like John Glenn in the *Friendship 7*, aimed upward into space, and he decided it was the first moment of the day that he had actually enjoyed. This chair might just have been the one good thing about working for the A.G. Maybe he would take it with him when he left. Or maybe he would never leave; he could just hang on here in a dingy state office, a lifer, the type that knew the precise date when his pension would vest.

Outside, something changed.

There was a modulation in the white noise of the city. A shrill siren whined, and another. A car drag-raced, making a perilous clatter in a city of close streets. Michael went to the window. Night had fallen. He saw nothing, of course, nothing but the yellow-brick rear of the State House, the ranks of office windows. But he knew by the change in pitch that something was wrong, some disaster, maybe close by, reflected off the mazewalls of the city. The air thrummed with it.

Heavy steps in the hall, the jingling of keys and equipment, and Conroy was in the doorway, grim and massive. "Bad news, Michael. We got to go. It's Joe."

"What?"

"Come on, we got to go. It's bad."

"What happened?"

"It's— Look, there's no other way to say it. I'm sorry—Joe's dead."

"What!"

"He got shot. That's all they know. I'm sorry."

"What?"

"Come on, Michael, right now, we got to go."

And this was how suddenly it happened. This was how Joe died, for Michael, with those two electric words: *He's dead.*

Then Michael was following Conroy down the hallways. Blood rushed in his ears.Objects seemed to swim—office doors with pebbled-glass windows; a janitor with a mop bucket on wheels; smudgy photos of stern, bushy-bearded politicians from the last century.

Out into the street, where Conroy had an unmarked cruiser waiting. For some reason Michael went to get in the back seat, as if the black Ford was a taxi, and Conroy had to tell him to sit in front. "Come on, Mike, you gotta keep your shit together, Mike. Your mother needs you here." Michael did as he was told, he sat in the front seat, and even now he detested Brendan Conroy—the worldly paternal tone with its hint that Michael would play novice to Conroy's mentor; the repetition of his name, Mike, Mike, Mike, as if he had learned the habit in a Dale Carnegie course. *Call me Michael, you prick.* But he was too bewildered to maintain his contempt.

Conroy rushed the car down the back slope of Beacon Hill and shot across Bowdoin Square.

Michael thought: He should have turned right, to make his way west to Boston City Hospital. Joe must have been taken to Mass. General instead. Maybe when a cop got shot even the remorseless

Yankees there would find it in their hearts to let an Irishman in the back door. But again, Michael's cynicism evaporated almost immediately. He could not hold a thought in his head. His mind continually emptied itself.

The siren made its clarinet wail, and a blue flasher strobed on the dashboard.

"They found him on Washington Street," Conroy was halfshouting, "right in his car, right there on the street. Can you believe that? I mean, can you believe the balls on these guys? The unmitigated balls on these guys." He clenched the steering wheel at nine and three o'clock, arms stiff.

Once they crossed Cambridge Street, the view through the windshield went black, like looking out over water at night. Then the buildings beside them disappeared and they sailed off the map, off the street grid, into the empty space of the old West End site. The road faltered. Conroy killed the siren and the blinking blue lights. They bounced over the rocky surface.

"Jesus, Brendan, what the hell, where are you going?"

"Hospital."

"*This* way?"

"Yeah, sorry, I know. Shortcut. Cambridge Street's a mess. Just let me drive. We'll be there in a minute. You alright, Michael?"

The answer was no, he was not alright, he was very definitely *not* alright. A late night at the office had exploded into a catastrophe, and the strangeness, the shock of it, left him feeling unmoored, as if that reclining chair in his office really had been the *Friendship 7* and Michael had been rocketed into outer space. He covered his mouth with his left hand and repeated, Joe is dead, Joe is dead, to convince himself of it. How recently had he taken a similar ride, in Joe's car, to bring similar news to Ricky after Amy was murdered? Six months before. Then, the mantra had been: Amy's dead, Amy's dead . . . What the brain cannot fathom, it simply rejects as untrue.

In front of them stretched a vast empty field, the fifty acres of the old West End razed to the dirt. The light of the moon and the surrounding city illuminated the ground with pale fluorescence. A rubble field of rocks and sandy soil and construction scrap, no trees, no roads. Before them the desolate irradiated landscape sloped gently away to sea level, a quarter mile away, where it ran out into the darkness. Looking over it you could imagine some conquering army had swept across and consumed it. The only things they had left behind were the enormous mounds of building materials heaped up like cairns, bristling with two-by-fours, the remains of demolished buildings. On the far side of the wasteland, lights burned in clusters at Mass. General and, farther away, at the construction site of JFK Park, Farley Sonnenshein's dream city of the future. The New Boston.

The car yawed and hopped over the rocks. Stones clattered in the wheel wells and chinked against the bottom of the car. Here and there, Conroy had to slow to a crawl to avoid bottoming out on the debris.

Michael tried to gauge his location, but the streets had been completely effaced. So he surrendered to disorientation and simply gawked at what was close: the haystacks of two-by-fours that rose to four and five times the height of the car; the scraps strewn on the ground, concrete, metal, brick; the odd personal item, a mangled baby carriage, a shoe. And stones—stones everywhere, the same rocky untillable soil the ancient pilgrims had found here. He thought—as everyone thought and everyone commented, because the memory was so near, the comparison so irresistible—that it all looked exactly like the old newspaper photos of bombed-out cities in Europe. And this thought, too, led back to Joe. Joe who had marched across Europe all the way to Berlin, only to die here. Joe was dead.

"Who did it? Are there witnesses?"

"Yeah. But don't you worry about that, Michael. We'll get the guy. You worry about your family."

"I should have done something, shouldn't I? I don't know; you know? I should've helped him."

"Can't think like that, boyo, can't do that to yourself."

"I should've—"

"Nothing anyone could do. Joe got himself into it. It's nobody else's fault. It's over now anyway."

Conroy picked his way over the rubble. In some places where the roads had been, the ground still bore their impression. On the ghost road of Chambers Street, he could move a little faster, briefly, until it vanished. He aimed the car toward the lights of Mass. General, tacking left and right

494

around obstructions. Near the middle of the expanse St. Joseph's Church stood alone, islanded. A hunkered-down Romanesque church—it looked more like a mausoleum for a secret society than a church. St. Joe's had not been designed for splendid isolation. It was a city church, meant to be hemmed in by narrow streets. Now its plain sandstone walls looked unfinished. The car beetled past it and kept on, bearing north through the debris field.

"What do you mean, Joe got himself into it?"

"Huh?"

"Joe got himself into what? How do *you* know?"

"I just know, is how I know. It's no big secret."

"No? So who else knows?"

"Michael? Jesus, would you give it a rest? The hell does it matter now?"

As they neared the northern edge of the rubble field, the lights of Mass. General approached and, to the right, the JFK Park construction site. Construction was already under way on two of the apartment towers. Framed with I-beams that formed ladders and cubes in the air, the towers seemed impossibly high. Barely begun, they were already among the tallest buildings in the city.

Conroy jerked the car toward the construction site. The rear wheels spun out, and the car fishtailed. Rocks chunked off the undercarriage.

"The fuck, Brendan!"

"Hang on."

"What are you doing! The hospital's—"

Conroy skidded through an open gate into the construction site, among the skeletal towers. He drove clumsily, hampered by the darkness and the narrow beam of the headlights and the rough surface.

The car slid to a stop at the edge of an enormous pit which had been excavated for yet another apartment tower. A bubble of pale light illuminated the pit, cast by buzzing portable arc lights.

The buildings in JFK Park were named for famous local politicians, in keeping with the presidential theme. This particular hole in the ground would eventually become a tower called Adams. For now it was just a crater, about half the size of a city block and two or three stories deep. The foundation walls were not poured yet; the pit was lined with corrugated steel walls. A dozen I-beams rose above the pit like ships' masts. These were the steel piles that would carry the weight of the building in the soft subsoil. A crane loomed, and a towering pile driver to ram them into the ground.

"What the fuck is this?" Michael asked. "What are you doing?"

Conroy bolted out of the car.

Michael saw a man walking toward them. Round-shouldered bull of a guy in mod slacks and short jacket zipped over a bulging belly. He tossed away a shovel.

Conroy dogtrotted around the front of the car, through the field of the headlights.

The second man produced a pistol from inside his jacket.

Michael struggled to connect these things, to

make sense of it, but already the door was flying open beside him and Conroy was tugging on his arm saying, "Get out here, get out here," and he heard this other man say, "Come on, get him the fuck out of there already. We don't have all fuckin' night."

Michael dove toward the steering wheel and grabbed it, first the ridged plastic wheel and then the steering column itself, and he hugged it, held on. He heard himself say, "No! No! No!"

The second man came around the car to the driver's side and smashed Michael's hands with the butt of his pistol until Michael's grip loosened and he was dragged across the bench on his belly, out of the car—

his forehead banged against the doorsill—

and he lay on the ground, shivering with cold and shock and fright.

Above him, Conroy grimaced like a man getting down to an unpleasant chore.

The second man was coming back around the car, crossing through the headlights as Conroy had a moment before, and— impossible—racking his pistol, and it was that sound, the metallic *clack-clack* of the slide that obliterated all thought and sent Michael scrambling ahead on all fours, toward the pit. It was impossible— impossible—impossible. It was just impossible to die. But Joe was dead. Is this what Joe had felt in his last moment, this frantic denial of one's own annihilation—impossible!— together with a subsiding sense that one was already gone?

The man was coming on, the gun extended now in one hand, expressionless, mindless.

Michael clambered forward fast, beating ahead on hands and knees. The soil was cold and wet under his hands, it seeped through the knees of his wool pants. Pebbles bit his palms. Left hand, right hand, left hand, right hand, then he set his left hand down on—

nothing—air—

and the hand went down into the hole, and his arm and shoulder went down after it, then his head was pulled in too. The lip of the steel retaining wall scraped his belly and he tumbled over it, into the black space in the pit, and he was in the air, turning.

Conroy said, "Jesus. Get down there and finish this. For Christ's sake. For Christ's sake."

The second man glowered. "Go finish it yourself, pig."

"I've got a homicide scene to get to."

Michael plummeted through darkness, wind drumming past his ears. The steel retaining wall invisible but perceptibly close; he could sense it beside him. There was a moment of weightlessness, no up or down—aware he was moving through space at fantastic speed, but with no sense which direction he was traveling. Where was the ground? He flailed, then stiffly he dropped through an atmosphere of thickening blackness and wintry cold.

Then the earth drove into him.

On the floor of the pit, thirty feet below the surface,

gloom collected in corners and pooled at the base of the high walls. The darkness in these shaded places had a texture, a moist blue density so thick you wanted to dip your finger in it. Overhead, the steel piles tapered upward. The blue dome of the sky was illuminated from beneath by the city's incandescent light, and some of that radiance washed back down into the pit, even reached the floor, weakly. But none penetrated as far as the corners.

The man with the gun foraged along the base of the steel wall. He paused, looked up its sheer face to estimate his own position and the spot where Michael Daley had gone over the side. He figured that the body ought to be here, right here at his feet, crumpled, dead or dying. But he must have gotten it wrong; again and again he looked up to re-calculate. In the gloom, dim silhouettes came forward which might have been bodies in various back-broken poses. But each, upon closer inspection, turned out to be something else, a rolled-up canvas tarp, a toss-pile of debris, or nothing at all, just a wrinkle in the darkness. Shit, what he wouldn't have given for a flashlight! Without one, there was no choice but to work his way along the wall, pausing now and then to crane his head forward for a better look or to nudge at something with his toe.

A rock chattered nearby. To his left. A few feet away, low in the shadows.

He jerked his gun around and fired, fired, fired, eager for release, as if he had been holding the bullets uncomfortably in his body.

The noise was deafening. The corrugated crazy-angled steel walls echoed the sounds and, it became clear, the bullets themselves.

The man cringed at the ricochets, crouched down, and it was in this position that he felt his right shinbone crack in two, heard the dry snap, then—after a delay, an extended moment—he felt a burst of pain in his leg. He looked down to see his shin grotesquely segmented, his leg two-kneed like an insect's. He stared, uncomprehending. His right foot lay flat on the ground, instep down. It reminded him of an empty boot dropped on its side. He understood, briefly, that the rock had been tossed to distract him, but already he was toppling onto his back.

Above him, Michael Daley hoisted a sledgehammer a second time. Michael shouted in pain as his arms reached ten o'clock and his shoulder—smashed in the fall—dialed upward. The pain made him dizzy. But the longhandled sledgehammer seemed to know where it was going, as if its design compelled it along a predetermined arc, and so Michael lassoed it above his shoulder and brought it down on the man's upper chest, just below the hollow of his neck.

The blow shook the man's body. His arms and legs jumped.

Michael tugged the sledge but it stuck, or seemed to. The illusion held for a moment—it felt like the hammer was sunk in the man's chest, like an ax head in a fat log—until Michael realized what had actually happened: His own shoulder had failed.

He could not budge his right arm, let alone the weight of the sledgehammer. The impact with the ground minutes before had spread open the bones of the shoulder, and now he could feel the displacement in his own skeleton, the ball of the humerus dislodged, grinding the rim of the socket, the arm dangling light and unsprung. The pain, though, was not confined to the area of the jumbled bones. It was general, radiant, a cold electrical current that chilled his entire side. The last two fingers of his hand tingled, as did his neck. Silently he chanted his old migraine prayer: *I am not my body; I am in my body*. He would master the pain.

With great effort, the man rolled onto his elbows and scraped forward, apparently unaware of the gun he had dropped or the heavy sledgehammer sliding off his body. His breathing was clutched and whispery.

Michael limped around him, crouched, and demanded, "Where's Conroy?"

The man belly-crawled a few feet toward the center of the pit. For a moment he did not move, then he raised up on all fours and pawed ahead. Stopped. He arched his back, opened his mouth wide, and released a gush of vomit with no more effort than a dog opening its mouth to drop a ball at its master's feet.

Michael picked up the gun. Surely it had been emptied, but he did not know how to check. He gathered up the sledgehammer as well. (Should he leave the tool in the pit where he had found it? Mix it in among the others left here by the workmen? Or take it away to avoid leaving evidence?) With these implements, the gun in his right hand, sledge-hammer in his left, he felt absurdly well armed and capable. He felt himself grow stronger under their influence.

The injured man was stock-still, on hands and knees. His breathing was shallow.

"Where's Conroy?"

No response.

Michael raised the gun uncertainly. Where to place it? The man's head was bowed, so Michael pressed the nose of the gun against the back of his scalp where it nestled in the dense black plush of his hair. "Who are you?"

"Like you don't know."

"I *don't* know. Tell me."

"Vi-Vincent Gargano."

Michael paused. Until now he had known Gargano's name and reputation but had never seen him. Vincent The Animal Gargano. Holy shit.

"Why are you doing this to me?"

No response.

"Where's Conroy?"

Gargano lay in the mud, silent.

"Is he here?"

"No."

Michael's finger tensioned the trigger, but he paused. "Is Joe Daley really dead?"

"Yeah."

"Who killed him?"

"I did, you d—" Gargano wetcoughed, then

labored to suck in a shallow, congested breath. "Dumb fuck. I did the both of 'em."

"The both of . . . who?"

"I clipped your old man, too. Last year. Now I did the other. Ha! Two Joe Daleys. I—" He did not finish, or could not.

Michael snapped the trigger back decisively. The gun hopped in his hand with a springy clack. Empty. He tossed it away.

"Can't even f—can't even fuckin' count."

"Is anyone here with you?"

No response.

Michael shook his head. He felt a lethal sense of detachment. He was indifferent to the man at his feet, to consequences, to his own former self. The killing mood. He tugged the sledgehammer up and guided it through its parabolic course again—he yelled again as the handle lifted his arms excruciatingly—and he brought it down squarely on the small of Gargano's back, where the belt of his jacket had pulled up to expose a bulge of soft flab and a cirrus cloud of black body hair. The impact made a fleshy smack.

Gargano's limbs held him up a moment, then he collapsed.

"Are you alone here?"

Gargano wheezed.

"Are you alone?"

"Yeah."

Michael sat down carefully in the dirt. Just lowered himself down. The hammer moved off his lap, drawn away by the weight of its heavy head.

He cradled his injured arm with his good one, holding it across his belly. In this position the pain was reduced almost to nothing, although the nerves still shivered with the memory of it. His mouth was particled with dirt and stones. A raw scrape burned down his cheek. On the right side of his scalp was a cool wet sensation, as if a flap had been opened and the interior of his head lay exposed to the air. It was not painful. Far from it, the breezy window in his head, if it was that, was rather pleasant.

He closed his eyes and imagined those footsteps again, *shick-shick-shick-shick-shick*, whisking along the pavement. He dreamed Joe Senior sprinting down that alley as Conroy dropped back, with a grimace of Judas's remorse on his face. Joe Senior coming around that corner, scuffing to a stop, confronted by a gun, the four-shot derringer, panning up to the face of—this man, Vincent Gargano.

Michael struggled to his feet, shielding his injured arm. With his good hand, he pat-frisked Gargano's body.

Nearby a hole had been freshly dug, a deep tube drilled straight down in the earth to receive the next pile. The piles were arranged in a grid; the next would be planted here. A crane and an enormous pile driver loomed above it. Michael stood over the hole and looked down. He could see ten feet or so, after that it fell away into darkness. Michael knew about these piles. Everyone who worked downtown did. When the piles were being driven, windows shook in offices a half mile away and people kept their windows closed to muffle the raucous clanging. Gargano had intended to dump Michael's body in this hole. Tomorrow morning, according to the plan, with each smash of the pile driver, Michael would be rammed down and down.

For now, the scene was quiet, so quiet that Michael could hear the wind fluting softly past the piles. He dropped a pebble into the hole to gauge its depth. He didn't hear it land.

Gargano gasped. He said something which Michael could not hear until Michael stood right over him: "I c-can't breathe."

"Why," Michael said, "did you do this? Why me?"

"I c-can't breathe."

"Why me?"

"Orders."

"From who?"

"Capobianco."

"Capobianco? But why me? Why *me*?"

"Conroy said—"

Gargano's corpulent body shuddered. When it stopped, he said in a breathy rasp, "Conroy come to Capobianco ... he said you knew ... said you knew about the cop, your old man. Said you accused him right to his face. You even told him you thought Capobianco ordered it. That's not something you say out loud."

"So Capobianco ordered the hit on my old man? Why? What did he ever do?"

"Look around you, you d—dumb fuck."

"I don't understand."

505

Gargano sniffed. He turned his head slowly. "You're standing in money. These people are making fucking millions. Fortunes. *Fortunes*."

"What's that got to do with Capobianco?"

"It's his money."

And finally, by degrees, Michael saw it. He saw it. Gangsters not just working construction but doing the strong-arm work to clear the neighborhood for demolition, roughing up the holdouts, rolling up the lame and the halt and the stubborn—work that could take months, even years if it was left to the government. *Delinquenti*, Mrs. Cavalcante had called them. *They say, "You gotta go, Mrs. C, you gotta go. It's not safe for you here no more."* Capobianco had deployed his troops to evacuate the West End. That some of the soldiers happened also to be policemen was an incidental fact. Cops had acted like gangsters because they *were* gangsters—they were on Capobianco's pad, paid to protect his interests. It all made sense only if Capobianco had an investment in the West End, because Charlie Capobianco didn't do anything, didn't even cross the street, except for money. He worshiped money as only a truly poor kid would. He wanted this project built, by any means necessary, and for reasons that had nothing to do with some fatuous fantasy of a New Boston. Charlie Capobianco did not give a Chinaman's fart about Boston, new or old.

"How much does Capobianco have invested in all this?" Michael asked.

But Gargano was weakening. He lay flat on his

stomach and his torso moiled about in the mud. His jaw chewed the air a moment until words came out: "I—I can't breathe. I need a hospital."

"You're not going to any hospital."

Gargano looked up at him with an expression of spite which softened, second by second, into spiteful submission.

"How big a piece of this did Capobianco take?"

"The fuck should I know?"

"What did it have to do with my father?"

"Conroy said— Conroy said he was gonna blow it up."

"Blow it up how? My father wasn't the type. He never squawked about cops on the sleeve before."

"He wanted out. Said he didn't work for Capobianco, didn't want the money. They asked him to do some things; he said no. Didn't want to go any further. All of a sudden he don't want to go any further? *Shh!* After all those years he took Mr. Capobianco's money? Now he's gonna blow it all up, this *chiacchierone*? Nobody was gonna let that happen. If Daley had went and ratted about cops on the pad in the West End, or Mr. Capobianco having his fingers in the West End, he would have took down this whole thing. What politician is gonna stand up for a buildin' owned by Charlie Capobianco? And everybody wants these buildin's to go up. Everybody. The city, the feds, the developers. Too much money to stop it. Too much fuckin' money. Your old man was like you: wasn't smart enough to keep his fuckin' mouth shut."

"And Amy?"

"What Amy?"

"Amy Ryan. The reporter."

"Oh. Whatever. She was gonna write it. Loved crooked-cop stories, this fuckin' bitch, that's what Conroy says. Course Conroy didn't give a shit about nothing except himself anyways; he just didn't want her writing *his* name in the papers. That piece of shit wouldn't last a week in Concord without his badge. So he comes back and says we got to clip her, too. Otherwise she's gonna spill the whole thing in the newspapers, and, y'know, prob'ly the whole project gets stopped. So we did. We hit her too. No choice."

"Who . . . killed her? All the things they did to her?"

"That was Conroy's idea. Dress it up like the Strangler, he said. He gave us all the details, all this shit we were supposed to do, tie a bow around her neck, whatever. He knew the newspapers'd go crazy for it."

"And the broom handle? Conroy did not give you that; the Strangler never did it. Whose idea was that?"

"Mine."

Michael nodded, accepting this boast. The sadistic indifference of it.

He hefted the sledgehammer again, patiently. The hammerhead was cast iron, barrel-shaped. Its weight pulled Michael's arms into a rigid V. Together with the dangling hammer they formed a Y, and the Y rocked back and forth, back and forth, back and forth. A nerveless energy began to build,

508

fed by the rocking and the vision of Amy crucified on her bed.

"And Joe, my brother? What'd he do? He told me he was helping you. Why kill him? He was already on your side, you already had him."

"You can't have a cop know that much about your business, see it from the inside. Longer it goes, the bigger the risk. Whole thing was crazy. Someday he'd have burned us. End of the day, a cop is a cop. He woulda woke up, someday. He walked away with too much of Mr. Capobianco's money anyways. He was lucky he stuck around as long as he did. Dumb shit."

"How do I know you're telling the truth? How do I even know Joe's really dead?"

"Bullet in the forehead," Gargano said. "Check it out, you'll see. Third eye—keep the other two shut."

"And the gun?"

"You just threw it over there somewhere."

Michael surveyed the massive pit. The chilly gloom. The forest of piles rising overhead. This place was not part of the city, he felt. It was not part of the earth.

Gargano tortoised forward on his elbows a few inches before laying his head back down, exhausted. "My throat. I think you . . ."

"Why in the hell," Michael said, "would Capobianco put his money in this? Since when is he in construction? What does he know about it?"

"Nothing," Gargano said. "But he runs a cash business, and he can only put so much on the street.

He's got to put it somewhere. He needed a legit investment, a big one. You know how much cash he pulls in? More than you can imagine. Your dad was a cop? *Pff*, believe me, you can't imagine."

"Try me."

"It's so much fuckin' money, the state's gonna start up its own lottery. You believe that? All these years the government tries to get Capobianco, then they turn right around and go into the numbers business. That's how much money is in it."

"And Sonnenshein, how much does he know?"

"Sonnenshein doesn't know shit. The money's invested without Capobianco's name on it, through a trust or whatever. Capobianco always owns things through trusts so the feds can't take it."

"So why's Capobianco interfering? He's already invested. Why not just watch the project go forward?"

"With that much money riding on it? You don't know Mr. Capobianco. He don't take those kind of chances. He's gonna protect his investment. These buildin's are goin' up." Gargano faltered. He coughed, then spat in an intricate way. "Mr. Capobianco don't bet. That's the secret. The book never loses, only the suckers."

Another fit of racking coughs tossed Gargano's body. When it was done he lowered a thread of drool from his mouth until it adhered to the ground, like a spider launching a filament out of itself.

Michael laid the hammerhead on the back of Gargano's head.

Gargano shook it away and dragged himself a few inches.

Michael rested the hammer on Gargano's head again.

Gargano began to snort in angry dumb protest.

Michael tamped twice, lightly, as if setting a nail in a board before driving it in.

Out front a cruiser and an unmarked car, a detective's car, were double-parked.

A uniform cop stood guard at the front door, one of the bulls from the nearby stationhouse. He looked Michael up and down.

"This is my mother's house," Michael offered.

"Go on in."

Michael was no stranger to police uniforms, of course. Monkey suits, Joe Senior had called them. Still, in the presence of this uniform Michael hesitated.

"You okay, sir?"

"Yeah."

The cop opened the screen door for him.

And so it would go, Michael thought. There would be no reckoning for what had happened in that pit. No one would ever know. Because Michael was wearing a uniform too: clean khakis, a clean buttondown shirt. (He had stopped at his apartment to wash up and change clothes.) To all appearances he was a grieving brother and a dutiful son. Not a murderer at all. What had he expected this cop to see?

Inside he found Margaret and Kat in the living

room and he bent to kiss them. Kat's eyes were red-rimmed, her complexion splotchy. Little Joe sat stone-faced, absently turning a penknife in his hand. Michael bent to kiss him, too, though the teenager did not move to offer his cheek so Michael lightly kissed the crown of his head, with its brush of short soft hair.

"Where's Ricky?" he asked quietly.

"In the kitchen," Margaret said.

"Is he okay?"

"Why don't you go ask him?"

Michael nodded. They didn't know what he meant; that was his answer. Ricky had not been hurt. Even Ricky had no idea what had gone on in the pit. Michael alone knew everything. How close Michael had come, how close.

He drifted into the kitchen, where Ricky leaned against the counter, arms folded, speaking in murmurs with Tom Hart.

Hart, seeing Michael's blank expression and apparently misperceiving the shock of a victim there, came across the room to lay a consoling hand on Michael's shoulder.

Michael flinched at the contact. "Sorry, Tom. Hurt my shoulder the other day. Still a little sore, I guess."

Ricky's eyes narrowed.

Hart spluttered awhile about how sorry he was, he didn't have all the right words, Joe was a heckuva guy, just a heckuva guy, and he didn't deserve a goddamn thing like this, and of course it wouldn't bring Joe back but they were going to find

512

the guy who did this thing if it took the rest of Hart's goddamn life.

Michael thanked him. There was a silent moment during which Michael wondered again whether the detective could sense something was wrong.

"I know it's a terrible time," Hart said tentatively. "I hate like hell to do this, you know. But you know how these things go, Mike. The first few hours, *you* know."

Margaret drifted into the kitchen, then Kat. They knew what was coming, they'd been through it already. Margaret crossed one arm across her belly, and with the opposite hand she covered her mouth, as if she knew, as if she already knew, what Michael was going to say.

"You know how I feel about the lot of you," Hart was saying. "You too, Mike. But I'm on the job, you know."

"It's okay, Tom. Ask what you got to ask."

"Okay. Okay, then. You know the question, Mike: Is there anything you can tell me about what happened to your brother tonight?"

Michael felt a little grip in the muscles of his jaw.

"Anything at all?"

"No."

"You're sure, Michael? Sometimes the smallest thing—"

"No. Nothing."

"What about the thing we talked about, Amy Ryan and—?"

"Alright then, Tom," Margaret broke in, "you got

your answer. You don't need to give him the third degree."

Hart hesitated. A policeman's wife would not be surprised by the questions. He glanced back at Margaret then at Michael.

But Margaret insisted. "It's been a hard enough night for everyone. Just let us alone now, Tom. This is a family time. I'm sure you've got a long night ahead o' yuz, too."

Hart held Michael's eyes in his own for a long moment. Then: "Yeah. Okay, I'll leave you folks alone. I'm sorry, you know, I'm real sorry for your loss. I guess you've had your share."

"Thank you, Tom," Margaret said. "You go on now and do your job."

"We'll keep a cop out front, Margaret, just in case. All night, if you want."

"Go."

From the kitchen door Margaret watched the Homicide detective let himself out. When the Daleys were safely alone, she went to the sink to wet a dishrag. She came to Michael's side, draped the towel over her index finger, and wiped Michael's neck below the right ear. Inspecting the towel, she frowned, then showed Michael a red-brown smear. "Is this what I think it is, Michael?"

He nodded.

"Who did this to you?"

"It's not mine."

Next morning.

The ground trembled under Michael's feet.

514

Vibrations entered the soles of his shoes and shivered his legs, his trousers, his testicles.

"Hey!" a construction worker shouted to make himself heard through the concussed air. "Hahd hats only!" He pointed at his yellow helmet then jiggled one upturned thumb: *Get lost*.

Michael gave him a friendly little uncomprehending wave. Just a dumbass lawyer with his coat flipped over his shoulder, shirtsleeves rolled up past his elbows. Just some dumbass enjoying the spring morning and the sunshine and the spectacle of a pile driver.

That gorgeous pile driver! The clocklike regularity of its movements. The slow ascent of the dropweight, a little hitch, then the weight released to ride down a chute and crash into the I-beam. Each blow rammed the massive pile a few inches farther into the ground. Each clang rattled in Michael's ears and sent those tuningfork shivers up his legs. All night, he had worried the corpse would erupt out of the ground the moment the pile driver began its work. He had envisioned the construction stopped, the site teeming with cops. But here it was. Not a cop in sight, nothing out of place. Workers shuffled about, came and went—with no idea what they were really doing. Which was this: they were ramrodding the body of Vinnie "The Animal" Gargano down into the earth forever.

Michael fantasized the dead man under the bottom of the pile, speared, pinned to bedrock. The truth, no doubt, was not so picturesque. Boston does not sit on bedrock like New York; the subsoil in Boston is mostly muck. The body would roll with the soil's turbulence or grind along the side of the I-beam. But those were technicalities, mere facts. Who cared? In Michael's mind, the building would foot down square on Vinnie Gargano for a hundred years.

Yet for all that, on the morning after, Michael still did not feel much of anything about Gargano. Certainly not remorse. Gargano was dead—murdered, alright; call it what you want—but he wouldn't be missed or even remembered. Someday, no doubt, Michael would forget, too. He would forget the jet of blood that splashed him like warm bathwater, he would forget the way the corpse rolled willingly headfirst into that deep hole. Someday, Michael would gaze up at Farley Sonnenshein's completed white tower, silent as a pyramid, and it would not seem strange that a man lay underneath it. We are promiscuous forgetters.

At Margaret's house, they would be waiting for him. Another family meeting, another wake and another funeral to plan. Well, let them wait a while more. Joe would have understood: You do not bury your dead until the battle is over.

Before leaving, Michael took a deep contented breath. When had daylight ever looked so clear, or the sun felt so fine as it reached through the morning chill to warm his forehead? When had this grubby old city ever looked so rare? The priests, of course, would inform the Daleys that Joe had gone on to a better place. But a morning like this, Michael thought, gave the lie to the sanctimony of priests. Lay out a priest on his deathbed, let him feel the danger approach, its wings beating close, and watch how he fights.

Charlie Capobianco glared. "You believe this guy? Are you threatening me?"

Michael shook his head.

"Hey, you speak American, you fuck? I asked you a question. Are you threatening me?"

"No. Sir."

"You come in here, to my place of business, and give me some story about I got money in this thing, and I did this and that in the West End, and to top it all off I had your brother *and* your father killed— and you're not threatening me?"

"No."

"Then what in the fuck do you want?"

"I'm asking you to let us out. My brother Ricky and me, the both of us—just let us walk away. That's all we want."

They were in Capobianco's shabby Thatcher Street office. Michael sat in a vinyl chair. Charlie Capobianco stood nearby, glowering, chin tipped up. Charlie's brother Niccolo listened from a couch nearby. Consigliere Nick was keeping his distance, in both senses.

"What are you shakin' for?" Charlie said.

"I'm not shakin'."

"You are. I see you. You get all this from Gargano?"

"Yeah."

517

"Why would he tell you anything?"

"He was hurt. Maybe he thought he was dying."

"Why would he think that?"

"He was hurt pretty bad."

"Who hurt him?"

"I couldn't say."

"Ah, fuck Gargano. He can take care of himself. But you can't fuck *me*, hear me, Paddy? Your brother owes me money. He took those stones. He's gonna pay me my fuckin' money."

"He says he didn't take them."

"He can say he's a fuckin' elephant—doesn't mean it's true."

"He says he didn't take them."

Capobianco sat down next to Michael and leaned in close. His breath had an eggy stink. "Why would I do this for you, some Paddy off the street? I don't know you."

"You let us out, you keep your money. I'll take the whole story to my grave."

"I could make that happen sooner than you think."

"I've made arrangements. A reporter has the story, someone I know, in case I go to my grave any too soon. If that story comes out, you'll lose all your money one way or another. A grand jury'll find it. It doesn't matter how you invested it, how you kept your name off it. They'll open up those trusts and find you. The pols'll probably stop construction, too. Either way, the money's lost. It's more than me and Ricky are worth. All you got to do is just let us out. Sir. Just let us out."

From behind Michael, Nick interjected, "Okay. You're out."

But Charlie Capobianco, the boss, was not quite finished. "What kind of guy are you, Paddy? You come in here and tell me I killed your brother, your father, but still you're willing to make deals."

"There's someone else who's more responsible than you."

Conroy had spent the night working the Joe Daley homicide. An all-night vigil was typical of the critical early hours of a homicide investigation; it was pursued with a special mission in this case, where the victim was a cop. Night-for-day meant nothing. Almost immediately they had searched for an organized-crime angle. The stink around Joe Daley and the brazenness of the hit pointed the way as clearly as fingerposts. They swarmed out to press witnesses and rats, and in the whisperings a single name swirled continually: Vincent "The Animal" Gargano.

For Brendan Conroy the direction of the investigation was worrisome. If Gargano ever did start talking, who knew where it would lead? But the situation could be managed. In the end, there was no chance Gargano would talk; these North End guinea hardcases didn't operate that way. That was all that mattered. Conroy was insulated. For now there was nothing to do but stay out front. Over the next few days and weeks in his dual roles as detective and grieving "stepfather," he would be a paragon.

He got home around nine A.M., but only f⋅⋅ a quick stopover. A hot shower and a good stropping toweling-off and a clean shirt, then he would head off to Margaret's house to join the mourners. He stood in the tub shower, let the water pound him awake, thought of Margaret and of various graceful condolences he might dispense over the next few hours. His position with the Daleys, with Margaret in particular, could only be strengthened by his performance today. He would radiate his imperturbable strength and they would be grateful. How could they not be? It was no good, a manless woman, a manless family. He would lead them. But softly, softly. No need to overstep. Jesus, his back and knees ached. Getting old. His brain was the only goddamn part of him that wasn't breaking down. Every other goddamn thing, knees and cock and shoulders and eyes and feet, the whole damn thing was starting to go.

He turned the water ice cold—he believed it closed the pores and thus warded off sickness—and withstood the blasting freeze for a full thirty seconds, then turned it off. He yanked the shower curtain back with its metallic screech.

He froze. Shocked, he worried he might piss; his bladder was suddenly engorged, quivering, another betrayal by his aging body.

But he recovered himself to say, in a loving tone—because surely there was still a deal here, a way to talk his way out—"Well now, look at you. And where did you get that?"

* * *

It was from the newspapers that Michael learned, later, what sort of gun he brought to Brendan Conroy's home that morning. It was a Smith & Wesson Model 39 nine-millimeter with a blue-black finish and wooden grips. The newsmen were keen to identify the gun precisely, just as the newspapers had been full of Oswald's *6.5-millimeter Mannlicher-Carcano carbine*. In the absence of meaningful information, minor data can be spun to create an illusion of knowledge. Sometimes it's the best you can do.

Michael did understand the gun's logical significance, its value to the detectives who would puzzle over it. Here was the same weapon used to kill Joe Daley the night before. The magazine bore prints of Vincent Gargano's thumb, index and middle fingers, protected from smudging inside the pistol grip. They would conclude—what else?— that Gargano had killed both Joe Daley and Brendan Conroy. They would not wonder for long over the motive, either: "Two Cops Slain for AntiMob Bravery," the reporters would write. The story would be an easy sell. It is a cop's job, after all, to stand in a criminal's way.

Better still, as Amy used to say, that headline would move paper. And who would ever step forward to complicate the official version? Not Gargano, certainly; Vinnie The Animal, it would be widely assumed, had gone underground. Not the cops; still bruised by the bookie-joint controversy and the gossip about mishandling the Strangler case, the Department would happily lay the blame

521

on an olive-skinned baddie in order to close the cases. Michael understood all that. Every murder plays out first as a whodunit—people can't stand not knowing—and only then as a tragedy. So Michael had been canny enough, even in the hysteria of hammering Vincent Gargano to death, to resolve the whodunit for them. He had retrieved the gun. He had found an extra loaded magazine in Gargano's jacket. Using the dead man's wormy fingers, he had rolled the fingerprints onto the magazine. Its smooth oiled finish would hold the prints nicely. When he was finished here at Conroy's apartment, Michael intended to leave the gun for them to find.

The apartment door was unlocked.

In the living room was a cheap tin snack table on metaltube legs. Water was dripping somewhere, *pink, pink, pink*.

It was not too late to stop, of course. He could turn around and walk out and no one would be the wiser. But he had determined to do this thing, and the idea pulled him on. He took Gargano's gun from his coat, and the gun seemed to lead him by the hand toward the bathroom, toward the sound of the water.

The door was ajar and Michael glimpsed a hairless bone-white knee above the rim of the bathtub.

He did not like to think of that knee—it was naked and animal— and so he focused on the gun in his own hand and what a supremely well-designed tool it was. The way it nestled in his palm. How naturally his fingers curled around the grip, how perfectly sized it was, smaller than a tennis racket handle, thicker than a knife handle. What a sensuous pleasure to raise and point it. It felt like a part of him, an extension of his hand. When he raised the gun and sighted along its barrel—

when he tapped the door open with it—

and he beheld Brendan Conroy—round and white and lightly haired, his head lumpy and small under wet hair, his legs incongruously skinny, the little pale-pink rosettes of his nipples, the spatters of orange freckles—an old fat man on his back in the bathtub—sprawled—the vulnerable fleshy clump of his genitals—

it felt as if the gun barrel was an eleventh finger or, more exactly, as if it were his own index finger extended to absurd length, telescoped outward—

and didn't every child know—didn't—

He was distracted by Conroy, by that sly shit-eating grin, as if they were sharing a little joke, the two of them. *Hey there, boyo, now what did you mean to do with that thing?*

Didn't—

didn't every kid in the playground who had ever formed his hand into a gun and said *pshoo!*—

Conroy, a pinkish blob in the background of the gun sight—

didn't every kid know that pointing your finger and pointing a gun were essentially the same gesture? But how godlike, to kill with nothing more than a pointed finger! Like a wizard pronouncing a curse, you had only to point and wish someone dead—you had only to decide it, and bang.

"Bang," Michael whispered aloud. He lowered the gun.

Conroy was already dead. A single bullet hole in his chest, at the heart—where, Amy had once said, a lucky marksman could kill a man with one shot. Already dead.

The tub spout dripped. *Pink, pink.*

Michael stared. Would he have done it? Yes, he assured himself. Maybe. He thought he would have. Then: No, of course not.

He came to the side of the tub.

Dark wet blood was gelled over the hole in Conroy's chest. No blood or damage on the walls of the shower stall; the slug must still be inside the body. Conroy had been standing naked in his tub when he took the bullet into himself, absorbed it in the thick mass of his torso. Another remarkable thing, that: The bullet had emerged from inside the gun only for a millisecond before burying itself again inside this man, leaping from one host to the next. Then Conroy had fallen, or sat, and died with this ambiguous expression on his face, not so much wounded as astonished. There was water beaded on his skin, and pink watery streaks of blood that marbled his belly in intricate thready patterns like veins.

There was still work to do, of course. It was not enough that Conroy was dead; the murder had to be explained, the whodunit resolved, the story spelled out.

So Michael pulled the shower curtain closed, feeling fastidious and cunning both, but not really deciding anything now, just following through on a course he had already committed to—finishing. The curtain rod screeched.

Carefully, so as not to disturb the fingerprints, he slipped the magazine out of the pistol grip, pried up the top bullet with his finger, and dropped it in his pocket. True, the slug already in Conroy's body would not match the slugs fired from Gargano's Smith & Wesson, but it would take a careful ballistics test to reveal that. It would require no special knowledge to count the slugs, though, and to realize that Conroy's body held one more bullet than Gargano's gun could have fired.

Ready now, Michael chambered a round, wrapped his arm inside the shower curtain, and tensioned the trigger. But the trigger pull was tight and the gun did not fire.

An inch or two from Michael's nose, the shower curtain— an opaque sunflower-yellow vinyl stamped with a flower print— reflected the sound of his frustrated sigh.

He plunged his finger down hard, once. The thunder echoed in the small bathroom, amplified by the tiles, and an afterexplosion in his ears, trailed by a ringing sound. The spasm of the gun's recoil sent a wave of pain through his injured right shoulder. The bullet casing carelessly tossed away. The homey, smoky-fireplace smell of the burned powder.

He had the feel of it now, he thought, and he pulled, pulled, pulled, pulled, pulled the trigger, and this time he counted, as Gargano had instructed. Seven rounds. One fewer than the magazine in a Smith & Wesson Model 39 could hold.

Michael slipped into church and glanced about, as if he meant to steal the candlesticks.

The pews were nearly empty. Two old men sat far apart from one another, barely moving. Michael recognized them both as parishioners at St Margaret's. He'd seen these oldtimers here a thousand times, back when Michael was a kid and going to Mass regularly, but now he could not for the life of him remember their names. They seemed to be waiting, these old men, though for what Michael did not know. It was midmorning. No Mass was scheduled.

He slunk down the center aisle, clearing his throat softly, selfconscious about the rustle of his clothes and the shushing of his shoes.

Seated in the front row, characteristically, was Michael's mother. From the back, her shape and posture struck Michael as very old-looking. Her spine and shoulders were beginning to warp. Even so, she was still very much the iron lady, the morning after her son was murdered. She gave Michael a brief glance, then turned her attention back to the altar. There was no trace of tears on her face.

"You okay, Mum?"

"Yes."

He sat down.

Margaret's black pocketbook stood between them on the bench. A big black faux-patent-leather thing with a stiff strap for a handle. Michael eyed the handbag, then he picked it up and opened the clasp.

Margaret gave him another sidelong look but did not protest. Her expression suggested to Michael that she was not defeated, she was not giving in to him; she simply did not care what he found in the purse or what he thought. *Go on, then,* she seemed to be saying, *see for yourself*.

He opened the purse and looked down into it. Joe Senior's service pistol was nestled inside, among the clutter of balled-up tissues, the compact and lipstick, the wallet and keys. The gun lay on its back. Michael was transfixed a moment, before he realized the risk and clicked the pocketbook shut. The clasp, with its overlapping gold beads, reminded him of a schoolgirl's crossed knees. He put the pocketbook back down on the bench.

Beside him, Margaret had willed herself—her face, her posture— into a resolutely ordinary pose. She had nothing to say about Conroy's multiple betrayals, of her husband and her sons and of Amy, and she made no excuses for the pistol in her pocketbook—down one bullet, surely, and mustn't Brendan Conroy have been dazzled by the sight of her taking aim square at his breastbone. She picked up the purse and threaded her forearm through the strap.

"Come on, Ma, we got to go. There'll be people at the house."

"All night and day there'll be people over to the house, talking us half to death, eating us out of

527

house and home. We'll all be fit for the loony bin before it's over."

"Okay, Ma."

He stood and offered his elbow, which she took, and as they processed down the aisle she nodded at the two old parishioners who, she informed Michael in a stage whisper, were a drunk and a philanderer respectively, though the one still drank like a demon while the other's philandering days were long behind him. The two of them together, she said, didn't have enough sense to tie their own shoelaces. But the Lord is in no hurry to come collect His fools. Only the good ones like Joe He comes for. Only the good ones. "Only my Joe," she whimpered, and Michael felt her weight on his arm and he stiffened his elbow to support her.

1963 and the first half of '64 had been murderous years. Michael's father, his brother, Amy, even Brendan Conroy—all dead. But they had not quite left. Michael had the feeling that any of them might wander into the room at any moment. They left their things around, too: Joe Senior's coat still hung in the hall closet, Amy's handwriting lingered in a notepad. When the newspapers were filled with the Gulf of Tonkin question, Michael wanted to hear Amy boil it all down with her cheerful cynicism. It came back to him that of course Amy was dead; the memory still carried a faint sting of surprise.

Yet life went on. The summer and fall of 1964 were strangely normal. In Michael's presence, people pretended nothing had happened. They were determinedly cheery and superficial, until the merest mention of tragedy, any tragedy, started them stammering. The possibility that Michael might launch into a discussion of his losses terrified them. They would rather whistle past the graveyard—better yet, they would rather not acknowledge the graveyard at all. They wanted to go on pretending that murder could never touch them. The truth was, Michael felt hardly anything at all. He was as hard, or at least as numb, as a stone.

Michael felt no remorse for the blood on his own hands. The only question was: Could a man go from ordinary citizen to killer and back again? He assured himself that he could. Soldiers did it all the time. And if Michael were ever called upon to pass from citizen back to killer again? Well, he thought, soldiers did that, too, and so, if need be, could he.

So went 1964, or most of it.

On Christmas Eve, that desultory semi-holiday, Michael closed up his office in the middle of the afternoon. He had spent the day working, with no particular pleasure or urgency, on an eminent domain action: a few parcels around Scollay Square, which was already being razed to make way for a new "government center." It was good, dull work. Michael made his way through the gloomy, nearly empty corridors of the State House.

At the Strangler Bureau, Tom Hart and a couple of the BPD Homicide detectives were lugging cardboard boxes out to the street.

"They're shutting it down," Hart said.

"Shutting down the Strangler Bureau? They haven't even charged the guy, never mind tried him."

"They're not going to charge him. There isn't going to be a trial." Hart grabbed a box labeled *Feeney, J., 11/22/63*, and he hoisted it into Michael's arms. "Here, make yourself useful."

Hart took a box of his own and together they made their way out to the street.

"So," Michael said, "the Boston Strangler is going to walk."

"DeSalvo's not going to walk. He's doing life, on those rapes. He'll be parole-eligible in ten years, but let's face it: No parole board is ever going to release a guy who the whole world thinks is the Boston Strangler. DeSalvo is going to do life."

"But if DeSalvo's the wrong guy . . . ?"

"If DeSalvo's the wrong guy . . . I'd rather not think about it."

"So what happens to the cases?"

"Nothing. They sit. Technically, if the A.G. does not want to pursue the case, it comes back to us. But realistically it would be impossible to convict anybody on these murders now. Where are you going to find a jury that doesn't already 'know' DeSalvo is the Strangler? No prosecutor is going to touch it. The Strangler cases are closed."

"So they wait till Christmas Eve to announce that the case against DeSalvo is going to be dropped. And hope no one notices."

"The stranglings have stopped. If DeSalvo is the wrong guy, then the real Strangler has probably moved on. Or he's in custody. No sense telling everyone the Strangler got away. It'd just start a panic."

"Come on, Tom, listen to you. It's politics."

"No, it's government."

"What's the difference?"

The detective thought it over. "There is none."

They came out into the cold. Gray, sunless New England winter. Sunset coming earlier and earlier, daylight already beginning to dim in midafternoon.

"So what happens now, Tom?"

"Byron runs for governor or senator or whatever. DeSalvo sells his story to the movies. The rest of us just go about our business."

"It'll never work. They can't keep it quiet forever."

"The only one who could blow it up is DeSalvo. But he'd have to recant the confession, and he's not going to do that. He'd rather be the Boston Strangler than be nobody at all."

"A few years in Walpole will cure him of that."

"Maybe." Hart slid his box into the back seat of an unmarked cruiser, then relieved Michael of his box. "Merry Christmas, Mike."

"Merry Christmas, Tom. Let's hope the guy coming down the chimney tonight is Santa."

"Oh, I wouldn't worry. Whoever the Strangler is, he's probably skipped town. He hasn't made many mistakes. I bet he's someplace far away, someplace no one is looking for him."

"There's no way this stays quiet. No way in the world."

"Michael," Hart said, "this isn't the world. This is Boston."

"Hey, you wanna see something cool?"

Michael was staring at *The Tonight Show*, a Christmas Eve special with Gila Golan and Woody Allen. He had been watching long enough that his eyes were glazed. His crossed feet, in sneakers, were on the coffee table.

"Hey," Ricky repeated, urging him to wake up, "wanna see something cool?"

They were slouched at opposite ends of the couch. On the cushion between them was a green glass ashtray.

Michael said without turning, "Yeah. What?"

"Get your coat. We got to go for a drive."

"Oh, forget it. I thought you were just gonna— Forget it. I'm going home. The hell time is it?"

"Twelve-thirty."

"I'm going home, Rick. It's been a long day. I've had enough." Michael swigged from his bottle of beer and sat up.

They would both need a good night's sleep. Tomorrow was Christmas, and Margaret was determined to snow them all under with presents and food and self-conscious cheer so they would not think about Joe. The tree, next to the TV, was over-trimmed, over-lit, over-everything. Ricky advised that no one look directly into it, for fear of burning the retinas.

"Forget it, Ricky. Mum's a loon. She wants us back here at eight. You probably don't even remember what eight in the morning looks like."

"Am I missing anything?"

"Not really."

"Come on, then. Sleep when you get old, right?"

"You know what you look like when you look like that? A mouse. Anyone ever tell you that? Beady little mouse."

"Come on, big brother, don't be a fag. Get your coat. I want to show you something."

"Some other time."

"No, it's gotta be now. It's a Christmas thing."

"A Christmas thing. What do you know from Christmas?"

"I'll show ya."

They drove into town, Ricky at the wheel. At Park Street, near the State House, he pulled over. "Come on," Ricky said.

They strolled into the Common, hands jammed deep in their pockets to hide them from the cold. The trees were loosely strung with long saggy strings of Christmas lights that swayed in the wind like women's necklaces.

At the Nativity scene, Ricky took a quick glance around, then stepped into the manger and grabbed the figurine of the baby Jesus out of His straw bed.

"The fuck are you doing? Put that back."

"Just wait, Mikey."

"You can't take that. It's . . . God."

"Would you relax. It's not God. It's just a little statue. God is within you."

"No, He's not. He's in your hand. Now put Him back."

"Come on. Don't be such a baby."

Michael looked up at the sky to address the Lord. "I have no part of this."

They walked back to the car with the statue stuffed inside Ricky's coat.

"You know,"Michael said,"I think there's a special part of hell for people who do this."

"Yeah, okay, Mikey. Whatever. Come on, get in."

Inside the car, Ricky took the statue out again and looked it over, front and back.

"What do we do now, Rick? Make a sacrifice to Beelzebub?"

"Something like that."

Ricky wrapped his hands firmly around the baby's torso and with a swift up-down he smashed the back of its head on the dashboard. The head snapped off neatly. It rolled on the floor at Michael's feet.

"What the f— What are you doing? Look what you did!"

"Put out your hands, Mike."

"Holy shit! Ricky!"

"Put out your hands."

When Michael did not respond, Ricky wedged the statue between his legs to hold it upright, then cupped Michael's hands together. He tipped the statue and poured from its open neck. Stones. Cold and heavy and roughedged in Michael's palms.

"Jesus saves." Ricky smirked.

Michael lifted his hands to see better in the light. Diamonds.

Coda

Ypsilanti, Michigan. August 8, 1967.

It might be a deer, all hulked up and leathery and melting with rot, or a dog. Animals are always going and getting killed around here, like stupes, as they flash across Geddes and LaForge Roads from one farm field to another then off into the trees. The carcass is small for a deer, though, and big for a dog. And it's too far from the road to have been launched here by a car, so it must have been put in this spot, just like, set down in this weedy place near the sagging foundation of a farmhouse and a silo. But why here? This spot is a hangout. A stand of box elder trees shields it from the road. Kids park here to drink and make out. They prowl around the old foundation, toss their beer cans and cigarette butts into it. Why dump a deer carcass here? A joke? A stink bomb?

A boy sidles toward the thing. He is fifteen and burned brown from working his father's farm all summer. He wears a T-shirt and cutoffs and a filthy Tigers cap with the visor pulled down so low that

537

he has to raise his chin just to see where in the hell he's going. He rotates his chest, unconsciously, so that his left shoulder is slightly forward, as if he means to sneak up on the deer.

At a distance of twenty feet the air is foul, even out in the open like this. The dungy stink of decay. The carcass is old. It is manuring, crumbling in the summer heat.

Another mystery: The boy was here just a week ago—this place is next to his family's farm, the fields run right on up to it—and he did not see a carcass here, though you could hardly miss it now. So if the animal was moved here recently, it must have been good and rotten already. Who would touch it then?

Closer now, the boy can hear the flies buzz. They are swarming, excited. They hop up and down on the carcass, they jerk around in the air. Their electric zzzzzzz harmonizes with the grumble of a tractor off somewheres, and that is the sound of summer of hot afternoons, that insect-buzz coming in waves.

Standing over the carcass, though, all the boy can hear is the hum of flies. The black surface of the carcass is seething with them. He can't see the thing clearly.

The head is misshapen, melted. It seems to have collapsed like some sodden, rotting, black piece of fruit. The flies are clumped thick on it, feasting on the sweet meat inside. The boy gazes at the head a moment until a shape at its center, a little flower of whorls, becomes a recognizable shape—a human ear—and the boy is sprinting, startled, back across the field.

Then the cops come. Sheriffs from Washtenaw County and state police from the Ypsilanti barracks and someone over from Eastern Michigan University where a coed went missing about a month earlier. They close off the roads. They comb through the weeds until they turn up a baggy orange dress and a torn bra and a sandal.

These are sensible men. They have daughters and granddaughters, and they do not like to look at the body—it lies at the center of all this activity; it cannot be moved until the M.E. arrives to handle it—because when they look at the shape on the ground, they see that it is a girl. She lies on her side, nude, her face turned down toward the earth. Once their minds have made this picture, the black carcass seems all the more ghoulish. (It is missing both feet and one forearm. Its chest is riddled with thirty stab wounds.) So they hang back from the corpse. Tight-lipped, they turn their backs to it. They gather on the road to have a smoke and wait while the search continues and the M.E. makes his way over.

A quarter mile away, at the periphery of this scene, well away from the body itself, away from the charged atmosphere, a cruiser is parked across the road and a young deputy directs traffic away.

A car rolls up to this roadblock. The windows are open. The driver is a man, midtwenties. In the afternoon heat, his blond hair is matted and his cheeks flushed. He wears a damp shirt. The temperature is near eighty-five. "What's going on?" he says.

"You'll have to turn it around, sir. Road's closed."

"What happened?"

"There was a murder."

"A murder! Oh my God. What happened?"

"They don't know yet."

"A murder! Is it that girl, from E.M.U.?"

"What makes you say it's a girl?"

"What do you mean? She's been missing, the poor girl. It's in all the papers."

"Well, like I told you, they don't know."

"How'm I gonna get back to Ann Arbor?"

There is a distinct honk in the man's voice, a nasal foreign accent, *Ann AH-buh*, which catches the deputy's attention. He walks to the back of the car. Massachusetts plates.

"You mind if I ask what you're doing here today, sir?"

"Heading back to school. I'm at U of M."

"May I see your license?"

"My license? What'd I do?"

"Just routine, sir."

"Routine." The young man makes a skeptical smirk. He knows he's being harassed but he is willing to play along. The cops are hopped up about a murder in town. It's understandable. He gets his wallet out of a back pocket, and the license out of the wallet.

The deputy reads, *Kurt Lindstrom, 50 Symphony Road, Boston*. "This license is expired."

"Is it? I'm sorry, I hadn't realized. I moved here

540

pretty recently. So much to do, you know? So much paperwork. Guess I'll need to get a Michigan license."

The deputy considers, then he relents and offers the guy a friendly little smile, and hands the license back. Today there are bigger fish to fry. "Take care of it right away."

"Oh, I will. Thank you, Officer."

"You're from Boston?"

"That's right. Ever been?"

"No."

"Well, you should go someday. Not in winter, though. It's murder."

"Alright, then. I won't."

"Good, well," Lindstrom holds up his expired driver's license, "thanks for the break. I'll take care of this, I'm gonna get right on it."

"Welcome to Michigan, sir."

Lindstrom executes a cautious threepoint turn. But before he drives off, he stops to share a last thought with the deputy. "Hope they catch the bastard that did this."

THE END

Author's Note

This is a work of fiction. The Boston Strangler cases have been the object of sensationalism and myth-making almost from the start. This novel makes no attempt to solve them. The same holds true for other aspects of the story. The West End was razed. A bloody mob war was fought. These are matters of historical record. The book in your hands obviously is not that record.

So, the rules of engagement. Where actual historical figures appear in the novel, I have tried to render them as accurately as the evidence permits. Their dialogue and actions, however, are invented. All of the central characters are products of the author's imagination, with no intended resemblance to actual people. Among those invented characters are all police and prosecutors and all of the victims of the Strangler murders. The timing of actual events, too, has been altered to serve the story.

I am deeply grateful to Captain John Daley (retired) of the Boston Police Department for sharing his memories of the city and the cop life in the 1960s. (That Captain Daley shares his surname with the family at the center of this novel is a coincidence. Again, no similarity is intended.) Another retired policeman, Ed Tobin, generously related stories of the old West End and the Boston PD, some of which appear in the book. I am also indebted to the following books and authors: *The Boston Stranglers* by Susan Kelly, *The Underboss* by Gerard O'Neill and Dick Lehr, *Building a New Boston* by Thomas H. O'Connor, and *Migraine* by Oliver Sacks. Finally, I thank Maura Driscoll for an invaluable suggestion; Kate Miciak and Alice Martell; and above all my wife Susan for her constant support and encouragement.

William Landay
Boston, 2006